ALSO BY

GENE KERRIGAN

Fiction
The Midnight Choir

Non-fiction
Hard Cases
Never Make a Promise You Can't Break
Another Country
Nothing But the Truth

LITTLE
CRIMINALS

Gene Kerrigan

LITTLE CRIMINALS

Europa
editions

Europa Editions
116 East 16th Street
New York, N.Y. 10003
www.europaeditions.com
info@europaeditions.com

First Publication 2008 by Europa Editions

Library of Congress Cataloging in Publication Data is available
ISBN 978-1-933372-43-3

Kerrigan, Gene
Little Criminals

Book design by Emanuele Ragnisco
www.mekkanografici.com

Prepress by Plan.ed – Rome

Printed in Italy
Arti Grafiche La Moderna – Rome

This is for my daughter,
Cathleen Kerrigan

LITTLE
CRIMINALS

From where he lay, with only the light from the street-lamp outside his flat Stephen Beckett could see the gun on the bedside table. The Colt .45 pistol rested on the red and white hand towel, level with his gaze. Old and worn, big, grey and ugly.

A bit like me.

It was some time after two o'clock. If he didn't get some sleep, it wouldn't matter what he decided in the morning. He wouldn't have the strength to hold the gun, let alone use it.

He closed his eyes, but that didn't help, his mind was still full of the gun and all it meant.

He opened his eyes and forced himself to turn over on to his back. The tiredness seemed to have hollowed out his bones. Some fool drove by too fast and the roar of the engine was accompanied by a pattern of light gliding across the ceiling.

It has to be done.

After he'd come to bed and spent most of an hour thinking about what he had to do, he tried to push his mind on to something else, in the hope that he might drift off to sleep. No chance. There was no other thought strong enough to gain space in his head. This thing crowded out everything else in the world and he knew that was a mark of how messed up he was.

The little fucker.

There were people who took shortcuts through other people's lives, didn't give a damn what harm they did. Sometimes, what mattered wasn't just the damage they left after them, it was the reckless contempt of it. It's like some lives matter and other people exist just to populate the landscape.

It has to be done.

Stephen Beckett had lived too long to mistake this urge for anything other than what it was—the need for revenge. At any other time of his life, he might have found a reason to step back. Now, the way things were, his sense of caution was feeble and there were more important things than right and wrong. Stuff like that belonged in another life, before the shooting began.

1.

The shooting began in the small town of Harte's Cross, a few minutes after ten o'clock one chilly summer morning. At first, only a few people knew there was anything wrong, and they were all in Sweeney's Pub.

The pub owner was pleading for her life. She was a small-town throwback, aged about fifty, wearing heavy spectacles and settled into her plumpness, with the hair and the clothes of her mother's generation. She hardly saw Frankie Crowe standing in front of her. Instead her gaze was fastened to the big black gun in his hand.

"Please, mister," she said. Frankie Crowe was twenty-eight.

Frankie Crowe had a Homer Simpson baseball cap pulled down low on his forehead, a large pair of thick-rimmed glasses hiding the shape of his face. Under his bulky beige anorak, he might have been thin or fat or anything in between. The large automatic he was holding was pointed at no one in particular, but it was the centre of attention.

There was just the one barman on duty, just as Leo had said there would be. And he was no problem. Hands flat on the counter, carefully avoiding eye contact with Frankie Crowe.

Of the three customers in the pub, two were sitting in a booth across from the bar, old men with faces the colour of stale porridge. One of the wrinklies, a pinch-mouthed little man with a stained and misshapen felt hat, had his arms held rigidly above his head, not that Crowe had given him any instructions. The old man knew, from the Bogart movies he'd seen more than half a century ago, that that's what you do when someone pulls out a gun.

The other man was bigger and well built, with a slight stoop to his back that disguised his height. One hand cradled a teacup as he stared at the gunman without emotion.

The third customer was a young woman with very short black hair, a ring through her left eyebrow and a baby held in a sling on her chest. She was sitting at a table near the window, her own coffee and the baby's half-empty bottle in front of her. When she saw Frankie Crowe come in with a gun in his hand she stood up and made for the door, but Frankie just shook his head and used his gun hand to wave her back to the table. The woman sat down, one arm supporting the baby's sling.

She didn't even see Martin Paxton, standing just inside the door, a dark baseball hat worn low on his forehead, a handgun held down by his leg, until Frankie said, "Keep an eye," and took the pub owner into the office behind the bar.

Nothing complicated, Frankie said. In and out and back home to Dublin with a rake of money, maybe fifteen grand, before anyone knows we've been there. Not the kind of take that would make a difference, but enough to keep things ticking over.

It was a Monday morning. "Saturday night, they make a bundle, Sunday too," Leo Titley said. Leo was the tip-off. "The icing on the cake is, Saturday night coming up they have a concert. Old man Sweeney, before he died, bought out the kip next door, broke through, fixed it up with a stage. They do a gig every month or so and it takes maybe five hundred punters."

"The bank has a night safe?"

"None," Leo Titley said. "That's the beauty of it. They lodge the takings next day. Mrs. S. does it herself, noon on the dot. Local cop walks her down the street. Guy I know used to work there a few years back, said there's a safe in the back room. Two nights' takings and the gig money, waiting to be banked Monday morning."

And the great thing about the gig, Leo said, was it was nothing special. If it was a name act, there'd be advance booking. This was all money at the door. A couple of losers from a boy band that never happened. It broke up and three of them went back to scratching their arses, the other two were earning peanuts hawking their out-of-tune cover versions around the provincial pub circuit.

"Money at the door. The pubs love it, taxman never sees a cent."

And Monday morning, before they can get the cash into the bank, Frankie Crowe and Martin Paxton are sitting in the pub car park in a stolen Primera.

"The pub opens at ten thirty," Leo said. "You go in, wave a gun and the safe opens."

That was the plan.

The old bitch's legs were trembling when she came out of the back room, so Frankie gave her a shove to hurry her up. The woman moved as fast as she could, putting the counter between herself and Frankie.

"Time lock, she says," Frankie said.

Martin made a pissed-off noise and hit the door with the butt of his gun.

"Says she can't open it for another hour and a half. She's bullshitting." He pointed his gun at the barman, his hands still flat on the counter. "You know the combination?"

The man swallowed, shook his head. He was wearing a short red waistcoat that showed his white shirt bunched up at the top of his trousers. His voice was thin, like he was squeezing the words out through his fear. "She's telling the truth. She got the new safe last year, couple of young fellas broke in one night, nearly got the back off the old one." He looked at Frankie as if he was judging how his story was going over. "Can't be opened until twelve o'clock. That's when the garda comes, to keep an eye while she's banking it."

"Bollocks."

Frankie looked at Martin and said, "Old bitch is lying, this cunt, too."

"Please, mister! For the love of God, this is all there is!" The woman had the register open and was holding up a handful of notes.

She held the money out towards Frankie. When he got within reach he knocked the money out of her hand and grabbed the front of her blouse. She closed her eyes as he screamed in her face. "Open the fucking safe!"

The young woman with the baby made soothing sounds and cradled her bundle in front of her. Its head tilted sideways, the baby stared with frank interest at the angry man and his colourful hat.

Over at the door, Martin Paxton said, "Ah shit," then he leaned back against the door, opening it slightly. "Come on," he said. He waited, and when Frankie ignored him he pushed the door open and walked out.

Crowe shouted, "Bitch!" and let go of the woman's blouse. She was close to passing out, sweat rising on her forehead and along her quivering upper lip.

The tall elderly man who hadn't raised his hands had a loud voice. "Leave her alone, you. Leave her alone."

Crowe turned and saw an old fool, a hillbilly with big, gnarled hands, untidy hair and a face pitted with time.

The old guy stood up. "Coming down here, waving a gun. Why don't you work for your money, the same as the rest of us?"

Crowe looked at him like the old man was a peculiar species he hadn't yet come across. He walked slowly towards the booth, until he was no more than two or three feet from the old man. "Who the fuck're you, grandad? Sir Galahad?" He pointed the gun at the old man's crotch. The hillbilly tried desperately not to flinch. Crowe grinned.

"You have balls, grandad. You want to keep them?"

The old man stared. Beside him, still sitting, raised hands trembling, his small friend kept his gaze fixed on the surface of the table in front of him. Frankie made a dismissive sound and turned back to the pub owner. "It's make your mind up time." He pointed the gun at her head and his voice was casual. "One, two—"

The shooting came at the end of a period—more than a year—in which a lot of things didn't quite work out. By now, Frankie Crowe and Martin Paxton were supposed to be on their way somewhere. Instead, they were here in a small town in County Meath, still scrounging for the rent.

The town's kids were at school, the farmers and their labourers were off in the countryside doing whatever farmers do. It was mostly women shopping, and mostly elderly women, that were to be seen on the streets that morning. There was a drinks lorry delivering a palletload to Harte's Cross's only hotel. A couple of old lads squinting at yesterday's results in the window of a bookie's. A limping man pushing a Calor gas cylinder in a child's buggy. Two dogs being walked by a white-haired old woman in a scarlet tracksuit.

And one cop.

The garda was standing alongside a car about twenty yards down the street from Sweeney's Pub, chatting up a young woman.

He hadn't been there when they arrived. Now, Martin Paxton got into the Primera in Sweeney's car park and kept an eye on him.

The cop had a Boy Scout face. Uniform a little on the loose side. He was watching the woman's backside as she leaned into the car to drape a collection of dry-cleaned clothes across the back seat. Paxton smiled. Naughty boy. The woman, it seemed to Paxton, was too pretty and too sure of herself for a chinless wonder of a culchie cop fresh out of Templemore. She sat halfway into the driver's seat, smiling, nodding, idly touching the ends of her loose blonde hair as the garda leaned on the car and rabbited away at her.

Across the street, in the window of a clothes shop, a shop assistant was fitting a flowery summer dress to a mannequin. The shop, like the MegaMarket and the petrol station halfway down the street, belonged to the pub owner's family.

A mud-spattered tractor chugged past, towing a trailer from which dripped a steady trail of something dark, green and smelly.

Two elderly women, all headscarves, knowing eyes and fluttering lips, stood outside Tubridy's newsagent's, dispensing more gossip than any combination of the trashy magazines on the shelves inside.

Most people within hearing range paid little attention to the first shot. It was a flat smack of sound that could have been several things. Martin Paxton looked to the mirror and saw the garda push himself away from the woman's car and glance around, unsure of himself.

Not even the boy copper could mistake the second shot for something else.

Somewhere in the distance, there was the sound of someone screaming.

The garda moved into the middle of the street, looking up and down, trying to decide what to do, knowing that civilians nearby were looking in his direction. The woman he'd been talking to swivelled round in her seat and pulled the door of the car shut.

Martin Paxton started the engine of the Primera and waited.

Inside Sweeney's Pub, one of the owner's hands was clasped

across her mouth, the other was holding on to her hair. Her eyes were closed, her lips tight, her breathing fast. There was a bullet hole in the Guinness mirror behind the counter. A second bullet had shattered the display screen of the cash register.

The barman was bent forward, hands on the counter, head to one side, as though he was determined not to see whatever happened next. There was a burning smell in the air.

The woman with the baby had turned her back and was cowering, putting the slender width of her body between the gun and her child. The small pinch-faced old man with his hands up had pissed himself, leaving a big dark patch all down his white trousers. The ballsy old hillbilly had raised his hands.

Frankie Crowe fired three more shots—one into the wide-screen television set high up on the end wall of the pub, two more into a second screen in an alcove. Another two bullets hit an electronic quiz machine. The eighth shattered a bottle of vodka a foot from the pub owner's head.

Crowe made a noise of disgust. She was out of it, so far into fear that she was beyond threats. Besides, what was the fucking point? She had to be telling the truth.

Crowe picked up the banknotes from where the old bitch had dropped them on the counter. As he reached the pub door, he put the money and his gun into his anorak pockets, made sure Homer Simpson was firmly in place, then he opened the door and stepped outside.

After the second shot, the two gossips shuffled into the newsagent's, glancing back as they went, already shaping the anecdotes they would harvest from the drama.

The garda had decided he knew where the shots had come from. He began running towards Sweeney's Pub. He was into the car park when he heard the second flurry of shots. He stopped ten feet from the stolen Primera. Martin Paxton tugged his baseball hat so the peak was shading his face, opened the door and got out of the car. He held the gun casu-ally down by his side.

The garda looked from the pub to Martin Paxton. The gun-man just shook his head.

The door of the pub opened and Frankie Crowe came out.

He stopped just outside the door and used the index finger of one hand to rub his nose, the hand partly obscuring his face.

The garda was a riot of uncertainty. No obvious course of action was acceptable. Do something—that was stupid. Do nothing, Jesus—

End up with the lads at the station calling him a fucking eejit for having a go, or a no-balls coward for being sensible? He knew that right now heroics were dangerous and pointless. He knew too that if he backed down, no matter how long he lived there would never be a day when a part of him didn't squirm at the memory.

Frankie Crowe walked as though he was setting out on a stroll to see the town sights. He stopped a yard away from the garda.

The thing to do, Garda Joe Hanlon knew, was to play it cool. Do nothing to give the thug a reason to use the gun. Take everything in—the face, the build, distinguishing marks, the other one standing by the car. Get the number as they drive off. Take it all in, survive, watch them run, then deal with them. Branches all over, he used to joke—outfit I work for, we've got branches all over.

Garda Joe Hanlon held his chin up.

Across the street, in the window of the clothes shop, the shop assistant stood as still and as pale as the mannequin she was dressing.

The thug was smiling. "Morning, garda. Soft day, thank God."

The thug held the gun up, moved a finger and the magazine dropped from the handle into his other hand. He held the garda's gaze as he put the empty magazine into a pocket and took out a new one. Garda Hanlon heard it click into place.

"You from around these parts?" the thug said. He had a Dublin accent. He was holding the gun down by his side now, as though to put the garda at ease.

"You know there's nothing I can do." Garda Hanlon was surprised that his voice carried no tremor of the dread he felt. "Just take whatever you got and fuck off out of here."

He didn't see the thug squeeze the trigger.

For a moment, there was nothing inside his head except the sound of the gun going off. It was like the biggest door in the universe slammed shut an inch from his ear. Then his mind was flooded with panic.

No, please wait—

The garda realised he hadn't been shot. The thug was still holding the gun down by his side. He'd fired into the tarmac surface of the car park. The garda was already turning, and in seconds he was fifty feet away, his head still echoing with the gun's explosion. When he stopped and looked back, the gunman was standing there, gun poised.

Garda Hanlon reached up and touched his bare head. He hadn't noticed his cap fall off, but it was there on the pavement just outside Sweeney's car park.

"Frankie, for fuck sake!"

Martin Paxton lurched in behind the wheel of the Primera. Frankie was walking towards the garda now, big smile on his face. The garda backed away, turned and ran a little more, then looked round and stopped.

Martin watched Frankie pick up the garda's cap. Frankie walked slowly back towards the car. He threw the garda's cap into the back seat, climbed inside and took off the thick-rimmed glasses. It was like the anger had been diluted by the shooting. He smiled. "Whenever you're ready."

Paxton revved the car and drove across the car park, towards the exit. He saw the garda turning and running fast down the street.

Frankie Crowe was looking towards the pub. The old hillbilly who had challenged him was standing in the doorway. Crowe lifted the baseball hat in salute and smiled.

2.

It was a gift, an ability to close his eyes and immediately drop off to sleep, and an instant clarity on waking. Justin Kennedy was sitting in his favourite chair, in his living room, it was late evening and his wife and two children were asleep upstairs. His briefcase and his jacket were on the sofa, carelessly thrown there when he had arrived home. The vodka and tonic he'd poured sat on the side table, untouched. He'd surrendered to the tiredness, collapsed into the chair, let the drowsiness take him for a few minutes. Now, his mind clear, he looked around the room. From where he was sitting, everything he could see spoke of quality. The furniture solid, the walls expensively embellished, there was an unmistakable balance to the room. It was mostly Angela's doing, her and that fruit she'd hired.

Justin dipped a finger in the drink, put the cold tip of the finger to his tongue. He lifted the glass and took as much pleasure in the weight of the crystal as he did in the sip of vodka.

He enjoyed this. The late-night working, the tiredness, the knowledge that he was stretching himself to the limit at work and had a place of comfort to which he could return.

He watched a drop of moisture fall from the glass on to the dark cloth of his suit trousers. He smoothed the damp spot into the material. Justin's business suits were mostly Ermenegildo Zegna, but he had recently ordered a suit from Brioni. It was his friend Daragh who put him on to Brioni. It cost maybe three times as much, but that wasn't the point. "It's not about fashion," he told Justin, "and it's not about showing off. It's about positioning yourself in the market."

At forty-one, when the first millimetres of grey had recently appeared, Justin had his hair touched up to match his natural dark brown. Laser treatment allowed him to dispense with glasses, but that, he was convinced, made the puffiness under his eyes more noticeable. He had a pair of clear-glass spectacles made, but he felt foolish and wore them only once.

For a while, he regarded the unmistakably inflated belly that softly pushed out over his belt as a correctable failure of discipline. As time went by, he'd come to think of it as an acceptable indulgence of his prosperity. The secondary chin that had gradually accumulated over the previous few years was more of a worry. Mostly when he looked in the mirror he unconsciously edited out such blemishes and noticed only a slightly older version of the handsome striver he had seen in his youth. Over the past year, however, he had winced at occasional photographs in the business pages of the newspapers, and at social-page snaps of his appearances at a couple of charity events. He worked out a little at home, but lacked the necessary discipline. He signed up with a gym but after three weeks of early-morning sessions he decided he couldn't spare the time. It was a problem that strayed into his thoughts with increasing frequency.

He let the ice touch his lips and took another sip of the vodka, then he put the glass down carefully and made a satisfied sound as he pulled himself to his feet. Upstairs, he looked in first on Luke, then on Saskia, both fast asleep, before entering his own bedroom. His wife had fallen asleep with the bedside lamp on. A hardback book, one of her reading-group novels, was open beside her on the pillow. In her sleep she had shrugged off the duvet and he stood there a moment, looking down at her with approval and pride.

Succulent.

It was a word he would never use to anyone else about Angela—and certainly not to her—but it was the word that came to mind when he first saw her, and when he first took her to bed, and at the steps of the altar as he was about to marry her ten years back. Now, the word came to him again, as he evaluated his sleeping wife.

She was eleven years younger than he and although these days he could see a slight creasing under the eyes, it was still a face that drew admiring glances wherever they went. Her dark brown shoulder-length hair had recently been cut shorter than he preferred, but not troublesomely so. Her breasts, slightly on the small side, were the precise shape and weight of the idealised breasts that had most readily stirred his libido since puberty. She was long and lithe and toned and he didn't begrudge the annual gym fees that ensured she stayed that way.

When they'd met, her job in PR required her to spend a certain amount of time and money maintaining an appearance. Throughout their marriage, the budget for what she called "upkeep" was agreed without negotiation. Angela was on his books as an assistant, so most of it could be written off.

Succulent.

As he gently pulled the cover over her, Angela stirred and said something he didn't catch. He whispered, "Night, love," and switched off her lamp.

Just over two hundred, it came out as. Fuck sake.

Frankie Crowe was still angry about it next morning, still doing a bit of pacing in the small living room of Leo Titley's cottage. It was a combined living room and dining room, cramped, with a dining table in the centre. It reminded Frankie of the poky little living room of the house he'd grown up in in Finglas.

"Wanker," he muttered, when the door closed behind Leo.

They were a couple of miles from Harte's Cross, at the isolated farmhouse where Leo lived alone. It made sense to torch the Primera and go to ground locally. It meant sleeping overnight in lumpy armchairs in Leo's manky cottage, and eating his greasy food, but they could take their time travelling back to Dublin, instead of making the journey while the Meath bluebottles were agitated by the robbery.

Repeatedly, Frankie ran his hand back and forth through his curly black hair. He was medium height and he was fit without being obviously muscular. His even features were diminished by a permanently querulous expression.

He had done a couple of things with Leo in the dim and distant and it was Leo's urging that had brought them to Harte's Cross. A hatful of money, he said, no security worth talking about. What he didn't say was, no fucking money worth talking about.

Frankie did a bit of roaring and shouting when they got back to Leo's place after the balls-up, then Martin said it was their own fault. Do a quickie, no checking, you take your chances. Frankie snorted. The knowledge that Martin was right didn't help.

"I've got some whiskey," Leo said, as though that might help. Frankie waved a hand. No booze. That was a Frankie Crowe rule. Keep a sober head until you're well clear of trouble. Celebrate when it's over.

Not that there was anything to celebrate. It wasn't like they'd been expecting a fortune, but two fucking hundred.

This morning, Leo was on his way into Harte's Cross, to see if things had settled down, and if it looked OK the others would take off and be back in Dublin by lunchtime.

"Risking everything," Frankie said, "for beer money."

Martin Paxton was a tall man in jeans and a Manchester United shirt, almost thirty and already balding. He was soft-voiced and gave an impression of rounded edges. Whenever he had to lie about what he did for a living he said, "Software," and he looked the part. When he did occasional straight work it was mostly chasing and plastering for his electrician brother. Doing that, he could put in the best part of a day for a couple of hundred into his hand.

Paxton said, "OK, it's not the Crown jewels, we'll have a go at them next week."

"Smart-arse."

By the time Leo came back from Harte's Cross to say the coast was clear, Frankie had decided there was no point splitting two fucking hundred. He left it with Leo.

On the road to Dublin, in the anonymity of the heavy traffic, Frankie said, "I never want to see that wanker again." From behind the wheel, he looked across at Martin. "Risking our lives for loose change. Fuck sake, this is no way to be."

Martin Paxton knew the rest of the routine. Starting with We're not kids any more, moving into It's there to be taken, and finishing on something like All we need is the balls. He'd been hearing it from Frankie at least twice a week for the past three months.

Martin Paxton had known Frankie Crowe for over twenty years. They grew up on the same housing estate, mitched from the same school, got into trouble on the same streets, and met again when they were doing time in Mountjoy. And there was never a time when Frankie didn't have notions. "There's moochers and there's doers," he used to say. "Moochers take shit. Moochers don't know they're alive."

Over the past few months, the ambition had taken shape. You could hear it in Frankie's tone.

"It'll always be this way, unless we do something about it. You keep putting things off, what happens—you wake up one day your arse is dragging on the floor, you're still living on loose change and it's too late to do anything except crawl into the coffin." He poked a finger at Martin. "Or, you pick a target, put a price on it, do the big one."

"You know how long you get in the funny house for kidnapping?"

"If you get caught. And you get caught because you dawdle—way I want to do it, there'll be no dawdling."

Three days later, Frankie was talking like it was all agreed.

"Just the two of us?" Martin said.

"Three, four maybe. Dolly Finn if he's up for it, maybe Brendan Sweetman."

Martin nodded, then he said, "Something like that, it's not just the cops we have to worry about."

Crowe tapped his chest. "Leave Jo-Jo to me. He owes me. Big time. Jo-Jo's cool."

Martin Paxton reckoned there wasn't much point in arguing. This was where Frankie was headed. And the way things were, cutting loose from Frankie Crowe and striking out on his own wasn't an option. There wasn't much point heading into this kidnap thing with half a heart.

"You got the target picked out?"

"It's down to four or five," Frankie said. "Eeny, meeny, miney, mo."

B rendan Sweetman knew that the chubby blonde's name
was Nina and that she was a brunette in a wig. That
afternoon, she was with two other women in their late
thirties. They were fashionably dressed, and had all put a lot of
work into their hair. Each carried a large handbag. Sweetman
didn't recognise the other two women, but seeing as they were
with Nina, there was no doubt they too were shoplifters.

In the four hours since Sweetman came on security duty at
noon, he'd already refused entry to eight people he knew to be
strokers. He stepped away from the shop door, shifted his
chewing gum from one cheek to the other and held his hands
up and wide. "Sorry, Nina, not today, love."

"I beg your pardon?"

"Piss off, Nina, take a hike." He grinned. With her hooked
nose and her over-plucked eyebrows, the poor cow was unmistakable, no matter what she wore on her head. The days when
she'd get away with stuffing other people's merchandise down
her jeans were few and far between.

"How dare you! Who d'you think you're talking to?"

"On your bike, Nina."

"I want to see the manager!"

Sweetman's smile broadened. "Go on, Nina. You're sussed.
Take it like a lady and fuck off quietly."

All three of the women erupted in obscenities. Brendan
Sweetman didn't take it personally. As they snarled at him, he
stared in turn at the two he didn't know, imprinting their faces

on his memory. The three walked away. Until they rounded the corner into the main street, they took turns hurling the usual curses back at him.

Sweetman was in his mid-thirties. He'd worked the front of one store or another in the city centre on and off for almost five years, and for the past year he'd been full-time at it. Some security personnel found it boring, standing around for hours, using their walkie-talkies to share info and dirty jokes with neighbouring bouncers, using their mobile phones to text friends, or just shuffling their feet and chewing gum. Brendan Sweetman loved the job. Some of the thieves waited until near closing time, knowing the bouncers were likely to be tired, bored and inattentive. Brendan Sweetman was as lively at five minutes to six as he was when his workday started.

Hair cut so tight it was little more than a shadow, he was short and wide and made up in bulk what he lacked in height. He tended towards plain black T-shirts along with plain black trousers that he had made by a tailor in Ringsend. Although he was eligible for staff discounts, the shops he protected didn't sell much in Sweetman's size. Jeans big enough to go around his waist were several inches too long for his legs, and had to be taken up at the ends. Shirts that accommodated his neck had sleeves too long for his arms. Much of his bulk was muscle, and few who came across him dared make any of the obvious fat jokes in his hearing. No one had ever done it twice.

The idiot two doors down was jabbering into his radio again. "The tart in the yellow top, look at the tits on that!"

Brendan Sweetman didn't reply. That kind of unprofessional carry-on, passers-by could hear shit like that, it gave the business a bad name. He'd just spotted Frankie Crowe standing with his back to a nearby shop window. Frankie mimed drinking a pint and Brendan nodded. Frankie poked a finger in the direction of Coley Street, then gave the thumbs-up. Sweetman went in search of the manager, to arrange a break.

There were two pints of Guinness on the counter in front of Frankie when Brendan arrived ten minutes later. Crowe held out his hand.

"Looking good, mate."

"Jesus, Frankie, it's good to see you. It's been, what—"

It had been three and a half years. Sweetman had been the back-up muscle on a successful job across in Terenure, a jewellery thing organised by Jo-Jo Mackendrick and carried out by Frankie. That was just before a garda raid on the Drumcondra house where Frankie then lived turned up a stash of stolen cigarettes and Frankie went away for two years.

"Been a long time, Sweets," Crowe said. Brendan sat on the next stool. The pub, which used to be called Maguire's or Malloy's, something like that, had recently been extended and renamed Vesuvius. A lot of work had gone into the volcano motif, with predictable consequences for the price of drink. Everything seemed to have a hard, shiny surface, including the barmen. The male customers tended towards long hair and long black overcoats. The women customers more often than not were insistently blonde and had fashionably surly mouths.

Frankie Crowe said, "You retired? Someone told me you were full-time at the security game?"

Brendan Sweetman grinned. "You know how it is." He picked up his pint. "Cheers."

Frankie Crowe held his pint and watched Sweetman take a long swallow. Frankie moved his beer mat a fraction of an inch, so it was exactly parallel to the edge of the counter. He put his pint down in the exact centre of the beer mat.

He said, "You're not open to suggestions, then?"

"Nothing wrong with talking."

When she became pregnant, Brendan's wife told him she wouldn't ever visit Mountjoy, and if he ended up there so would the marriage. Which was fair enough. After fifteen years of stroking, with only two short spells in the Joy, Sweetman owned his own house and the security job was pulling in a steady wage, so he made her a promise.

When Frankie told him about the kidnap, Sweetman took another long swallow of Guinness. "Interesting," he said.

He asked about the when and the where and how long it would take and who else was on the crew and Crowe explained. Then they talked money.

The thing about the straight life, as far as Brendan Sweetman was concerned, was it took away the anxiety. You knew more or less where things were going. There wasn't the chance that one day you'd come out of a bank or a jeweller's with a shotgun in your hands and find half a dozen trigger-happy cops waiting to blow you away. You weren't taking a chance you'd spend a few years in a small room with bars on the window and some bonehead wanking and farting his way through what passed for a life.

Other hand, though, you knew things would never get much better than they were. There'd always be some rich asshole looking down his nose while he short-changed you, and the money you took home would never amount to more than it took to keep you exactly where you were.

Was a time the risk was worth it, so that's the way he went. Lately, life was comfortable, and the downside of stroking wasn't worth the kind of money you got to take home.

"You're talking about real money."

The kind of take Frankie was talking about could shift life to a different level. One big jump. Then the security work would keep things motoring along. Have to give Frankie credit. Comes a time when you either get out of this business or you make something of yourself. Brendan Sweetman was out of the business, living cool. Which didn't mean he couldn't see the benefits of a one-off that makes a difference.

Frankie said, "This isn't just another job. Know what I mean? Kind of money we're talking about, we don't get that for standing around looking menacing. I'm just making sure you know what might be involved."

Brendan thought about that for a moment, then he said, "I know what you're talking about."

Frankie nodded. Brendan hadn't gone soft. Give him time to think and he'd make the right decision. A job like this, you need people around that don't have to be told how the world works. Frankie finally took a sip of his pint.

Three days later, early evening, Frankie Crowe was across the river in Temple Bar, sitting at the counter in Top Nosh, a cup of coffee in front of him. The place wasn't busy. A couple of stools to Frankie's left, a fat-faced priest was finishing a sandwich. At the sole window seat, a colour-coordinated couple in their twenties were having a quiet but fierce argument. There were three other people in the coffee shop, all sitting separately. Frankie sipped his coffee and opened the leather-bound notebook that served as organiser, diary and memo pad. Over the two months since the Harte's Cross mess, he had put together the guts of a promising project. The three Ts— target, timetable, team. Surveillance information, lists of things to do, phone numbers, sources of supplies and support. He leafed through pages that had nothing to do with the snatch, and came to a page on which was written FC, MP, BS, DF, Mky, TS.

He had already check-marked his own initials, Martin Paxton's and Brendan Sweetman's.

Another—what?—a month, maybe. Even less. No point screwing around. This one works, he told himself, everything changes. This one doesn't work, everything changes.

"An organised man."

Frankie looked at the priest, who was smiling with proud modesty, like he'd just said something that let slip his cleverness. His face was shiny, soft, his accumulated chins quivering.

He nodded towards the notebook. "An organised man. Everything in its place. A sure sign of an ordered life." His voice was Kerry or thereabouts.

If he was cruising he'd have ditched the collar. Just a moocher in need of conversation.

Frankie said, "What's it to you?" He closed his notebook.

The priest blushed. It took him another couple of minutes to pay his bill, carefully ignoring Frankie, then he gathered his leather shoulder bag and his fold-up umbrella and shuffled off without glancing back. Frankie looked at his watch. Dolly was late. He picked up the *Irish Independent* the priest had left behind. The paper was open to a page on which a politician deplored anti-American tendencies in modern Ireland. Such attitudes, he wrote, lead to a cowardly abdication of international responsibilities. Frankie decided the guy was right.

"Fuck off."

The female half of the arguing couple was walking fast towards the door. The man sat there, his face red, staring after her. Frankie watched him. It was hard to tell if he was upset about the row, or just embarrassed that it had happened in public. After a moment, the man threw some money on the table and hurried out after the woman.

Frankie moved to their table, beside the window. He watched as a waitress cleared the table and took the money, then he ordered another coffee. From a pocket in the inside back cover of his notebook, Frankie took a folded wad of paper. When it was unfolded, there were three pages clipped from magazines.

The thing about the really rich bastards is that as soon as they clock up enough funds they piss off out of Ireland to live in mansions in the Caribbean. Frankie Crowe had started with a *Rich List* magazine that came free with a Sunday newspaper. It took him little more than an hour to select five possible targets.

There were a hundred people on the list. He went down

through the ones with the hundreds of millions and most of them were tax exiles, only dropping back to Ireland now and then to make a fuss about giving money to charity, or to watch their favourite racehorse win a cup.

He went down through the people with tens of millions, ticking off possibles—some of them did a lot of their business in London and Eastern Europe and spent most of their time there and that was no good. Then it occurred to him that he was going about this the wrong way.

No matter how rich these people are, he told Martin Paxton later, they're not going to be able to get their hands on more than couple of million in a hurry. "So, if you're taking a million from someone, and you want to do it quickly, it doesn't matter whether he's got six million or six hundred million. Matter of fact, the more he has the more difficult it gets. Fortresses some of those bastards live in, you'd need a couple of tanks to get in, and a squad of commandos to bring them out."

So, he went past the bottom of the rich list, to where fifty rich people were listed in a section headed "Bubbling Under." There he found his five possibles, all of them said to be worth around thirty million. He asked at his local public library and was directed to the Business Information Centre at the ILAC Library, and there he spent an afternoon looking through press cuttings on business and businessmen. One magazine story was headlined THE CELTIC TIGERS WHO GOT THE CREAM. It listed ten up-and-coming entrepreneurs who made fortunes during the boom years, two of whom were also in the "Bubbling Under" rich list. What clinched it was a sentence in another magazine story, about property deals. "Justin Kennedy is, of course," it said, "best known for the breakthrough that came when he landed Bryton, the small private bank."

"Couldn't ask better than that," Frankie told Martin. "A small private bank—a direct line into the money. Last thing I want is we get into some kind of back-and-forth, me and the family. That's the way they like to work, the cops. Tie you up in chat, the money just out of reach. Negotiators spinning things out, trick cyclists analysing every fucking word you say, looking for a handle. Fuck that." He kept his voice calm and deliberate. "Short deadline, let them cough up or pay the consequences. They fuck around, someone else'll know better next time."

Now, at the counter in Top Nosh, he again read the page from the *Rich List* magazine. The piece on Justin Kennedy mentioned his "new home on Pemberton Road," and it carried a picture of the lucky man. Soft-looking fucker with a double chin and bags under his eyes.

What David Finn—known since childhood as Dolly—liked about the narrow cobbled streets of Temple Bar was the smell of the food. Everything else you could stick, particularly the people. He didn't mind the middle-aged Yank tourists, taking pictures of one another in front of supposedly quaint pubs and streets. Mostly they were polite and kept to themselves. He moved off the pavement to avoid a dozen women unleashing a blizzard of squawking laughs. Their English accents and tight pink T-shirts announced they were a hen party celebrating "Ellie's Weekend in Dublin." The cobbled streets were full of local posers throwing shapes, people who'd gone to endless trouble with their hair and their clothes to impress passing strangers with their coolness.

When Dolly arrived at Top Nosh he was listening to Billy Frisell on his iPod. Finn was a tall, skinny man, with a long, thin moustache that drooped down each side of his mouth, making his hollow-cheeked face seem even longer than it was. He was in his early forties, with thinning fair hair brushed right back. Under a grey waistcoat, he wore a white collarless shirt with the sleeves rolled up over his bony forearms.

He paused in the doorway to switch off the iPod. He looked around: Frankie's kind of place, all right. City's full of them. All chrome and shades of gray. Shitty coffee, rip-off prices, throw a piece of bacon into a bread roll and call it a panini. None of them give a fuck, all waiting for Starbucks to come along and buy out the lease.

Frankie spotted Dolly and waved him to a seat at his table by the window.

When a brusque waitress appeared beside the table, Frankie Crowe ordered a panini. Dolly Finn ordered a chicken salad and a mineral water. In a quiet voice, Frankie started explaining the job, the way he reckoned it would go, the team, the money. Dolly was looking out across the narrow street, his attention caught by a skinny youth sitting on the doorstep of a shop that sold expensive leather clothes. The kid's head was slack on his shoulders, threatening to pitch forward, as though he was overcome with tiredness. His pale skin was pockmarked, his clothes shabby. He'd been sitting there a couple of minutes when someone from the leather shop, a wispy woman in a leopard-skin top and a long black skirt, came out and told him to move. The kid looked up at her like he couldn't figure out where the voice was coming from.

"Fucking junkies," Dolly Finn said. "They're everywhere. Used to be a decent town, now look at it."

The kid made it to his feet and shuffled off down towards the river. Frankie Crowe said, "Poor bastard."

Dolly shook his head. "It's all about self-control."

The food arrived. Dolly used a fork to poke at his salad, searching through the lettuce until he found a piece of chicken.

Finn was from Cork city. His mother was dead, his father had scarpered to England three decades ago and he didn't know if his three brothers and one sister were still alive. He joined the army and did two tours with the United Nations in

Lebanon. When he'd been out of the army a year, most of it on the dole, a former army associate named Johnner Mulligan offered him a place on a team doing a hold-up at a credit union in Lucan. Since then, occasional projects of that nature financed the purchase and upkeep of his riverside flat and the small shop he owned, around the corner from his flat. The shop opened for a few hours a day, selling jazz albums to a small, dedicated clientele. From among them, he drew on the few others he needed for companionship. Three or four times a year he travelled abroad to attend jazz festivals and concerts. Dolly had no partner, and didn't see the need. He first had sex in Lebanon. He didn't like it. Twice after he came home, he went to prostitutes in Dublin. He hadn't bothered since. His shop lost money, but it was the centre of Dolly Finn's life, subsidised by his occasional work with people like Frankie. He had only once been arrested and charged with anything, and the case was dropped before it came to court.

"When?" Finn was looking at Frankie, eyebrows raised.

"Have to spend a bit of time sussing out the guy's house, take care of a few things."

Finn nodded. "Just so I have a couple of weeks' notice."

"You're in, then?"

Dolly nodded. A thing like this, if it worked out, would mean he didn't have to take any more criminal jobs for—depending how it worked out—maybe five or six years. Dolly Finn reckoned he had a simple life, simple needs. The less time he had to hustle to pay for his overheads, the better.

Out on the street, Dolly shook hands with Frankie, inserted the iPod earphones and set off back towards his shop, his stride in sync with the rhythm of Billy Frisell's "Del Close."

4.

It was just after eight in the evening about two weeks later when Frankie Crowe walked up the stairs of his apartment block in Glasnevin carrying a heavy holdall. As Frankie reached his own landing, the chatty fucker across the hall was on his way out.

"I hope the music wasn't too loud last evening?"

Crowe shook his head and walked past. You live in your own house, you don't have to share space with dickheads who want you to notice their existence. The Glasnevin apartment block in which Crowe had lived since his marriage broke up was awash with bubbly young things from down the country, junior civil servants and college students living independent lives by the grace of Daddy's chequebook. The kind of people who took it for granted that apartment life is a great shared adventure. Crowe had spent the previous evening in a pub and he hadn't a notion whether the chatty fucker had been playing music. If it was ever too loud, he wouldn't have waited for a casual meeting in the hallway to let him know about it.

Inside his flat, Crowe left the holdall on an armchair, made coffee and sat at the kitchen table with his leather-bound notebook. Of the six sets of initials, four were ticked—FC, MP, BS and DF. Crowe now added a tick to TS.

The one unticked entry on the list was Mky.

Crowe took out his phone. The kitchen was a corner of the tiny apartment. The living room was another corner. A thin partition wall enclosed the one bedroom, and the miniature bathroom was an enclosed nook within the bedroom. There were neighbours above, below and at three sides, and you could hear every cough and fart.

Frankie Crowe liked the flat. It was as much as he needed. Right now, life was a thin echo of what he'd had with Joan and Sinead. If he couldn't have that, he'd as soon live in a box that was easy to manage. Some day, when he'd put together a cushion of money and the kind of reputation that comes with pulling off hefty jobs, maybe it would be different. He never allowed himself to indulge the flicker of hope he sometimes felt when he thought of Joan and Sinead, but neither was it an emotion he would allow himself to kill.

Meanwhile, a gaff like this was just the job. If you didn't have a place for everything and made sure that everything went in its place, you ended up living in a tip. Crowe liked the discipline of it.

"Yeah?"

"Milky?"

"Yeah."

"Frankie. How are we fixed?"

"I've had a look around. I can manage it."

"We'll be there two days, maybe three, should be no more than that."

"No bother."

"Good man. The cars?"

"The easy part."

"Good man. We're on, then?"

They were on. Milky mightn't be fancy, but he was reliable. Crowe sipped his coffee and looked again at his list of things to do. He added a note: JJ?, and drew a circle around it. Once that was done, everything would be in place. Just shows. You do the work, you get the results. Within hours of the Harte's Cross fuck-up, he'd convinced Martin to go ahead with the kidnap. Couple of months later, the target was sussed, he'd recruited Brendan Sweetman and Dolly Finn, Milky was on board to supply cars and a hideout and they'd pretty much settled on a ballpark price for that. He'd fronted the money for Tommy Sholtis and today he'd made a visit to Tommy to collect the gear. All that was left to do was finesse Jo-Jo, pick a date, do it. Enough fucking about. Step up to the life.

Crowe opened the door of the closet in his bedroom. He didn't have many clothes. When he tired of a garment, he disposed of it and bought something new, usually dark in colour and conservative in cut. Most of his clothes came from River Island, and once a year he bought a suit at Brown Thomas, almost always Armani.

He knelt and took his spare pair of shoes and his Nike trainers from the floor of the closet and moved aside two cardboard boxes in which he kept personal documents and family photographs. He got a fork from the kitchen and used it to prise loose a section of the floorboard. He fetched the heavy holdall he'd collected from Tommy Sholtis and took from it four revolvers, three automatics and a sawn-off double-barrelled shotgun. He got eight Tesco plastic shopping bags from a drawer in the kitchen and used them to wrap each weapon individually, before storing them under the floorboards.

Pistols were the basic tools, if there had to be shooting on a job, up close and final, but there was nothing like a sawn-off to scare the shit out of would-be heroes. Someone waving a shotgun around, if he looked the part—and Brendan Sweetman looked the part—wiped out any heroic thoughts that might simmer in the head of any dumbo civilian. Which, when you think of it, reduced the odds that there'd be any shooting at all, which was in the civilian's interest.

When he replaced the floorboard, Crowe poured another coffee and sat down at the kitchen table again. On a fresh page of his notebook, he made a list of the weapons, using Ct for Colt, R for Ruger, H&K for Heckler & Koch, and Gk for

Glock. He thought about it for a moment, then he assigned a piece to each crew member, writing their initials alongside the weapons. He flicked back through the pages until he found the list of initials and put a final tick beside Mky. A busy day, a lot done. Do the work, get the result. No big deal.

He tapped out another number on the phone.

Martin Paxton put down the phone and put on his sheepish face.

Deborah said, "Ah, no."

"Look, I'm sorry."

"Martin, for Christ's sake—"

"I won't be long. He just needs to—"

Deborah walked out of the room, shrugging off her denim jacket as she went. She dropped it in the hall and slammed the door of their bedroom.

Paxton waited a few minutes, let her get rid of the first wave of anger. He and Deborah had been at the door of the flat, on their way out, when the phone rang. It was the second time in the past couple of weeks that Frankie had blown an evening out by ringing at the last minute.

"Deb?"

Standing outside the bedroom door. From inside, a blast of music. Fuck it. When she started throwing George Michael at him, there was no answer to that. He picked up Deborah's jacket, hung it on a hook near the front door and pulled on his pale blue Hugo Boss jacket. When he left he pulled the door gently shut behind him.

When Martin Paxton arrived at the pub, Frankie Crowe was sitting at the bar, working on a beer mat. He folded it in two, broke it apart along the fold, then folded the two pieces again. He did it once more, and he now had eight small, rough-edged pieces of cardboard. He placed each carefully on top of the other, forming a little tower, beside two similar cardboard constructions.

Standing at Frankie's shoulder, Martin noticed that his whiskey hadn't been touched. He said, "They did a survey of barmen once, and you know what their number-one pet hate is?"

"What'll you have?"

"That," Martin pointed at the torn cardboard, "they hate that. A pint."

Frankie pointed at a free table near the back. "I'll bring it over to you."

The pub was having a quiz night, conducted by a DJ who read each question in a country-and-western accent. "To what section of the orchestra does the timpani, the timpani, belong?" In between the questions, the DJ played what he referred to as funky music.

After they'd been sitting at the table five minutes, Martin knew that Frankie'd been out to Walkinstown to get the hardware from Tommy Sholtis. "And Milky's got a couple of places picked out. He'll source the cars."

"Fair enough."

Mostly Frankie spoke, mostly Martin listened, and they were happy with that arrangement. The only thing Frankie had to say that mattered was that he'd decided they were asking for too little. They'd always intended to go for a million. Frankie had been mulling it over.

"Break that down between the four of us, and take out what we have to shell out to Milky and Tommy Sholtis, we're talking not a lot more than two hundred grand a head." Frankie shook his head. "That kind of money, fuck sake, what's that worth these days? Wouldn't even buy a decent house in this town, even on the Northside."

You have to think ahead, Frankie said. The kind of money you get from a score like this could take you up to the premiership. He knew people, came across them all the time, who were crying out for investors. Bankroll a shipment, the white stuff flows in from Amsterdam, you take a margin, sell it on, leave the distribution to the people who want to take that risk. A slice of the profit goes back into the next deal, and the next and the one after that.

"It's like planting a money tree."

The million ransom, after the split, was too skinny for what Frankie had in mind. "Guy got himself a bank, the job must be worth two million. We double the ransom."

Martin Paxton didn't think it mattered. If it worked, it was a big piece of money, either way. If it didn't work, *sin scéal eile*. He just nodded.

There wasn't much else to discuss about the job. Nothing that couldn't have waited until next day. It was just the way Frankie needed to go over things again and again.

Frankie took a long drink. "Two million. That's real money. A long way from napkin rings."

Martin raised an eyebrow.

"First thing I ever stroked," Frankie said. "From Lenehan's in Talbot Street." He shook his head. "Napkin rings. Me and a couple of the lads went into town. Barely out of short trousers. Security guy was giving us the evil eye. Maybe if he hadn't been such a pushy fucker I wouldn't have bothered. They were just there, the napkin rings. Customer asked him something, whatever, he looked away, the napkin rings went up my sweater and we were out of there."

"Johnny Dillinger'll never be dead, what?"

"I didn't even own any napkins."

The pub DJ was reading out the answers to a section of the quiz. He punctuated the questions with bursts of throbbing music. Martin was about to suggest they get the hell out of here when Frankie held up a finger to the Asian lounge girl and then pointed to their almost empty glasses.

"OK," Martin said, "but I have to go after this one."

"She's got you rightly domesticated."

Martin grinned. "Fuck off."

"Can't say I blame you. This the big one?"

Martin never felt comfortable talking about that kind of thing. "You know, it's fine."

Frankie nodded. He seldom asked about personal shit and he'd met Deborah only twice. "Nice," was all he said to Martin after the first time he met her. After Frankie's trouble with Joan, he and Martin had only once talked about what happened. It was a drink-sodden evening that ended with Frankie curled up on the floor of Martin's flat, sobbing.

"I could have ended up down the juvenile, and off to the happy house for stealing fucking napkin rings."

"Kind of hard to shift on the black market."

"I once tried to add it all up, what it comes to, a dozen years of stroking. It's more than I'd get stacking shelves at Tesco, right enough. But not enough to make it worth the time you spend slopping out your potty in Mountjoy. You know what I mean?"

Martin shrugged. "I make a decent enough living. We both do."

"I'm not knocking it. All I'm saying, it's time to step up, Martin."

The quiz DJ was into the next round of questions, asking the name of the current US Secretary of State for Defense.

Martin said, "Still planning on running this past Jo-Jo?"

"It's the wise thing to do. Once we're OK with Jo-Jo," Frankie said, "anyone tries to take advantage, they know they've got him to worry about, too."

After the kidnap, word would get around. It usually did after a big job. Nothing solid enough to give the police a handle, but enough to point scavengers in the right direction.

"And what if Jo-Jo says no?"

"One thing clear. Whatever Jo-Jo says, this is going ahead, even if we have to take whatever shit he hands out afterwards. It's not like we need permission. Talking to him, we're just doing what's the right thing to do."

Martin didn't say anything. What he was thinking was that if Jo-Jo put a damper on the job and they went ahead, things could get very uncomfortable, very quickly.

Deborah had two glasses of red wine ready when Martin got back to the flat. They kissed. After a while, he said he was sorry, she said something similar and they left the wine alone for a while. Later, she brought him his glass in bed. Martin could have done without the wine, after three pints of Guinness down the pub, but he reckoned it wouldn't be terribly sensible to mention that.

"Cheers," he said.

"This thing, it's definitely on, then?"

"Don't worry about it."

Deborah looked like she was deciding not to say something, then she said it. "He's a strange man, Frankie Crowe. I know you don't—"

"Please," Martin said.

"Is he lonely or what?"

"Look, Deb, in the first place, if it wasn't for Frankie, I wouldn't be around to fuck up your evening."

"That's not true."

"You were there, were you, on the next landing?"

"I know you, you'd have survived. You've got strength, Martin. You're strong enough to have done it without Frankie."

She had no idea.

Martin had once tried to explain to her about how men relate to each other in prison. The best way to protect yourself is to come across like you're a guy that others need protection from. Back down, even on something that doesn't matter, you mark yourself as a fall guy. They'll be queuing up to use you as a demonstration of how tough they are.

"It wasn't so much that Bomber Harris had it in for me. It was more like, when he wanted to show people he was hot shit, the easiest way to do that was give someone a walloping, and I was the chosen one."

Martin closed his eyes. "Someone beats you down like that, you lose your nerve, they own you." He was quiet for a moment. Deborah watched him. Then he said, "Bomber Harris owned me. Frankie came along, he was Abraham Lincoln, you know what I mean?"

Debbie said she did. Then she said, "That doesn't mean that Frankie has to own you, either."

He looked at her. "You've no idea," he said. "You really don't."

Martin's wine glass was empty. He fetched the rest of the bottle from the kitchen and filled his glass, leaned across Deborah and saw that her glass was still almost full.

"It's not Lent, is it?"

Deborah picked up her glass, took a small sip and put it down again. She waited a moment and then she said, "That'll have to do me for a few months."

Martin said, "Oh," and sat on the side of the bed. He said nothing for a while, then he said, "You sure?"

She nodded.

"How long have you known?"

"Just today."

They hugged and talked in whispers for a while and Deborah told him she'd already worked out dates. They talked about that, about the things they'd have to do. In the middle of this, Martin shook his head and softly said, "Jesus Christ."

"Scary, isn't it?" Deborah said.

They agreed not to tell anyone for a while. Deborah's parents had immediately taken a liking to Martin, a polite chap with a job in software being an appropriate match for their librarian daughter. Then Martin was pulled in for questioning about a job he didn't do. The police let him out next day, but Deborah's mother had been there during the raid, mouth open, face pale. After that, her parents made no effort to disguise their loathing.

Martin took a slug of wine. He put the glass down and said, "That's it for me, too. For the duration." He leaned over and kissed her. "You're a genius, that's what you are."

5

There was a plate of biscuits in the centre of the table. No chocolate ones left. Lots of pinks and yellows and a few of the round brown ones, with the sugary white cream sandwiched in the middle. Eeny, meeny, miney, mo. Justin Kennedy was chewing the third and last of the chocolate biscuits from the plate. He gestured to young Faraday, who hopped up and hurried over to the table in the corner of the room. He came back with the coffee caddy and refreshed everyone's cup.

Albert Gibson was still yammering on. Albert Gibson was a fool, and that was just one of the many things Justin Kennedy was grateful for.

They were in the main conference room of the offices of Justin Kennedy & Co., on the top floor of a building round the corner from St. Stephen's Green. The building was owned by, and the offices rented from, Flynn O'Meara Tully & Co., the legal firm with which Justin Kennedy had made his name as a mergers and acquisitions expert, with a promising sideline in property. Six years earlier, Kennedy had amicably parted from Flynn O'Meara Tully, having built a reputation as a good man to have on side in any major deal. If you were assembling a site for development, buying or merging a company or taking it to the market, putting together a consortium or sourcing finance for a deal, Justin Kennedy could be relied on to save you a lot of grief.

There's security in being a prized performer at a place like

Flynn O'Meara Tully, but no matter how much they pay you there's always some no-talent gobshite further up the corporate food chain taking a bigger share of the proceeds and the credit.

From independent advising and consulting, Kennedy moved to taking a percentage in the deals he handled, and increasingly to initiating his own projects. As yet, he saw himself as merely moving out of the base camp of the higher peaks of the Dublin financial landscape, but he knew precisely where he was going. The current deal was a routine but high-fee transaction that would pay the rent.

Behind Albert Gibson, the window of the conference room ran almost the length of the room and more than half the height. It framed a panorama of the Dublin skyline, where a familiar sprouting of cranes decorated the city. From where he sat, Kennedy could see three tall buildings commemorating deals in which he had been involved, and from which he could remember the billing totals to the cent. Two of the cranes were markers for similar deals-in-the-making. Before this takeover thing was done and dusted, he'd be up to his neck in the next deal and getting another couple out of first gear.

Kennedy had been shepherding such deals for the best part of a decade. The work involved connecting ideas people with money people and identifying obstacles before they became problems. Once the numbers were credibly established, every deal had its own logic. It was all about recognising the pattern the negotiations would take and staying ahead of the curve, preparing responses before the opposition thought of the questions. Kennedy had figured out the pattern of this one weeks ago.

An Irish company, Kwarehawk Investments, was merging with an American corporation. Like lots of such developments since the economic boom peaked, Kwarehawk was merging in the sense that a fat little fish merges with the gaping jaws of a shark. Over the previous ten years, successful Irish businesses, having prospered for a while, queued up to be sold off to large foreign outfits, mostly British and American. Whatever the business—newspapers, PR firms, hotels, radio and TV stations, phone companies, pharmacy chains, electronics stores—as soon as it established a feasible profile it was rushed to the global marketplace. The founders of successful Irish companies tended to take the money and run. Maybe it was what Justin Kennedy thought of as the chicken factor—an absence of long-term confidence—or maybe just an impatience to get hold of the loot. Whatever, smoothing the way for such deals had become a significant part of Kennedy's business.

Justin Kennedy's firm had been hired to guide the Yanks through the intricacies of Irish company law. Two American lawyers had come over to earn big money for being told what to say. Gibson had brought along three sidekicks to pad out his firm's fees. Kennedy had young Faraday for the same reason, but mostly to pour the coffee. Helen Snoddy, a freelance consultant on contract to Flynn O'Meara Tully, was sitting to Kennedy's left. Tall, thin, brunette, primarily Prada, with a touch of Vuitton, just twenty-seven, smarter than anyone in the room and aware of it, she supplied specialist advice on tax matters. Sometimes an aspect of a deal had to go through three or four shelf companies and a couple of offshore jurisdictions before the tax liability was small enough to please the players. And Helen always knew the shortest route between any given deal and the nearest tax sanctuary.

Kennedy adjusted his face to display mild interest in Gibson's meandering, and let some coffee wash down the last crumbs of the chocolate biscuit. Gibson was chubby and bald, the kind of bald where the remaining tufts of hair are fluffed up and teased and treated with the care given to rare plants. It had taken him two weeks to prepare his figures, based on two months of negotiations. Another week to get his PowerPoint presentation to his liking—although the figures could have been printed off on one side of A4.

One of the Americans asked a question about the timescale of an assortment of software licences. Justin Kennedy nodded his approval. Inwardly, he groaned. The short answer was that the software licences were irrelevant, applying to material already obsolete. But Gibson would never give a short answer. Helen Snoddy glanced at her watch. Kennedy could see that the top of the page open on her legal pad was decorated with doodles, prominent among which was a quite impressive caricature of Gibson, with a clown's nose.

Kennedy took another mouthful of coffee and tried to stop his gaze drifting back towards the biscuits. He decided to exercise restraint. Another twenty minutes of this and his secretary would intervene to announce that lunch was ready to be served.

At two thirty on the dot, the kids of St. Ciaran's National School spilled out the doorway, draining the last of their drinks from their beakers, dragging jackets along the ground behind them. The boys used lurching shoulders and swinging schoolbags to continue the little skirmishes left over from lunchtime in the schoolyard. The girls mostly came in bunches, clustering, chattering.

Little more than a week back at school, Sinead was already settled down and loving it. Over the summer, the school's old prefab classrooms had been demolished and a row of new prefabs had been built. Frankie Crowe wasn't happy that his daughter was being educated in a shanty schoolroom, but he had to admit that the prefabs were at least clean and warm. The main school buildings were more solid, but shabby. Despite the voluntary donations and the kids' sponsored walks, there wasn't money for plaster on the breeze-block walls, and some of the classrooms had no ceilings, just steel girders beneath a corrugated roof.

Sinead came running. These days, whenever he came for her, at school or at the house, she ran to him. Another year or two, a welcoming hug for her dad would be out of the question when her friends were around. She handed him her schoolbag and ran to catch up with Carla and Patsy, her best friends at school. Frankie walked behind, the schoolbag over one shoulder. Only when they got to the main road and the other two turned right, did she wave them goodbye and drop back to walk alongside Frankie.

Frankie Crowe collected Sinead from school once a week, on Wednesdays. Sometimes at weekends he took her into town for a treat and she slept over at his place in Glasnevin, but she didn't much like the cramped flat, so he didn't push it too often. She was eight now, she'd been four when he went into jail and six when he came out, and it had taken her over a year to get to know him all over again.

The Wednesday routine varied little. McDonald's, then whatever Sinead felt like. Today there was a Disney movie she'd seen twice and had to see again. "Mam promised she'll get me the video as soon as it comes out."

It was a cartoon thing, several steps up from Sesame Street, Teletubbies and all the other bright, cheerful things that once made her giggle but were now deeply uncool. She was a passionate Barney fan when Frankie went to jail. By the time he got out, she was treating the chuckling dinosaur with undisguised scorn.

Sinead changed his point of view about doing a stretch. It used to be that jail was tough, but it came with the territory. "You're doing the crime," Jo-Jo Mackendrick said to Frankie when he was still a teenager. "Sooner or later, you'll do the time. If you can't handle that, now's the time to find yourself a job stacking shelves down the supermarket."

Frankie could handle it, and had done so three times. Long before he went down for the two-year stretch, he had taken small hits—probation, probation again, then a few weeks inside. He coped. Get into the right frame of mind and you could even get something useful out of it, like a soldier racking up the campaign medals that gave him credibility with his peers. Stay on the straight and narrow, be an upright John Citizen, you spend how many years locked up in a job that eats a big hole out of your life, pays buttons and bores you into an early grave. Follow your own path and you stay free, live well.

The way Frankie added it up, even doing all the hard time that comes with the life, you spend a lot less dead time in jail than John Citizen spends shovelling shit for shit wages.

What he hadn't counted on was the massive chunk that the two-year jail term gouged out of his relationship with Sinead. Those two years amounted to half the life she'd lived before he went inside. It was like time changed pace when kids were involved.

And when he came out, the split with Joan had torn away the permanence of his relationship with his daughter, reducing it to this daddy-by-appointment routine.

As usual on Wednesdays, they cut across Rockwood Park, on their way to McDonald's. Rockwood was a stretch of green in the centre of a housing estate, peppered with untidy clumps of carelessly placed trees and bushes. In the middle there was a flat, glass-strewn tarmacked area where kids played football in the daytime and gangs of teenagers drank cider at night. Throughout the day, people drove to the park, took their dogs out of their cars and set them loose to shit on the grass.

On these walks from the school, Sinead regularly surprised Frankie with her knowledge of trees and plants, her carefully phrased nuggets of information about animals and insects. He didn't know enough to be sure if her lectures were accurate, but he loved the way she brimmed with new information and couldn't wait to pass it on. Today it was knock-knock jokes.

"Knock, knock."

Frankie grinned. "Who's there?"

"Luke."

"Luke who?"

"Luke through the keyhole and you'll see."

Halfway across the park, Crowe saw the squad car. It came out of a nearby street, turned parallel to the path on which Crowe and Sinead were walking and slowed down, matching their pace. Bastards must have spotted him earlier, now they were timing it so they'd pass the exit just as he came out the other side of the park. Gobshites.

Sinead was telling him about a schoolroom crisis that developed after some graffiti was found in the toilets. "The toilet incident," she called it. Teacher was pretty mad, and she wanted whoever did it to own up, or they'd be in deep trouble.

They were twenty feet from the park exit, and Crowe could see that the squad car was coming to a stop. He recognised the driver from the local garda station. Used to run into him over in Rialto. What was it? Hennessy, Flannery, something like that. Big ignorant culchie bollocks.

"I think it was probably Katy O'Neill. She's a goody-two-shoes when teacher is looking, but she doesn't fool me."

"How a'ya, Frankie." The culchie bollocks had the window rolled down and was leaning out with a big grin on his face. "Proper family man these days, what?"

Sinead hadn't noticed the squad car until now. Her cheeks went red, her gaze flicking here and there. She slid her hand into Frankie's grip.

"Just keep walking, sweetheart."

"What do they want, Dad?" Her voice was low, diffident.

"Nothing to worry about, love."

The squad car moved slowly, keeping up with them. "Off to the supermarket, Frankie? Fill up another trolley, what?"

Frankie stopped walking.

"What does he mean, Daddy?"

"He's just stirring it, sweetheart. Don't worry about scum like that."

"You sure you don't need anything at Tesco's, Frankie?"

Crowe saw that the other cop, on the passenger side, a young guy, was staring fixedly ahead, at nothing at all, as though wishing he was anywhere else.

Fennelly, that was it, the culchie bollocks. Garda Fennelly.

Crowe hunkered down and took Sinead by the shoulders. "There's nothing to be afraid of, love. Just a stupid man making a fool of himself. Just stand here, OK?"

"Daddy, please—"

Crowe stood up, turned and walked over to the squad car. His tone was conversational. "Fennelly, you can mouth all you like, but you'll always be a slag. They all know you." Standing close to the car, he bent down and spoke across Fennelly to the young cop. "He used to ride the hoors, d'you know that? When he was over the south side. Pretend to arrest the poor bitches, take a freebie and let them off."

The young cop stared daggers at Crowe. Garda Fennelly went red.

"Did you know that? Ask your mates. Everyone knows about Fennelly, but most people don't like to say it out loud."

For a moment, Frankie wondered if the two cops might be wound up enough to get out of the car—even with all the houses around—and give him a seeing-to.

But Fennelly was rolling up the window. The squad car accelerated away.

"Down the canal—they all know him!" Frankie shouted as the squad car slowed to turn into a side street. "Go on, Fennelly, you fucking muppet!"

"Daddy!"

When Crowe turned back, there were tears running down Sinead's cheeks.

In McDonald's, fifteen minutes later, as Sinead dipped a chicken nugget in the little rectangle of curry sauce, Crowe tried to think of something to say about what happened, but he couldn't think of anything that wouldn't make things worse. Sinead had adopted a stubbornly casual air that only made her anxiety more obvious. He asked her if she had much homework, and she said it was more of the same. He asked her what part of the movie she was most looking forward to seeing again and she said all of it. He asked what games she'd played in the schoolyard that morning and she said they were the usual ones.

Crowe stirred his coffee. Back in the old days a friend of his used to collect McDonald's little plastic stirrers. There used to be a tiny spoon at one end, perfect for measuring a hit of heroin. When they found out how their stirrers were being used, McDonald's started making them flat at the end.

Crowe asked Sinead what she wanted for her birthday, a month away. She picked at her chicken nuggets and said she hadn't thought about it. Frankie knew the thing to do was give her time to settle. She spent a while tinkering with the plastic toy that came with the Happy Meal. Twist the knob at the back and something was supposed to pop up out of the top, but it didn't.

"Another dud," Frankie said. Sinead nodded.

She was finishing off her strawberry milkshake when she said, "Knock, knock."

"Who's there?"

"Cook."

"Cook who?"

She cackled. "Come on, open the door and stop making bird noises."

Frankie didn't get it for a second, then he threw his head back and laughed.

The legal meeting on the Kwarehawk Investments takeover

ended at 5 P.M. Justin Kennedy spent most of the next hour making phone calls and reviewing progress in other matters. At 6 P.M., he was in the dark and noisy downstairs bar of the Westin buying Helen Snoddy a drink.

"We could have had this deal wrapped up a week ago," she said, "if that clown would just sit down, shut up and pass the papers to his principals for signing. And they wouldn't be one cent worse off, either."

Kennedy shook his head. "You're being logical, again. Gibson is a clown—business is full of them. Without the clowns, we'd all have a leaner time of it. Thank Christ for clowns, is what I say."

Helen had some sort of family commitment, so there would be no spending the evening back at her place in Sandymount.

"You have time for a quick bite?" Kennedy asked.

"As long as I'm on my way by seven."

"You're on."

Ten minutes later, as they were being seated in a tapas bar, Kennedy called home.

"Gibson's about to run out of shite to spout," he told Angela. "Home at a reasonable hour for a change."

She asked, as she always did, about whether he had eaten, should she have something ready? He told her he'd grab something on the run, not to bother.

On the walk home from the cinema, Sinead explained to Frankie, in complex detail, the plot of a movie she'd recently watched on video at the home of her very best friend. He was thinking of something else, but he paid enough attention to get away with the odd meaningless interjection—"That's pretty scary," "Cool move, right?"

He took her for granted sometimes, then he got taken aback by her energy and the countless surprises that popped out of her changing personality. He had helped create her, but sometimes he wondered how much he'd had to do with making her the person she was going to be. It was like there was so much more to her than could have come from him and from Joan.

In the first hour of her life, nineteen-year-old Frankie had been stunned by the purity and simplicity of his own protective reaction. He made himself promises about how this clean, innocent bundle would become the centre of everything. Nothing would be allowed come between Frankie and the warmth he felt towards this blanket-wrapped mystery. Things happened, things came up, and Frankie found himself in places he never intended to go.

They came to a low wall surrounding the Ring, the green space in the centre of the Sweetlake estate, five minutes from her home. Sinead made him sit on the wall while she finished her story. When she was done, she looked him in the eye and said, "You haven't been listening to me at all, have you?"

"I'm sorry, love. I was thinking of something else."

"What?"

"I was thinking about the day you were born."

"What about it?"

"I was just remembering."

"I know, I know," her face exaggerating in mock weariness. "It was the best day ever in the history of the world."

She grinned and Frankie held his arms out and said, "C'mere," and she stepped forward. He held her close, aware of her smell and the sound of her breathing, the feel of her hair, the movement of her little body, the years of joy and pain that lay ahead of her, and he closed his eyes and he loved the very air that hung around her.

Joan Crowe wore blue jeans and a plain grey T-shirt. She was slightly thinner than was fashionable. Her hair was cropped tight. Not for style, but for convenience. One less thing to worry about. For the same reason, her nails were trimmed short. Beyond a few quick strokes of lipstick, she didn't bother with makeup. The lines at her eyes and the extremes of her mouth bowed downwards, as though pulled by gravity, or something heavier.

Once it turned six o'clock she found herself, as usual on Wednesdays, drawn to the front bedroom, where she could see far down into the lane along which Sinead and Frankie would come strolling. There was no need to be anxious—whatever else about him, Frankie was a good father. He'd have her back safe and on time. It was just that so much of Joan's life was bound up in the child that even the routine separations left her feeling edgy.

Feeling edgy was part of the job of trying to raise a kid in this place. It was a way station for Joan, after Frankie and while building up to something better. People who couldn't afford anywhere else settled for the Sweetlake estate. People who got evicted from other places ended up here. Girls, old enough to get pregnant, too young to hold together a relationship, raised their kids here, coping with the remnants of the lives they'd thought they had. The Sweetlake was heavy with prey. Kids went out of control early, and too many of them enjoyed their ability to frighten the shit out of the vulnerable. Raising kids around here meant protecting them from the brutes and deflecting them from becoming one. A neat trick, when it could be a struggle just to pay the gas bill.

When Sinead started school, Joan got a job on a checkout at the local Dunnes Stores. Mostly nine in the morning to one in the afternoon. Occasionally, Joan's mobile rang and she had to get someone to cover for her while she went to the school to collect Sinead. One day last winter it was because the ancient heating system finally broke down. The kids were just three days back in school this September when a rat came strolling out from a hole in the wall and climbed on to the window sill to take a leisurely look around. The school was closed for a couple of days, and Joan left Sinead with a local childminder while she went to work, which put a crimp in her income that week. The supermarket wages weren't great, but a bit of cash went into the credit union every week. Over the past few months the house was showing the difference, and this summer she'd managed to arrange a week's holiday outside Dublin. The aim was to shift out of this estate before Sinead was ready for secondary school.

From the bedroom window, Joan could see the remains of the stolen car that got burned out last night. First time in a while they'd done that. Used to be a regular event. The kids stole something fast enough—an Audi or a Volvo, maybe—and they took it to the Ring, the circular grassy area in the centre of the estate. They drove around the Ring, revving noisily, doing handbrake turns, until someone called the police. Then they taunted the cops until they got a chase out of it, swerving in and out of Sweetlake's narrow streets. Very occasionally they killed someone, another driver, a pedestrian, a garda or most likely themselves. Mostly, when the kids got tired of the chase they lost the cops and, as a final spectacle before they went to bed, set the car on fire.

It was always boys who did the driving, so Joan didn't have to worry about that. All she had to worry about was a very few years from now Sinead becoming a passenger on one of those jaunts. Or becoming pregnant by one of the little fuckers doing the driving.

Like me.

The burned-out car would sit there for a few days. Things got broken quickly around here—street lights, railings, gates, garden walls, windows, side-passage doors—and the council was slow to fix them. Things got covered in graffiti and the council didn't bother doing anything about it because the city officials didn't see the point of an expensive redecoration just to give the little bastards a clean canvas. The police came to kick ass when something happened; they were never there to prevent it.

The part of Finglas where Frankie and Martin and Joan came from used to be like that, before it settled down. It was usually Frankie did the driving, Martin in the passenger seat.

Joan Crowe was standing at the open front door, a big smile attached to her face, as Sinead and Frankie arrived at the front gate. "Was the movie as good as the last time you saw it?"

"Better!"

Sinead was carrying the striped paper bag that held the last of the sweets Frankie had bought her as part of the cinema routine. She ran up the path, winked at Joan as she passed, and powered up the stairs at a noisy, swaying gallop.

"Hi," Frankie said.

"You'd better come in."

Frankie left Sinead's schoolbag on a chair and looked around. Joan had put up new wallpaper in the living room. A kind of foggy pink colour. Everything else was the same. Frankie hadn't been in this room for over six months. Shitty neighbourhood, the best Joan could afford on her checkout job. Frankie'd offered, but she wouldn't allow him to give her anything. He bought the schoolbooks and uniforms, and he was allowed to take Sinead out shopping for clothes, toys, books, whatever she wanted, but Joan took care of the day-to-day.

"Everything OK?" Frankie asked.

"Not a bother."

She seemed thinner, wiry, strong. Kept herself busy. She didn't take care of herself, that was Joan's problem. Cheap clothes. Lines starting around the mouth. No effort. Take a little trouble, she'd be everything that knocked him out first time he laid eyes on her. Even now, he could see the shape of her underneath the kind of crap she wore these days and something flared inside him, a surge of memory—the small movements in dark rooms, urgent words and glimpses of shapes that made the breath stop in his throat. Nothing and no one had ever come close.

"She's taken a lot of time with this," Joan said.

"With what?"

Joan just nodded towards the door.

Sinead's footsteps were clattering down the stairs. She was flushed, her eyes alight, as she ran into the room. She held up something flat and a foot square, wrapped in flowery paper that had fluorescent "Happy Birthday!" printed all over it. "I did it myself," she said. "Happy birthday." For a moment, he juggled dates in his head.

"How did you—"

"Mam told me!"

When Frankie peeled away the wrapper from the birthday card, the front showed a detailed drawing of a large sunflower, with "Happy Birthday" in a half-circle around it. Sunflowers were Sinead's trademark. Few of her drawings were without one. He opened the card and saw an elaborate sketch—two figures, himself and Sinead, she holding a stick with a fluffy cloud on the end, and carrying a teddy bear. There was a mountain behind her. He recognised the scene at once. The day they'd spent in Bray that summer, the candyfloss, the bear he won for her in a crane contraption in the amusement arcade. Above it all, the sun, and the rays from the sun shooting down on to everything.

"Ah, sweetheart, it's only gorgeous."

She was holding out a small, badly wrapped package and when he unwrapped it he found a black imitation-leather wallet with "Dublin" stamped in gold on the front. "I bought it with my own money," she said. Frankie hugged her and she held on to him, proud and pleased.

"It's special," Frankie said, "just like you." She was blushing. "I'll always treasure it, sweetheart, always."

Joan said, "Time for homework, love, while I get your tea ready. Say goodbye to your dad, then get changed, OK?"

A minute later, Sinead was skipping up the stairs. She was humming a tune from a TV advert for a DIY superstore.

"Jesus, she's great," Frankie said. "There's real talent in that drawing."

"She's been working on it, off and on, for the past week. She'd take no help at all. All her own work."

There's something there still, Frankie thought. There had to be. Joan reminding Sinead about his birthday. Despite it all, there had to be some feeling left.

"Listen, Joan, thanks for—you've been really great, the way you help keep things going between Sinead and me."

Joan stared at him. Then she looked out the window as she spoke. "Just because I can't stand having you near me is no reason why she shouldn't be on good terms with her father."

"Ah, Joan—"

"I've got to get her tea."

"OK, fuck it, no need to make it so obvious. I'm going."

Now that Sinead was out of earshot, there was no trace of the gloss of normality Joan had adopted when he'd arrived at the house. She was always good at that. Putting on a face she could hide behind, then coming on like a fucking martyr. Doing that, it was like Frankie was the total shit, like none of it was her fault. Most of it, when you got right down to it, was her fault. If she hadn't been such a cold-hearted bitch.

He started for the door, then turned. "About Sinead. I'm not sure about the next couple of Wednesdays. Two, three, I don't know. Something's come up, I've got to do something. I'll be away."

He paused, but she didn't display any curiosity. Fuck her.

"Not sure how long it'll take. I'll give you a buzz when I know. OK?"

"Have you told her?"

"Yeah, she knows. I think I'll be OK to pick her up from school the Wednesday after that, but I'll let you know. That's not going to mess things up for you?"

"I'm here, one way or the other. I'm always here."

"Well, I'll do my best."

"I've got to get her tea."

Frankie nodded. Going out the door, with the birthday card and the present held against his chest, he called up the stairs to Sinead and she returned the goodbye and added one last "Happy birthday." That thing with the culchie bollocks, it was like it never happened.

Before he was halfway down the path to the front gate he heard Joan close the front door behind him.

In the car park at Flynn O'Meara Tully, Justin Kennedy and Helen Snoddy kissed.

"Tomorrow night?" he asked.

"I'm off on my travels. Remember?"

"Of course. Give me a buzz when you know how you're fixed."

Madrid, of course. She'd told him a while back. Home for a couple of days, then she had to accompany some client to meetings with bankers in two jurisdictions, she was speaking at a weekend seminar in Galway, then she was taking a few days in London. She didn't say, but the London thing was probably business, though he supposed there might be a bit of personal stuff. He never asked about her personal life. He knew there was a boyfriend of sorts, and her family was important. She never asked about his family, or his relationship with Angela. It wasn't the first bit of offside fun that Kennedy had enjoyed. Fifteen months into his marriage he had realised that being happy at home didn't mean he had to deny himself the pleasures of bachelorhood.

The thing with Helen Snoddy began two years back, an off-

and-on thing. When it was on, Kennedy didn't look around for any other diversions. He wasn't sure that was true of Helen. He never asked and he didn't much mind. This kind of thing was as much a part of Kennedy's life as his occasional lunchtime indulgences in the small, expensive restaurants that catered to the business trade in this area. It was pleasant, it added something to his life, it made him feel good about himself. It was going nowhere and neither he nor Helen wanted it to.

As Helen's maroon Chrysler Crossfire pulled out of the car park, Kennedy unlocked his Merc and threw his briefcase on to the back seat. When he sat at the wheel, he paused for a moment, allowing himself the ritual indulgence of enjoying the moment—the achievements and the pleasures of the day, the evening yet to come, not least the feel of the car, the way it fitted into the life he had built around him. It would be nice to get home at a reasonable hour. The kids would still be up.

6.

The house lights went off within a few minutes of ten thirty. They could see just one light now, in an upstairs room at the front, but it was too far away to see anything useful. Frankie Crowe and Martin Paxton spent three evenings parked in a lane from which they could see the Kennedy house, but Frankie thought that kind of thing was too risky. "One snoopy copper and it's all fucked up." Tonight they were just cruising the neighbourhood, stopping for a few minutes down the street from the target house.

They drove by the house several evenings, sometimes up to half a dozen times, getting a handle on the routine. Twice they saw the target arriving home in his Merc. Other than that there was very little to see.

Every house in this part of Ballsbridge cost at least two or three times the price of the average Dublin home. Every house on Pemberton Road cost at least twice the Ballsbridge average. The Kennedy place was bigger than any of its neighbours. It was a double-fronted red-brick Victorian, bay windows all over the place. The front of the house was almost completely clothed in creeping vines. Each corner of the roof was dominated by a chimney, making it look a little like a small castle. Although set in a busy neighbourhood and parallel to a main road, Pemberton Road managed to retain a placid atmosphere. The house was set well back, behind an array of bushes and trees, with plenty of space on either side. Private, or—from another point of view—isolated.

As they drove away from Pemberton Road, Martin said, "Ready for Jo-Jo?"

"Tomorrow. He'll be OK."

"You're up for it, then, a bit of crawling?"

"Fuck off, Martin, we're not crawling. Jo-Jo's no problem. He owes me."

It was starting to rain as Angela Kennedy closed the bedroom curtains. The weather had been fitful through the summer, rain never far away. Angela enjoyed the certainty of the approaching winter, the cosy feeling she got closing curtains against the elements. Soon, they'd be on the run-in to Christmas, their second Christmas in this house. She had enjoyed the two weeks in New York with Justin and the kids, and the week in Barbados alone with Justin, but she welcomed the coming winter just as much. More, perhaps. The summer was pleasure, the winter was intimacy. Just a few years back, when drink and parties and the frippery of social conquest mattered, she could never have imagined the depth of happiness to be found in the weeks of long nights at home, snuggled with the kids and—when he could manage it—Justin. The fire blazing, games or crayons or a last video before bedtime, reading and hugs and all the stuff that sounded too trivial until it became the centre of everything. There were enough nights on the town with Justin or with friends to make a contrast. Knowing it would be just a few short years before the kids became too old or too cool for that kind of thing only made the intimacy more intense.

By the time Angela slid between the sheets, Justin was locking up downstairs. The kids were already asleep. When Justin came out of the bathroom, Angela said, "Saskia has your birthday present already. Luke wants me to take him into town at the weekend, he has something in mind for you." She paused. "I know you'll make it home early."

"It's not for another—what?—two weeks."

"They're counting on it. You'll be there?"

"I'll be there."

"Sometimes I regret you're not a bit more humdrum, drawing up wills for pensioners. We'd get to see more of you."

He got into bed. "You'd soon get sick of the sight of me."

"Never," she said, embracing him. They kissed. She let her fingers loiter on the back of his neck and brushed his lips with hers again. Justin returned the kiss, then he reached down for a green folder on the floor beside the bed. Settling back on the pillow, he opened the folder.

Angela hesitated. The signal hadn't been bare enough, and he was tired and distracted. She could make it more obvious, or leave it for now. She said, "Goodnight," and he murmured a reply, already skimming through a column of figures.

7

They parked around the corner from Jo-Jo's house. "What's the worst he can say?" said Martin Paxton. "No. He can say no, that's the worst he can say. And how bad is that? I mean, it's not like this town isn't brimming with loose money waiting to be picked up."

"What's wrong with that old bitch?" Frankie Crowe was looking at a fat, middle-aged woman, her hair dyed jet black, who was backing her car out of the driveway of the house outside which they were parked. As she edged past, she glared resentfully at the two men.

Martin smiled back at her. "We're poking our grubby little motor car into her personal space, that's what. People around here, they like their personal space."

"Fuck her."

Although the woman couldn't hear them, she revved aggressively as she drove away, as though in response to Crowe's remark.

"I'm off," Crowe said, opening the door. After yesterday's rain, the weather had swung round and the sun was bringing out the autumn colours in the trees.

Paxton wound down the car window. "Don't stay for tea and cakes, right? Remember I'm out here cracking my knuckles. And good luck."

Walking up the path to Jo-Jo's house, Crowe pulled at the hem of his leather jacket, making it taut at the shoulders. He used both hands to tug the collar of his shirt straight. He recognised the gesture as one of nervousness and felt annoyed at his deference. No big deal. There was a way of doing things, a necessary display of respect, and that's all this was.

Jo-Jo's place was a large detached red-brick, off the Howth Road. Lots of greenery around the outside, big gardens front and back, enclosing the house in a cocoon of privacy. When Crowe pressed the button, the bell played the first few notes of the theme from *Star Wars*.

The bodyguard's name was Christy something. Crowe had met him in company a couple of times, had a drink with him, but they'd never worked together. Christy was tall and solid. He wore jeans and a dark blue checked shirt, his sleeves rolled up over thick forearms. Unlike most men who shave their heads, Christy wasn't masking the symptoms of encroaching baldness. The bald, hard look was more suitable for his position as Jo-Jo's primary minder. He nodded a welcome and closed the door behind the visitor.

"What's the mood?" Crowe asked.

"You know Jo-Jo, mate. Take him as you find him. One minute he's a cuddly bear, next minute he's pulling your spine out through your ear." Christy grinned. "Relax, Frankie. He likes you. Always did. You need something?"

"No, just keeping in touch, more or less. I don't want to step on any toes."

"Always a good idea," Christy said. "Wait there, Frankie, back in a mo." He went out through the kitchen.

The hall was wide and high, the floor was black marble, the walls were oak-panelled. Off to the right there was a games room and bar. There was a snooker table at one end of the room, at the other an array of PlayStation, GameCube and Xbox consoles. The bar came with optics for dispensing spirits and old-fashioned long-wooden-handled pumps for pulling pints. It had high stools, beer mats, all kinds of glasses, little bowls for cherries and olives and slices of lemon, a bowl of peanuts and a variety of drinks ranging over half a dozen shelves. Frankie wasn't very clear about the kind of life he was working towards, but it included a games room like this. The kind of place where you could pull a pint when you had your mates over for a frame or two.

Frankie had last played snooker here with Jo-Jo eighteen months back, two days after he got out of prison. Jo-Jo was the kind of snooker player who chalked his cue before every shot. He'd assessed the lay of the blue, first from one side of the table, then the other. "There's always room on my crew, you know that," he told Frankie. Jo-Jo bent low to judge the probable track of the white, then went to the top of the table to see if there was a follow-on pot. After staring at the balls for a while, he decided on a safety shot and sent the white gently up the table, where it softly kissed the blue and spun off to stop within a hair of the top cushion.

Frankie had explained about the plans he'd made with Waters and Cox, two hard men from Rialto that he'd hooked up with in the Joy. Partners, they said, three partners with a big future. This was before experience proved what fucking eejits they both were. Jo-Jo understood the need to move on, to start over.

"Come see me any time, Frankie. You know you're always welcome in this house."

With nothing much on, Frankie went for the remaining red down the other end of the table. He hit the white hard, the red jangled and the white had enough speed left to touch three cushions before glancing off the red again and leaving it hanging over a centre pocket. Jo-Jo cleared the table.

Later, standing in the hall when Frankie was leaving, Jo-Jo produced an envelope and tucked it into the inside pocket of Frankie's jacket.

"A little welcome-home present." He winked. "Get you up and running."

On his way home, Frankie checked the envelope and found three grand. That night, they left Sinead with Joan's mother and Frankie took Joan for a slap-up at *La Stampa* and they spent the night at the Shelbourne.

As the Waters and Cox thing went pear-shaped, Frankie talked on the phone with Jo-Jo a couple of times, met him in this house with a roomful of others for Christmas drinks. It was understood that Frankie was still trying to find his feet as an independent, but within the glow of Jo-Jo's goodwill.

There were lots of others who saw Jo-Jo as a mentor, but only Frankie Crowe had stood with Jo-Jo Mackendrick in the front room of this house, just over ten years earlier, when death came crashing through the window. Not yet out of his teens, Frankie was rooted to the floor, white-faced. Jo-Jo scrambled to a desk drawer and came back in a hurry with two handguns, one of which he held out to Frankie.

A hard man from Blanchardstown, figuring there was a shortcut to writing off the debt he owed Jo-Jo, had sent two assholes over Jo-Jo's garden wall with shotguns. After the front window was blown in, Jo-Jo and Frankie stood shoulder to shoulder, blazing away, while the dark figures in the garden crouched in the bushes and fired one more volley before their nerve broke and they legged it. The trouble ended a few days later, when Jo-Jo sent a crew to Blanchardstown and the hard man had his debt cancelled in the most permanent way possible.

The events of that evening made Frankie more than just another crew member, which was why he now felt confident that Jo-Jo would look tolerantly on any new direction he wished to take. Jo-Jo was old stock, came up the hard way, one of the pioneers. Maybe a bit laid-back these days, maybe a bit out of touch with the younger scene, but Frankie knew he was a fair man.

"Frankie! Frankie Crowe!" The fragile, high-pitched voice

came from behind him. Crowe turned and saw Jo-Jo's mother coming through the kitchen doorway. Pearl Mackendrick, once a legend of inner-city Dublin, the hard-nosed widow-woman, a pitiless moneylender. Now she was celebrated as the proud mother of two of the most feared gangsters on the Northside. Her ancient face seemed too slender for all the wrinkles it had to accommodate.

"Pearl, you're looking great!"

Her smile broadened.

Pearl was in her mid-eighties. Hair dyed a discreet blonde, fingernails an imprudent scarlet. The Ralph Lauren blouse and skirt, a trophy of her annual shopping trip to Harrods, hung a little too freely on her thin frame.

"It must be a year, Frankie! No, I tell a lie, it was Christmas, and that's an age."

"Pearl, you're looking younger every time I see you. Must be all the toyboys keep you fit and healthy."

She laughed obligingly and as they embraced he was surrounded by the sweet perfume with which Pearl drenched herself each morning as soon as she rose. Obnoxious as it was, it was an improvement on the carbolic smell Frankie remembered from his teenage days, hanging around the Mackendrick house, carrying messages for Jo-Jo and Lar. Even back then he'd figured there was no future in freelance knocking-off, the real money was in the organised outfits that were coming together. Pearl was a permanent presence through the years when Frankie served his apprenticeship with the Mackendrick brothers. Her husband, an anonymous little mouse of a man, his purpose in life served by providing Pearl with sons, drank himself to death before the boys were out of their teens.

"How's the little one? She's only gorgeous!"

"She's thriving, Pearl, thriving."

"You'll have to bring her round to see me. Listen, did they offer you a cup of tea?"

"Thanks, but not this time, Pearl. Business. Your young fella's expecting me. Sure, I'll look in and say hello before I go."

Pearl put her hand on his arm. "I mean it, love, bring the little one round here some afternoon next week. It's great to have the youngsters around. It's like I'm soaking up a bit of their energy, God bless them."

"I will, Pearl, she'd love to see you."

As Pearl moved slowly towards the stairs, her arms folded, her slippers making a slapping sound on the marble, Christy came to the door of the kitchen and crooked a finger. He led Frankie through the kitchen and out the French windows, into the back garden. About thirty feet away, Jo-Jo Mackendrick was slouched in a chair beside a wooden garden table, phone at his ear. He wore black shorts and a dazzling white FCUK top. There was a glass of white wine on the table, beside a hardback book—a John Grisham—open and face down.

Jo-Jo finished his conversation and waved at Frankie to come over. Christy stood by the French windows, arms folded, in sight but out of hearing. In his mid-fifties, balding, with a slight paunch, Jo-Jo still had the build of the construction labourer he once was. He'd had an extension built on to the side of the house, a gym where he did half an hour each morning on the bike, reading the *Irish Times* and the sports pages of the *Mirror*, and three mornings a week he followed the bike with half an hour on the weights. His three sons were grown up, two of them with kids of their own. Since his wife had died of breast cancer five years ago he'd lived alone here with his mother, wintering in the Caribbean but always spending Christmas week at home, holding open house for his friends and their families. Jo-Jo retained overall control of the business, while his older brother Lar handled most of the day-to-day concerns—what Jo-Jo called "operational matters." The core businesses were cigarette smuggling, protection and three brothels. The firm also took what Jo-Jo referred to as "royalties" from a number of operations managed by others, such as diesel laundering and credit-card fraud. A car-ringing scam had recently closed down due to police attention. The Mackendricks still sponsored the occasional armed robbery, but Jo-Jo preferred the steady income from what he thought of as the wholesale and service sectors. Although the brothers had provided finance for occasional heroin and cocaine imports, they decided early on to avoid the hassle of direct involvement in drug distribution. Wholesale was safer, leave the retailing to the hobbits. Three small, legitimate building companies, unconnected and working in different parts of the city, were used for laundering money.

"Your mother's looking well, Jo-Jo."

"She's terrific. New hip, had the veins done. She's off the smokes and her blood pressure's like a teenager's. Doc says she's so healthy we'll have to shoot her."

"Old trouper."

"That she is. Sit down, Frankie." He gestured to a chair. "Might as well get a bit of sun while it's still here. Poxy summer." Crowe sat down and waited while Jo-Jo took a sip of wine.

"See the missus at all?" Jo-Jo said.

"When I see the kid, once, twice a week. Otherwise, that whole thing's dead."

"Fine-looking woman. Shame the way that went." He picked up the wine glass and took another sip. The obligatory personal chit-chat was over. "Now, what can I do for you?"

"Thanks for seeing me like this. I mean, I know it's short notice, but I've been setting up a major piece of action. So, I thought I'd better run it past you. Out of respect."

"That's decent of you."

Fuck you, too, Jo-Jo. You could make it easy, wave it through, instead of which I have to make like I'm asking for a favour.

"You know I've been marking time since I split with Waters and Cox? Little jobs, nothing special."

"You and Martin Paxton."

"That's right."

"And?"

"We've been working on something a bit more ambitious."

"Go on."

"It's a kidnap. Guy's got a private bank."

"A snatch?"

"I know exactly what—"

"Frankie, no one does kidnaps any more. Too fucking—"

The edge of a cliff. Please, Jo-Jo, don't bring me here.

"Jo-Jo, the kind of money there's around these days—"

"Jesus, Frankie." Jo-Jo began ticking things off on his fingers. "One—you can't make a thing like that pay unless you take someone who's really loaded. Two—this country, anyone loaded the chances are they're connected. Three—someone gets snatched, and all the things the cops don't have the time to do, they suddenly have the time to do. Four—every tout in the country goes on a premium rate. You know what that means for people like me."

Don't do this, Jo-Jo.

"I've earned the right, Jo-Jo, you know that."

Jo-Jo stood up. He walked a few steps, turned and pointed a finger at Frankie.

"You do a post office or a credit union," the finger jabbing, "a bank job if you can handle it, fair enough, you're taking care of your overheads." Frankie had seen this done to others—the swagger, the finger, the casual and unconscious display of contempt—but he'd never felt it. "Something as big as this—and a banker, Jesus—it brings the cops down on top of everyone. If they nick you, they'll connect it to me."

"They know I haven't been working for you since I got out, Jo-Jo, they know that."

"Maybe they do. And maybe they make a connection anyway, or invent one. Very tempting for the bluebottles, to connect me to something like that. So, I end up being dragged into
something I don't control. And that's not on."

Crowe just sat there, resisting the urge to look away from
Jo-Jo's unwavering stare. There was saliva in his mouth and he
wanted to swallow, but Jo-Jo would see that and read it as a
sign of weakness.

Play it cool, take it easy. Whatever happens, leave on good
terms. This job is going ahead, even if we have to take
whatever shit Jo-Jo hands out afterwards.

"It would never come to that, Jo-Jo. I've a right to step up."

"We all find our own level, Frankie."

Jo-Jo sat down. He took another sip of wine.

"Look," he said, "people do what they have to do to live the
life they want to live. I understand that. But there comes a time."

He looked impatient, as though everything had been said,
time was ticking, he had a book to get back to. His feet tapped
rapidly to the rhythm of music only he could hear. When he
spoke, his words came in the tone of a man resigned to taking
his responsibilities seriously.

"You start off, Frankie, you want to do everything there is to
do, ten times over. Women, drink, gambling, travel, go everywhere, do everything. That stage of your life, you have dreams,
you have ambitions. When you're young you believe you can do
it, whatever it is, and that's right and proper." He held up a finger. "You get to a certain age, Frankie, you have to know what
you can do well. You have to live within that."

Jo-Jo gestured at the garden around him. "That's where I
am, these days. No dreams, Frankie. No fucking about. I make
sure I'm not a problem for anyone else. I do what I'm good at.
Money, advice, connections. A dozen businesses in this town
would've gone down the toilet if I hadn't helped out, and most
of them I don't take nearly as much as I'm entitled. I read my

books, listen to my music. Old friends come visit. I take Ma to a restaurant, make a fuss over the grandkids. I keep an eye on the business. And the last thing I want is someone I like turning into a problem I don't need." The finger again, one emphatic poke. "You're old enough now, Frankie, to be thinking about what you're good at, what matters to you."

He shook his head. "Stay dreaming too long, you become an embarrassment. I'm sorry, Frankie."

Jo-Jo picked up his glass of wine.

Crowe said, "This isn't fair."

"I know that, but it's the way it is."

Crowe didn't want to sound desperate, but it was all he could think of. He said what he didn't want to say, what had always been unspoken.

"You owe me, Jo-Jo. When your back was to the wall—"

"I know, Frankie, and I'm grateful. You're twenty-four carat. That doesn't make me blind." He put down his wine, leaned forward, his palms on his knees, and spoke quietly. "You need direction. You're a weapon, Frankie. And a weapon—a weapon is something to be pointed. Guided. Directed."

"Used."

Jo-Jo stared for a moment, then shook his head. "No need to get snotty. We all find our own level. What you do, it's a good living. You want to step up, good people like you and Martin—there's always a place on my crew."

Once a moocher.

Frankie kept an even tone. "I'm putting this thing together. And if that's a problem for you—"

"Go."

Jo-Jo picked up his book.

"I don't need your fucking blessing, Jo-Jo."

"Go!"

"I just need you to stay out of the way."

Jo-Jo closed the book again, and put it down on his lap. "Go!"

His eyes narrowed, his lips peeled back from his teeth. "Fuck. Off. Frankie."

Over at the French windows, Christy moved forward a couple of steps. He had his right hand behind his back, under his loose shirt. Jo-Jo lifted a hand, gesturing to Christy to stay back.

"Frankie's going," he said. "Aren't you, Frankie?"

Crowe swallowed. "I'm sorry I lost my temper. Really, Jo-Jo. No offence. I apologise. Can we talk about this again?"

Jo-Jo seemed to consider this. He nodded.

"Of course we can. Give it a year or so, we'll talk."

A year or so.

"OK, then. Listen, no hard feelings." Crowe despised his own instinctive urge to mend fences.

"Of course not," Jo-Jo said, and his cold tone made a lie of his casual words. "Come see me, we'll talk. For now, Frankie, I think it's best if we give ourselves time." As Crowe stood up, Jo-Jo began flicking through the Grisham, looking for his page.

In the kitchen, Crowe asked Christy for a glass of water. He sipped from it, drew deep breaths, trying to calm the nerves that were stretching the muscles around his mouth.

"I blew it," he whispered. He put the glass down on the kitchen counter and stared at it.

Christy shrugged. "It's not personal, mate."

"He owes me, Christy. Everyone knows that."

"I know he can be a right bollocks, Frankie, but Jo-Jo has to look at the big picture. He doesn't—"

Crowe hit Christy in the throat with the edge of his right hand. Christy floundered, gasping. He grabbed at his throat. Crowe kicked him in the balls. Christy made a loud, harsh noise and fell to the floor. Crowe raised his right foot high and stamped down on Christy's head. There was a crunching sound. The bodyguard lay still.

Crowe reached down, plucked a small black revolver from the holster at the back of Christy's belt and walked quickly back out into the garden, cocking the weapon.

Jo-Jo was already standing, tense. When he saw Crowe he dropped his book and picked up his chair.

"Frankie, you're fucking mad!"

Crowe squeezed the trigger once, twice—still walking quickly towards Jo-Jo—three times, and two patches of blood appeared on Jo-Jo's chest, a third on his stomach. He went down, knocking over the table on the way.

Crowe stood over him.

Jo-Jo was lying face up, damaged but alive and very afraid. His face grey, his lips quivering. Every breath was a harsh sucking sound. He looked up at Frankie.

"Ah, Jesus," he said.

Crowe pointed the gun down at Jo-Jo's head.

"We all find our own level, right, Jo-Jo?"

There was a scream.

Crowe looked up. Jo-Jo's mother was standing at an open bedroom window. She screamed again.

Crowe was still looking up at Pearl, looking into her eyes, with the gun pointing straight down at Jo-Jo's head, when he squeezed the trigger. One second Jo-Jo was a quivering mess of muscle and blood, with fear and hatred blazing in his eyes, then Crowe looked down at him and there was a hole in his forehead, his eyes were vacant and his body was as limp as a discarded costume.

Crowe stood there for several seconds, until Pearl's "Nooooo!!!" pierced through the fog that had for a moment enveloped him. He glanced up at the bedroom window. Pearl stopped screaming and jerked her head back inside.

Crowe moved fast, back into the house, stepping over

Christy, hurrying through the kitchen, across the hall at a run and taking the stairs two at a time. He kicked in the door of the first bedroom he came to. Nothing, wrong room.

By the time he got to Pearl's bedroom she had managed to pull something, some piece of furniture, halfway across the door. Crowe pushed hard and there was a scream as the door opened and the piece of furniture—it was a chest of drawers—toppled over.

Pearl was lying on the floor, one foot caught under the chest of drawers. Her throat was making little noises. Glancing up at her son's killer, she pulled her foot free and struggled to rise.

"Oh, Jesus, Mary and Joseph! Frankie—"

Crowe hesitated. From her position on all fours, Pearl made eye contact, the expression on her ancient face a mixture of rage and guile.

With his left hand, Crowe swept a yellow satiny dressing gown off the bed and threw it over Pearl's head. She screamed, rising from her knees. Crowe put the gun close to the shape of her head and fired once. A rosette of blood blossomed on the dressing gown and she collapsed instantly.

He went down the stairs.

In the hall, approaching the front door, he put the gun away and composed himself. He curled his fingers inside the sleeve of his jacket and used the sleeve to grasp the knob of the front-door lock. Then he remembered the glass. He went out into the kitchen, stepping over Christy's, found the glass he'd used, emptied it of water and put it into his pocket. He went back out into the hall and again carefully grasped the knob of the front door.

There was a groan from behind him.

At the door into the kitchen, Christy—barely conscious—was trying to stand up, his hands grasping ineffectually at the door and the walls. The left side of his face was a sheet of blood, the eye closed, the mouth pinched. The other eye glared wildly at Crowe.

Crowe took the gun from his pocket and went back across the hall, his heels clicking on the black marble floor.

* * *

Crowe didn't tell Martin Paxton what had happened until half an hour later. "Drive," he said when he got into the car, and he sat there, breathing hard, as Paxton steered them away from the area. A couple of times, as they drove, Paxton looked across at his friend, but didn't say anything. Frankie was rubbing the heel of one hand hard against his forehead.

After a while, Crowe realised he still had Christy's gun. He found a tissue and wiped the gun. They stopped at a bridge over the Royal Canal and Crowe got out and leaned across the parapet, while Paxton drove on and waited in a nearby side road. Crowe glanced around, saw no one looking his way, and let the gun and tissue fall from his hand. Then he took the glass from Jo-Jo's kitchen out of his pocket. He smashed it against the inside of the parapet wall and watched the pieces fall into the water. Crowe hurried after the car and they drove on towards Finglas.

After a while Paxton asked, "What happened?"

"Nothing," Crowe said.

They parked in the grounds of a church in Finglas and walked in silence down the slope to the long, hilly, bare stretch of open space just south of the housing estate. The green space between Finglas and Cabra West had once been vast and full of hollows and thickets within which local kids could find adventure. As children, Frankie and Martin had played cowboys and Indians around here, down by the canal, under the bridge and over where the public swimming pool used to be. They played rounders, football or hurling, they had fights, sometimes with each other, and later they took diversions through these fields while walking their girlfriends home. Now, the expansion of the housing estates had narrowed the gap until only this stretch of green was left, where the occasional football game was played, and teenage urban cowboys let their clapped-out horses roam free.

There, Frankie Crowe—still coming down from the chemical surge that had flared through his veins during the killings—told Martin Paxton what happened.

For more than a minute, Paxton didn't say anything. He just hunkered down and pulled repeatedly at tufts of grass. Then he said, "Jesus Christ, Frankie, what the fuck."

"I know."

"This wasn't supposed to happen."

"It happened."

"This changes everything."

"It changes nothing."

"What the hell do we do?"

"Nothing. We do nothing. There's nothing to connect it to us."

Paxton stood up, brushing pieces of grass from his fingers. Working hard to keep his voice normal, he said, "You can't be sure about that, Frankie. Someone might have seen you leaving the house. Jo-Jo might have told someone he was meeting you. These things always get out."

"No one saw me."

"Jesus, Frankie, it wasn't the end of the world, Jo-Jo saying no. We could have done something else, something that would've been OK with Jo-Jo."

Crowe made a derisive sound. "The only thing that Jo-Jo would've said yes to was whatever kept us bowing and scraping to him. If we went ahead, and him saying we shouldn't, who the fuck knows what he'd have done. Grassed us up, maybe. Put the word out we were flush, and he wouldn't take offence if we got done over." He held his arms wide. "We're playing in a different league now, Martin. That means doing what has to be done. And fuck anyone who gets in the way. That's the difference. Being ready to fuck anyone who gets in the way."

Frankie walked away, maybe twenty feet, stood there calming himself. When he came back he said, "It's the difference between being a loser and being someone who matters. Being ready to fuck anyone who gets in the way."

"Frankie, this didn't start out, it's not what—"

Crowe came up close and spoke quietly into Paxton's face. "From here on in, we're dealing with a fat, soft, civilian target that'll shit money at the first sight of a gun. We've done the homework, we know the layout, the routine. We have the crew, the money's there for the taking." He moved away and made a fly-swatting gesture. "Jo-Jo couldn't be helped. It happened. It shouldn't have, but that's done now. It's done now, Martin, the shooting's over. From here on, we're dealing with civilians and the job couldn't be simpler. You can't back off now, Martin."

From his silence, a stranger might have imagined that Paxton was thinking it over, coming to a decision. But that decision had been made a long time ago. Paxton tried a smile, but his face didn't quite make it. "I'm not backing off, Frankie. I'm just saying, Jesus—" Then he said, "Ah, fuck it."

Crowe was suddenly all bouncy energy, running his fingers back through his hair. "It can't be this week, OK? Not now, after this. I mean, this is going to cause a few heart attacks around the place. We're going to have to put it off for a week or so. Breathing space, OK?"

"OK," Paxton said. Then, because he had to ask, he said, "Tell me the truth, Frankie." He hesitated, unsure of how Crowe would take this. "Tell me the truth. Going in, going in to see Jo-Jo, did you have this in mind, is that what you decided to do, if he said—"

"No," Crowe said, shaking his head briskly. "No, I swear to

you, Martin. It wasn't like that. It just happened. It just happened."

Paxton didn't say anything for a while, then he said, "OK."

Crowe took a long, deep breath and when he spoke his voice was just above a whisper. "I don't think so, Martin. To be honest with you. I don't think so. I think it just happened."

Paxton didn't say anything. After a moment, he reached out a hand and he touched Frankie on the shoulder.

They were leaving the green space when Crowe remembered something. The energy that had stirred him seemed to have ebbed.

"About Jo-Jo. Only me and you know we'd anything to do with that, Martin. Let's keep it that way. Not a word to Dolly or Brendan. It's not something they need to know."

"Course not," Paxton said.

"What we say, we tell them there's a small hitch, the target's routine changed, we'll have to put things off for a week or two. We tell Milky the same, OK?"

Martin Paxton nodded.

Silent again, the two friends walked slowly back up towards the church and the car. Sheep as a lamb, Martin Paxton told himself. Sheep as a lamb.

8

T he removal service ended with the parish priest thank-
ing the mourners for coming and he reminded them
that Jo-Jo Mackendrick and his mother would be laid
to rest after ten o'clock Mass next morning. The paying of
respects began. The centre aisle filled with people, settling into
a queue that inched its way from the back of the church up
towards the altar. The crowd at this evening's ceremony, for the
arrival of the remains at St. Anthony's Church in Clontarf, was
unusually large.

Just in front of the altar rails, resting side by side on metal
trestles, there were two coffins. Jo-Jo's family sat in the front
row, receiving the condolences of the stream of mourners.
Although it slowly shuffled up the church, the queue hardly
shortened. More joined at the back, as those at the front paid
their respects to the family and moved back down the side
aisles.

Outside the church, more than half a dozen surly policemen in uniform stood around, making no effort at all to appear
respectful of the occasion. From across the road, on the
seafront promenade, four detectives from criminal intelligence
eyed the mourners as they arrived at the church. They
attempted in vain to find some significance in who turned up
for the funeral and who stayed away. In the six days since the
murders of Jo-Jo and Pearl Mackendrick and Christy Powell,
the police had methodically interviewed surviving members of
the family, as well as Jo-Jo's friends and associates, and were

none the wiser. It was hard to tell if Jo-Jo's people thought they owed loyalty to some form of underworld code, or if they just didn't know anything. The neighbourhood had been canvassed and every tout on the Northside was given an opportunity to ratchet up credit with the police, and no one had anything helpful to say. Autopsies revealed nothing useful. Although Technical fine-combed the house for three days, it soon became clear that there was little for them to work with.

"Most likely?" Assistant Commissioner Colin O'Keefe asked a conference of senior officers, reviewing the case on the afternoon of the removal.

The lead investigator looked uncomfortable. "Hitman, probably. Hired by—probably someone who got their toes trodden on by Jo-Jo."

"Indications?"

"Well planned. They went in and out without leaving a trail or a witness. Clinical stuff."

"Candidates?"

"No one obvious. Jo-Jo was on good terms with most of the Northside operators. And he didn't really do much across the river, not in recent years. Anyone he had serious trouble with, he either patched things up with them or they're not around any more."

"What about the IRA? That's what some of the newspapers are saying."

"Possible. A couple of their people had a run-in with Jo-Jo, but that was five, six years back, and we thought it was sorted."

O'Keefe turned to a Special Branch officer. "Anything to tell me?"

"The chuckies have long memories. Our contacts say there was definitely nothing official, and I believe them."

"But?"

"But that doesn't mean it wasn't some Provo hardcase nursing a private grudge."

A recently promoted chief inspector leaned forward into the table, then waited until he got the nod from O'Keefe. "There's a whole rake of gangs now, sir, small outfits, hard men in a hurry. Type of people who see guys like Jo-Jo as dinosaurs. I reckon it's most likely someone had an itch."

"Nominations?"

The officer looked like he wished he hadn't said anything. "Could be any one of—I don't know—dozens."

"To sum up what we know for certain, then," O'Keefe said, "a pro job, by someone who's been waiting in the long grass. Agreed?"

He looked around the table. No one said anything.

O'Keefe sighed. "Or, to put it another way—what we know for certain—fuck all."

The killings played big in the media for several days, and this morning's papers had a photo taken at Christy Powell's cremation at Glasnevin cemetery the previous day. It showed Christy's girlfriend clutching their two kids to her. Just in front, Christy's brothers and mates carried his coffin. There was no real political pressure on the police for results. The Minister for Justice made a statement about how such savagery would not be tolerated, and the opposition claimed that crime was out of control. The newspapers peddled pages of gory details, some of them accurate, but already the story was fading. No civilians had been hurt, it was an internal gangland affair, so the public found the killings more exciting than shocking. The city's leading investigative journalist wrote an authoritative piece, based on garda and underworld sources, that pinned the killing on a teenage gangster, a former McDonald's employee who worked as a hitman for an up-and-coming gang in Dolphin's Barn. For legal reasons, and to add a touch of glamour, the newspaper christened the alleged killer "the Chef." Once the funerals were over the story would be parked. If anyone was ever charged, or someone came up with a new angle, it could be revived for public entertainment.

Most of Jo-Jo's friends turned up for the funeral, and some of his enemies. Business associates, both criminal and legitimate, rubbed shoulders with neighbours, members of Jo-Jo's golf club and kids from the GAA club where he'd played hurling as a youngster. There were lots of elderly people from the old neighbourhood where Pearl and her sons were revered as locals who had bettered themselves. Two nuns living in the old neighbourhood turned up. Jo-Jo had for several years financed their meals-on-wheels effort for pensioners down on their luck. There were plenty of gawkers, too. Some of them brandished disposable cameras as the coffins were carried into the church. The media was there, using long lenses from way down the street. A few months earlier, at another underworld funeral, a photographer had come too close and had three cameras broken and one arm.

Frankie Crowe was halfway up the aisle, shuffling along with the queue. A few yards ahead, he spotted Oscar Waters, with whom he'd worked briefly when he got out of jail. Waters' partner, Shamie Cox, had recently been given another three-year stretch. Right fuck-ups that pair turned out to be.

The coffins were covered with flowers and Mass cards. One whole side of the altar overflowed with wreaths and bouquets, stacked in rows. In the centre of the display was an arrangement spelling out "Grandad."

In the front row of the pews, to the right of the aisle, Lar Mackendrick welcomed each mourner with a nod and a handshake. Mostly he sat, now and then he stood up, leaning on the rail in front.

Occasionally the queue was held up for a minute or so as one of the chief mourners whispered with some family friend. Frankie saw Oscar Waters shake hands with Lar and move on to sympathise with Jo-Jo's grown-up kids.

None of Jo-Jo's three offspring was in the family business, and all seemed awed and out of place. They shook hands with their father's friends and accepted sympathy, but they represented only their own grief. Formal recognition of the family's loss, and respects to the family status, were being accepted by their Uncle Lar.

After another couple of minutes of shuffling, Frankie was extending his hand, whispering the standard phrases of commiseration.

"Frankie Crowe, good man." Lar Mackendrick didn't just shake hands, he stood up and embraced Frankie. The front of his white shirt was stained with lipstick, a remnant of an earlier sympathetic hug. Lar had made an effort at shaving, but his chin was rough. The whites of his eyes were streaked with tiny red rivulets and there was sweat on his forehead. His whole face seemed raw. His suit was expensive but too tight for his bulky frame. His tie had been loosened and his top shirt button was undone. Beside him, his wife May kept glancing at Lar, as though fearful for him.

Frankie said, "Sorry for your trouble, Lar. Shocking, it was. Terrible."

Lar took Frankie's right hand in both his own. "Every now and then he'd talk about that night, Frankie, when those two fuckers came to the house with shooters. If they were all as reliable as Frankie, that's what he said to me, many a time."

Frankie waited, then he realised he was expected to speak. He said, "He was good to me. Jo-Jo was a good friend."

Lar's voice sounded like something inside him had been stretched until it bled. "The two of them, Frankie. Jesus, the two of them, to go like that."

Frankie felt his eyes sting. "There's no words, Lar. If there's anything I can do, y'know?"

Lar nodded. He continued to clutch Frankie's hand, as though clinging to a fragment of his dead brother's life. He said, "Thanks for coming, Frankie, talk to you in the morning, right?"

Frankie nodded and his hand was released. Lar sat down. Frankie shook hands with May and with Jo-Jo's kids and moved on and the queue inched along in his wake. He found himself briefly sympathising and shaking hands with other relatives, some of whom he didn't recognise. There were tears on both his cheeks and he used the back of his hand to wipe them away. As he walked back up the side aisle, he noticed people looking at him. He felt a pride in having been so publicly welcomed as an intimate of the family.

Frankie was looking forward to the funeral in the morning. He liked the idea of mixing with the family, being seen to be connected. There was a price to pay. After the Mass and the ritual at the cemetery there would be the inevitable and unavoidable wake at some hotel, and the kind of drinking that would put him out of action for most of the day after. Which was OK, because the kidnap job wasn't scheduled for another six days.

9.

In the corridor outside the Circuit Criminal Court, a woman opened her blouse and offered a breast to her baby. A young, skinny, uniformed garda, one hand clasping the other behind his back, watched for a moment, then strolled over to the mother and told her to take it outside. She told him to have a heart and her brother, a five-foot-three bundle of muscular animosity, hurried over and told the young garda not to act the bollocks. The woman told her brother to go away, she was OK. Then she continued feeding the baby.

The garda looked around, as though considering which of the eight colleagues hanging about the hall might best be called upon to help him restore law and order.

Sitting on a bench several yards away, Detective Sergeant Nicky Bonner muttered, "Asshole." Beside him, Detective Inspector John Grace looked up from his Evening Herald crossword, clocked the situation and nodded.

It was pushing seven o'clock in the evening, the company of performers from the Circuit Criminal Court—police, lawyers and civilians—was hanging around waiting for the jury to make up its mind. Otherwise, the Four Courts complex was closed for business.

John Grace watched the woman cuddling the child, the curve of the nourishing breast just visible between the baby's face and the open edge of the pink blouse. Dolores Payne was a shoplifter whose workrate added half a shift to at least one inner-city police station. She was here to offer moral support to her boyfriend, the defendant in the manslaughter case John Grace had been attending, as senior investigating garda, for the past three days.

The case was a stupid one, the kind of not-for-profit crime that filled more cells than any number of criminal master plans. Close to closing time in the defendant's local, someone cracked wise about something or other, someone else called the wise-cracker a wanker, someone pushed someone and the sensible people left the pub in a hurry. Dolores's boyfriend, seeing himself as the senior Big Shot on the premises, stepped in as a peacemaker. One of the combatants, a distant cousin, told him to fuck off and by the time the police arrived Mr. Big Shot had to be dug out of his estranged relative. Decades of half-remembered internal family resentment popped up out of nowhere, resulting in one set of bloody fists and a distant cousin who lasted six days on life support before he gave a sudden shudder, woke up and said to the nurse who was changing a dressing, "Tell Sheila I want to see her." Then he closed his eyes and died. He had no relative, friend, neighbour or workmate named Sheila, no Sheila worked in the hospital, his wife was named Marian and no one in his family knew who Sheila might be.

For the detectives at Turner's Lane garda station, the case involved little more than turning up and arresting the guy everyone was pointing at, Mr. Big Shot. This kind of stupid killing was as old as alcohol. It was one of eight serious assaults that detectives at Turner's Lane dealt with that week. It was the only one to end in a fatality.

"It's the new Ireland," Nicky Bonner was fond of saying. "Since we got prosperous, everyone's more tense and no one feels the day's complete until they get marinated." Nicky had a theory. "Used to be the Church set limits to things," he said. "That's all gone. All the old landmarks are gone. Even the IRA are wearing suits and discussing gross national product. It's all about money now, and grabbing your share and a bit of the other fella's."

People had become more efficient at getting revved up. A few pints, maybe into the jacks to do a couple of lines, then another few pints and everything's faster, louder, closer to the edge. For the detectives at Turner's Lane, there was increased business in the form of black-and-blue women, tanked-up kids driving cars into walls, and young men determined to assert their individuality by kicking the shite out of anyone who looked crooked at them.

The case now being adjudicated in the Circuit Criminal Court was the kind that in the old days would have been marked down as an assault causing bodily harm. These days, that kind of thing often developed into a homicide, with consequent long hours of boredom for gardai waiting for a jury to come back.

Facing a long stretch in the Joy, Mr. Big Shot was fighting the charge, just on the off chance that his mouthpieces could bring off a miracle. His defence—that he was merely protecting himself against an unprovoked attack—might have stood up if most of his punches hadn't been delivered when the victim was unconscious.

Dolores's husband, one of the nicest, most obliging junkies in the North Strand, went down in one of the AIDS waves that culled the city's heroin addicts. Her boyfriend, the argumentative Mr. Big Shot, was also HIV positive, as was Dolores's aggressive brother and his girlfriend and their eldest daughter, aged six. Dolores and her two kids had escaped the virus. To John Grace, Dolores might be technically a habitual criminal but in truth she was a decent sort who did her best with one of the few income-producing options open to her. To add to her shoplifting revenue, she occasionally earned some extra money selling information to the police.

The young garda came back for another bite at Dolores. He said something about public decency.

"Christ," Nicky Bonner sighed, and hauled himself up to

his considerable height. He crossed to the young policeman, hands in the trouser pockets of his grey suit, looking every inch the nightclub bouncer he'd been when he needed to boost his wages during his early years on the force. He smiled as he approached the skinny young garda and took the paragon of law and order by one elbow. Nicky leaned over and said something in his ear, then turned, nodded to Dolores and walked back towards his seat. The young garda stood there for a few seconds, his face flushed. He looked over towards John Grace, then he ostentatiously looked at his watch and quickly headed down the corridor towards the jacks.

Sitting back down, Nicky said, "It's a good sign, four hours."

John said nothing. He was the same height as Bonner but lacked the bulk. Although he was in his mid-forties, his face had a placidness that made him look younger. Since his earliest years on the force, he disliked the impression of sensitivity that his soft features created. These days, his short-cropped hair was almost totally white, adding a fatherly air to his good-natured features. It could be, he concluded, that it helped with the more gormless criminals that he had a face that implied more sympathy than he felt.

"They'd have done it by now," Nicky said, "if they were going to acquit. You reckon?"

"The tank is empty in America?"

"Sorry?"

"Three, two, three. The tank is empty in America?"

"Give me a break."

John lowered his crossword. "Juries are like next summer's weather, you know that. Predictions are for fools. It's always fifty-fifty. Jury's out for days, it might be bad or it might be good. They come back after ten minutes, it might be good or it might be bad."

"I reckon the longer the better."

"You might be right. You might be wrong. Fifty-fifty."

Waiting for a jury to come back had no upside. The joys of coffee in the local pubs soon faded. Then it was down to mooching around the court corridors, accumulating dead time. Even if they quickly made up their minds, a jury usually liked to take at least a couple of hours, so no one would think they weren't taking their duties seriously. Waiting for a jury that might come back five minutes from now or five hours was a recipe for heartburn, unless you found a way to blank it all out.

"Out of gas."

"Sorry?" said Nicky Bonner.

"The tank is empty in America," said John Grace. "Three, two, three. Out of gas." He inked in the crossword.

The court clerk appeared at the door of the courtroom and gave a thumbs up.

Grace and Bonner stood, Dolores put her tit back in her blouse, her boyfriend rubbed his palms together, and they all started moving towards the courtroom.

Grace watched Mr. Big Shot shuffle towards his fate. A bulky little man with a pout. Since the pub fight, the poor clown had come close to a nervous breakdown, and doubts had been raised about whether he was fit to stand trial. Grace felt sorry for the stupid fucker. Putting him in jail wouldn't do anybody any good. Sure, he was a danger to society. So are most people who get tanked up, and you can't lock them all up. But that's the job. If someone gets thumped and they die, the law ordains that you arrest the thumper and bring him before His Lordship. The charge should be stupidity and bad luck, but they don't have laws against things like that, so the nearest that fits is manslaughter.

"He's not looking such a smart-ass now, is he?" said Nicky Bonner.

John Grace grunted.

On a bench at the end of the corridor, a thin woman sat with an elderly couple. The victim's wife and her parents. No one else from his family had attended the trial. They rose slowly, as though dreading entering the courtroom, their faces as strained as the defendant's.

Angela Kennedy glanced at the small TV at the end of the kitchen counter. The nine o'clock news was on, something about a government minister denying something categorically. Angela was racking plates in the dishwasher. Out in the dining room, Justin and the kids were on their second portions of birthday cake. Angela had decided to skip it. She had cooked Justin's favourite meal, a lasagne, and had herself eaten only a small portion, filling out her plate with salad.

It was the first evening in weeks that all four of them had sat down together for dinner, and it took Justin's birthday to accomplish that.

Without the kids, Justin would insist on ignoring his birthdays, seeing them as unwelcome reminders of a finite and dwindling supply of time. For Luke and Saskia, aged eight and nine, any anniversary was a cue for a fuss, and they treasured being allowed to stay up a little later than usual. The kids were still slightly bemused at the dullness of adult birthday parties. No decorations worth speaking of, no games, just a token cake and hardly any goodies.

"Adults can have anything they want," Saskia said. "Daddy could have a party in a disco, or on a yacht, adults can do anything they like. But their birthday parties are always so boring!"

As Angela left the kitchen, carrying two cups of coffee, there was something on the TV about a verdict in a manslaughter trial. The kitchen door swung closed behind her as the screen showed a fat little man with a sweaty face being led out in handcuffs, climbing cautiously into a van.

An hour later, the kids were in bed—it was a Wednesday, a school night, they'd been up later than usual, and there were no stories, no reading, they were both ready to drop. In the living room, there were candles alight on the mantelpiece, Angela was pouring the last of the wine, and Justin was wearing Luke's present—a Dublin GAA football team shirt—and sliding Saskia's present into the CD player. As the first track of the Elvis Presley greatest-hits album swaggered out of the Bose speakers, Justin sprawled on the sofa and looked up at Angela. He admired the burgundy dress, the colour and the flattering cut, what it did for her, and for him. He held up his arms and she went to him and they kissed, at first with affection and then with passion.

He made his eyebrows do a Groucho Marx dance, and whispered, "You wait till I get you upstairs."

She smiled. "Ready when you are. I'll deal with the rest of the mess in the morning."

Justin held up his left wrist, watching the light from the candles reflect in the gold watch. His mixed feelings about Angela's gift made him feel a little guilty. For a few weeks he'd had it in mind to buy himself a Patek Philippe, as a little personal celebration now that the Kwarehawk deal was completed and two other projects were tick-tocking towards a lucrative finale. That really wasn't on now, since Angela had given him the Rolex. What the hell, no big deal.

"Thanks again, love," he said, and smiled warmly at Angela. "It's splendid," he said, and the doorbell rang.

10

T he idea was, go in just before bedtime, when they're tired and sleepy, before they turn on the alarm.

"Lights out is ten thirty, give or take. We go in about ten," Frankie said.

"What if they've got visitors, or they go out for the evening?" Brendan Sweetman asked.

"Something like that, babysitter shit, there's no way of knowing. It happens, we deal with it."

There were no such obstacles. Frankie Crowe and Martin Paxton, both wearing suits, went to the front door. There were two bright overhead lights in the porch, and a CCTV camera poking down from the front of the house. Dolly Finn and Brendan Sweetman waited in the car.

There was a risk here. Masks were out of the question at this stage. The people inside might check the CCTV picture before opening the door. They would certainly be cautious about answering unexpected callers at this hour, and even if the CCTV was for show there were narrow glass panels running down each side of the front door. Frankie was wearing glasses with heavy frames, Martin had a false moustache. The disguises were flimsy but they'd have to do. If it came to it, a decent defence lawyer could rip apart an identification made from a nighttime glimpse on a doorstep.

From the other side of the door, a man's voice. "Who is it?"

"Gardai, sir. Detective Sergeant Courtney." They'd agreed that Martin should speak. Frankie's accent was too Northside.

"Sorry about the time of night, sir, but a serious matter has arisen in connection with an associate of yours. We're hoping you can help clear it up."

"Christ sake."

When the target opened the door, Crowe and Paxton flashed the ID cards Martin had printed off from his laptop. "Shouldn't take long, sir."

The target, in a blue Dublin GAA football shirt, jeans and bare feet, didn't try to conceal his irritation. "Couldn't this have waited until morning?"

"Not really, sir, if we could just—" Paxton made a hand gesture, suggesting they be invited in, and the target stood back and said, "Let's make this as quick as we can."

Once inside the door, Frankie—his face turned away—took off the glasses and pulled on a balaclava. Then he showed the target his pistol.

"Say nothing, do nothing, don't panic, just stand there for a minute."

The target's face was frozen. He took a step backwards, crossing his arms, just as quickly uncrossing them, then standing with his arms down by his sides.

"Say nothing, do nothing," Frankie repeated. "It'll all be all right, believe me."

Martin Paxton, his own balaclava now in place, stood in the doorway, pointed a small flashlight towards the street and clicked it on and off. Within half a minute Dolly Finn and Brendan Sweetman, wearing dark overalls and already pulling masks down over their faces, were closing the door behind them. Dolly had a holdall containing two more empty holdalls, Brendan's shotgun and a change of clothing for Frankie and Martin. The holdalls were necessary because a house like this, apart from the target, would be worth trawling for portable valuables.

All four of the raiders were wearing gloves. Crowe, Paxton

and Finn had pistols, Sweetman took the sawn-off shotgun out of the holdall. The target reacted appropriately. His stance was unnaturally stiff, his fingers plucking at his jeans.

"Where's your wife?"

The target looked confused. "Why?"

"Where is she?"

"Look—"

Crowe pointed at the shotgun. "You think if that thing made a big noise, she might come out here to see what it was? You think so? I can arrange that. Now, where's your fucking wife?"

"Inside, she's inside, over there, the room on the right."

"The kids?"

"They're in bed." The target was breathing deeply, like he was trying to get the hang of a stress-relief technique he'd picked up from a magazine. Crowe turned to Paxton and nodded. Paxton and Sweetman moved quickly across the spacious hall. The hall was two-storey, full of dark wood, and dominated by a wide, central staircase. Paxton whistled softly. "Gone with the fucking wind, what?"

They met the target's wife coming out through a doorway. Her hands shot up to her mouth and her eyes widened.

She was wearing a wine-coloured dress, low-cut and clingy. Martin Paxton was impressed.

The target moved over to stand beside his wife, speaking as he went. He was making a big effort to sound like he'd just discovered the solution to an unexpected problem. "Listen, I think you have the wrong house. There's no one here you want, you've mixed us up with someone else."

Gobshite thought they were here to do him.

"Now," Frankie said, keeping his voice low and calm, "just so you both know. This is about money. Nothing personal, so don't get scared. No one here has any reason to do anything drastic."

"In there," Paxton said, gesturing towards the room from which the wife had emerged. The target and his wife touched hands briefly as they moved into the living room. They stood close, looking from one masked face to another, from one gun to another, shaken, pale and disbelieving. Down by his side, the target kept making a fluttering movement with the fingers of his right hand, like he was rinsing it in an invisible finger bowl.

"The kids asleep?" said Crowe.

The woman, her voice thin and low, said, "They were dozing off when I checked a while ago."

"Keep things quiet, then, and they'll never know we were in the house."

The woman jerked around as she heard a whispered Whuh! sound behind her. Dolly Finn was standing by the mantelpiece, blowing out the lighted candles.

"What do you want?" The target was agitated, getting his nerve back. "And what gives you the goddam right to come into my home, waving guns around?"

Crowe said, "Where's the CCTV, the tape machine?"

"Fuck this!" the target said.

The woman said, "It's in the garage. Out through the kitchen."

"The alarm's not turned on, right?"

"What the fuck is this about?!" The target's voice was high-pitched, barely in control. Crowe said to Dolly Finn, "Show him." Finn reached into a pocket and took something out. He held it up and there was a click and the blade of a knife appeared from the small black handle. He held it casually.

Crowe said, "There doesn't even have to be a bang, no noise at all, OK? Any trouble—" He made a gesture, his thumb drawn across his throat.

The woman said, "Look—"

The target said, "OK, OK, I'm all right."

"Just so you know," Frankie said. He leaned forward. "You cooperate, you don't see our faces, there's no reason to hurt you."

The target, white-faced, nodded. His eyes found his wife, who was shaking her head slowly.

Frankie spoke to Dolly Finn. "The CCTV tape. Then find a bedroom that overlooks the front, keep an eye." He turned to Brendan Sweetman and pointed to the cordless phone on the sofa. "Leave that one, kill the rest. And do it quietly, don't wake the kids." Both gunmen left the living room.

Crowe said to Martin Paxton, "Let's get this thing moving. Make sure there's no surprises." To the target he said, "Show this man the house, upstairs and downstairs. And speak when he asks you a question. Otherwise, shut it. You," he spoke to the woman, "sit down and say nothing." The woman sat down in the armchair to the right of the fireplace.

Martin Paxton took the target by an elbow and moved him towards the door. "This won't take long."

The target turned to his wife. "I'll be back in a minute. Are you OK?"

She nodded. "I'll be all right. Do as they say, we can get through this."

"Sensible woman," Crowe said. When the other two had gone, he said, "Your mobiles?" She told him hers was in her handbag, on a table in the hall. Justin's was charging, on the counter in the kitchen. He found them, pocketed them, and sat down in the matching armchair facing the woman, his gun resting on his knee.

Mostly it was a rich blue carpet. Thick, bouncy stuff. Any thicker, Martin Paxton thought, we'd need skis to get around. The same carpet, right through the house. Except for the hall—all dark wood, including the floor—and the tiles in the kitchen and the bathrooms. This fucking place had more bathrooms than most houses had rooms. One downstairs, one at the top of the stairs, four more attached to four of the six bedrooms.

The kitchen was wide and long, with a dining table and chairs on one side. Almost the entire outer wall of the kitchen was a window, with a view out on to the long garden, the boundaries now marked by lines of softly glowing lamps.

It seemed to Paxton that the target was unable to conceal his pride, as he took his captor on a tour of the house. First, they checked out the cars. Through the kitchen, out a connecting door to a large garage. There were two cars there, a Saab and the Merc in which the target had arrived home on the evenings they kept watch on the house. The target opened a side door of the garage and showed Paxton a LandRover, parked in a passageway alongside the boundary hedge.

"We'll take the Saab," Paxton told the target, who nodded as though taking the Saab was obviously the sensible thing to do. Probably dotes on the Merc. And, right enough, it was the kind of flash wheels Paxton wouldn't mind taking for a spin, but it would be silly to take the target away in such a high-profile car. And the LandRover, no.

The house seemed to go on forever. It was like they thought up something they'd like to do, so they'd add on another room to do it in. Watch television, listen to music, lie around on a sofa. There was a room for the kids to play computer games, one with an exercise bike, a small bench and some weights, and a room with three computers, an array of desks and leather chairs, and several filing cabinets. One room, bigger than Martin Paxton's living room, was just shelves, all around the walls, floor to ceiling, and all of them stacked neatly with labelled boxes.

A large room with two long sofas facing each other across a big coffee table opened into an even larger conservatory. The fuck these people do, use their mobiles to talk from one end of the room to the other? High ceilings, fireplaces wide and tall, paintings on the walls, huge leather couches, chunky furniture, chandeliers, crystal all over the place and everywhere the thick blue carpets. In the dining room, Martin reckoned you might just manage a game of five-a-side football on the long table, though that would kind of take the shine off it. There were a dozen high-backed chairs around the table, and the walls were lined with large paintings that mostly showed people sowing and reaping in sunlit fields.

At the top of the wide staircase, the target stopped and said, "That's my daughter's room, there, and my son is in the next room down. Please be quiet."

"Church mouse," Martin Paxton said. He passed along the corridor, glancing at the framed photographs of the family. There was one of the target shaking hands with a wide man with a thick gold chain hung around his neck and curving down across his belly. Paxton opened the daughter's door and peeped inside and across the darkened room saw there was a shape on a bed. He nodded to the target, closed the door, then went to the next room. Same routine. He closed the door softly and he said, "OK, mission accomplished. Let's take you straight back to Mama Bear."

Halfway down the stairs, Paxton said, "I'm impressed, mate. My mammy was right. Go into the banking business, son—you're never short of the folding green."

The target stopped. Paxton raised the gun slightly. "Nothing naughty, now, OK?"

The target looked at his captor for a moment, then he took a deep breath. "Look, I think there's been some kind of mistake."

Martin Paxton said, "That's what he said." He had his balaclava off, now, as had the other three, and he threw it on to the kitchen counter.

"What's this mean?" Brendan Sweetman asked.

"He's trying to pull one," Frankie Crowe said.

"Seemed genuine enough."

"Fuck!"

"Will someone please—" Brendan Sweetman looked at Dolly Finn, made an enquiring gesture with his open palms, and turned to the others.

Martin Paxton said, "Take a banker, you have a direct line to the money, it speeds things up. Now, the guy says he's not a banker."

Frankie Crowe wasn't listening. He opened one of the holdalls and found the suit he'd changed out of. From an inner pocket he took one of the magazine clippings about the target, the one with the photograph. He'd brought this in case he needed a photo of the target and had brought neither of the other two clippings. One of those referred to "his Bryton Bank triumph." The other quoted a friend saying, "When Justin brought Bryton to the table he became a player." Further down it said, "Acquiring Bryton Bank was the cherry on his cake." Frankie read again the clipping he'd brought. It explained how Mr. Fucking Wonderful had prospered in property deals, and how his breakthrough came "when he landed Bryton, a small private bank." Fucker was trying to pull one.

Frankie put on his balaclava and headed towards the kitchen door.

The Kennedys were sitting in the living room, in the armchairs flanking the fireplace. After the tour of the house, the leader's sidekick had brought Justin back to the living room and the tall, skinny gunman, the one who'd shown them the knife, had used thin plastic strips to tie their hands in front of them. The sidekick told them, "Just sit there, OK? We'll be back in a minute."

Then the two gunmen left the living room, taking the cordless phone away with them. Justin heard the click of the kitchen door opening.

"Are you OK?"

Angela nodded.

Justin said, "When I saw the guns, Christ, I nearly lost it. I thought they'd come to shoot me."

Angela said, "Is there anything you're involved in?"

"What do you mean?"

"A deal, a client—"

"Christ, no. Jesus, nothing that could possibly—this is—"

"Do what they say, then. They mean it, it's money they want. Let them take whatever they want, as long as we all—"

"Of course, of course. I think it's going to be OK. This is a mistake, they know that now, I think they'll just leave."

"What happened upstairs?"

"They think I'm a banker."

Angela stared at him.

"The fellow who took me upstairs, I told him there was a mistake, and he brought me down, back here."

"They've come to the wrong house?"

"Something like that. I suppose he has to consult with the others, that's why they tied—"

The door opened. The leader came in with his sidekick trailing behind. The leader said, "Bryton Bank, right?"

"Look, there's been a mistake," Justin said.

"In a magazine last year, it said Pemberton Road, Ballsbridge. Justin Kennedy, big-shot what-the-fuck entrepreneur. Dublin's upmarket Pemberton Road, that's what it said. I checked the voting register. Justin Kennedy."

Angela said, "I assure you, Justin is not a banker."

"Bryton Bank, right?"

Justin said, "I've nothing to do with Bryton, I swear."

"You're lying." He fumbled in a pocket and held up a page torn from a magazine. Justin could see his own face staring out from the page. "'When he landed Bryton, a small private bank.' That's what it says."

The target was shaking his head. "You've got hold of the wrong—Jesus, I see, look—let me explain."

Jesus Christ. Sitting here, fucking handcuffs, giving lessons in capital finance to a stupid thug in a balaclava.

Bryton was almost two years back. With the Dublin property market oversubscribed, increasing numbers of investors were buying in Britain. Justin was managing the smallest of three consortia manoeuvring to clinch a city-centre development in Edinburgh. The business pages depicted his syndicate—mostly barristers looking to put tribunal money to profitable use—as "quixotic," which in business journalism roughly translated as losers. Then, approached by Bryton for advice on securing a new headquarters, Justin instead convinced Bryton to come into his consortium and take on the Edinburgh project. It immediately changed the dynamics of the deal and within a month the losers had clinched the development.

"I brought them into a consortium—there was—" He took a deep breath. "Look, I'm a solicitor. I mostly, these days, organise property deals. I persuaded the owners of Bryton Bank to join a consortium—a group of investors—and because they did we beat a couple of bigger outfits to a deal. And I got the credit. That's it. We made money from it, but I swear— beyond that I've nothing to do with Bryton. Jesus, that was nearly two years ago, it's probably eight, nine months since I talked to anyone from Bryton."

The gang leader stood there, unmoving, for the best part of a minute. Then, Justin Kennedy said, "It's true," and immediately felt like a schoolboy offering an implausible excuse.

The leader turned sharply and walked out of the room. The other gunman said, "Look—" He had a soft voice. "Don't worry," he said, "it'll be all right." As he moved past her, towards the door, Angela caught a whiff of a musky aftershave. When he left the room, the gunman closed the door quietly.

* * *

When Frankie Crowe and Martin Paxton came back into the kitchen, pulling off their masks, Brendan Sweetman was agitated. "What the fuck, Frankie? What's the story?"

Frankie Crowe said nothing. He stood, hands gripping the countertop, staring down at the dark marble, as though he could see something scrawled there. Dolly Finn looked at Martin Paxton and raised his eyebrows. Paxton shook his head.

"We calling it off, Frankie?" Brendan Sweetman said. "Cut our losses?"

"He convinced me," Martin Paxton said to Frankie Crowe. "Whatever else he is, he's not a banker. But, maybe we shouldn't get hung up on that? There's an option, Frankie."

Frankie Crowe didn't say anything.

Martin gestured. "Look around you. You don't buy a place like this with loose change."

"Ready money," Frankie said, quietly. "We take a banker, we squeeze his people and they can reach out and grab a bundle of money right away. That was the plan. Solicitor, it's not like that."

Dolly Finn said, "I don't see the problem. Rich fucker, he has money, doesn't matter what his job is."

Martin said, "It's a point, Frankie. Kind of money we're talking about. So, it takes an extra couple of days—"

Frankie Crowe said, very quietly, "There was a plan." He reached up and opened the cabinet door in front of him. It had a double-doored glass front, and glass shelves, and an array of little halogen bulbs lighting up a whole cabinet full of Waterford crystal. Frankie took down a heavy piece, a brandy glass, and held it for a moment. Then he dropped it on the slate floor. It broke into a number of pieces. He took down another glass and did the same. And another. He kept dropping glasses—brandy, whiskey, wine, whatever—and the top two shelves were cleared. By then, Martin Paxton had left the kitchen. Dolly Finn and Brendan Sweetman followed him out. They stood out in the hall, not talking. Dolly Finn finished a cigarette and ground it out on the dark wood floor. The sound of breaking glass began again.

Martin Paxton donned his mask and went into the living room and checked on the Kennedys. They looked frightened. Paxton said, "It's OK," but he could see that didn't help at all.

He went back and stood with the others and after a while there was silence from the kitchen.

Inside, Frankie stared at the bare shelves, a glaze of sweat across his forehead. The soles of his thick black shoes made crunching noises on the snowdrift of broken glass. He kicked at the shards and they made a sound like small bells tinkling.

Crowe stood there a moment, breathing hard. Then he closed the cabinet doors and took a heavy blue mug from a rack on the counter and used it like a hammer to smash the glass in one of the doors.

Outside in the hall, Paxton, Sweetman and Finn stood silently, not looking at one another. After a while, Frankie came out. There was a cut on his right cheek, a trickle of blood oozing down. Frankie pulled on his mask. He said, "We take the lawyer."

In the living room, the leader said to Justin, "We're taking you."

Angela said, "No, please—"

Justin said, "Look—"

"Give me the name of someone we can talk to, someone who can get their hands on your money. You have partners, accountants, what? Your wife, can she handle it?"

"It isn't like that—"

"Tell me what it's like."

"Look," Angela said, "we can give you money, right now. There's a couple of thousand in a safe, there's jewellery, there's Justin's watch, it's a Rolex and it's brand new."

"Let's see," the gang leader said. He held up Justin's bound hands and examined the watch. There was a click and the watch came off Justin's wrist. The gang leader took off and pocketed his own watch and put on the Rolex. He held out his arm, admiring the watch.

"The jewellery is worth a few thousand," Angela said.

The gang leader spoke to Justin. "We're taking you."

There was a silence, then Justin nodded and said, "OK, we need to work out the details."

The gang leader took a leather-bound notebook from inside his jacket. "A name, give me someone reliable who can handle the ransom."

Angela said, "I need to go to the bathroom."

The leader turned to her, his head jerking in annoyance. He went to the door and called out to one of the others. "Take her to the toilet." Angela held up her hands, showing the plastic binding. The leader jerked his thumb towards the hall. "They'll untie you, just go." He watched as Angela crossed to Justin and kissed him on the cheek. Justin arranged his face in the shape of an encouraging smile. The leader stood aside as Angela quickly left the room.

Then the leader said, "We want a million."

Justin said, "Holy Christ, how can I—"

"That's peanuts for someone like you, fucking peanuts."

"I assure you—"

"I'm not negotiating. A million. That's half what we figured when we thought we were getting a banker. This is a compromise, OK? We keep it down to that, your mates can cough it up quick enough, we get this thing over with."

Justin said nothing for a moment. Then he nodded. Resistance was pointless, and these people had too much of an edge for any negotiations to be worthwhile. Work out the terms, agree the deal, get it done.

"Here's how we can do this—"

The leader's fist shot out and punched Kennedy on the shoulder. "The fuck you think you are? You're telling me how we can do this? You—you've got no say in anything right now, fuckhead. You got that?" His finger poked Kennedy in the chest. "You got that, fuckhead?"

Kennedy held up his bound hands in a gesture of submission. "Look, I'm not telling you anything. I'm just suggesting how we deal with this."

"Suggest nothing. Just—" and the leader let out a scream of rage and pushed Kennedy out of the way. He darted to the base unit of the cordless phone, resting on a sideboard near the door, picked it up, found the lead connecting it to the phone socket down on the skirting board and jerked it out of the wall. Then he turned and ran out of the room. A physical shudder ran through Kennedy's chest as he heard the leader scream, "Where's the bitch?"

They both knew where this was going, even before Justin put it into words. "They're going to take me," he told Angela.

For a while they hoped that the confusion about Bryton might abort the whole thing, then they heard the sound of glass breaking in the kitchen. The relentless shattering noise baffled as much as frightened them. This didn't make any sense, even in the extraordinary circumstances in which they found themselves. Neither of them spoke for a long time. Then Justin said he knew they were going to take him.

"It's what I'd do. I mean, they must have put a lot of work into this. They're not going to walk away empty-handed."

"Can we just give them some money? Jewellery, things—

there's cash in the safe, a few thousand. That and the jewellery—"

"Listen carefully. Daragh O'Suilleabhain, his home number is in my book. When we're gone, ring him. Don't say anything about this on the phone, he doesn't need to know details. Just tell him you're speaking for me, he has to do exactly what you say—"

As Justin spoke, Angela remembered the second handset for the cordless phone. She didn't say anything, just listened to Justin giving her the instructions she was to pass on to Daragh O'Suilleabhain. Daragh would know what to do—Justin could work out the reimbursement once this was all settled. Follow whatever instructions the gang leader gave, do it all through Daragh. "It's the best way, the quickest way to get this over and done and back to normal."

The gang had disabled the phones around the house, and taken the mobiles. They'd taken the handset of the base unit in the living room. The second handset—Angela had finally remembered where she'd left it—was in the bathroom next to Saskia's room. She'd used it there, she'd been drying Saskia's hair after her shower, when her sister rang from Paris. Had the gang found it when they looked around the house, or when they were disabling the phones? If not, did she dare get to it?

Too risky.

Even if she got away with making a call, what if the police came stomping all over the place, panicking the gang? What if the gang started shooting and the police fired back? Maybe there was another way, maybe they could be convinced.

That's when the leader came in and said, "We're taking you."

Angela offered them money. It amounted to several thousand, in cash and goods, and they might take it. Not bad for an evening's work. But the leader just took Justin's new watch and carried on making his plans.

So, Angela decided, there was no point delaying any longer. Don't do this and however it works out you'll for ever despise your weakness.

She said, "I need to go to the bathroom."

The tall, skinny one who had tied their hands used his knife to cut the plastic strip open. He followed her upstairs and stood outside the bathroom. As soon as she went inside, she saw that the small black handset was on the shelf beside the shampoo. She closed the door.

"Emergency services."

It was only then she remembered the green light that glowed on the base unit when a call was being made from either of the handsets. She kept her voice low.

"Police, hurry."

"Which service do you require?"

"Get me the police!"

"Please hold on and I'll connect you."

A few seconds later the line went dead.

Half a minute after that, when the gang leader jerked open the bathroom door, Angela was washing her hands. She had pushed the handset into the middle of a stack of towels on a shelf beside the bath. Screaming that she was a stupid bitch, the leader took her by an arm and pulled and then pushed her out on to the landing and left her there. It took him a very short time, ransacking the bathroom, to find the handset. He brought it out on to the landing and began smashing it against the banister.

A door opened and Saskia's frightened face looked out. Luke's door opened, he came out on to the landing.

Saskia said, "Mum?"

"Go back to bed, love, it's all right." Angela turned to the gang leader and said, "For pity's sake, can't you—" and he slapped her hard across the face. Luke screamed. The gang leader grabbed the front of Angela's dress, bunching it in his fist, and dragged her towards him. "You want it like this? You want to be a player? OK, you're a player. Fuck you, you asked for it."

The other gunmen were in the hall, now, looking up the stairs. Saskia and Luke were calling their mother.

The gang leader turned to the soft-voiced one and said, "Take care of the kids, Martin, get them to shut the fuck up," then he pulled Angela by one arm, moving fast, bringing her down the stairs behind him.

In the living room, Justin was standing, with one of the gang holding him from behind. The gang leader pushed Angela across the room until she stood beside her husband. Then he turned to Justin and said, "You're off the hook."

For a second, Justin's face reflected his relief. Then the gang leader said, "We're taking the bitch."

11.

It makes sense," Frankie told the others, in the kitchen. "Take him, we have to work through his missus, or whoever can get their hands on his money. Take her, he can get the money quicker. And that's what it's about. Don't give them time to get fancy on us."

Dolly Finn was nodding. Brendan Sweetman shrugged.

Martin Paxton couldn't think of anything else to suggest, so he said nothing.

It's like every step we take, we're moving further away from what we planned.

"Get the car ready," Frankie told Dolly.

The woman was allowed to take the children to her bedroom, to speak with them. Frankie took the man out to the kitchen.

"First things first. You see this?" He held up his pistol. The man said nothing.

"What I have here, it's a Heckler & Koch. German, about twenty years old, maybe more. Takes eight rounds. One of these pieces of lead, I punch it into your wife's head, it turns her into a sack of waste. Something goes wrong, that's your best-case scenario."

He pushed the man back against the counter and put his face up close and spoke in a whisper.

"Everyone plays ball, it's over in no time, we take the money and you get your happy little life back. It goes the other way, I'm put in a tight corner, she goes first. No question. So, you do what I say, all it costs you is money. You understand?"

The man just nodded.

"I swear, any fucking around, I'll find out and I'll cut my losses and bury her somewhere and you won't even get to give her a funeral. You understand?"

He put the gun away.

"No need for that. No percentage in that for me. But I'll do it if I have to, you know I will."

When the man spoke his voice was low, thick.

"Whatever you say, I'll follow it to the letter. Can I ask a question?"

"One question."

"Please, will you take me instead?"

"No."

"Why—?"

"That's two questions."

"Christ, look, it makes more—we can arrange—"

"Shut the fuck up, OK? Understand this, big man. You don't get to say what's what, not on this gig."

The man just stood there, silent.

"You won't hear from me for forty-eight hours. No point getting in touch with you before you have the money ready. Forty-eight hours, got that?"

"Forty-eight hours."

"Have the money ready then."

"I'm not sure I can—"

"You'll have the money ready. A million. In fifties. We do the business, it's all over in hours. You try to drag it out, you play games, fuck you, she's gone."

The man stared.

"Get me? She's fucking gone."

"Please, I'll have the money, I'll do—"

"Here's your mobile." He handed it over. "I'll get your number from the missus. Maybe I'll call you on that, maybe your home phone'll be fixed. Don't go too far from home, right?"

"OK. Listen, there's one thing." He waited as though seeking permission to continue.

"What?"

"I have a fairly structured life—I'm expected places."

"Take a few days off."

"That's what I mean. Business associates, family—someone's liable to notice there's something wrong. What I'm afraid of—if the police get word—"

Frankie said, "You call them, you tell the cops yourself. Take the "what if " out of it. I'll take it for granted they're looking over your shoulder. You can tell them what you like but you'll do what I say. And you wait until morning to contact them. No sooner than nine o'clock, OK?"

"OK."

"I'll know. I have ways of finding out. You say a fucking word to the cops before nine o'clock tomorrow morning, you know what happens."

"I won't, I swear."

Frankie said, "One other thing—there was something about jewellery, and your missus said there was money in a safe, shit like that?"

The man slowly nodded. "I'll show you."

"Good boy. Then we get your missus and the kids down and you tell her goodbye. The sooner we get going, the better."

Some hours later, lying awake on a bare mattress, on the floor of a cold room in a building on the Northside of Dublin, Angela tried to understand why she hadn't been paralysed with fear when the gang leader said he was taking her. All along, from the moment she first walked out into the hall and saw the men in the masks, it was like there was a low-voltage current running through her insides. It was fright and dread and uncertainty, but when the gang leader said what he said, her mind pushed the fear into some hidden crevice and narrowed itself down to the tasks at hand. Calming the kids, and calming her husband.

"Mum?"

Luke was the immediate problem. Saskia seemed to have decided that this, whatever it was, was too big for her to figure out. It was something for the adults to deal with. Her lips tight, her arms folded across her chest, she shut herself off from whatever was happening.

Luke, a year younger, was on the edge of hysteria, his eyes watery, his cheeks red.

"The man was shouting because he's in a hurry, Luke. You know the way grown-ups can get flustered when they're in a hurry and things aren't going well?" It wasn't working. The doubtful look on Luke's face deepened. The explanation, even coming from his mother, didn't come close to accounting for the ferocity he had witnessed. Needing to give him something to build a hope around, Angela continued. "I have to show him the way to where he wants to go. And then I'll be back, OK?"

"No, Mum—"

It took a while, and Angela knew that at any moment the gang leader might come storming back up the stairs, shouting. She spoke quickly, soothingly, and she knew that no words would do the job, that there was a price the kids would have to pay and nothing she could do would change that. She stayed with them as long as she dared and when she brought the kids down the stairs, one each side of her, their hands in hers, Justin and the four gang members were in the hall, waiting. She saw that Justin's hands were now unbound.

Luke couldn't look anywhere but at the four masked faces, his mouth open, his hand tightly gripping Angela's hand. She tried not to imagine what this sight was doing to the children.

At least there were no guns on view. Angela had to pull gently to ease Luke down one step and then another.

At the bottom of the staircase, Angela gently disengaged from Luke and Saskia. Justin hugged the kids tightly and took their hands. As she backed away, their eyes stayed on their mother. Justin didn't dare release his grip on them, even for the time it would take to briefly touch his wife. His voice a strained imitation of normality, he said to Angela, "We'll, you know, we'll go sit down." With his head, he gestured towards the living room. Angela nodded. They held eye contact for some moments, then Justin was gone, shepherding the kids away. The sound of Luke's sobbing could be heard as soon as the living-room door closed behind him.

"Please," Angela said.

"Change into that," the leader said. He threw something on to the floor in front of her. She recognised her purple two-piece tracksuit. A second later her Nike trainers bounced awkwardly on the floor beside the tracksuit. Angela stared at him.

"Here?"

"We let you go off, find another phone stashed somewhere, right?"

The leader's sidekick said, "I'll do this." To Angela he said, "This way," pointing towards the kitchen. Angela picked up the tracksuit and went with him into the kitchen. He turned his back. Angela looked at the sparkling sea of broken crystal. As fast as she could, she shed the burgundy dress and pulled on the tracksuit.

"OK," she said, and he turned round.

"What's your name?" he said.

She said nothing. A pair of socks was stuffed into one of the trainers. She pulled them on, then the shoes. She took her time tying the laces.

"We've got to call you something."

"Look, why do—"

122 - GENE KERRIGAN

"We've been through that and this is how it's going to be."
There was an undertone she couldn't recognise.

"Angela," she said. "Angela Kennedy."

Out in the hall again, the gang leader pulled out a balaclava.
He said, "It's best that you don't see any faces, OK?"

"Please—"

When he pulled the mask down over her face, it was turned
round so that the eyeholes were at the back. Her wrists were
taken, pushed together and she felt a plastic strip tighten
around them. A hand took her by the elbow and steered her to
the front door and held her there. She heard the door open,
then the gang leader say, "Go ahead," and a single pair of footsteps moved off quickly. After a minute, she heard a car starting up, somewhere outside on the street. Then the gang leader
said, "Let's go." She could hear more footsteps crossing the
front yard, while the steady hand held her where she was. The
sound of car doors opening. There was silence after that, with
just the hand on her arm to let her know that she wasn't alone.
The sound of a car passing in the street. She noticed the scent
of the musky aftershave. It was the leader's sidekick. She recognised his soft voice when he spoke. "Everything's OK, just take
it easy."

She thought she could hear Luke sobbing.

"Please," she said.

"Come on."

"Oh, Jesus, please."

"Time to go, Angela. This way." His words were wrapped
in an exaggerated gentleness. "Come on."

She heard him close the front door behind them. Then she
was being guided away from the house. The hand tightened on
her elbow and she stopped. A second hand touched her shoulder and she was gently pushed into a sitting position, on to
something narrow, sharp. "Take it easy," the voice said. "You're
sitting on the back of the car, the boot's open, I want you to

swing round, feet up, OK, and ease yourself into the boot. There's a holdall there, you can use that as a pillow. OK?"

She did as he said, his hands guiding her, lowering her until she lay on her side, her head resting on the holdall, her knees pulled up, her bound hands tucked in under her chin. She realised she could feel her pulse beating wildly where her fingers touched her throat. It was like touching her body's terror. She moved her hands slightly so she couldn't feel it any more.

"OK?"

She said nothing. She felt herself being sucked towards some dread-filled part of her mind and knew that if she went there she would never come back.

Don't even think about that stuff. Slow it all down, take it a minute at a time, a problem at a time. Don't even think about the things you can't do anything about.

She knew it was impossible, but she thought she could still hear Luke's sobs. Then the boot slammed shut.

The door of the room was heavy, solid wood. The window was covered by a sheet of thick chipboard, screwed in place. First thing they told Angela was if she tried to mess with the window she'd leave marks and they'd know about it and they'd break her fingers. Then they took off her balaclava. There were two of them, both masked. The leader and the tall, skinny one.

She'd been in the boot of the car for well over an hour. There were things in the boot—Luke's plastic bucket and spade, from a summer visit to the beach, a pair of Justin's wellington boots, something metal she couldn't identify— things slid and rattled at every lurch and turn of the journey. Every movement of the car seemed more abrupt than it would have been if she were seated. The driver left every use of the brake and the accelerator to the last moment, and then compensated with the violence of his touch.

She'd started off trying to figure out, from the twists and turns of the car, where they might be heading. She gave that up and tried to keep a rough track of time. It was all stop and go, city noises, not the straight run and the swishing motorway sounds she'd expect to hear before too long if they headed south from her home. Probably they'd gone through the city and towards the Northside, maybe west.

The gang talked non-stop. They sounded excited. Angela could hear the voices but couldn't make out the words. Eventually, the car stopped and the lid of the boot opened and the one with the gentle voice helped her out. She could hear some kind of heavy gate being closed, a shriek of metal as a bolt was thrown, a padlock clicking. Then she was taken inside. A wooden floor, she could tell by the noise. Then, a hand on her elbow.

"There's a stairs, right? Up you go."

He guided her forward and up, coming up a step behind her. Someone else was ahead of her. She counted, twelve, thirteen, fourteen steps.

"That's it."

When they took the mask off she saw she was in some kind of storeroom with a bare wooden floor and dirty, yellow walls scarred from floor to ceiling with dustlines and empty screw holes where shelving had been removed. Light came from two long fluorescent fittings hanging unevenly from the high ceiling. The room smelled like the door had been closed and the air hadn't been stirred in a long time. If she had to put a name to the smell it would be putrid.

The leader laid down the rules. No messing with the window, no banging on the door, no screaming. "Fuck around with us, we'll break you. You understand?"

Angela looked at the eyes behind the mask. They were brown, very dark and pitiless. Maybe all eyes look that way, behind a mask, isolated from the humanity of the face.

"You understand?"

She willed herself not to answer him, not to nod. If he was aware of her attempt at insolence, his voice didn't show it.

"You want to go to the toilet, knock hard on the floor, we'll hear you. You can sit or stand, but no walking around up here, no noise. No talking unless you're asked a question."

He threw the balaclava on the floor. "You're told to put that on, you put it on. Put it on backwards. Whenever you're told to wear it, don't take it off without checking with us that our faces are covered. You don't want to see our faces, OK?"

Angela nodded.

At the door, the leader turned back. "That happens, we don't have a choice about what we do. You understand?"

Then they left, locking the door behind them.

There was a single mattress on the floor, no sheet, just a child's Pokémon quilt and a pillow with a stained pink pillowcase. There was no furniture in the room. Angela lay down and after a while she felt cold, so she pulled the quilt over her and stared up at the cracked ceiling. The door opened. It was the gang leader. He stood there looking at her for a moment.

Behind the mask, he might have been angry, sympathetic, threatening, amused or lecherous. Angela wanted to say something, anything, to provoke a response that might suggest which it was.

He reached out and switched off the lights, then he closed the door and apart from the thin lines of light at the top and bottom of the door, all was darkness. At the edges of her mind Angela could feel the fluttering of the swarm of thoughts that she knew she must not allow any closer. They were thoughts about all the things that might happen, the things she might dread and the things she might hope for, and they were too strong to confront. They were the kind of thoughts that cannot visit a mind without colonising it.

She had to think moment by moment. Neutral thoughts. Thoughts about things that didn't matter.

Memories were OK, as long as she chose them carefully, so she didn't end up weeping. And thinking about practical things. She had to stay clean. She would ask for a hairbrush. A radio. That would pass the time. It occurred to her that she might well hear about this on the radio. That's how her friends would hear about it. Someone would hear it on the radio, the phone would start hopping. The notion of her friends hearing her name on the radio in connection with a major crime was so absurd that she almost enjoyed it. There were no words or images in her mind to which the thought could connect. Nothing in her experience made sense of this.

Tomorrow, Thursday, the routine was drop Saskia and Luke at school, drive on down to the gym. Would it be on the radio that soon? The regulars, talking about her, pedalling side by side on the stationary bikes.

The gym.

She wouldn't make it tomorrow. An hour sweating with the girls, a shower and lunch. While that was happening, she'd be—what?

She'd exercise. Wasn't much else to do, if she was going to be stuck in this glorified closet. Can't sit on your arse all day. Get up and move it. The gang leader had said no walking around. Have to talk to them about that. She'd have to be able to loosen up, run on the spot, that kind of thing.

Jesus God. The way I'm thinking, it's like this is going to go on for days and days.

Jesus, no.

Please.

It already seemed like days since Justin's birthday, the cake, the presents, the doorbell ringing. She wished she'd looked at her watch before the gang leader switched off the light. It must have been, what, ten o'clock, at least, when this started.

Eleven, probably half eleven when they left the house. That made it—say an hour, maybe more, getting here—one, maybe two o'clock in the morning.

Justin would be on to Daragh first thing, start the wheels turning, soon as he had the kids sorted. The kids—and here she was skirting close to forbidden thoughts—best if they go to her mother, so Justin would be free to do what he had to do. The kids would be fine. Once she was back with them, Luke would—no, leave that alone for now, stay focused.

Make-up. She was still wearing make-up. She'd need some facial wipes, get the warpaint off. She'd make a mental list of things to ask them for in the morning.

Some magazines. Drinks, fruit. She was still compiling the list when she found her mind fogging with tiredness. She levered off her trainers without unlacing them. She thought she should perhaps take the tracksuit off before sleep claimed her, or she'd feel grubby in the morning, but the cocoon of tiredness was too comfortable, the alternative too bothersome, and she drifted off.

12.

F rankie Crowe was up first next morning, making coffee, listening to the radio. There was nothing on the morning news, nothing at seven o'clock, nothing at eight. The husband would be on to the cops within the hour, if he followed orders. The cops would keep the media out of it for the time being. They'd spend the first couple of days beating the bushes, trying to get a handle on this. Touts would be rousted this afternoon, tonight, threats made and favours called in. No chance. Only five people knew that Frankie was involved—and four of them were in this house. Milky was the fifth, he'd be here later. Tommy Sholtis knew that Frankie had got tooled up, but he didn't know what the job was. Anyway, Tommy was as tight as a drum.

The cops would still be getting into gear by the time the money was handed over and the whole shebang would be game, set and match.

Frankie was sitting in a makeshift kitchen, some kind of staffroom at the back of the building. Beneath the layers of dust, grime and grease, the walls were painted a dull cream. It was a big room, with some cupboards and a fridge, plus a cooker and a short countertop, a microwave, several chairs. In one corner, there was a large matt silver television on a stand, with a matching video machine underneath. Not new but close enough. Milky had done them proud. There was no cable or satellite, so the viewing was limited to the two RTE stations. An archway led to a massive walk-in fridge, and there was a toilet at the end of the corridor.

It was a two-storey commercial building, off a side street in Phibsboro. There was a yard at the back, not overlooked, which was ideal for getting the hostage out of the car and into the building.

The door to the staffroom opened and Dolly Finn came in. He was wearing his black tracksuit zipped up to his chin.

"Morning."

"Where d'you think you're off to?"

Finn's eyebrows pushed up, wrinkling his forehead.

"I always go for a run, first thing."

"Sit down, have a coffee. No one leaves the house."

Dolly paused a moment, then he said, "Fair enough," and got himself a coffee. He sat across from Crowe and the two sipped their coffees and for several minutes nothing was said. Then: "She OK this morning, no hysterics?"

Crowe said, "I looked in on her twenty minutes ago, still fast asleep."

Brendan Sweetman came into the staffroom, sleep in his eyes, a heavy shadow on his jowls. "Any breakfast? I'm famished."

"Corn flakes," Crowe said.

"Fuck sake."

"Milky'll be here later, put in your order."

There was silence for a long while, then Dolly Finn said, "No going out at all?"

"Safer that way."

Dolly nodded.

"Long day ahead," Brendan Sweetman said.

Crowe said, "There'll be nothing stirring today. He has forty-eight hours to get the money, then we'll see how fast we move. That's the thing. No hanging around, no negotiations, just bang-bang-bang, and we're gone. Today, tomorrow, we just bide our time while hubby makes a withdrawal."

Martin Paxton was last to come down from upstairs, yawning. He said, "She'd like a cup of tea."

"There's some tea bags there."

"And she has a list."

"She has what?" Crowe was grinning.

"A list. She has a list of things she'd like us to provide."

"I like it! I like it!"

"Toothbrush, toothpaste, that kind of thing."

Frankie said, "Candelabra on the table, place mats and silverware, right?" Brendan Sweetman laughed, a series of hiccupping sounds.

Paxton shrugged. "She's just, I reckon she's just trying to cope, just trying to get along."

"What it is," Frankie said, "is you can take the bitch out of the mansion, but you can't take the mansion out of the bitch. Fucking list."

Martin filled the kettle. "Tea, anyone?"

Coming up to eleven o'clock in the morning, the Round Hall of the Four Courts was like a major train station at the start of a holiday weekend. Crowded, noisy and tense. The circular floor was thick with robed and wigged barristers conferring with each other, with solicitors and with clients. Around the edges of the hall, people sat on curved wooden benches. Others leaned against the pairs of tall pillars that flanked the doors to each of the four principal courtrooms surrounding the hall. The black Druidical garb of the barristers set the tone. The accumulated chatter rose like invisible steam high up into the massive dome above the crowd. Despite the airs and graces of the place, it had the unmistakable character of a marketplace.

Detective Sergeant Nicky Bonner was standing on the steps of Court No. 3, his eyes sweeping the crowd, watching for the arrival of Desmond Cartwright, Senior Counsel. He'd tried

Cartwright's mobile, with no response. The barrister might have had to go into a huddle with a solicitor or a client before the 11 A.M. court session. In which case he wouldn't be available until the courts adjourned at lunchtime.

Lawyers clutched untidy bundles of documents to their chests, as though they were shields. Clients glanced repeatedly at the huge clock over the entrance to the deeper recesses of the building. At eleven o'clock, when their cases began or resumed, years of worry, months of preparation, would come to a climax. The lawyers displayed their trade's confident nonchalance. There would be another case tomorrow, next week and the week after. The clients might fret about the outcome, but for the lawyers, win or lose, there was nothing personal involved, it was just another eddy in the never-ending stream of business.

The crowd parted as a short procession of jailers and prisoners came through the front doorway and crossed the hall towards the stairs down to the waiting room. Lawyers ignored them. Gardai checked them out. Civilians cast quick glances at the defendants, handcuffed creatures from an exotic underworld. Litigants in civil cases, for whom winning or losing meant a financial penalty or a windfall, were merely consumers of legal services. The major criminal cases, murders and rapes, were usually one-offs, products of anger or passion. The career criminals, the thieves and the drug peddlers, in their uniforms of the Nike and Reebok armies, seemed for the most part unresentful of their probable fate. Their repeat business made them the reluctant underwriters of the prosperity of the legal business.

Bonner recognised one of them that he'd done for burglary a few years back, a shuffling loser from an inner-city flats complex, still playing out the hopeless hand he'd been dealt. He didn't know any of the others, fresh-faced hoods who kept a touch of arrogance in their stride, even while handcuffed. It was as though graduation to this plateau of justice, from the rough and tumble of the district court, was some kind of promotion. A sign of getting old, Nicky Bonner reckoned, when the criminals start to look young.

"The man himself." Desmond Cartwright was suddenly at Nicky Bonner's side, emerging from the crowd. He was a small, fat, bald man, with the cultivated air of a nineteenth-century aristocrat who just happened to find himself working at the Bar in twenty-first-century Dublin, and was perpetually amused by this turn of events.

"Mr. Cartwright." Bonner held out his hand and Cartwright shook it. The Waterford background they shared was tangential. Mr. Cartwright was leaving boarding school, on his way to Trinity and Kings Inns, around the time that Nicky was quitting his factory job to join the guards.

"Perhaps we could—" Cartwright stopped and turned to one side. The crowd parted, this time to allow a judge to proceed across the hall towards the side door to one of the courtrooms. A robed tipstaff, carrying a long wooden rod, preceded the judge. The barristers all turned and bowed their heads towards His Lordship, who acknowledged the deference. His serial nodding, along with his bulbous jowls, made Bonner think of one of those plastic dogs that used to sit in the back windows of cars.

"Perhaps we could adjourn to a more—if I might use the word—judicious location, sergeant?"

Cartwright, his robe hanging precariously from his shoulders, his wig tilted slightly, led the way out of the Round Hall, across a vestibule and down a corridor.

As a young man, Cartwright had made a solid reputation in the criminal courts, with occasional forays into commercial law. His fees grew in proportion to his experience, and his girth in proportion to his fees. Representing a leading businessman at a long-running tribunal of inquiry, Cartwright graduated from merely very wealthy to unassailably rich. He was now on retainers from two other businessmen who feared that a current line of tribunal investigation might reveal their interest in one of the more controversial property deals of the previous decade. Such work was so lucrative that Cartwright's involvement in criminal cases was now sporadic. His fortune made, and his interest in fighting routine cases waning, he had recently put out feelers in political circles and was hopeful of an appointment to the bench within the next year.

He found a window nook opposite the office of a Supreme Court judge. There, underneath a No Smoking sign, he lit up a Benson & Hedges. "It's done?"

Bonner nodded. "He's a decent lad."

"That's not the description that leaps to mind when I recall the manner in which he treated me."

"Just doing his job. And you can't deny you were wearing the wobbly boots that day."

"A touch over-refreshed, perhaps, but I was quite capable of looking after myself."

To hear the arresting garda tell it, Cartwright came out of his gentleman's club with both eyes in the one socket. Middle of the afternoon. Wouldn't take a friendly warning, insisted on climbing behind the wheel, and then did a runner.

Nicky Bonner said, "Not to worry. It seems he's mislaid the notebook he used on that occasion."

Cartwright took an envelope from an inside pocket and handed it to Bonner. "The avaricious little shit didn't need too much convincing, I take it?"

Bonner put the envelope in an inside pocket.

The lawyer took a second envelope from his pocket, and said, "A little something for yourself, just a small token."

Bonner shook his head. "Put that away, Mr. Cartwright. The garda is risking a reprimand for making a balls of a routine drink-driving. So, it's only fair that he gets compensation.

I'm just a go-between. Seriously, I wouldn't dream of taking a penny off you."

Cartwright put the second envelope away. "Thank you, my friend. Decency, I'm glad to hear, isn't entirely obsolete, even in the rapacious little nation we've regretfully become."

Bonner said, "Mother Ireland, she's not what she used to be, right enough."

Cartwright raised an eyebrow. "Do I detect a note of sarcasm, sergeant?"

"Not in the least, Mr. Cartwright."

"Don't patronise me, sergeant. I'm quite aware that what we're doing is ignoble. It's a question of proportion. I'm a fine lawyer. I'll be a great judge. Not one of the time-servers appointed to the bench because they licked party envelopes and ministerial arses. I have the intellect and I have the guts to do what's right for this country. I won't be anyone's lapdog. The question is, do I throw all that away because I've had a drop or two and some little fascist wants to meet his quota of motoring offences? Do I slink away and let one more slot on the bench be filled by some nonentity who hasn't two original thoughts to rub together? Or do I do the sensible thing?"

"No offence intended, Mr. Cartwright."

Nicky Bonner watched Cartwright purse his lips. Smug fucker.

"None taken, sergeant." He looked at his watch. "Showtime."

They shook hands, Cartwright said something about having a jar one of these evenings and that was that. Two minutes later, in a cubicle in the jacks, Nicky Bonner opened the envelope and counted the money. Well worth it to a lawyer whose career expectations might not survive a drink-driving conviction.

It made sense for Bonner to turn down the bonus. The second envelope couldn't have contained more than a few hundred, maybe a grand at most, and that was a small price for the lawyer's future goodwill. This way, he turned a considerable profit and kept a stain-free reputation with someone who mattered. In years to come, there might be occasions when it would do a detective sergeant no harm to have a judge feel a sense of obligation.

Nicky Bonner left the Four Courts and strolled down the quays towards O'Connell Street. Next week he'd arrange the split with the arresting garda. Two grand from the five in the envelope would see the youngster right.

There was a time when Bonner had offered John Grace a cut from the two or three strokes he pulled in a year, but Grace had a conniption. "Do what you do, but don't involve me in that fucking stuff, OK?"

"No problem."

"I mean it, Nicky. I know nothing. I want to know nothing, and if you get caught—"

They both knew there was very little chance of that. The way Nicky Bonner saw it, a hard-working policeman got a very occasional and well-deserved bonus. And decent citizens such as Mr. Cartwright retained their well-deserved respectability. Nobody got hurt. And Nicky Bonner brought home to his wife and four kids something like the kind of money to which a man of his experience and dedication was entitled. He owned two houses in Waterford, bought before property prices went crazy, set out in flats and earning big. The plan was to go back there when he took early retirement.

Past Capel Street Bridge, he hailed a taxi and as he climbed inside he was thumbing the keys of his mobile, checking in with John Grace. Unless there was something pressing to attend to, Bonner intended taking the rest of the day off.

13

Milky came just before lunchtime. He had the *Star*, *Mirror*, *Sun*, *Daily Mail* and *Irish Independent*, three rented videos, the makings of a fry-up, apples, oranges and bananas, a dozen cans of Coke, a dozen assorted sandwiches from a local deli, milk, sugar, a packet of tea bags and a jar of Maxwell House. The label on the sandwiches had the name of the deli, so Martin scraped it off a ham sandwich before taking it up to the hostage, along with an apple and a glass of milk.

Frankie Crowe took a bite from an apple. Brendan Sweetman immediately gave Milky a list of food he wanted for an evening meal.

Milky took his time lighting a cigarette, an untipped Player, then he said, "I hope it keeps fine for you." He offered Dolly Finn the packet of smokes. Finn shook his head and tapped his own packet of Benson & Hedges on the table.

Brendan said, "Fucking corn flakes, that's all I've had."

"Your cut from this job, you can spend half the year in the Canaries. All the room service you want." He went out to his car and brought in a cheap holdall containing a couple of changes of clothing for the four members of the crew.

Milky was in his late fifties, with a full head of hair dyed black. He was still fit and not too padded by the years. He was wearing his usual gear, a check jacket and a plain shirt and tie. Milky had a selection of check jackets and plain shirts and ties and Frankie had never seen him wear anything else. Today's jacket was primarily green, the shirt was yellow, the tie was brown. Although his wardrobe had once included a balaclava or two, Milky had long ago stepped up to another level. He owned a garage and a pub, purchased twenty years back on the proceeds of a series of armed robberies. He occasionally dabbled in small Dublin properties and lately he'd bought three beachfront properties in Cape Town. He maintained a sideline in providing facilities for occasional projects carried out by criminal associates.

"No need to slum it," Brendan Sweetman said. He picked up the sausages, rashers and pudding and took a frying pan from a shelf and began wiping the dust off it.

Frankie took another bite from the apple and gave Milky a nod. "Got some stuff to shift." The two left the staffroom and went into the front of the building, a former butcher shop. The window was covered by a grubby once-white blind that filtered all strength from the daylight. There was an old-fashioned ornate cash register and a mechanical scales. On shallow shelves underneath the counter, the top sheets of a stack of white wrapping paper were yellowed and turning up at the edges. There was some kind of metal dispenser at the end of the counter, holding a roll of plastic bags, a length of the roll hanging down almost to the floor. The bags each had an illustration in dark blue ink. It showed a fat, cheerful butcher and the slogan, "There's No Meat Like Rafferty's Meat." Against the back wall, there was a worn, scarred, well-scrubbed butcher's block. The shop hadn't functioned for over two years, but the smell of dead meat lingered. It was like someone had tidied up one weekend and everyone forgot to come in the following Monday or ever again.

The site had twice been purchased by companies that pulled out of the deal when business slumped and survival took precedence over expansion. When he rented the place for a month, Milky used two cut-outs between himself and the people who owned the building.

"You reckon what," Milky said, "a week, no more than that?"

"Three, four days," Frankie said, "no stalling." He pressed a key on the register and watched the drawer spring open. It was empty. "What I need now is a dozen mobile phones, ready-paid, clean and untraceable, kind I can use once, and then bury."

Frankie took another bite out of the apple, dropped the core into the cash drawer and slammed it shut.

Milky gestured at the bulky holdalls on the floor near the counter. "This them?"

"Some jewellery, small electronic stuff—Palm Pilot, a couple of laptops, digital cameras, silverware, shit like that. A few decent watches, too—I'm keeping a souvenir." Frankie held up his wrist and Milky nodded appreciatively at the Rolex.

"Everyone should have one."

Once the portable loot was shifted by Milky, and passed to a fence, it would bring enough of a cash bonus to take care of running expenses.

Martin Paxton came through from the back room. "Just the man," he said, and handed Milky a piece of paper torn from a notebook. "I jotted down her list." He put his hands on his hips and smiled.

Milky raised an eyebrow and glanced at the list, his tongue flicking at his half-open lips. "Facial wipes? Fuck sake." He shook his head, passed the list to Frankie and grinned. "Madam keeps this up, maybe you ought to jack up the ransom by a few grand."

Frankie read the list. "No radio. Don't want hubby sending messages through some helpful disc jockey. Rest of it, what the fuck. She's going to pay her way, before this is done."

Milky came back to the former butcher shop that evening carrying two plastic shopping bags, the air around him reeking of fish and chips. He dumped one bag on the table in the staffroom and said, "Dinner is served, gentlemen." The smaller bag he left on the floor by a wall. "Her ladyship's delivery."

Brendan Sweetman took charge of dividing up the individually wrapped portions from the chipper. Dolly Finn asked, "Is there nothing else?"

Milky looked for a moment as though he might be about to say something waspy, then he just said, "No." Dolly turned away and went to the fridge, where he found one of the sandwiches that Milky had brought earlier. He sat down, opened the *Mirror* and nibbled at the sandwich as he read.

Frankie Crowe unwrapped a packet of fish and chips and asked, "Anything unusual going on out there? Cops putting up roadblocks, that kind of thing?"

"Not that I've heard," Milky said.

"Raids, searches?"

Milky shook his head. "Nothing out of the ordinary, I think I'd have heard." Brendan, already halfway through his own food, reached over for the packet of fish and chips that Dolly had disowned and moved it closer to his side of the table.

Martin Paxton emptied a bag of chips on to a plate and added a portion of cod. He got a bottle of Ballygowan from the fridge and took the food upstairs to the hostage.

"Milky," Brendan Sweetman said, "where in the name of fuck did you get those videos? *Titanic*, for Jesus sake. And that other thing, Jack Nicholson. I mean, what about something made this century?"

"What's the matter, Sweets—" Milky adopted an American accent, "—you can't handle the truth?"

"Fuck it, I'll go out later and get something worth watching."

"No one leaves here," Frankie Crowe said. "We don't want locals noticing a parade of strangers coming and going. Milky comes in and out, one guy, nothing odd about that."

"Just the once. Down the street, get a few videos, no big deal?"

"It's a couple of days, Brendan, that's not a big deal. Then, we collect the ransom, and you can be up to your bollocks in DVDs."

Sweetman made a grimace of displeasure. He finished his own food, screwed the wrapping paper into a ball and threw it across the room, missing a waste bin by a couple of feet, then he unwrapped Dolly's untouched chips.

Milky said to Frankie, "You're not tempted to ring, see how the money's coming along?"

"He's sensible, he'll be working on it. If not, fuck him."

When he got home from Turner's Lane garda station that evening, Detective Inspector John Grace went to his home office, a converted spare bedroom, and spent an hour reading the file on a case that was due to start in the Circuit Criminal Court the following Tuesday. It had been fourteen months since he supervised the investigation and many of the details had become blurred. In the witness box, he'd have to provide instant, clear answers that gelled with those of other officers.

Around eight o'clock, his wife Mona came in and asked if he was OK for taking Sam to bed.

"My turn," John Grace said.

"You haven't eaten yet," Mona said. "I'll take him up."

"Not at all," Grace said. "My turn."

He valued these evenings, reading his grandson to sleep. Married at twenty, he had three children of his own before he was thirty. Now, at forty-six, he'd been a grandfather for almost six years. Of his own kids, Jocelyn had an engineering job in Birmingham and David was studying economics at UCD. The eldest, Jess—Sam's mother—had a flat in town and worked as a freelance illustrator. Because Jess was single and working, John Grace and his wife helped with the raising of

Sam. Grace was enjoying it, aware that when he was a young policeman pursuing an ambitious career, he'd missed a lot of the pleasures of parenthood.

He tidied up his desk, locking the case material away in a file drawer. Sam sometimes used the computer in the office, to play his Pingu and Bananas in Pajamas games. Raising his own three kids, Grace had become scrupulous about never leaving documents or crime-scene photographs lying about. There were times when he brought home the kind of stuff that would give a kid nightmares.

Until recently, Grace had never lived in a house big enough to offer a separate room as a home office. Then, two years ago, he and Mona had moved to a house near the sea, at Sutton. With the two oldest kids moved on, they had more room than they needed. The home office was twice the size of the shoebox he shared with another detective down at Turner's Lane.

Sam stayed over most Friday and Saturday nights, sometimes a couple more nights, depending on his mother's work and social schedule. He liked to change into his pyjamas himself, and if he sometimes got them inside out, that didn't matter. John Grace sat on the child's bed and watched the awkward ballet of sleeves and trouser legs until Sam was ready for bed.

"Where were we?"

Sam had already fetched the book from his shelves. "We were going to start the cat story tonight."

"Fair enough, lie down there and we'll start." Grace watched as Sam wormed his way under the bedclothes. The simple beauty and innocence of the big brown eyes in that soft oval face never ceased to amaze him. He'd seen that quality in his own children, and watched as it was washed away by incremental waves of maturity. There wasn't a face on the planet, no matter how hardened, weary or cruel, that hadn't at one time, and however briefly, glowed with that same beauty and innocence. Grace opened the book in his lap. "Sunny's Big Adventure, Chapter One."

* * *

Angela was lying face down on the mattress when the kidnapper with the soft voice brought the meal of fish and chips and a bottle of water. She looked up, saw the food, then turned so she was facing the wall. She heard the click of the plate being placed gently on the bare floorboards.

"Don't be silly, love. You have to keep your strength up."

The smell from the fish and chips was heavy and inescapable, filling every corner of the room.

The day had started with the same kidnapper looking in on her, yawning. He'd brought her a cup of tea. When she rapped on the floor he came and took her to the toilet, down a short corridor, past doors open on what seemed like a couple of makeshift bedrooms. She could see mattresses on the floor, bedclothes thrown untidily on top. The toilet was dim and dusty. The man stood outside. There was no window in the toilet; the bare bulb was low wattage. There was graffiti on the back of the door and on the walls, some crude, mostly just names. Some kind of workplace.

Later, when the same gang member came up with a sandwich, an apple and milk for her lunch, he scribbled a note as she recited a list of things she needed and he said he couldn't promise anything.

She opened the sandwich but couldn't eat it. Nothing wrong with it, ham with a sliver of limp lettuce, but she suddenly wasn't hungry. She ignored the apple but drank some of the milk.

Her plans for organising her thinking came to nothing. Her mind seemed clogged and slow, incapable of pulling together coherent thoughts. It wasn't fear and it wasn't distress. More a kind of indolence. She lay on the mattress most of the afternoon, in something close to a daze. Hours passed in which she did nothing but lie there. Her eyes seemed to have acquired the ability to consistently focus on some point in mid-air.

The gang looked in on her every halfhour or so. Always the same, checking that the sheet of wood covering the window hadn't been interfered with. A glance around to see that everything was as it had been, then they left. None of them said anything, except the one with the soft voice, the leader's sidekick, who made a point of being friendly. Everything OK? Warm enough? Fancy a Coke? She ignored him.

The small fat gunman was easy to read, even with the mask. Every movement, everything he said to her, dripped with irritation and resentment. It was like he wanted her to know that she'd done something that personally hurt him. In the afternoon, he came up after she knocked on the floor. When he took her to the toilet he used single words, his voice coarse and abrupt. "OK," he said, holding the door open, when she told him what she wanted. When they got to the toilet he said, "There."

When she closed the toilet door, he roughly pushed it open again and said, "No." She didn't see the point of this. "Are you trying to humiliate me?" she said. This time, he used two words. "Fuck off." He stood out in the corridor, off to one side of the door and out of sight, while she used the toilet.

At some stage that day she took off her watch. Whenever she looked at it the time on its face seemed to bear no relationship to the time that had surely crept by. She'd left the watch on the floor several feet away from the mattress and she hadn't the energy or the will to get up and check it. The day merged into a dull, featureless length of time, a disabling fear leaking out of her every pore.

Now, in the evening, the smell of the fish and chips reminded her that she had hardly eaten all day. The satisfaction of her insolent non-response to the gunman who delivered the smelly food had faded. She turned over and looked at the food. She made a face. Christ, even a McDonald's would be better than this. It was old-style fish-and-chip-shop food. The gnarled brown batter in which the fish was encased was visibly saturated with grease. The thick chips were little better, but they were edible if she took sips of the Ballygowan. There was no fork, so she used her fingers. Once she got used to the taste, she ate more eagerly. By the time she finished the chips the edge had been taken off her need, but she was still hungry. She broke the fish in two. The grease had penetrated the batter and coated the surface of the fish. She split the batter away from the fish and tried a piece of the white flesh. It was hard to discern a flavour under the taste of the grease, but she ate it all. When there was no more fish she ate some of the batter. When she squeezed a piece of batter she saw the grease run out of it, which was when she pushed the plate away, took another mouthful of Ballygowan and lay down on the mattress.

After a while, the chatty gunman came to collect the plate. "Good girl, well done." He left a plastic shopping bag on the floor. "Stuff you asked for." Again she ignored him.

When he was gone, she emptied the bag. A couple of celebrity magazines, a copy of *Cosmo*, a hairbrush, tissues, facial wipes, a three-pack of knickers, toothbrush and paste, a sponge, two small bottles of Coke and a litre of Ballygowan. She used the wipes to get the grease off her fingers, then cleaned her face and neck and under her arms.

When John Grace's home phone rang, he had just come down from the child's bedroom and Sam was no more than ten minutes asleep, not yet beyond the reach of a persistently ringing phone. Mona was in the kitchen. Grace hurried across the living room and picked up the cordless.

"John Grace."

"I'm told you're the man to talk to about a thug named Frankie Crowe."

"Sorry?"

"Colin O'Keefe. I need to talk to you about this Frankie Crowe fella."

For a moment, Grace was puzzled, then the name clicked. He had met Assistant Commissioner Colin O'Keefe at a retirement party for a colleague, a superannuated super. He doubted if the AC remembered him. Given the general level of intoxication at the party, he hoped not.

"What's he done now?" he said.

"How soon can you get up here?"

"That bad?"

"Tell your missus not to wait up."

When Martin Paxton came downstairs after checking on the hostage, there was a bullshitting session under way. Brendan Sweetman was telling Frankie, Milky and Dolly the story of a burglary he did in Rathmines, the one about the big dog coming howling up the stairs. "The hound of the Baskervilles, no kidding. Big as a bleeding donkey." The story ended with Brendan locking the dog in a closet and screaming at the owner to get the fuck back to his bedroom and count to five hundred.

"Halfway down the stairs, I was, when the gobshite opened the closet. The dog came flying out, mad as a hen with piles." He paused for a beat. "Started biting the legs off yer man."

Frankie laughed, although Martin knew that he'd heard it at least once before. Dolly's face adopted what might have been a smile.

Frankie contributed the tale of the fuck-up at Harte's Cross, and how he and Martin got a tip-off from Leo Titley and toddled off down to do a pub in Hicksville and how Titley fucked up the info on the job and they ended up with a lousy two hundred.

"Not surprised," Brendan Sweetman said. He did a job with Leo once. "Culchie wanker."

"There was a bit of crack, mind," Frankie remembered. "Old bollocks in the pub, he looks at me like I've landed in a flying saucer. Put away that gun, he says. Middle of a job, the local yokel decides to come to the rescue of the oul bitch that runs the place. Leave the lady alone, says he, standing there like Rambo's grandad. So I let him see the business end. You want to keep your balls, Sir Galahad?"

Brendan Sweetman laughed.

"Shut him up, right off," Frankie said. "Another old guy, when I let off a couple of rounds to encourage the bitch to cough up some money, know what he did? He pissed himself. Standing there with his hands in the air, big wet patch all the way down his trousers."

Martin Paxton stood up. "I need one last coffee. Anyone?" Only Dolly nodded. As Martin left the room, Frankie looked at Brendan, pointed at the ceiling and said, "Lights out."

When the small fat gunman came to switch off the light Angela said, "No, please, just a while more."

He switched the light off.

"Fuck you," she said.

He stood there, silhouetted in the doorway. She could hear the noise he was making chewing gum. After a few moments, he gave a grunt and turned away, pulling the door shut behind him.

"Bastard!"

There was a second's silence, then there was a very loud noise, and Angela could almost feel the concussion ripple through the room as the door shook from his kick. She sat up on the mattress her arms crossed in front of her body, clutching her elbows to stop herself shaking.

Someone shouted something from downstairs and she could hear the fat little man grunting a reply. When she heard him going down the stairs she sank back down on the mattress. A little later she heard loud male laughter from downstairs.

She took long, deep breaths. Again, she made an effort to hold at bay the thoughts she had resolved to shun. She tried to make sense of the chatter coming from downstairs, but it was muffled and disjointed, punctuated by laughter.

She turned on her side, knowing she was a long way from sleep. She heard a toilet flush, a door closing. It was like when she was a child, lying in the darkness of her bedroom at night, waiting for sleep, random thoughts floating in and out of her mind as she listened to the noises the adults made downstairs. It was the sound of life continuing. It was one of the ways she began to understand the size and the complexity of the world, and that she wasn't the centre of it all, and that it didn't stop when she went to bed and fell asleep.

With the knowledge that others' lives go on even as we surrender to sleep, came an understanding of how the world goes on whether we're there or not. It was an understanding that intrigued her in childhood and terrified her as a teenager, when she began to measure her own mortality.

Angela turned her face into the pillow and closed her eyes. She recognised that she was on the verge of admitting some of the thoughts she'd sworn to banish. She needed to think other thoughts. Very deliberately, she began trying to visualise what the small fat one looked behind his mask. She imagined that face, chubby and sweaty, vacant and slack-jawed. And in her imagination, she spat on it.

When Brendan came back downstairs, Martin Paxton was trying to encourage Milky to tell the others how he got his nickname.

"Ah, Jesus, leave me alone," Milky said, but he was grinning. He liked the story. He lit up a Player's, used a thumbnail to remove a flake of tobacco from his tongue. "You tell it," he said to Martin.

"What were you, twenty, something like that?"

"Eighteen, nineteen. It was the first gun I ever got my hands on. A starting pistol. A newsagent's out in Bray, up the town," Milky said. "And I did a bookies before that, same starting pistol. Stroked a couple of grand that time."

"Anyway, Milky walks into the newsagent's, no customers, one bird behind the counter. Hand it over, he says, and your woman squeals and when he gets her to calm down he says, Give me the money, all of it. Now, there's nothing she'd like to do more, and get Jesse James out of her shop, but there's only a handful of notes in the register, fivers and tens, and she throws them on the counter. Anything over a twenty goes straight into a drop safe, she says, there's no way she can get at it. So, Milky picks up the money and puts it in his pocket and stands there, the gun in his hand, big scarf over his mouth, your woman licking her lips. You know what he did?"

"I couldn't think of anything else to do!"

"He grabbed a handful of chocolate bars and ran for the door."

Brendan Sweetman snorted. "Good man, Milky!"

Milky shook his head. "Big GAA slob coming in, just finished practice, a hurley in his paws, takes a look at the starting pistol in my hand, gives me a smack in the mouth with the hurley and when I woke up the cops were standing over me, breaking their shite laughing."

Martin said, "Tell them, when you were wheeled into the Joy, what the screws christened you."

Milky sighed, looked up at the ceiling. "The Milky Bar Kid."

There was a high-pitched hooting laugh from Dolly Finn, a series of short honking noises that came as much from his nose as his mouth. It was the first time any of them had heard Dolly laugh. The sight and the sound of Dolly laughing stoked the others and Milky threw his head back and chortled, Frankie Crowe's shoulders were heaving. Martin looked across at Dolly and saw that he was blushing.

"Jesus," Brendan said, "I'd love a pint. That's what an evening like this needs, a bit of lubrication."

Frankie shook his head. "Take it easy, lads. This whole thing, it could go like click-click-click, and we walk away with a bundle. Or, maybe we already did something wrong, and the cops are outside putting on their bulletproof vests."

"We're cruising," Sweetman said.

Frankie said, "It happens. Whatever way it goes, best chance we have, keep clear heads. There's lots of time later for cracking bottles."

Dolly Finn said, "How long you reckon?"

"We're got a schedule—short and sharp. So far, we're on track."

Brendan Sweetman poked a finger in the direction of the ceiling. "That one? What you reckon's the safest thing to do with her?"

"Don't see why we can't hand her back spick and span. She hasn't seen any faces, right? No names? Should be OK." Frankie shrugged. "I mean, you can't be a hundred per cent on a thing like this, but the way we're going, no reason we can't pat her on the arse and send her home to hubby."

14.

There were two gardai in the kitchen of the Kennedy home, with the telephone-monitoring equipment. Two more were on permanent duty in the hall. All armed. There was little likelihood of the gang coming back to the house, but it wasn't the kind of thing anyone wanted to take a chance on.

Justin Kennedy was in his bedroom, mooching around. Nothing to do. Too tense to sit for more than a few minutes. It was—what?—he checked his watch—after ten o'clock. Twenty-four hours since this—Jesus, Angela had been kidnapped—since this began. Another twenty-four hours to the deadline—the phone call from the kidnappers. The instructions for the ransom. Nothing would happen until at least then.

The important thing was, no panic. This could be handled. There was a problem. We have something they want. They have something—and the fact that it's Angela can't be allowed get in the way of dealing with the problem—they have something we want. There has to be a transaction. Take it in steps, no surprises, nothing to make them jumpy. This can be managed.

After the gang had left the house, Kennedy was up all night, comforting the children until they dozed off, then drinking coffee and pacing the hall, mobile in hand. He made a phone call at 6 A.M. Then another at six-fifteen, to Angela's sister in Paris. He told her what had happened and asked her to take a flight home that morning, to organise the family end of things, to break the news to Angela's mother, to help with the kids. Elizabeth was a first-rate organiser, with the deepest love for her younger sister, and she'd handle this end of it so well he'd never have to give it a thought. She agreed to come immediately.

It was not until precisely 9 A.M., in obedience to the kidnappers' orders, that Kennedy contacted the police. Through the night, he thought carefully about how best to do this. He made a phone call to a senior adviser in the office of the Minister for Justice, a man on whose invitation the Kennedys recently attended a major charity event for Down's syndrome children. Justin explained what was happening, and asked that the garda commissioner be informed, and that the strictest confidentiality be maintained. Within ten minutes, the first gardai arrived at the front door.

In the hours since they'd been contacted, the police had fixed the phone line, wired it for monitoring and put a protective team in place. A specialist team of officers in white overalls went through each room, photographing, fingerprinting and searching. The living room and the kitchen were still out of bounds to Justin. A chief superintendent—Hogg, his name was—had come to the house and told Justin that the gardai had never yet lost a kidnap victim.

"We have to advise against paying a ransom, Mr. Kennedy," Hogg said. "The principle is well established. Paying the ransom creates an incentive, so this kind of thing happens again. Maybe not to your family, but that's what happens." He looked Justin in the eye. "What we find, generally, in this situation, is that people listen carefully to this advice." He paused, then he said, "And they make private arrangements for the ransom to be ready. Just in case. It may never get to that stage. And it's not something we encourage, but I'm aware we're dealing here with human beings."

152 - GENE KERRIGAN

"If it was your family?"

"Happily, that's hypothetical."

Justin nodded. "I'm still staggered by all this, but I think I know what I have to do."

As it happened, the first call Justin Kennedy had made, three hours before contacting the authorities, was to his friend Daragh O'Suilleabhain, principal partner of Flynn O'Meara Tully & Co. He explained what happened. O'Suilleabhain said, "Jesus Christ," then he said "Uh-huh" a few times, otherwise he waited until Kennedy finished speaking. Then he said, "Sit tight, Justin. Whatever it takes, we'll get Angela back."

They agreed that O'Suilleabhain would take charge of raising the million in cash. By the time the police arrived at Kennedy's house, O'Suilleabhain had contacted two directors of the principal bank through which Flynn O'Meara Tully & Co. did business. He swore them to secrecy and the job of sourcing the ransom cash was begun. O'Suilleabhain rang Kennedy twice, keeping him informed of progress. During the second call, he told Justin he had confidentially briefed a psychologist who did work for the company. When Justin thought the time was right, counselling would be available for the children, and for Angela.

Now, Chief Superintendent Hogg was saying to Justin, "I must ask you to inform my people of each and every step you intend to take, relating to the ransom demand. As I say, we'd find it difficult to interfere, but we must know what's happening, or—well, you can imagine."

Kennedy's first instinct was to hold back from telling the police about his contact with Daragh O'Suilleabhain. Angela's safe return was Kennedy's only goal; the police had wider ambitions. Part of their strategy would be aimed at catching the gang. Cutting the police out of this made sense up to a point. But trying to keep the arrangements secret from the them, even as they listened to his phone calls, was to invite disaster. Kennedy told Superintendent Hogg about the preparations already being made through Daragh O'Suilleabhain, and the detective wrote down the details.

That evening, Elizabeth brought the kids from her mother's house to see Justin. Saskia seemed to be OK, though she said little and she kept her arms folded across her chest throughout the visit, hugging herself. Luke cried when he ran to Justin's arms. He clung to his father and his gaze never left Justin's face. He sobbed as he left over an hour later, his Bear Factory toy clutched fiercely against his neck. Elizabeth managed to distract him with a promise of a sleepover in Granny's living room, in his cuddlesack. Then, once the children got into the unmarked police car, the tears started again. Luke clutched his auntie, Saskia sat alongside them in the back, her arms still folded, staring at the house as Elizabeth did her best to find comforting words. Two armed gardai drove them away.

There was a painting on the wall opposite Justin and Angela's bed. It was a fairly innocuous thing by a Dublin artist who for the past decade had been described as promising. It was the first picture they hung when they moved into Pemberton Road. The painting had been in a similar position in the bedroom of their previous home, ever since Justin bought it at a charity auction four years back. That was some night, the night he bought the painting.

Justin sat on the bed. Tension and tiredness sapped the strength from his muscles and he lay back and let the mattress take his weight.

That painting was something special for both Angela and him but he couldn't remember ever discussing that night with her. They didn't have to. They both knew it to be a landmark on the way to where they were.

"One thousand?"

The auctioneer, an RTE celebrity, acknowledged a bid from

a table up near the front of the large, chintzy hotel dining room. Most people had been a couple of drinks up when the charity dinner began, each table had four open bottles waiting when the guests sat down to eat, and the waiters were now unobtrusively ensuring that no glass stayed drained for long. The bidding went up in five hundreds and the sixth time that the auctioneer asked for any advance on three thousand, Justin poked a finger in the air.

"Thank you, sir, three and a half."

The painting was OK—light blues and glittery whites, with the odd coil of dark colour scattered around the lower third of the canvas. It might have been a messy beach or something to do with the spirit of winter—whatever, Justin thought it hung together nicely in its grey, blotchy frame. He liked the notion of being listed as a purchaser, and it was for a good cause—a machine for some hospital or other.

"Three and a half, I'm bid three and a half."

Justin looked around and across the table and found Angela smiling broadly at him. Silently she mouthed the words, Go for it!

Someone bid four. Why not? Justin thought. This was fun.

"Five," he said. There were six people at Justin's table, and at least two of them murmured encouragements.

"Six thousand," a throaty voice said. Justin looked across the room and grinned. "Tommy Hederman, fuck sake!" he said to no one in particular. Blond-haired, treble-chinned and usually smiling, Tommy was a property man, son of a property family that had used Flynn O'Meara Tully's legal services for over twenty years. Tommy was a bit of a legend around town, with a devoted wife and three loving sons, and an equally devoted mistress and two equally loving daughters. Apart from his family homes—one in Dublin, one in Sligo—he had an apartment in New York, a country house in Wicklow, a farmhouse in the Languedoc region of France

and a private jet to get him from one to another. His attractive personal assistant was fairly familiar with most of the
alphabet, and his mobile phone's ring tone played "The Ride
of the Valkyries."

Justin had worked with the Hederman family on a couple
of deals. He and Tommy had shared a flat briefly in their college days and up to a year or so back they'd played the odd
game of lunchtime squash. Then Tommy developed breathing problems that limited his physical activities. It was
known within business circles that Tommy's health troubles
derived from a cocaine binge that left him in the Blackrock
Clinic for a week. He remained one of the country's most
cunning moneymen, specialising in quietly buying up options
on city-centre locations, using fronts, then developing the
assembled site at rates of return that would generate envy if
Tommy wasn't such a well-regarded guy. Invitations to generous weekends at his imitation Gandon country house were
prized within Dublin business circles. On such occasions,
Tommy provided as much recreational medication as his
guests might require, but these days he never touched the
stuff himself.

Across the room, Justin and Tommy exchanged smiles of
genuine affection. Tommy held up his right hand and cocked
his thumb like it was the hammer of a pistol.

"Seven!" Justin said loudly.

"Seven, I'm bid seven."

Someone behind Justin shouted, "Go on, ya-boy-ya!"

Tommy took his time, letting the RTE celebrity rattle out a
few Am-Ibids to build tension. Finally, he popped up and sat
down again, staying on his feet just long enough to shout, "Ten!"

The room erupted in appreciation of Tommy's timing. This
wasn't just about money, it was about flair, style, grace.

All those at the two men's tables, and at tables in their vicin-
ity, adopted each as a favourite. People at tables further away

cheered impartially, and each bid was greeted with a roar of approval and expectation. Twelve, fourteen, sixteen—

"Eighteen!"

"Twenty!"

When it got to twenty-five Justin stood up. He paused, his cheeks flushed, his smile taking over his whole face. On standing, he noticed a balding man a couple of tables away, a man he recognised as something minor in a firm he sometimes used down at the IFSC. They'd never had any more contact than a ride in a lift together and right now the man was staring sour-faced at Justin, like he deeply resented something or other.

Bollocks. Everywhere else, faces were alight with the excitement of the moment. One in every fucking crowd.

It felt as if every particle of air in the room had been connected to a generator. Justin was surfing on a wave of nothing less than joy. He looked over towards Tommy's table and his voice was loud and firm when he said, "Fifty thousand!"

The loudest hubbub yet, and before it died Tommy Hederman stood up, put his arms down by his sides and bowed to Justin.

The resulting roar dissolved into a clamour of applause and when Justin turned around he saw Angela looking at him with love and pride and delight for him and in him. That moment, he decided later, and all that surrounded it—the money, the applause, the social approval—even the impotent disapproval of the sour-faced fucker from the IFSC—the friendly tussle with Tommy, the clarity of Angela's love for him, the joy of it all—was the very best moment of his life.

Jesus, that was some night. It was like everything came together in one sweeping rush—his peers' public recognition that he had arrived as a serious player, his deepest feelings about himself, his ambition, his achievement and the world of possibilities awaiting him. And the intensity of the love he felt for Angela that night made him see clearer than ever the sheer rightness of their marriage.

Justin jerked up from his restless half-sleep, his hand instinctively reaching for the bedside phone. Then he realised it was his mobile, across the room on the dressing table, that was making noises.

"Yes?"

"You busy?"

It was Helen Snoddy's way of asking if he could speak openly.

"Jesus," he said. Justin sat down on Angela's side of the bed.

Since this began, his grasp of the world had shrunk to this house, Angela, the kids and The Crisis. He remembered now what he'd said to Helen last time they'd been together, when they'd kissed in the car park—Give me a buzz when you know how you're fixed.

Jesus.

"Look, Helen—"

"Is everything all right?"

"No."

There was a long pause. He didn't have the words, and he didn't have the energy or the will, to say more than that. Whether he offended her, whether he saw her again or not, none of that mattered. Things that normally took up most of his day—his work, his firm's place on the financial leader board, his car, his office and his goddam double chin—now seemed to matter as much as the choice of where he might dine during some distant lunchtime. There was nothing in all of that, nothing outside the core of his life, that couldn't be fixed or replaced or done without. And the realisation that that core might melt down in the next day or two drained everything else of meaning.

"I'm sorry, Helen—"

"Sounds like really a bad time. Talk to you soon. Bye."

"Bye," he said, but she'd already rung off.

When he looked up, there was a detective standing at the bedroom door.

"Anything of relevance, sir?"

Justin said, "No, nothing."

15

The office wall behind Assistant Commissioner Colin O'Keefe was a hymn to his career. There were framed certificates of this and that, along with photos of a younger O'Keefe standing beside senior officers and politicians. O'Keefe's reputation as a man who knew how to gladhand his superiors hadn't damaged his reputation as a solid copper. It was pushing midnight and the rest of the Phoenix Park complex was dimmed, but O'Keefe looked like he was here for the night.

O'Keefe introduced the heavyset man in his forties seated in front of his desk. "Detective Chief Superintendent Malachy Hogg. He's running this case. He could use the benefit of your experience of Frankie Crowe."

Hogg didn't rise. He nodded to Grace, who returned the gesture. They hadn't met, but anyone who knew the politics of the garda hierarchy knew about Malachy Hogg. His success as a district detective was spotted early on and he'd been drawn into the Phoenix Park elite. He was a couple of years younger than John Grace and no one doubted he'd be running the force by his early fifties.

O'Keefe nodded towards an empty chair in front of his desk, then said, "How well do you know this Crowe prick?"

"Frankie's given us a fair bit of business. Protection, robbery. Took a couple of falls early on." John Grace sat down. "Recent years, I pulled him in after three different hold-ups. No results. Finally put him away about—what?—three, four years back."

"What for?"

"We raided him after he beat up a pub owner who got stroppy about paying protection. Got the pub owner's back up, he came to us."

"A brave publican?" Hogg said.

"It didn't last. Couple of days later, he withdrew his complaint, but by then we'd found a rake of dodgy cigarettes in Frankie's attic. He went away for a couple of years."

"Loner?"

"He was one of Jo-Jo Mackendrick's boys for a long time, then he went with a couple of losers from Rialto—name of Waters and Cox. Tried a few solo runs, nothing much. What's he done now?"

O'Keefe drew a deep breath and steepled his fingers. "Twenty-four hours ago, give or take, Frankie Crowe kidnapped a woman named Angela Kennedy."

"Personal or is this a money thing?"

"The message is, have a ransom ready within forty-eight hours or he kills her."

John Grace raised an eyebrow. "The thing about Frankie Crowe, he's a small-timer but he doesn't know it. This kind of stuff, it's out of Frankie's league."

O'Keefe was tilting back in his chair. When he spoke it was as though he was talking to himself. "Half the world's troubles are caused by people who don't know their limitations."

"Who's the victim?"

"Wife of Justin Kennedy. Hotshot solicitor. Out Ballsbridge way."

Grace shook his head. "No bells."

"You won't have come across him down the Circuit Criminal. He does commercial, high-end stuff, property deals and the like." O'Keefe paused, then—in a deliberately casual tone—he said, "He's connected. We first heard of this through the Minister for Justice's office. Well known on the social circuit, probably on the list when the party begging bowl goes out at election time."

Grace hesitated for a moment. Political connections, sensitivities—was he being invited to comment on how this might influence the running of the case? No, probably not. Just absorb it, be aware of it.

Grace said, "He can afford a ransom, then."

Hogg said, "They're asking a million, he's willing to pay it. I've given him the official line on paying ransom, and the unofficial line."

Grace said nothing for a moment, then he asked, "How do you know it's Frankie?"

Malachy Hogg's voice was deep and unhurried, as though he was recounting an interesting tale he'd heard last night in his local. "My lads retrieved some CCTV footage from a house close to the Kennedy home, shows part of the street. Four men arriving in a Hyundai. Two of them in suits, left the car, followed a while later by two others in tracksuits. Timing's right. Has to be the same people."

"And Frankie's one of them?"

"The tape's shit quality. But there was a Hyundai Accent reported stolen that evening, found next morning near Broadstone. Without the CCTV we'd no reason to link it to the kidnap. Once we got the tape we put Technical on the car. Most of the prints are the owner's. We got two orphan marks, Frankie Crowe and some little shit named Brendan Sweetman."

"I know him. He does front-of-house security in the city centre."

O'Keefe said, "The incident room is at Carbury Street station. Right after this, I want you to brief Malachy's lads—about Crowe, and any of his mates that might be involved. You'll be having a late night."

Hogg said, "And I'd like you to come in on the case as a

consultant of sorts, since you know the little shit." It was as polite an order as Grace had ever had.

O'Keefe said, "I'll arrange for your caseload to be transferred within the station."

"I've got one coming up in the Central, Tuesday."

"Leave the details, I'll have a word with the judge."

Hogg was looking at his watch. "We should be setting off. I've called my lads in for an update in about half an hour, give or take. OK with you?"

Again, an order delivered tactfully. John Grace nodded.

O'Keefe said, "One thing strikes. No one does kidnaps any more. We went through that in the old days—the IRA, some other ambitious bastards, no one made it pay. Hold up a bank and there's a team of policemen after you. Kidnap someone, you've got the whole force on your back. How dumb is this Frankie Crowe?"

Grace said, "Frankie's not stupid, but he tends to do what feels right at the time, whether or not it's in his best interests."

"Has he ever done serious damage?"

"I take it you don't know about the supermarket trolley?"

O'Keefe made a face. "Something tells me we're not talking about shoplifting."

John Grace took a breath. "A week after Frankie came out of the Joy, back with his beloved family after two years pulling his wire, a friend of his, Timmy Pocock, was taken out of the Royal Canal. In a supermarket trolley. With a screwdriver in his ear. Round about then, Frankie's wife turned up in Beaumont A&E with a technicolour face."

Joan Crowe's face had been one big wound—swollen, lopsided, bruised and bloody. Grace remembered the physical strain it put on her, in the hospital cubicle, just listening to his questions, never mind refusing to answer them.

"He did this to you, Joan? Frankie?"

She said nothing.

"Far as I know, Frankie's not a thumper. Maybe he thinks he had a reason?"

She didn't even look at him.

"What do you know about Timmy Pocock? Was that Frankie, too? That's what I'm hearing. You and Timmy, is that right, Joan?"

The story going around was that Frankie was a week out of the Joy before he found out that Timmy and Joan had been at it.

John Grace adjusted his features to add a quota of compassion to his natural air of sensitivity. "You don't have to let him get away with this, love."

She turned her gaze on Grace briefly, assessed his sympathetic expression, then looked away. She was too disinterested to be irritated, like he was some tight-ass Mormon trying to sell her a change of religion.

"Make a complaint. I'll have him locked up by the end of the day. He'll never lay a finger on you again."

It took an effort for her to open her lips, and when she did he could see that an upper tooth was missing. Her voice was low, hoarse, exhausted and not at all angry, when she told him to fuck off.

Frankie and Joan split up, but although John Grace tried a couple more times to get her to talk about the killing of Timmy Pocock, she remained unresponsive.

Grace said, "It was one of those things where we all knew the score, and I could never touch him for it."

"You believe him when he says he'll kill the hostage if he doesn't get the money?"

"He doesn't know we're aware he's involved. In the wrong circumstances, he's capable of anything."

At the top of the incident room there was a white notice-board, with photographs of Frankie Crowe and Brendan

Sweetman just below a photograph of a smiling dark-haired woman in her late twenties. The two criminals' images were mugshots. The victim's picture was no informal snap. Her hair had the casual perfection that comes with painstaking design. Her teeth were American in their flawlessness. The yellow of her blouse perfectly complemented the greens and browns of the background. And the abstraction of that background, artfully thrown out of focus, was a perfect setting for her crisp beauty. It's not just that she looks like she hasn't a care in the world, Detective Inspector John Grace decided. She looks like she lives in a world where cares are an alien concept. Mind you, she's had twenty-four hours in the company of Frankie Crowe and his merry men. No matter how this works out, it'll be a long time before she'll smile like that again.

Apart from Grace, there were fourteen detectives in the briefing room, ranged around a long table, with Chief Superintendent Hogg standing at the top of the room. All the detectives but two were male, all younger than Grace, and they had the bristling confidence of the ambitious. Hogg's men were young strivers, hand-picked for fast-tracking. Although it was after midnight, they were all wearing suits and none of them looked like they'd spent a long day on a hot case. There was no coarse language or mocking camaraderie, none of the careless office jumble, the small forests of Styrofoam cups and displaced files, that John Grace associated with intense late-night group work. Mostly these people looked like they were on their way to a nightclub, or at least a parish hall ceilidh. John Grace was beginning to regret his open-necked shirt and the casual jacket he'd thrown on when Colin O'Keefe called.

Hogg was wearing a beige suit, his tie loosened and his two-tone shirt open at the collar. As the meeting began, Hogg introduced Grace, bringing him to the top of the room, to stand facing the rest of the detectives. Then he took a series of updates from his squad. All routine stuff, the process of collecting evidence, seeking leads, and carefully recording every step for possible use in a prosecution. Most police work involved going to all the obvious people and asking all the obvious questions. Eventually, two or more pieces of evidence didn't fit together, so someone got leaned on with diminishing levels of politeness, until there was enough of a case to bring charges.

Several members of Hogg's team were reporting back on the various areas of work they'd been assigned. An exhibits officer was in charge of maintaining the chain of evidence, another detective was drawing up a questionnaire for a house-to-house. A third was liaising with Special Branch, the Technical Bureau and district stations. A fourth was maintaining contact with the Emergency Response Unit, as the chances were before this was over they'd need an armed squad to wallop someone fast and hard. The necessary equipment had been immediately assembled in case it was needed for a siege—audio and visual fibre-optic snoops, to be inserted in walls, and the technicians to operate them, along with an assortment of rams, gases and communications equipment. A negotiator and a couple of psychologists had been put on standby.

The rest of the team had been checking possible leads assigned at a previous conference. Ballsbridge, being a parish with clout, was well policed. Uniforms who had been on duty on the night of the kidnap and over the previous week had been painstakingly debriefed by Hogg's detectives and ordered to scour their notebooks for any incident that might provide a lead. About two-thirds of the CCTV tapes retrieved from businesses and houses in the area had so far been assessed.

Two detectives were combing through a list of traffic tickets handed out in the streets adjacent to the Kennedy house over the previous month, checking reg numbers against known or stolen cars.

Two more detectives made contact with the previous owner

of the Kennedy house, now living in Portugal. He agreed to see them, and they had flown out that morning. Chances were he knew nothing about anything, but there was a possibility that he'd been threatened before, or got some hint that someone might have been keeping an eye on the house.

Was the victim's husband involved? Money problems? Marital? Either of them playing away? Business rivals? Personal enemies? Threats? Kennedy's family and business associates were canvassed to see if anyone thought this might be retaliation for something he had done? Did she have any enemies?

At the start, every possible angle had to be considered, the case a foggy swamp with little solid ground. The family's Saab turned up abandoned in Lucan and got the works from Technical, with no useful results. Then the mist cleared. The CCTV footage of the Hyundai parked near the Kennedy home was put together with the stolen Hyundai found with Frankie Crowe's print. The kidnap was no longer a riddle without boundaries, it was an identifiable problem with specific targets. Frankie Crowe, Brendan Sweetman.

One by one, Hogg's team reported. Hogg's style was brisk. Pay attention, catch it first time. No room for slackness in this outfit. Puppies, John Grace thought as he watched the eager detectives bringing back titbits to impress their boss. The sparse details were outlined, sketching a picture of the Kennedy family as well-off and trouble-free. The detectives would continue checking off possibilities, just in case, but Crowe and Sweetman were in the investigation's cross-hairs.

"Sweetman we have an address for, a semi-detached out beyond Coolock," Hogg said. "The files have nothing current for Frankie Crowe. Can you help?"

John Grace nodded. "These days, Frankie lives on the second floor of an apartment block in Glasnevin—Temple Road, Temple Avenue, something like that. One of those poky little high-rent places. I'll get you the details."

Grace hadn't noticed until now that Hogg's somewhat wispy hair was browner than it ought to be. Been at the Clairol, have we? Not the kind of thing you'd imagine would concern an up-and-coming chief superintendent. On the other hand, maybe it was a peculiarity of the breed.

Hogg turned to Grace. "OK, then, let's have the full SP on Frankie Crowe."

Grace told the detectives about the years Frankie worked for Jo-Jo Mackendrick, the failed alliance with Waters and Cox. "Frankie's in his late twenties, separated, one kid. He's as vicious as he needs to be. His previous is mostly routine thuggery—protection, muscle, small-time armed robbery." He told them about the murder of Timmy Pocock, the screwdriver and the way Timmy was worked over before he died.

Hogg said, "Family, brothers, cousins? Anyone we should keep an eye on?"

Grace shook his head. "Estranged. His dad had a van, delivered vegetables out Finglas way. Respectable type. Started his own little shop. Dead now. Frankie was a bit of a tearaway. Started serving his time as a mechanic, never took to it, had a falling-out with the family. He has a couple of sisters, one brother, mother's still alive—no contact with any of them for years, far as I know."

"Sweetman?"

"A bouncer, city-centre security. His dad ran a protection racket twenty years ago out in Ballymun, taught his lad everything he knows about being an all-round thug. Brendan was with the oul fella in the old Watering Hole pub when someone came in wearing a motorcycle helmet and carrying a shotgun. They found bits of Daddy sticking to the ceiling."

Hogg said, "There were four of them in the raid on the Kennedys. Apart from Crowe and Sweetman, any notion of who else might be in the frame?"

"I'd be surprised if Martin Paxton isn't in the crew. He and Frankie go way back."

"Another thug?"

"Used to be a hospital porter. Break-and-enter, smash-and-grab, maybe a stick-up or two. He can turn his hand to most things crooked."

"Who do you reckon for number four?"

"Could be any one of a hundred third-rate Dublin heavies. That's the circles Frankie moves in."

Hogg was nodding. "We'll need addresses."

"Crowe lives alone, Paxton lives with a woman. Deborah something. Sweetman is married to a woman who had a couple of kids by someone else, Sweetman took them on. Then his wife got pregnant, had a kid about a year back. The complete family man. Word was he wasn't stroking any more."

Some of Hogg's detectives were bent over notebooks, taking down every word. They all looked like they were prepared for a long night's work. John Grace's feet were aching. He wanted to sit down, but he felt that wouldn't look too clever. He already felt like someone's grandpa being allowed to stay up late with the hip young things.

"Informants will be important on this one," Hogg said. "These gougers won't have an infrastructure. They'll need small-timers to arrange cars and safe houses, supplies, that kind of thing. Small-timers gossip. So, talk to your touts, twist arms if need be." He nodded towards one of his team. "And rustle up whatever we can get in the way of photographs, pass them on to Technical." He turned to another of the bright sparks. "Family addresses, known associates, talk to Grace here and get the lot, run the names. We're OK'd for as much back-up and overtime as we need, so anyone promising gets tagged for surveillance."

A hand went up. "We going to raid their gaffs?"

Hogg shook his head. "Not yet. We keep our distance. Not

a word to the neighbours. Chances are these gents don't know we've got their prints. If they turn up anywhere, we hang back, follow them, no heroics. We could be lucky and one of them takes us somewhere." He made a loud clapping sound with his hands and said, "OK, I think that's it. Anyone without an immediate task, get your head down for a bit. I've got the security correspondents first thing in the morning, get them onside for a media blackout. Any press enquiries, direct them to me. You all know what you have to do—conference here late tomorrow afternoon."

As the meeting broke up, Hogg touched John Grace on the elbow and said, "Well done." Grace felt like he'd been given a silver star on his school copybook.

It was pushing two o'clock in the morning. The pub was ten minutes from Carbury Street garda station and when John Grace tapped on the side window the pub owner himself let him in. He was a genial type who knew the value of soft-soaping certain classes of people. Two of the bar staff were cleaning up, and as on most nights a handful of off-duty policemen and a couple of journalists were having an after-hours jar or two before heading home. Apart from the drink, there was usually a buckshee sandwich on offer at this time of night, and Nicky Bonner was chewing on one.

"Well?" he said.

"Get me a pint and I'll tell you."

Immediately after O'Keefe's phone call summoning him to the briefing, John Grace made a call to Nicky Bonner.

Nicky was upbeat. "Looks like you've fallen on your feet there, boy."

"You don't suppose I'm being set up?"

Hang around management types long enough, Grace knew, and you'll notice that the most successful ones have a twin-track approach to every problem. First, they decide what they're going to do about it. Then, they arrange to have a patsy on-site that all the fingers can point at if something goes wrong.

Nicky's opinion was that Grace hadn't a choice. "Assistant Commissioner calls you in, you curtsy. Suppose you could always go sick. I was you, I'd go with the flow." The call ended with Nicky demanding that Grace meet him afterwards in the pub, whatever the time.

Now, after the conference, John Grace's wariness had evaporated. He told Nicky about the kidnap and the hunt for Frankie Crowe.

"What's Hogg's team like?"

"Young, energetic, going somewhere."

"It's the place to be seen, sure enough. Play your cards right, this could open up new avenues."

At forty-six, John Grace had long lost whatever professional ambitions he nursed when he joined the force. He had mastered the methodical routine of detective work and was sure of his abilities as a supervisor of those beneath him on the ladder. Those talents got him to a respectable level, at which he lingered. From early on, Grace recognised his lack of the political skills necessary for zigzagging to the higher reaches of the garda pyramid. He'd come to believe he was the type that gets his nose stuck into a job and by the time he remembers to look up and work out where he's got to, most of a life has gone by. Grace—processing a ceaseless stream of damaged people who committed stupid or desperate crimes—knew that where he was in his working life wasn't where he set out to be. He sometimes wondered if he and they hadn't been corralled in a ghetto on the outskirts of real life, condemned to endlessly act out petty games of cops and robbers.

Which was maybe why spending long weekends weeding the garden and watching his grandson Sam use his fingers to smear paint on sketchpads was an increasing part of his life.

Moving on was an option, but there were no great career moves awaiting a middle-aged copper of modest rank and reputation, and he was too young to take to the garden full-time. Nicky was right. This kidnap thing might open up opportunities. So be it. Perform well in a high-profile case, people who know people put your name around. When there's an opening, inside the force or otherwise, people remember. Ideally, a promotion, a couple of years at senior level, then maybe a move to a management position in private security. Put together a little pot of money before retirement. Cases like this made careers. Grace felt it was almost indecent to benefit from someone else's troubles, but in this business that was usually how it worked.

"Joining Hogg's team, it can't hurt."

"I'm not joining the team—he wants someone on tap with personal experience of Frankie."

"Keep in mind you're not the only one."

"I know."

"I mean it. You see an opening, give me a mention to the bossman. I know Frankie. I could be useful."

"I'm not exactly Hogg's right-hand man, Nicky."

"I'm just saying. If the opportunity comes up, right? I'm available."

"You never know your luck."

Nicky raised his glass. "Here's to Frankie Crowe."

16.

John Grace got home shortly after three in the morning, slept for three and a half hours and was back in the incident room at Carbury Street before eight. If Nicky had been around he'd have remarked on the crispness of Grace's best suit and made a crack along the lines of, "Holy God, someone stood up close to the razor this morning."

In the absence of Nicky, Grace silently mocked his own enthusiasm. If he'd been asked, he couldn't say if it came from a dutiful wish to play a part in getting the victim back to her family, or an eagerness to impress the bossman. He told himself that, whatever his motive, it worked out the same for the victim.

About half of Hogg's team were already at work in the office—as fresh and peppy as they'd been at the midnight briefing—the rest were out beating the bushes. Grace found a free keyboard and began typing up everything he knew about Frankie Crowe. He made phone calls, mentioned Hogg's name, and there was none of the usual We'll do our best. He had the records he needed delivered by garda courier well within the hour.

Halfway through the morning, a gofer from Technical brought in a folder of photographs of Frankie and the other suspects, along with snaps of relatives, associates and known hangouts. Grace got the job of adding details about the various players. Hogg wanted the completed folder printed off as a kind of match programme for the team of detectives.

It was a surprise to see Brendan Sweetman back in action. Marriage and fatherhood seemed to have made a solid citizen out of him. His wife was an obnoxious woman who had filled Grace's ear with obscenities the last time he made a routine visit for a chat with Sweetman. Obnoxious, but straight as they come. After years together, Sweetman remained obviously crazy about her. However this worked out, whoever got the job of raiding Sweetman's home could look forward to a right bollocking from his missus.

John Grace made a habit of keeping in touch with old clients. The last time he'd been in Frankie Crowe's Glasnevin flat was shortly before Frankie checked out of his partnership with Oscar Waters and Shamie Cox. It was an expensive little dive, one of the thousands of pygmy apartments thrown up in Dublin over the previous decade, built on the cheap and sold at a premium. They were the surest sign of an underdeveloped city, newly affluent, borrowing heavily and impatient to spend its money.

For a while, Grace had great hopes for Frankie. He recognised a type. Ambitious but not making any great strides. That kind, if they're tapped at the right moment, make the best informers. They've been around the scene, they know lots of people and what those people are up to. Not having reached the status they imagine is their due, they're bitter. A position as an informer gives an opportunity for revenge against those who prospered, and it gives the ambitious type a genuine role as a mover and shaker, which is half of what he's wanted all along. Their new-found status has to remain secret, but for that kind there's a pleasure in looking someone in the eye and feeling the thrill of superiority that comes from deceit.

Within ten minutes of making his pitch to Frankie Crowe, John Grace knew his timing was off. Frankie was still convinced of his destiny, disillusioned with Waters and Cox but still confident that his fate involved greater things. He was too upbeat to take the offer seriously.

The hell with it, Grace had told himself. Give him time, he'll bite.

"Do you ever feel guilty? The kind of things you do to people, walking into their lives with a gun in your hand?"

"I'm not a bad person, Mr. Grace. Mostly, the things I do, an insurance company coughs up. Big fucking deal. Thing is—look, if you want to do the best for yourself, sometimes you have to do something you know is just plain wrong. You do it because it's the only way to get you where you want to be. Don't do it, you stay a loser." He paused, like he was about to deliver a polished credo. "People with the balls to do what they have to do, they own the people who don't. So, you do what you have to."

"And you can live with that?"

"It's a bad thing, but doing a bad thing doesn't make you a bad person. It makes you a person doing a bad thing—one bad thing. You do it, maybe you feel bad about doing it, but it's that or be a loser. So, you do it. You do it and you move on."

In the report he was typing up for Hogg's team, John Grace didn't mention anything about Frankie's possibilities as an informer. In the time since he propositioned Frankie, the opportunity hadn't arisen again. Whichever way this kidnap thing went, the chances of Frankie Crowe ever again being in a position to rat on anyone were on the slim side.

Justin Kennedy was slumped in the back of an unmarked police car, one armed garda beside him, two more in the front, speeding through the bus lanes. It was a relief to get out of the house. In the thirty-six hours since this started, there seemed to be something like twice the usual number of minutes in every hour. The very air that he breathed seemed charged with some form of ominous energy.

From the speeding car, he took in isolated images of the city's daily routine, everything distinct, sharp and cut off from its surroundings. Glimpses of the normal world, operating at its usual pace, emphasised the strangeness of the landscape in which he now existed. An old woman standing at a bus stop, her thinned hair dyed bright red, her face lifeless, like she'd given up on something. A prat in a silver sports car, mobile clutched to his ear, steering one-handed through the traffic, almost clipping a cyclist.

When the police car stopped at a traffic light on Baggot Street, Kennedy watched a tall, thin, grey-haired man in a well-cut blue suit cross the road, placing one foot in front of the other with the care and attention only the truly drunk can bring to the task. Kennedy recognised the type, still clinging to the uniform of respectability while allowing himself the delicious irresponsibility of surrender. For a moment, Kennedy let himself envy the drunk, easing into the comfort of recklessness, letting go of everything that made life complicated and fraught. The joy and the hope as well as the pain, worry and fear. It was a thought that sometimes surfaced during times of stress—he quickly killed it now.

The police car passed through a narrow street of rundown shop fronts. Kennedy recognised the area as one that he and some associates had appraised with a view to development. Some of the shops were derelict, others had been re-opened on low rents and short leases. They were now run mostly by immigrants offering ethnic foods, colourful clothes and hairstyles, expertise in mobile-phone repairs or cheap Internet and phone connections to far-off continents. The boom had suddenly brought a wave of Asians, Africans and East Europeans to Ireland. Apart from staffing the pubs, restaurants and hospitals that found it hard to hire Irish workers, they were spawning old-fashioned commerce in the unlikeliest places. Kennedy had decided against buying up the site, but someone else did. Once the immigrants were evicted from here, they'd as quickly start businesses elsewhere.

Now, as the police car turned out of the street, Kennedy saw two black men standing outside a clothes shop, one rolling a cigarette, the other throwing back his head and laughing. Usually, whenever he encountered immigrants Kennedy wondered what their story was, what dangers they had endured in getting from some distressed country to this one. Now, he was surprised to feel a surge of resentment towards immigrants who didn't appear all that troubled. He didn't question or dispute the emotion but found a comfort in yielding to its spite.

The policemen remained in the lobby of the Flynn O'Meara Tully offices while Kennedy went up in the lift. Daragh O'Suilleabhain was waiting when the doors opened on the fourth floor. Daragh was in his forties, and had cultivated a slight Northside Dublin accent and a roughness around the edges, though he was pure Blackrock College. Daragh was known in Dublin business circles as "a bit of a character," which in his younger days had led a lot of people to underestimate him. After a while, his contemporaries began to realise the ease with which he could switch off the joviality and hand them their heads. He was seldom underestimated these days.

His first words on welcoming Kennedy set the tone of the meeting. "I won't waste time on sympathy, Justin. Let's get this done, give the bastards the money, and get Angela back." Daragh had been a year ahead of Justin at Blackrock College, and though they'd had little contact at school they had since developed a durable business and personal relationship.

Daragh led the way to a small conference room, where the occupants stood and greeted Justin with the uneasiness of distant relatives dutifully attending a funeral. There was a senior bank executive, and a Flynn O'Meara Tully accountant that Justin didn't know. As the firm's primary mouthpiece, Daragh O'Suilleabhain's job involved an amount of glad-handing, both inside and outside the firm, and he had developed a style to go with it. This morning, he shed the bonhomie like an unnecessary piece of clothing.

"To bring you up to speed, Justin, first thing yesterday, soon as you got in touch, I got on to the bank and they assigned two officials solely and exclusively to sourcing the cash, and they've done a superb job." He nodded to the bank executive, inviting a contribution.

The banker nodded. "We've got the money assembled, more or less complete at this stage—and given that we've got all today to finish the job, I can't see any problems."

O'Suilleabhain said, "I gather it's a pretty hefty package, and maybe we'll need to talk to the bastards about how they want it delivered."

"Pretty hefty," the banker said, "but portable. A million in fifties, we're talking about twenty thousand banknotes, which weighs maybe forty, forty-five pounds. It fits into two rather solid holdalls."

Daragh said, "What about getting the money to the bastards?"

Justin said, "I'm waiting—about half eleven tonight—to be told when, where and how."

"What about transporting it?"

The banker said, "We have several anonymous-looking, secure vehicles that we occasionally use for discreetly transporting large amounts. We've not yet talked to anyone about this, but these vehicles are already wired for GPS tracking, if we want to take that course."

Justin shook his head. "I don't know, maybe the police—"

Daragh cut the matter short. "It's an option."

The accountant led a brief discussion of the procedure whereby Flynn O'Meara Tully would reimburse the bank but Daragh brushed aside all but the barest details. Justin's assets, although more than enough to cover the ransom, were tied up in property and stocks. The bank's role was merely to provide the ransom cash in a hurry. Daragh wrapped up the meeting soon after, and when the two functionaries left he had a secretary bring in a couple of cups of coffee.

"You bearing up, old son?"

"Once I get instructions from the fuckers I'll know how long it's going to take to nail this down. The forty-eight-hour deadline is tonight, a bit after eleven o'clock."

"Angela's strong, Justin. She'll come through this." He put a hand on Justin's shoulder and his rough voice softened. "Hold on to that." Justin had seen it done several times, Daragh applying his professional vocabulary of concern. Being on the receiving end, he found himself totally convinced of the man's sincerity, and grateful for it.

He tried to discuss the mechanics involved in liquidating assets to repay Flynn O'Meara Tully, but Daragh shook his head. "Time enough for that. Money's how we keep score, but right now the game is suspended and money's just a tool to do a job. When it's all over, we can shuffle the paper around."

The best part of twelve hours later, after three further conversations with O'Suilleabhain, by phone, Justin Kennedy knew that everything was in place. Then, midnight came and went, and the forty-eight-hour point was passed, and the bastards didn't ring with their ransom instructions. Justin's face had a film of sweat. He was sitting in his kitchen, at the table, house phone in front of him, his mobile too, a couple of bored telephone technicians tweaking the monitoring equipment, and three gardai—including Chief Superintendent Hogg—standing around.

And the bastards didn't ring.

The gunmen had not only taken the Rolex that Angela had given him, but the watch he wore before that and two others of his that they'd found in a bedroom drawer. Justin checked the watch he'd borrowed from Daragh O'Suilleabhain. Twelve thirty-three. "Something's gone wrong," he told the policemen. "Wednesday night, they left the house at eleven-thirty, sometime around then. They're an hour late ringing."

"These are not businessmen, Mr. Kennedy," Hogg said. "We can't expect punctuality. I know it's difficult, but patience is important in these circumstances if you're not to wear yourself out."

It was all very well for the police. They'd been sympathetic, respectful, obviously efficient. They wanted to get Angela back safely, and get their hands on the kidnappers. Just as obviously, for them this was a professional task. The detachment was, he supposed, necessary. But, Jesus, it was like they were plumbers trying to fix a broken pipe.

Justin had done nothing wrong. He'd set about raising the ransom. The gang said it was OK to contact the police, they were expecting it. He'd done exactly as they said. And still the bastards hadn't called.

It was like every fibre in his body had been stretched, twisted and rubbed raw. He'd hardly slept for two days and yet he felt not tired but electrified.

"What the fuck are they up to?" he asked no one in particular.

One of the policemen that came with Chief Superintendent Hogg—they'd been introduced but Kennedy didn't catch the name—said, "I know these people, sir, and believe me, you wouldn't want to set your watch by them. Men like this, they say forty-eight hours, they mean two or three days."

Hogg said, "Detective Inspector Grace is right, Mr. Kennedy. This means nothing. Besides, it may be they're aiming to stretch your nerves, push you off balance."

Kennedy didn't reply. He looked at Daragh's watch. It was twelve thirty-seven, four minutes since last he checked the time.

* * *

Poor sod.

Grace reckoned there'd be no phone call tonight. You wouldn't want to set your watch by them was meant to comfort the hostage's husband, so it understated his own worries. Could be that Frankie Crowe said forty-eight hours because he thought it sounded good at the time, but he hadn't meant it to be taken literally. Could be that he'd gone on the piss, celebrating his criminal brilliance, and he'd wake up in the morning remembering there was something he was supposed to do last night. Could be that something went wrong and Frankie disposed of the hostage and was lying low, unaware that the police knew of his involvement.

If that's the way it's gone down, most likely Frankie will turn up at his flat one of these days and we'll take him and he'll roll over. And before long we'll be wearing white overalls and digging up a patch of earth in the Dublin mountains, with masks on our faces to filter the stench.

There was something different about this case. There was the possibility of disaster, yet there was also a sense of satisfaction. A sense of responsibility. Almost every case John Grace was involved with, from burglary to murder, required the police to pick over the debris of a crime and try to catch up with the culprit. As likely as not, finding the guilty party involved fairly simple logic. There were other times, when witnesses were too scared or too compromised to give evidence, or when the randomness of the crime made detection unlikely. Whichever way it went, nothing the police could do would change anything, even when the offender was caught and convicted. The deed was done, the damage, the pain and the fear had gone as deep as they were going to go, and the police job was one of clearing away the wreckage. This Angela Kennedy thing was different. What Grace and his colleagues did or didn't do might determine whether a woman came back to her husband and kids.

Grace recognised the feelings he'd had since this thing began. Excitement, interest, passion. It had been a long time since his work aroused such emotions.

What he'd come to recognise after a couple of years at the policing game was that the crime just kept on coming, and would keep on coming, and what he or anyone else on the force did wouldn't make a difference worth noticing. They could drive it away from one area and into another. Gangs frustrated by bank security would hijack lorryloads of computer chips. Break a protection racket and watch the gangsters start up a diesel-laundering scam. The way things were, when people didn't get the things they wanted or needed, some of them became beaten and sour, others just took what they could, where they could. All of them, whether they lived in ghettos or mansions, had their own vision of the life they were entitled to. And the urge to acquire whatever the vision demanded—money, sex, status, or just a rush of whatever drug best pampered a fucked-up mind. And if getting what they wanted meant breaking a law or breaking a head, so be it.

There were problems out there that no amount of police would solve. And, apart from the odd radical priest or social worker on the way to an early burn-out, no one gave a shit. John Grace sometimes felt like a glorified binman, collecting the week's rubbish and taking it out of sight. The police couldn't stop lawbreaking, any more than binmen could stop the accumulation of waste.

No one said it out loud, but there was an acceptable level of crime, maybe even a desirable level of crime. John Grace reckoned he made a better living out of the crime business than most lawbreakers. Only a very few criminals soared to the levels of prosperity enjoyed by the lawyers, the insurance companies, the newspapers, the top people in the firms supplying the alarms and the bouncers, and all the rest of the services that thrived in the hinterland of the crime business. Even if a criminal reached the level of a Martin Cahill or a Jo-Jo Mackendrick, the chances were that he'd rub a lot of people up the wrong way and eventually pay a price.

If they got this Angela Kennedy back alive—and the chances were that they would—the case would then become the familiar hunt for evidence that would store the bad guys away for a few years, with nothing much more at stake than professional pride. In the meantime, the prospect of getting her back safe, saving a family from even worse pain, aroused in John Grace an enthusiasm he hadn't felt since his early days out of Templemore. Afterwards, he knew, the stagnancy into which his career had drifted would seem less interesting than ever. But, for now, he felt a peculiar gratitude to Frankie Crowe for giving him this opportunity.

Poor sod.

The victim's husband was in rag order.

Justin Kennedy had been repetitively rubbing his face, as though the friction might distract him from his fears. Keep this up, John Grace thought, and you'll be fuck all use to your wife when push comes to shove.

"A cup of tea, sir, coffee?"

Kennedy shook his head. He stared at the two phones on the table in front of him, as though they'd become a special kind of enemy.

17.

It was noon on Saturday, sixty hours after the kidnap started, before Justin Kennedy got the call. There were no preliminaries, just a terse, "Have you got the money yet?"

"You were supposed to ring after forty-eight hours. Is—"

"Have you got the money?"

When the call came it was to the house phone. Detective Inspector John Grace was in the kitchen along with one other detective, two technicians and Justin Kennedy. Superintendent Hogg had gone home at two o'clock in the morning. Grace slept in a spare room, close to Kennedy's bedroom. Kennedy undressed and climbed into bed, for the first time since this began, and fell instantly asleep, his phones close by.

This morning he sat in the kitchen, ignoring the coffee one of the policemen put in front of him. On the counter, over beside the microwave, there were two large, heavy-duty holdalls, supplied by the bank. Half a million in each, in fifties. The presence of a million in cash in his kitchen would in any other circumstances have aroused in Justin Kennedy at least a measure of curiosity. He hadn't bothered to open the holdalls to look at the cash. He knew from Daragh O'Suilleabhain that everything was in order. The money was of no more interest than the holdalls it was in.

He knew that when the fuckers called the chances were slim that he'd get to say more than a few words to Angela.

He'd spent some time deciding what was most important, rejecting words and phrases until he had honed a single reassuring sentence. We all love you very much, the money is on the way, this will soon be over.

There were several phone calls that morning, all casual, family or business. Each time the phone rang, John Grace donned a pair of headphones, a technician started a tape running, Grace nodded and Justin Kennedy picked up the phone. By the time the call came from the kidnappers, just after noon, Kennedy was compulsively rubbing his cheeks, fidgeting in his seat.

"Have you got the money yet?"

"You were supposed to ring after forty-eight hours. Is—"

"Have you got the money?"

"I need to know if everything is OK with Angela."

"Are the cops listening in?"

Kennedy looked up towards Grace, then quickly said what had been agreed. "Yes, you said it would be OK to contact them. Is Angela all right? Can I speak to her?"

"About the ransom."

"Can I speak to Angela? How do I know—"

The voice took on an edge. "About the ransom."

"I've got it, it took a while, but it's ready. How do you want to do this?"

"Two million."

"Sorry?"

"Two million, fifties."

"You can't—"

"The Bryton Bank fuck-up kind of threw me, but I've been thinking. No need to go cut-price. Anyone can do the one can do the two."

"Now, wait a—"

"Two million. Another forty-eight hours. I'll be in touch."

He rang off.

There was an hysterical edge to Justin Kennedy's voice when he roared "Wait!"

One of the technicians was shaking his head. "Nothing," he said. John Grace took off the headphones. "Did the voice sound familiar, sir?"

"It sounded like, yes, it was the gang leader. How do I know he hasn't—why didn't he let me speak to Angela? Two fucking million!"

Grace was already tapping a number on his mobile. When Hogg answered, Grace said, "He rang, sir, and it was definitely Frankie's voice."

"Good."

"I'm afraid there's a complication." As he told Hogg about the increased ransom demand he was looking across the table at Justin Kennedy, who had tears in his eyes, mouth open, face flushed. Shit, that's all we need. Victim's husband has a nervous breakdown.

Frankie made the call from the south pier at Dun Laoghaire. You could never tell what kind of shit they were using to pin down mobile calls, so he needed somewhere that wouldn't point any fingers. Somewhere on the Southside. Somewhere it was easy to ditch a phone. He'd intended to make the call exactly forty-eight hours after the kidnap began. Then it occurred to him that standing on a pier in the hour before midnight wasn't a good idea. But he liked the pier idea so he decided it made more sense to leave the call until next day. And it was when he woke up that morning that the thought of doubling the ransom popped into his head.

Fuck it. One rich man's as good as another. OK, he doesn't have his own bank, but he's a flash lawyer, house like that—fuck him. Same price we set out to get for the banker. He can raise one million, won't be too big a stretch to raise two.

That meant it couldn't be wrapped up as quickly. No guarantee the guy'd be able to raise the second million as fast as the first, so this might drag things out. Fuck it. That kind of money's worth a little overtime.

Call done, he powered down the mobile and walked over to the edge of the pier. There were lunchtime strollers here and there. Frankie paused while a doddery old pair shuffled past, the woman holding the man's trembling elbow. Get to that stage, what's the point? The mobile was one of Milky's specials, no connection to Frankie, but the technology they had these days, they could work out who called who from what phone, at what time, from where. Even a pay-as-you-go, they could identify the area the call came from. Too many smart people ended up being stitched into a prison cell by some fucking telephone technician. Use it and ditch it. By the time the phone hit the water, Frankie had turned and was walking back down the pier, past the doddery pair.

At the counter in McTell's Bar, just off Dun Laoghaire's main street, Frankie ordered a coffee and a chicken sandwich. The lunchtime trade was building, the barmen brusque. Frankie had almost finished his sandwich when he noticed in the mirror behind the bar a reflection of the television screen high up on the wall behind him. It was showing a photo of the hostage, a big smile on her face.

Frankie turned round in time to see the photo replaced by a female newsreader, her lips moving silently. Then a shot of the outside of the hostage's house. Frankie turned back to the bar and stood up. There was a barman turning away from the cash register. "The sound," Frankie said, loudly. The barman looked at him, verging on irritation. Frankie said, "The TV, quick. Please." The barman looked around, found the remote control on a shelf and when Frankie turned back to the screen the newsreader was saying, "—garda spokesman had no further comment. A friend of the family told RTE News they remain hopeful that Mrs. Kennedy will be returned safely to her family, and asked that the family's privacy be respected at this difficult time."

Frankie left the pub and found a taxi. Bound to happen. Thing like this, can't keep it under wraps. It made it a problem, though, to use the old butcher shop for the extra time they needed to get the second million.

When he got back to the safe house, Martin Paxton, Brendan Sweetman and Dolly Finn were standing around in the kitchen.

"Did you hear?" Brendan said.

"We're out of here," Frankie told them. Four hours later, they were arriving at Rosslare Strand, a hundred miles away in Wexford.

* * *

Hail Mary, full of grace, the Lord is with thee.
Blessed art thou amongst women,
And blessed is the fruit of thy womb, Jesus.

Even before the small fat one slammed shut the lid of the car boot, Angela knew she was about to die.

They came to the room, two sets of footsteps hurrying on the stairs, the small fat one and the gang leader, and they didn't say anything when they came in, they just put the mask over her head, backwards again, and they weren't gentle when they tied her hands.

"What—" she said when the gang leader produced the mask.

"Listen—" she said, and they said nothing, neither of them, and when the mask went over her head she made pleading sounds, then a hand grasped her face, iron fingers squeezing her jaw, digging into the muscle. She stopped talking. She knew it was the small fat one, pulling her arm, guiding her down the stairs, the open air, abrupt movements, rough hands, pushing her head down. She could hear him grunt, a mixture of irritation and satisfaction, just before the lid of the boot came crashing down.

A different car, she got a smell of turf briquettes from the boot.

Holy Mary, Mother of God,
Pray for us sinners,
Now and at the hour of our death—

Something wrong. Something happened. Or didn't.

They didn't get the ransom.

Justin. Something happened. He did something, didn't do something, said something.

He wouldn't put her at risk, not deliberately. He wouldn't do anything stupid.

Something he said, they got hold of the wrong idea—maybe something they said, he didn't pick it up right—

Kill me. Oh, Jesus.

Dump me. A lane somewhere? A skip, bottom of some lane.

For a second she could see the skip and it was raining. She could hear the rain hitting the things, stuff, whatever, in the skip.

No. Not in the city. Find it—me—too quickly.

The smell.

They're taking me somewhere out of the way, bury me, maybe in the woods somewhere.

A cold physical surge of terror forced her head to jerk down and sideways, her eyes clenched shut. She let the wave of dread pass, a prickly feeling at the top of her scalp. She very deliberately tried to force her breathing into a regular, slow pattern.

Maybe they're just moving me from one place to another. Keep me somewhere else, until they get the money.

Why would they do that?

Could have killed me there, in that place, put the—my—body in the boot, dump it—me—somewhere outside the city.

The mountains, maybe.

No. If they get stopped, caught, now, and I'm alive, they get charged with kidnap.

If there's a body in the car, murder.

Murder.

Me.

Body in the boot.

Keep me alive until we get there.

Then.

The fear was an axe, chopping through her disconnected thoughts, slicing them into small pieces that tumbled one over the other, scurrying away from her mind's panicky grasp.

The smell.

Me. This body. Decay. Nothing.

The car stopped and started, city driving, then they were on a straight run, beyond the city, motorway, a constant speed, and her mind tried to steady itself and she was startled to find she'd dozed off. Then she wasn't sure if she'd been asleep or had fainted or had been awake all along.

After a long time, the car stopped, the lid of the boot opened. She was pulled out, unsteady on her aching legs, the ground rough. The mask was damp from the sweat on her face.

She could hear birds whistling, chirping. Air. Woods? The mountains?

Footsteps.

The gang leader's voice. "Breather. Stretch your legs."

Oh, Jesus, Mary and Joseph.

Please, God. Not here. Not now.

Time, please, a little time.

Saskia, Luke.

Justin.

Elizabeth, Elizabeth.

Of all things, she had a flash of a sunny afternoon in Galway, maybe fifteen years back, out in Salthill, Angela and her sister Elizabeth, flirting with two boys. Something about an ice-cream cone falling, the splat as it hit the pavement, the hysterical laughter.

Waste.

A word swelled through her mind, momentarily crushing every other thought.

Remains.

"Gardai said the remains were found—"

Jesus, Mary and Joseph.

Again, she fought to force her breathing into a slow, regular rhythm.

If they bury me here, never found. Weeks, months. No one will ever be sure. No body. No grave.

"Why isn't Mum back yet?"

"There's a delay," Justin will say.

Weeks, months. The kids will know. They'll know before anyone says anything.

The sound of liquid. Something being poured?

Someone pissing on the ground.

Will I feel it, the gun against the back of my head? The bullet? Will I feel it? Will I hear anything?

I won't know when. They won't say anything. Could be doing it right now.

Her head jerked, as though she could feel something touch the back of her neck. She took a step forward but her legs hadn't the strength to run. She bent forward, cringed.

Not to know. One second you're alive, the next, gone.

No, tell me.

"Tell me." She almost didn't recognise the dry croak of her voice.

Nothing. Perhaps they didn't hear her. Maybe they did.

They don't give a fuck.

She could hear them talking quietly. Just two of them. Some distance away.

The small fat one will do it.

Bastard.

"Bastard!"

They stopped talking. Seconds passed, then she heard the small fat one say, "Fucking ride."

All her limbs were trembling. Somewhere down in her gut there was a feeling of shifting fluid. Every intake of breath was sucking at the wool of the mask.

After a minute, the gang leader's voice. "You ready?"

Her mouth was too dry to speak. Footsteps approaching.

"Time to go. Only another hour or so, we'll be there. You want to piss? You want a drink? Pepsi?"

"What's happening? Tell me. I want to know before it happens. Not just—tell me—"

She screamed when the rough hands took her, pushing, dragging, her legs scraping along the rim of the boot, her body landing heavily, the lid slamming shut again. She sobbed as much in relief as distress. The engine started, the car moved. The wool of the mask stuck to her mouth and her nostrils as she took big gulps of air.

Holy Mary, Mother of God,
Pray for us sinners.
Now, and at the hour of our death.
Amen.

* * *

They were an hour out of Dublin, heading south on the road to Wexford, before Martin Paxton got more than single-word replies out of Dolly Finn.

"Suit yourself," Finn said when Martin said he wanted to

stop soon to get something to eat. Martin was driving, and he was looking forward to the break as much as the food.

"Jack White's?" Martin said. "That OK with you?"

Dolly Finn nodded. He'd been listening to his music since they left Dublin. Soon as they got into the car, Dolly inserted the earphones and pressed play on his iPod.

Once, Martin asked if Dolly would like to stop, get a Coke or a sandwich. Twice Dolly shook his head and kept on listening to the music.

When the heat got a bit much Martin rolled down the window and said, "That OK with you?"

"Yeah."

After a couple more attempts, Martin gave up. When Frankie and Brendan left with the hostage, Martin knew the journey south with Dolly Finn wouldn't be a social highlight, but the fucker made no effort at all.

Up ahead, just off to the left of the N11, Martin could see the two-storey building that was Jack's White's Pub. He wondered if Dolly would leave the earphones in over lunch.

Some people just have to yap.

You don't play Johnny Hodges in the background, something to fill the gaps in the conversation. If you listen, you listen. Even if Dolly Finn wasn't immersed in the music, he couldn't imagine what he might talk to Martin Paxton about. Nothing wrong with Paxton, seemed a decent sort. But Dolly Finn didn't have friends or colleagues or even associates in this business, he had contacts. He had a friend he saw three or four times a year, a man he went to school with. He sometimes went for a drink with customers who wanted to talk about the music. There was a collector in Nottingham who sourced a lot of the old Blue Note stuff for him. He'd put Dolly up in a spare room when he was in the area for a collectors' convention a few years back, and Dolly thought of him as a friend. Other than that, Dolly Finn kept himself to himself.

Johnny Hodges' sax strolled along the road laid down for it by Duke Ellington's band. Ellington's piano notes danced around Hodges' soaring, plunging melody, as though sprinkling a layer of petals in his path. This was one of those tracks Dolly Finn felt had become as much a part of him as his own flesh. Sometimes in bed at night he played the music back in his head, the individual instruments or the collective sound of the band, and it was still there when he woke in the morning.

Dolly paid no attention to the countryside through which he was passing. It was a foreign land in which he must labour until he could return to the life these kinds of jobs paid for. It could be tolerated, as long as there was a purpose to his exile and an end in sight, but it could never be enjoyed. The familiar music gave him comfort, and his companion's occasional attempt at chit-chat was a trial to be ignored.

When they pulled into the car park at Jack White's, Dolly switched off the iPod. He knew there'd be chatter. Martin Paxton flexed his arms behind his head and said, "Did you ever know her?" He nodded towards the pub.

Dolly's brow wrinkled.

"The one that used to own this place, the one that had her old fella snuffed? Ever come across her?"

Dolly remembered. He shook his head.

Martin said, "She served me once, behind the bar, few months after the shooting. Before she got arrested. Seemed nice enough. Brendan Sweetman swears she offered him the job, but he's full of bullshit."

Brendan Sweetman, in Dolly's opinion, was a brute. To survive in an evil world, everyone has to do what they must. For a brute, that's all there is. No wider view, no remorse, no hope for spiritual redemption. Just the slaking of brutish appetites. Dolly Finn had long accepted that his life must occasionally accommodate such people. He waited, unsure if Martin was finished yapping.

"Are you coming in for a bite?"

"No, I'll wait here." He decided to concede an explanation. "I want to listen to the next couple of tracks."

"It's good nosh."

"I'm not hungry."

"Suit yourself."

Dolly didn't read newspapers but he knew the bare bones of the Jack White's Pub killing from a radio report at the time of the trial. Sounded like she was just short of putting an ad in the paper, that one, asking around for estimates for doing the job on her husband. Any mugs that got dragged into a half-arsed thing like that, they deserved whatever they got. Dolly's brief involvement in hired killing ended seven years back, because of that kind of stupidity.

It was an incident he'd been thinking a lot about recently. Dolly believed he knew who killed Jo-Jo Mackendrick.

About eight years back, Dolly's army associate, Johnner Mulligan, offered him a job killing an elderly man—eight grand up front. There were people in Dublin who would kill someone for the price of a good night out, but Dolly didn't move in those circles. He figured if serious people want a proper job done they have to be prepared to pay serious money. Dolly kept it simple. No complicated schemes to go wrong, no guns to create forensic trails. He used a knife from the man's kitchen, and afterwards he tossed it into the Liffey. Dolly knew little of who the man was and nothing of who wanted him dead, or why. If the guy was in the business, which he probably was, he wasn't prominent. Just someone who stepped hard on someone's toes, and someone knew someone. Then, a couple of years later, Johnner offered him a second killing job.

"This one's different."

He'd have to do this one with another guy, and he'd need to use a gun, Johnner said. A back-of-the-motorbike job. Zoom in, bang-bang, zoom off, was how Johnner put it. When Dolly heard who the target was he shook his head.

"I'd have to think about that. And don't tell me—whoever's offering, I don't want names, OK?"

"Course not." Johnner was enthusiastic. "It's terrific money, way above the usual."

"Just Jo-Jo? What about Lar?"

"On his own, Lar's a wanker. Jo-Jo's the problem. Do him, Lar's nothing."

Dolly asked a few more questions, his casual air concealing the rage he felt. He offered Johnner another coffee. Stupid bastard. Didn't know the difference. Thought this was just another job. Thing like this, whatever way it goes, this was a no-loose-ends job, and Johnner was handling it like it was an afternoon's shoplifting.

Do it, you're a loose end. Pop.

Turn it down, maybe someone else does it, maybe not. Either way, when the dust settles there's a real chance someone's going to figure you for a loose end. Pop.

Maybe there's a balls-up and Jo-Jo leans on the trigger man or Johnner or whoever he can get his hands on. He puts a couple of razor blades in the guy's mouth, tapes up his lips, starts punching him in the belly, the chest, working up towards the face.

"There something you'd like to tell me?"

One of those Limerick wankers, that's what he did to some gobshite who got uppity. Did him over for a while, got tired of it, gave him one behind the ear. Dumped the body and when the pathologist peeled the tape off the stiff's mouth one bloody blade slid out. Pity about the nice firm fingerprint the Limerick wanker left on the tape, which is the kind of thing that Limerick wankers do.

Not the kind of mistake Jo-Jo would make. And if Jo-Jo comes out of this alive and puts on the squeeze he'll get the name of everyone this thing touched, including Dolly, and Jo-Jo'll shoot first and he won't even bother to ask questions later. Pop.

Soon as Johnner opened his mouth about this one, Dolly figured they were both already chin-deep in soft shit. He repeated that he'd have to think about it.

Dolly thought about it all that evening, made a decision and slept on it. He went to early-morning Mass, but found he couldn't concentrate. Went home, thought it all through again, then he went into the GPO and made a call from a phone box, got Jo-Jo's number, rang him and said, "You don't know me, but I've been offered money to kill you."

They met that afternoon and three days later the radio lunchtime news said two bodies had been found in a field round the back of the airport. Johnner was one of them, strangled. The second body had two holes in the head, entry and exit. Probably the other guy Johnner talked to about the job, the biker. Both of them had been worked on.

Dolly came home one night and found Jo-Jo waiting in a car outside the flat, a holdall on his lap with sixty grand in it.

What Dolly heard was that as soon as the bodies turned up near the airport an ambitious Southsider named Gerry Forbert did a runner. Ended up somewhere on the Continent, probably Spain. No one knew why, except it was for the good of his health. Over the next few months, one of Forbert's brothers and two of his associates turned up in fields round the back of the airport.

Over the years, Jo-Jo offered Dolly a couple of soft jobs, but Dolly's instinct was—if possible—to stay away from people like that. They were trouble.

What Dolly reckoned now was that all this time later, Gerry Forbert was homesick and what happened to Jo-Jo and his mother had to do with Forbert clearing the air before he came back to the old sod.

After half an hour, when Martin Paxton came out of Jack White's, Dolly nixed the Miles Davis track that was playing and browsed the iPod to find a sound more suited as background to the yap he could rely on from Paxton. As Paxton opened the driver's door, Dolly cranked up the volume on Lee Morgan's Sidewinder and felt the insistently upbeat music surge through his head.

* * *

The sun came out and Frankie Crowe got worried. They pulled off the road and found a quiet spot. When they took the hostage from the boot her tracksuit was sodden with sweat and Brendan Sweetman had to hold her upright. They put her lying across the back seat, with Frankie's jacket over her, and told her that if she fucked with them they'd kill her. Frankie reckoned that letting her out of the boot made more sense than maybe arriving in Rosslare with a dead hostage. Every time he looked back at her, the hostage was lying unmoving. Once, he said, "You OK?"

When she didn't reply he leaned over and shook her shoulder.

"You OK?"

Still silence. He flicked a fingernail against her ear and she made a dry grunt.

"Answer me. You OK?"

After a few seconds there was a sound that might have been "Yes."

Frankie said, "Drink this." He thrust a small bottle of Coke into her hand. She pushed the mask up beyond her mouth and made gulping sounds as she drank.

18.

W ithin an hour of the breakdown of the media blackout on the Kennedy kidnap, Chief Superintendent
Malachy Hogg was under instructions to have a
report on Assistant Commissioner Colin O'Keefe's desk before
nine o'clock next morning. Within two hours, Hogg knew as
much as there was to know about the cock-up, and within the
third hour had made a preliminary report to O'Keefe by
phone.

When he arrived at O'Keefe's office at the Phoenix Park
HQ at ten minutes to nine the next morning it was merely to
confirm this account in a one-sheet written report. Some busybody, most likely a neighbour of the Kennedys who knew the
extended family, got wind of what was happening and word
spread. Several tips to newspapers and radio stations vanished
into the media blackout organised by Hogg. Eventually, someone rang a morning yackety-yack show to complain about the
state of the country. Gutless government, decent law-abiding
people could be taken from their homes by armed thugs. The
idiot DJ made an event of it and the rest of the media panicked
and assumed the story was fair game.

O'Keefe was wearing Sunday casual. He had half a dozen of
his staff working the weekend along with him. There wasn't
much he could do, but if an executive decision had to be made
he didn't want to be at the wrong end of a bad mobile connection. "You're certain none of our lot had anything to do
with leaking it for a few shillings?"

"Certain."

"Can't be helped, then. We can live with it."

"There is one thing. Last evening, John Grace rang me with a suggestion. He reckons the public fuss might make Frankie jumpy. Might even spook him so much he decides to cut his losses, abandon the whole idea."

"And kill the hostage?"

"And kill the hostage. In case she saw or heard something. Far as Frankie's aware, no one knows who did the kidnap. He might decide to just bury her somewhere and go home."

"Grace thinks it's a serious possibility?"

"Very much so."

"And?"

Hogg's voice remained neutral, making it impossible to measure his opinion. "Grace reckons we should leak it that we know who's behind the kidnap. Takes away the reason to kill her."

O'Keefe drummed his fingers on his desk for a few moments. Then he shook his head. "Too many mights and maybes in that. Could just as easily push the little bastard over the edge. No, I don't think so." O'Keefe arched his eyebrows, inviting an opinion.

Hogg said, "Grace is a plodder, but he knows Frankie. There's that. But it's a risky thing to do."

Both men knew where the heaviest weight lay in this equation. Hang on, do nothing, and if something goes badly wrong it remains a matter of opinion about whether one initiative or another should have been tried. Make a chancy move and it goes wrong and your arse is out the window. Until an identifiable target popped up, from where O'Keefe was sitting the safest thing to do was hold fire.

* * *

About an hour later, Frankie Crowe waited until the hostage stopped vomiting, then he waited some more. Only fair to give her a chance to get herself together. After a while, he tapped on the bathroom door. He was wearing latex gloves. "I've a job for you." He heard the toilet flush, a tap running. He held up his wrist—fucking mask, didn't make anything easy—and glanced at his Rolex. Still not ten o'clock.

The bathroom door opened and the hostage came out. Have to give her credit. Four days, now—four and a half—and her purple tracksuit was creased and grimy, her hair tied back, her face pale and clammy, no proper wash, and from what the lads said she hadn't eaten much over the past couple of days. Then there was the stress of a couple of tough trips in the boot of the car, and being locked in a small room for the rest of the time. All that and you could still see she was a bit of a ride. He remembered, on the landing in her house, after the stupid cunt snuck off to try to make a phone call, grabbing the front of her red dress and noticing even in his fury the delicate lightness of the material, and the glancing touch of his knuckles against her breasts.

"I need you to write a note to your hubby."

He brought her back to the small bedroom where she had been held since the previous evening. The window was boarded up, but it was better than the old storeroom up in Dublin, cleaner, with a single bed and a bedside locker and lamp.

Frankie had already been getting antsy about the old butcher's shop. Fine as a hideout for a very short-term job, but the longer it went on the greater the chance of some nosy neighbour noticing unusual comings and goings. Once the kidnap went public, and busybodies all over the city were on the lookout for anything suspicious, it made even more sense to use the Rosslare place ahead of schedule.

The original plan was to use Rosslare as a halfway house, somewhere to rest, split the money and suss out the lie of the land once the job was over, the hostage released and the ransom in the bag. Rosslare was Milky's idea. He used a front to rent it for a month. "Holiday resort, so many people pass through, no one notices anyone. It's twenty minutes into Wexford, if you want to get some clothes, food, stuff like that." Far enough from the city to be out in the sticks, a whole other place, and near enough to drop back to Dublin when Frankie needed to. Today, Frankie could be back up in town by lunchtime, do the necessary, maybe spend the night in a B&B, maybe his Uncle Cormac's. By teatime tomorrow, phase one of the job should be done and dusted.

It was a four-bedroom bungalow, white-walled inside and out, bay-windowed, with a long path out to the gate. A couple of hundred yards from the beach, in a secluded area, with trees, brambles and high bushes in every direction. It had the cheap, transient feel of a house no one cared about, an investment built for renting to the holiday trade. A rash of holiday homes like this one had spread along the coast, built by people who needed something to soak up the spare cash generated by the boom. While the Dublin hideout meant everyone staying inside, depending on Milky for supplies, the sheltered setting of the Rosslare house, and the fact that the area was crawling with strangers who came and went after a few days, meant the lads would have more freedom to come and go. Milky had even provided swimming togs, draughts, chess and a stack of bootleg DVDs.

The hostage took the notepad and biro Frankie held out to her. She sat down on the bed and waited. Her face was flushed, but she looked less upset, almost calm. She looked like she'd reached a deal with herself.

"I talked to your hubby yesterday. I wanted to know if he had the money yet. Know what he said? He said, Fuck off, that's what he said. I can't raise that kind of money. That's what he said."

Frankie was pleased to see the unease creep back into the hostage's face.

He raised his eyebrows. "I don't know. Maybe he was telling the truth. Could be the kind of money we're talking about is out of his league. You think?"

He bent down, leaned over closer and Angela turned her head away. He spoke softly into her ear. "Couldn't be he's haggling, could it? I mean, it couldn't be he's trying to knock the price down, maybe get you on the cheap? That the kind of man he is, your oul fella?"

She sat there, waiting.

"It was me, I'd have the money by now, get you back. Maybe hubby's doing his best but he just can't get it together. What do you think?"

She said, "What do you want me to write?"

"Don't worry, love, I'm sure it'll all work out in the end."

"What do you want me to write?"

"A note to hubby. Your own words. Whatever you like. Within reason. Tell him you want to go home."

For a long time, she didn't do anything. Then she leaned over and began writing. The notepad resting on the bedside locker, she wrote slowly, the pen clutched awkwardly, close to the point, like it was an unfamiliar tool. She used her left hand as a kind of screen, to shield the page from his gaze, as though that mattered. When she was finished, she tore the page from the pad, folded it twice and gave it to him.

"Could I have some toast and a cup of tea?"

"Later," he said, and read the note. "Good girl." He stood up and walked to the door. "You get some rest, now."

Out in the corridor, Frankie stood for a minute, his ear close to the door. After a minute, he heard her crying, as he'd thought he might.

The banker was shaking his head. "I'm not saying there's a

problem. We're still on board, we can do this, but at the end of the day we're talking about shareholders' money and prudence demands clarity about precisely what it is we're committing the bank to—that's all I'm saying."

Daragh O'Suilleabhain nodded. When he spoke, his voice was even and temperate and if you didn't know him you mightn't notice that he was straining to keep his temper.

"Understood. Fair enough, and I'm not discounting the bank's responsibilities, but when we get right down to it, all the bank is required to do is provide a convenient facility in emergency circumstances. Flynn O'Meara Tully is underwriting the deal and we're good for the money."

Justin Kennedy had asked that this time the meeting take place at his home. The shock of having the kidnap become public had ebbed, but it left behind an increased reluctance to move too far from the phone. Daragh immediately agreed to come to Justin's house, and also drove the banker. Now, in the family room at the back of the house, with the games table at one end, the two long, deep sofas at the other, and the television screen hanging on the wall in between, the banker had a question. What was the extent of Flynn O'Meara Tully's commitment? Was it open-ended?

From the window, across the yard and framed by the huge kitchen window on the other side, two gardai were visible, having coffee at the kitchen table. The police had cleaned out the broken crystal and set up a base in the kitchen. They sent a regular supply of sandwiches to Justin, a couple of which he had eaten.

In the family room, Daragh and the banker shared one of the sofas. Justin Kennedy was standing behind the other sofa, hands in the pockets of his pale blue tracksuit, his head tilted back, his stare fixed on the ceiling, as though by sheer effort of concentration he could shut out anything he didn't want to hear.

On the wide plasma screen on the wall behind him, a Sky newsreader was chortling at something the weatherman had said. The sound was off. Justin knew it was unlikely the media would hear anything before he did, but he wanted the TV news on all the time, and he listened to the hourly radio bulletins, just in case.

"What if there's a further increase in the ransom demand?" the banker asked. He was a neat, shiny-faced man. "Do we go to three million? Four? How certain can we be that—" and he paused, revising his sentence "—that these people can deliver?"

"What you're asking," Justin said, leaning forward, his hands grasping the back of the sofa, "is, first question, how much—"

"Justin," Daragh said, "perhaps it's best—"

"—how much is Angela worth. Is there a point at which we say, no, she's not worth that much. And, second question, the second thing you're asking, can they deliver—when you say that what you mean is how do we know she isn't lying in a ditch somewhere with her throat cut. That's what you're asking, isn't it?"

The banker was trying not to show embarrassment. Daragh threw him a lifeline. "I'm sure the bank is merely looking at this thing from all angles—as it's duty-bound to do. But at the end of the day, we're all working towards the same goal—getting Angela back safely."

His mobile rang.

Daragh checked the phone's screen to identify the caller and immediately stood up. As he took the call he moved quickly away, towards the bay window looking out over the long, wide back garden.

"Thanks for getting back to me so promptly."

He listened, the fingers of his free hand running back and forth through his hair.

A minute passed before Daragh spoke again, and when he did there was emotion in his voice. "Listen, thank you. Thank you, my friend. This is a good thing you're doing. No—"

Listening again, he turned to Justin and smiled.

"I certainly will. And I know Justin appreciates—well, you're right, some things don't need to be said. Just so you know." He said thank you another couple of times, and when he came back to the table he said to the banker, with a deferential smile and in the friendliest of tones, "I wonder if Justin and I might have a moment?"

As soon as the banker left the room, Daragh O'Suilleabhain stood close to Justin Kennedy and spoke in a low voice. "There are two options and I think we ought to take the second of them." He was holding his mobile like it contained something precious. "That phone call changes things. If it hadn't come through, what I was going to suggest is that we use the Liechtenstein account."

Justin said, "It would take forever to get the cash—"

"With the Liechtenstein account in play, the bank would do a back-to-back, no doubt about it, and take a slice off the top. One thing you can rely on with those bastards—once the profit's guaranteed, there's no quibbles. They'll push the money at you, and if the deal involves a little creative accounting, what the fuck."

The Liechtenstein account was a tax-evasion scheme set up within Flynn O'Meara Tully in the early 1990s. The account was initially held at a Liechtenstein bank, with an array of cut-outs and buffers that made it as investigation-proof as these things get. Over a number of years, the firm's off-the-books earnings were channelled into the account, through a small private bank in Dublin, quietly building into a solid hoard of cash to be shared among a handful of the most senior executives. The money wasn't usually accessible and was traditionally retained for pay-out, through a separate offshore account in Jersey, when a senior lawyer left or retired.

"It's not ideal, but I've already had a word with a couple of the lads, and there'll be no problem accessing the account."

The Liechtenstein account was active until the turn of the century, when a High Court inspector inquiring into other matters saw a mention of it in a file and raised a query. Both the Liechtenstein and Jersey accounts were immediately closed and the assets transferred to the Virgin Islands, though the account was still known by its original name. New arrangements were made to facilitate pay-offs when necessary, but there was a moratorium on payments into the account until a safer scheme could be arranged.

By then, the political climate had become even more business-friendly and made tax evasion less worthwhile. Justin, who hadn't bothered taking his share when he left Flynn O'Meara Tully—seeing it as part of his pension plan—had no knowledge of the current pay-out arrangements.

"It's there, it's available," Daragh said. "It's a fall-back, but it requires careful handling. If we take the second option, Liechtenstein won't be needed." Daragh's smile was two parts deviousness and three parts triumph. "A confession—but I don't think you'll mind. I broke confidence. Last night, I rang Kevin Little. That was him calling."

"Jesus, Daragh—"

"Talking to Kevin, it's like talking to a priest in confession. It'll go no further."

"We've never met, I don't know him."

Daragh shrugged. Everyone knew Kevin Little.

"Why would he—"

"Kevin keeps an eye on the scene. Over the past few years, you've made a bit of a name for yourself. You're beyond up-and-coming, Justin. And Kevin—he's a global player, sure enough, but his heart remains at home. He pays attention to what's going on—Kevin sees himself as a kind of guardian angel. Thing like this, someone like yourself involved, he'll do whatever he can. I knew that, that's why I contacted him."

"Jesus, I'm not sure—"

"One word from Kevin, any of half a dozen banks will turn over the second million, no questions, no conditions, fast as they can put it together. Ten times that, if we need it."

"It's that easy?"

"I ring him back, he makes a phone call, it's done." Daragh gestured towards the doorway through which the bank executive had exited. "I'd like to call that fucker back in and tell him where the bank can shove its money—in the politest possible terms. But they have the first million ready to roll. It'd be stupid to piss them off now."

"So, we take their—"

"We take their million, and get Kevin to fast-track a two-million transfer right away. Pay off this shower immediately and have the second million within a couple of days."

Having Kevin Little involved, Jesus, it was like the heavy gang throwing their weight behind you. Tax exile, entrepreneur, a man whose steady advance to the outer reaches of fabulous wealth inspired a whole generation of Irish business-school graduates. There were kinks in Little's past. Deals that came halfway into the light, then faded from public scrutiny just as things were getting interesting. These days, Little was beyond all that. His wealth appeared so boundless that his skirmishes with legality took on the glow of youthful frolics. Libel lawyers ostentatiously patrolled the acres of media coverage devoted to Little, so it was seldom that anything embarrassing was published.

Now, when Little wasn't jetting in and out of the country to close a deal or squash a rival, or to deny a rumour that he was about to close a deal or squash a rival, he was modestly accepting applause for his latest philanthropic project.

"Is there a price for Kevin's help? I mean, I'm grateful, but what does he get out of this?"

"Nothing. Kevin gets nothing. Your goodwill, mine—something he might never need." Daragh leaned back in his chair, hands behind his head. "Way things are, Kevin bought a house in West Cork two years back. The furniture alone cost more than I spent on buying my place in Dalkey. He's never lived in it, never even been there, far as I know."

Daragh held up one finger. "It's an asset." He held up a second. "He's got a flat in New York that he uses about once a month." A third finger. "Another in Paris, he uses maybe once, twice a year. A place in Barcelona I know for a fact he's never seen." Both hands palms up. "Kevin likes to have assets, tucked away here and there. And your goodwill, and mine, this firm's goodwill, that's an asset. End of the day, we pay him back, and he's got something money alone can't buy—the goodwill of a couple of players in one of his playgrounds."

"How can I thank him—"

"I'll ring him back now, he'll make a call, whichever bank he chooses, end of business tomorrow, maybe early Tuesday, they'll have it wrapped and ready. When this is all over, settled down, Angela's back home and Kevin's in the country—some evening, I'll arrange a dinner."

"Thank him for me, when you ring. You, too, Daragh. You've been—"

Kennedy realised he was holding O'Suilleabhain's hand in both of his own. "Thank you," he said again.

A problem had been solved, he was a step closer to getting Angela back. Kevin Little's involvement wiped out any logistical hurdles to lining up the money. More than that, Justin felt as though—in an implicit way—he'd received some kind of promotion.

* * *

Jesus, Mary and Joseph, I offer you my heart and my soul.
Jesus, Mary and Joseph, assist me in my last agony.
Jesus, Mary and Joseph, may I— may I—

Fuck it.

Angela turned over onto her back and stretched to ease the muscles in her shoulders. *All that time with the nuns beating it into me, and I can't remember the damn thing now that it's appropriate.*

Appropriate, but not important. Not even now. The prayers she learned in school, seeming to carry such weight, turned into meaningless strings of words when the faith that sustained them evaporated. They were still carved into the memory, but less sharply, the edges rubbed away.

Jesus, Mary and Joseph, may I—

It was in the missal under the heading "Three Ejaculations," which gave the girls at St. Catherine's no end of chuckles. It was Sheila Brannigan who stood up one day in class, shaking her head so her long blonde hair danced on her shoulders, and asked Sister Dominica, "Sister, how many ejaculations are appropriate in any one session?"

It was anger the nun stifled, not embarrassment. Her weary "Sit down, girl," acknowledged the truth. Things were changing. There were always thirteen-year-olds who dared in private to mock the majesty of the cloth. Now, the schools were crawling with youngsters who wanted to publicly flaunt their moral and intellectual superiority to the Pope.

"The Prayer for the Grace of a Happy Death," Sister Dominica called it. Angela tried to remember if she'd ever, in her days of faith, truly believed that there were magic words that would help in the face of death. At worst, glimpsed in momentary thoughts she never entertained, death was an unexpected intrusion, the accident or disease that could suddenly cut across anyone's path. Mostly, the certainty of death was associated with the wrinkles and the cooled passions of an old age that wouldn't come for decades. Death would be something that would eventually meander into her presence, circling at a distance, allowing time for familiarity to breed acceptance. That comforting image had been swept away by the knowledge that her life was now a short thread, possibly measured in hours, minutes, or—as she'd felt when the kidnappers stopped in the woods on the way down here—seconds.

The thoughts she had carefully suppressed were now scuttling around her mind, mice in the skirting boards. There was something in the gang leader's rudeness, his indifference, above all the dismissive contempt of his voice, that was unmistakable. When he looked at her, when he spoke to her or about her, she felt disposable. There will be no ceremony. Any time she was in his presence she watched for the sudden movement that would tell her it was over.

Is Justin haggling?

The thought came unbidden.

That's what he does all day at work. Haggles, over words and clauses, dates and amounts of money. Justin haggles for a living.

Justin loves me.

Was the gang leader telling the truth? Was Justin haggling? Was he trusting his negotiating skills against people whose brutality was beyond his understanding? Was that why the gang needed the note, to put more pressure on Justin? Should she have been more emotional in what she wrote—should she have pleaded?

Justin loved her. She knew that. From the start, the open, flatly stated, frequently repeated, assurances of his love were wholly convincing.

She knew he loved her more than she loved him.

Do I love him?

She asked herself that on the morning of their marriage, and the answer she told herself was the same now as it was then.

She loved him—no, she loved being married to him—for what he was. His character and qualities, his assuredness, his generosity, his pride in her. She liked him for a lot of reasons. He was a good provider. He never embarrassed her. He was kind. She liked his confident advance through the business and social jungle, his lack of doubt in himself, in her, in them.

She appreciated him.

And his screwing around was part of that.

She had known about the women from early on. Without any evidence other than her understanding of the subtleties of their relationship. The unnecessary pause, the words spoken cheerfully but with a casually averted gaze. Very occasionally, the tone that said, Don't ask.

The evidence didn't come until three years ago, when she was saying goodbye to Elizabeth out at the airport. Sharing a coffee at a table on the mezzanine overlooking the departures area, seeing Justin come in through the sliding doors below. He was carrying a briefcase, with a short, over-cheerful blonde by his side. The blonde collected a large envelope at the Ryanair desk, took the briefcase from Justin and gave him a peck on the cheek. There was nothing obvious, he might merely have been seeing off a business colleague, but there was an intimacy, the hand on the blonde's forearm, the tilt of her head, the eye contact.

Elizabeth was chatting away, and Angela leaned back, casually moving her head out of Justin's line of sight, nodding in agreement with something her sister said. At first she thought her reaction sprang from a fear of being caught snooping, but she later realised she instinctively ducked away from the possibility that she might embarrass her husband. In the years before she met Justin, Angela had been PA to an up-and-comer in a brokerage. He was married with children and he treated Angela with impeccable professionalism. He was open about his girlfriend, and Angela came to understand that among his peers it was as routine to make casual remarks about the problems and joys of the extra-marital side of life as it was to commiserate about a particularly unfortunate golf score.

So be it. By and by, whenever Justin was engaged in one of his little adventures, Angela took care to stay out of his line of sight. There was nothing to be achieved by confrontation—just anger, pain and the end of everything. This was part of the package.

Angela's enthusiasm for her regular sexual jousts with Justin did not diminish. Her feelings for him and for their marriage didn't change. In a way, the knowledge that the marriage survived such assaults buoyed her. She knew what they had together. He knew it. It was what it was.

Do I trust him?

She knew him. She could trust him to be the man she knew him to be.

The gang leader was playing with her head.

Justin wouldn't haggle.

Not on this. Angela concluded she had absolute faith in her husband's love, and in his loyalty to her.

Jesus, Mary and Joseph, may I—

And it was suddenly there, faded but irredeemably etched in her mind. It came to her in Sister Dominica's brusque voice, and for the first time ever she envied the nun her smug, eternal certainties.

Jesus, Mary and Joseph, may I breathe forth my soul with You in peace.

19

Dolly Finn and Brendan Sweetman were walking on the Rosslare beach. Neither had much to say, which suited them both. They strolled the length of the beach and halfway back, then Sweetman said he needed to go to the jacks. Finn nodded and watched Sweetman climbing the steps to the strand road.

The pub.

Supposed to be against Frankie's rules, not that Dolly Finn gave a damn. He continued walking a while, then he found a quiet spot and sat down. Here and there kids were squealing, parents were snappy. The summer season over, few people were using the beach. The day was sunny, with a bit of wind, and Dolly Finn tried to remember when he'd last sat on a beach. Too long ago to remember when or who with. He lay back and felt the tension leak out of his shoulders.

Up in Dublin, Frankie parked in the grounds of the Church of the Most Precious Blood. He pulled on latex gloves, took from his pocket the note the hostage had written and used a pencil to add two lines of block capitals at the bottom. Then he went inside and planted the note.

Three hours earlier, shortly after he'd got the hostage to write the note, he'd taken off for Dublin. He'd probably be back in Rosslare tomorrow night. Maybe have another chat with Martin. The previous day, after all four of them, and the hostage, arrived from Dublin and settled in, Frankie and

Martin ended the day yawning over a couple of cups of coffee in the kitchen of the Rosslare bungalow. The chat didn't last long enough for Frankie to be sure, but it was like Martin was going soft on the plans they'd talked about in the months before this kidnap thing. Martin was talking about buying a house somewhere outside Dublin. Him and Debbie. Which was fine, as far as it went. But you have to think ahead, figure where you want to be ten years from now. And if you want to look to the long term, you've got to see this thing as the roots of a money tree. Speculate to accumulate.

"There's not going to be too many pay days like this. You want to squander it on home comforts, fair enough. But the kind of deals we talked about, you could end up buying a whole fucking street."

Martin said, "It's just, I'm not sure how long I want to go on living on my nerves. This works out, it's a big lump of money and it could be time to quit while we're ahead."

What Frankie wanted to talk to Martin about was ambition. Doing a thing just for the money—so you could have a bigger house or a new car or longer holidays in more expensive resorts—that was just greed. Doing a thing to get the money so you could step up to a new level, that was ambition. Long-term thinking. Consolidate, move on, you end up with fingers in all sorts of pies, many of them legit. That was the goal. It might well be that Martin wasn't—or wouldn't ever be—ready for that. Which would be a pity.

Driving out of the grounds of the Church of the Most Precious Blood, Frankie glanced at his Rolex. Lunch, then he'd ring the hostage's husband and give the cops something to do.

The one with the soft voice brought Angela's lunch. A thin slice of cold roast beef between a couple of pieces of cheap sliced pan, and a small carton of Tropicana. The gunman poured the orange juice into a paper cup and stood over by the door as Angela took a bite of the sandwich. He was wearing faded blue jeans and a white T-shirt and the brown woollen ski mask. Perhaps it was just that she'd become used to the masks but she no longer found them so frightening. The gunman looked like an overgrown kid playing a fancy-dress game.

The window, like the room in the first place she'd been held, was covered on the inside by a sheet of wood. When they arrived here the previous evening, they'd locked her in here with a bottle of Pepsi. It was after midnight when the tall skinny one came in and took her to the toilet. She'd had nothing to eat, and when she woke this morning she felt nauseous and had to bang on the door until the gang leader came and took her to the toilet to be sick.

After she'd written the note he wanted and he'd taken it away, when she was alone, the tears came and she spent a long while in a fog of depression. She hated them for creating her fear, she hated them for the horror they had invented for her family. Mostly, she hated them for saturating her in helplessness.

Fuck them.

The light bulb in the centre of the ceiling was a sixty-watt effort that was just bright enough to add to the gloom of the room. The sheet of wood that blocked the window was framed by a thin line of surging daylight that emphasised the feebleness of the artificial light.

She knew that whatever she wrote in the note to Justin would only add to the pressure on him. That was the purpose of the note. So, she'd kept it as short and as bare as possible.

Dear Justin,
They told me to write you a note. I am OK, but I miss you and Saskia and Luke and love you all very much. I know you are doing everything you can. Take care,
Angela

She felt hungry, but she knew it would be foolish to eat anything heavy so soon after being sick. As the gang leader read the note, she asked if she could have some toast and a cup of tea.

"Later," he said. It was well over two hours before the one with the soft voice brought the roast-beef sandwich.

Angela took small bites from it and chewed each one slowly. The meat tasted better than she expected, and in her mouth the flavours of the processed bread, the butter, the salt and the cold meat seemed both separate and perfectly complementary. She washed the last crumbs down with another mouthful of orange juice, and if she was imagining the physical boost the food gave her, so be it.

Christ sake, do something. Any fucking thing.

She was still wearing the same tracksuit, grubbier than ever. Her hair was stringy, her skin taut.

She'd heard a car drive away during the morning and from the lack of sounds of movement in the house, she guessed that she and the soft-voiced gunman were alone. When he took the empty plate, Angela rubbed her hands on the legs of her tracksuit and said, "Isn't there anything I can change into?"

"Maybe we can get something. See if there's a shop."

"Can I at least have a shower?"

He said nothing for a moment, his indecision reflected in tentative movements, a step back, a hand half raised, then, "I suppose—"

He brought her down a corridor to the bathroom. "You'll have to wear the same things, afterwards."

There was pebbled glass in the bathroom window. When he left her alone she touched the handle on the window, applied some weight, and it was like it was welded shut. Maybe it was. Anyway, what if this was some kind of test? What if they had one of the others outside, watching the window? She turned on the shower.

For a minute or two her nakedness made her feel vulnerable, then she began to enjoy the energy of the hot shower. It was as though the water was washing away a temporary and exhausted skin, allowing the fresh skin underneath to breathe. Streaming through her hair, down over her shoulders, the water drained some of the tension away. The brisk rubbing of the towel not only dried her body but left her skin flushed and fresh.

She was resigned to the used knickers, having already worn all those available at least once, but decided not to bother with the bra. It was the lacy thing she'd worn under the burgundy dress on the evening of Justin's birthday, and after four days it was stretched, grimy and uncomfortable.

She put on the trainers without the dirty socks. Dressed again, the tracksuit didn't seem as soiled, her movements seemed freer, her mind less fogged. The gunman was waiting in the corridor.

"Feeling better?"

She could see, at the other end of the corridor, past the door to her room, a door ajar. It seemed to lead out into a back garden. When she spoke, nodding towards the far door, she used a timid voice. "Could I go down to the kitchen, maybe sit at a table, have a coffee—maybe even go out into the garden, get some air?"

He began to shake his head.

"Please? It would mean so much."

He looked down the corridor to the door, back to her face, paused a moment, then shrugged. "Five minutes, no more than that. We come back in when I say so, understood?"

She gave him a wide, full smile. "I promise."

She went ahead of him down the corridor and caught a glimpse of a wide living room on the left, cheap furniture and a small television. She went past a kitchen on the right—she could see a draining board stacked with plates and cups—and out the back door.

A patch of yard and sixty feet of grass stretched away from the house. There were bushes along the bottom of the garden and all the way down both sides. A few clouds hovered in the distance, but the sun was bright in a blue sky that was mostly clear. She brushed her damp hair back from her face.

Behind her, the gunman stood just outside the back door, hands in the pockets of his jeans, the brown woollen mask looking even more absurd in the daylight. Angela took deep breaths. She could smell the sea above the scent of the grass. She could feel the weak heat of the sun on her face. As she rolled up her sleeves she could feel the breeze on her arms. She held the front hem of the tracksuit top away from her belly and waved it back and forth and felt the cooling air on her breasts.

The gunman said, "Must have been rough, travelling all the way down in the boot?"

She said, "Where are we?"

He hesitated, then said only, "Outside Dublin."

"I heard the sea, when they took me from the boot of the car. I can smell it now. Close."

Wexford, she guessed, somewhere around there. The sea, two, three hours drive from Dublin. Travelling all the way down, he said. Wexford, most likely.

He asked, "You still hungry?"

She looked at his masked face and she could see the eyes. Blue, blinking. Nervous.

"You don't hate me."

He didn't reply.

"The fat one, he hates me. Can't imagine why, but that's what he gives off. Hate. Like he's angry at me for something."

The gunman shook his head. "He's OK. There's nothing personal. It's just, for him, for any of us, it's just a piece of work."

She kept her face as blank as possible when she said, "The

tall one, the skinny one—he'll be the one to kill me, if it comes to that."

The gunman shook his head.

"Or maybe your boss will do it himself. Have you talked about that, among yourselves? Have you decided which one of you will do it?"

Still shaking his head, he came closer. "Nothing like that, I swear. That's not going to happen."

She was surprised at how easily the tears came. Not too much, no hysterics, just a catch in the voice and liquid at the edges of her eyes.

"Your boss—he told me things that my husband is supposed to have said. That he wasn't doing anything to get me back. You don't—is that true?"

"Look, he's fucking with your head. This is business. Your husband, big-shot solicitor, probably he's got insurance for this kind of thing. It's just a question of arranging things, that's all."

Angela was suddenly speaking quickly, urgently. "Let me go. Let me make a run for it."

"Ah, Jesus."

"You can say I knocked you down, took you by surprise, ran away."

"Jesus, come on."

"I can't identify you, I won't identify anyone. I'll pay you. More than he's asking for. I'll get it, I'll send it anywhere you say."

"Come on, that's enough." Thumbs hooked in the pockets of his jeans, his stance awkward and shifting.

"You know I won't double-cross you, I'd be too afraid." Angela moved a step towards him. He shook his head. She said, "Get me out of this, I'll send the money anywhere you say."

"That's what we're trying to arrange, a ransom."

"Ransom or no ransom, he's going to kill me."

"You've got us all wrong. This is business, no personal shit. What do they call you—Angela, Angie?"

"Angela."

"Angela. This is all about patience. This is all—"

"You're Martin, right?"

"How the fuck—"

"I heard the other man, that first night at my house, I heard him when he went wild, dragging me down the stairs, when he told you to take care of the children. He called you Martin."

He said nothing for a minute, just stared at her.

"I just heard the name. I haven't seen any faces. Listen, Martin, he's going to kill me! Even if he gets the money, he'll kill me."

"No—"

"Please. Turn your back for a few seconds, that's all it takes. Tell the others you tried to stop me—please, Martin."

He shook his head. "You're not making sense. Things don't work that way. And how long do you think Frankie would believe a story like that?"

Frankie.

He was agitated now, impatient. "Look, this is all wrong, this is fucking silly. Come on, inside—"

"Could I just—"

"Inside!"

"Please—"

"Stop fucking around. I know what you're doing. Just stop it, right now!" His voice was suddenly brisk. "Inside, right now, OK?"

In the corridor on the way back to the room she felt an elation. Fucking yeah!

She hadn't got very far. But, Christ, it felt good to do something, to try something, to be something other than a piece of lucrative meat locked in a small, gloomy room, waiting for that surly bastard, Frankie—Frankie! I know something you don't know I know!—to do whatever he intended to do.

Behind her, perhaps mistaking her slow gait as a mark of depression, he said, "It'll work out. I promise." She didn't reply, didn't even look at him as she went into the room and lay down on the mattress, face towards the wall. He waited maybe half a minute before he closed the door. She lay there, eyes open, breathing measured, refusing to look around. Only when she heard the key click in the lock and his footsteps move away did she turn over, sit up and clasp her knees, rocking back and forth.

The call came on Justin's mobile. He was in the kitchen, on the landline to Angela's sister. The kids were holding up, Elizabeth said. Luke was a bit teary, but Saskia was acting like there was nothing wrong at all, like she was on a normal visit to her granny's home and that was more worrying.

Justin said, "The police are here all the time, that would upset them, but maybe it would be better if—"

And his mobile rang.

Without preamble, the voice said, "There's a church called the Precious Blood." Justin didn't say anything to Elizabeth, he just hung up the phone and said into the mobile, "Who is this?"

"In Cabra. Cabra West. There's a note there, behind the statue of St. Theresa. Message from the missus. To prove my credentials."

"Please, tell me—"

"Did you hear me? What was the name of the church?"

"Precious Blood, in Cabra."

"Good man." And the phone went dead.

In less than half an hour, the police had collected the note and brought it to the Kennedy house. John Grace and Assistant Commissioner Colin O'Keefe were there when

Malachy Hogg pulled on a pair of latex gloves and opened the envelope. He glanced at the note and held it out for Justin, who read it and said, "It's her writing."

Pencilled at the bottom of the note, in block capitals, there was a two-line addendum.

CALL YOU IN A WEEKS TIME
CODE WORD—SUNFLOWER

20.

U ncle Cormac's sofa was damp. A dark wet streak ran diagonally down the light brown material of the back of the sofa, across the seat, looping around itself several times, and ending in a wide dark patch in the middle of the three cushions.

Frankie got another can of Coke from the fridge and swallowed noisily.

In the living room, Frankie unplugged the eight mobiles he'd put on charge when he got up this morning. He put them into his black Umbro overnight bag.

The previous day, having left the note at the church in Cabra and made the phone call to the hostage's husband, Frankie needed somewhere to stay. A B&B was an option, but he decided on Uncle Cormac's place. More potential for a bit of crack. Pity the little tosser wasn't there. Frankie had been thinking recently about family matters and what with one thing and another Uncle Cormac was well overdue another slap.

On arrival, he found the fridge as well stocked as ever and he made himself a beef sandwich, spent the evening watching shit on TV, then went to bed in Uncle Cormac's room.

Nice place, Uncle Cormac's new gaff. Four-bedroom house, halfway down Griffith Avenue, though what the bastard needed four bedrooms for. Proceeds of a lifetime of hard work in wholesale and a six-figure insurance claim when a warehouse went up in a fire that had Maguire & Paterson written all over it.

Uncle Cormac's was the only bedroom that was furnished. A second bedroom was used as a storeroom, the other two were bare. His uncle's bedroom was untidy, the bed unmade, clothes discarded across a chair. In a drawer of a bedside table, Frankie found a couple of wank-mags. Under the scented liner of the drawer in the mahogany dressing table, he found an envelope with a grand in small notes. Just-in-case money. Thank you, Uncle Cormac.

There was an Allied Irish Banks calendar on the back of the kitchen door, all the September dates and the first ten days of October filled in with scribbled reminders. Starting the day before, six days were filled in with the same word, London. When Uncle Cormac wasn't importing something he was exporting something else, usually something with paperwork that was close enough to pass for legit.

Having packed the mobiles, Frankie paused to look at a photo on the living-room wall. An older man and woman and a woman in her twenties, all relaxing on a beach somewhere, smiling for the camera. Frankie didn't recognise the young woman. The older couple were his parents. His dad, dead these six years, was grinning his old shit-eating grin, his mother displaying her stuck-up smile. His hands on his hips, Frankie stared at the photo and tried to remember a time when he hadn't seen through the phoniness of the whole fucking thing.

It was Uncle Cormac who made the move that brought everything crashing down, though Frankie had been on the outs with the old man and the old dear for most of his teens.

"Where'd you get this?"

Standing inside the door of the small living room, his mother held up a briefcase Frankie had left under his bed. The expression on her face wasn't curious or worried, it was triumphant, like she'd finally cracked a problem she'd almost despaired of. Gotcha.

Seventeen-year-old Frankie, lying on the sofa. Music pulsing from the television, Madonna arranging her arms in a succession of twitchy poses, her face rigid, vacant, staring straight out at Frankie. Frankie ignoring his mother, his father butting in, "Your mother's talking to you."

Which was when Frankie came off the sofa in a hurry, grabbed the briefcase and screamed that it was none of her fucking business. He tossed the briefcase across the room and his old man jerked his head sideways to avoid getting clobbered.

Frankie had found the briefcase in a car that he and two mates had taken for a ride a few nights earlier. He was getting out of the back seat when he noticed the case on the floor, took it, checked it out—a stack of typed pages, figures and scribbles all over them—useless shite that he threw high in the air, walking away as sheets of paper blew into someone's garden. He kept the briefcase for no reason other than it seemed too swanky to throw away. You never know.

Two days after the incident with his parents, the cops came for Frankie. That was Uncle Cormac's idea. Bring the briefcase down to the station, he advised Frankie's dad. Get the gardaí to give the lad a scare, frighten the waywardness out of him. Uncle Cormac was his dad's younger brother. The brains of the family. Bald and skinny and drippy as a soft-boiled egg, prying and fussy and full of big ideas. No wife or kids of his own, but never done sticking his nose in and bleating about black sheep.

And the shades took Frankie down the station, into a room without windows. Two culchie bastards, chins out, showing off what big men they were. Frankie told them to piss off. One of them stood watch by the door while the other gave him a bit of a going-over, but nothing to get worked up about. They didn't bother charging him.

That night, in the poky little living room, Frankie's mother told him about Uncle Cormac's big idea, a grin on her face as if daring him to let his anger take him where it might. Standing by the door, his dad said nothing. As if the room wasn't small enough—you couldn't take three steps without having to step around something—his older brother, big fat Seamus, was standing beside his mam, his arms folded, loathing written all across his big pouty face. Now and then, over the years, Frankie caught himself wondering why his mother decided to stir things up, letting him know it was Uncle Cormac's idea. There was something chronic going on there, his mam and his dad and his Uncle Cormac.

"My own family—called in the fucking cops?"

His mother enlarged her humourless grin. "Give you a taste of the real world, that's what Cormac said. Actions have consequences, he said. Bloody waste of time, far as you're concerned."

Frankie's dad said, "Now, wait a minute—"

Frankie walked out of the house. His dad followed him down the street, telling him not to be a fool. Frankie told him to get the fuck away or he'd get his stupid head opened. Frankie's dad stopped and stood there in the street.

Frankie walked the mile and a half to Uncle Cormac's house and when his uncle opened the door—"So, it's yourself—" Frankie smacked him in the face and stepped back to avoid the blood spouting from his nose. He kicked his uncle in the balls, then kicked him a bit when he fell down and curled up. Finally, with several of the neighbours watching, Frankie unzipped his fly and pissed on his Uncle Cormac.

Frankie never went back home, never went near any of them again. The day he knocked the bollocks out of Uncle Cormac, Frankie turned up at Jo-Jo Mackendrick's place, red-eyed and in need. Jo-Jo put him up for the night and got him a flat next day, paid the rent for a couple of months until Frankie found his feet. Frankie never even bothered collecting his stuff from home. Nothing there worth a fuck.

Later, his dad wrote to him twice, neat handwriting in blue biro on Basildon Bond, and Frankie tore up the letters, unread. His dad came round to see him and Frankie spat on the doorstep and closed the door in his face.

Half a dozen times, over the years, he'd been to see Uncle Cormac. More to frighten him than anything else. Couple of times, he just walked in, spent the night in a spare room, didn't open his mouth except to drink Uncle Cormac's beer and eat his food, and Uncle Cormac didn't say boo. Other times, he gave the silly bastard a slapping. When Frankie's dad died, Uncle Cormac came to tell Frankie about the funeral arrangements and Frankie told him to fuck off. Frankie didn't attend the funeral, but he got a little memorial card in the post, with a picture of his dad and a verse about how he'd never be forgotten. Poor dumb bastard collapsed down at the Smithfield Market, a sack of potatoes on his shoulders. Frankie was surprised to find out from the memorial card that his dad was only forty-eight. Poor gobshite, sweating for a lousy living, apologising for his existence, he was better off dead.

Looking back on it all, things had worked out for the best. But that didn't mean it wasn't a shitty thing to do, for a family to tout on its own kid.

Frankie took the photograph down from the wall. He smashed it against the mantelpiece and shards of glass glittered in the white shag rug in front of the fireplace. He took the photo out of the frame and tore it down the middle. Then he finished his third can of Coke and went into the kitchen to make himself a cheese sandwich and a coffee. Before he left the house, he pissed on the sofa again.

Uncle Cormac's brand new Pajero was sitting in the driveway; the keys were in a drawer in the hall. Frankie spent ten minutes working on the plates, then he drove across the city and found a place to park in Haddington Road. It was a couple of streets away from the hostage's house.

Sitting in the car, he listened to the mobile purring in his ear. When the call went through he said, "The code word is sunflower."

Justin Kennedy said, "The note said you'd call next week—"

"You have the money?"

"Listen, we need to talk."

"You have the money, you don't have it, which is it?"

"Look—"

"Do you have the money?"

"Dammit, I want to know—"

"Fuck off!"

Justin stopped talking.

"You said you had the money, time I rang."

"I have the first million. I told you the second million would take a little time. It's all fixed up, the bank is getting it together, it's nearly ready, another day or two and we—"

"Then we can talk about that in a day or two. I want the first million now."

"Look—"

"You said you had it. You lied?"

"No! I have it, it's here, but you said—"

"Put it in your car—your car, no one else's. The Land-Rover. Right now. Right this minute. Tell no one where you're going, bring no one with you, tell the coppers to fuck off. Got that?"

Justin was still trying to think of something to say when the gang leader screamed into the phone: "Have you fucking got that?"

"Yes, OK!"

"Take the car, your car, the Land Rover, turn right, right

again, heading straight out towards Dun Laoghaire. Bring your mobile with you."

"OK."

"It's important you do this right. You're being watched all the way, every inch. We've got sweepers. You use tracking devices, any shit like that, you bring an extra mobile to talk to the cops, you do anything to fuck me around, that's it."

"I just—"

"Step out of line, we do a fade. We're gone. And twenty years from now your kids'll still be having nightmares about whatever happened to Mammy, OK?"

"Please—"

"Leave the house with the money. Now. This minute. I'll call you on your mobile five minutes from now. You're not on the road, you're not doing exactly what I say, goodbye Mammy."

"You've got to tell—"

Justin realised he was talking to a dead phone.

One of the two cops in the house—Justin didn't know his name—fidgeted in the hall, all flustered and making like he was going to assert himself.

"Please, just stay out of the way," Justin said.

"Before you do anything, you've agreed to alert Chief Superintendent Hogg—"

"Stay out of it."

Justin turned away. He went to the kitchen and came back to the hall dragging the two heavy holdalls full of money. He set one down, fumbled in his pocket for the car keys.

"You have to wait, sir—"

"Fuck off." Justin realised, even in the heat of the moment, that he had bared his teeth. "This is my family we're talking about. You get in my way, you try to follow me—Jesus, I know people—you're all over the front page of the *Evening Herald*, the cop who put a mother's life at risk."

"Sir, the sensible thing—"

"I have minutes to do this. Catch them later, I don't give a fuck. I'm doing exactly what they told me to do."

The flustered one started stabbing out a number on his mobile. The other cop, a quiet fat man with a red face, nodded to Justin, grabbed the second holdall and shuffled with it towards the front door.

"Where are you? Precisely?"

"There's a Statoil filling station, it's just across the road." Justin looked around. He was parked, two wheels up on the pavement, where he'd pulled over when his mobile rang less than three minutes after he drove away from the house. "There's a newsagent's just ahead of me on the left, Wiley's newsagent's, and there's—"

"I'll say this once. You ready?"

"I'm ready."

"Drive straight ahead until you see a church on your right, big one. Drive in the gates, park. Got that?"

"I know the church."

"Leave your mobile on the ground, under the left rear wheel of the LandRover."

"Why? What's the—"

"That mobile's dead. You're going in to collect another one in the church. One mobile at a time, so you don't make any calls. When you get the new mobile, don't use it—I call you and you're engaged, she's dead."

"I won't. Tell me where to get the mobile."

"Go into the church, there's three confession boxes on your left, go to the first, the one nearest the door. There's two doors to each confession box, left and right. I'm talking about the door on the left. Inside, on the floor. Got that?"

"First confession box on the left, door on the left, the mobile's on the floor."

"Wait in the church, I'll ring you on that mobile, tell you where to go next, There'll be another mobile waiting, we'll keep doing that until I know it's safe for you to make the drop. I've got five more mobiles planted, and the schedule's going to be tight."

"OK, I understand."

"I mean it—you're being watched—do anything wrong—"

"I swear."

"You leave a note for the cops, anything like that, bye-bye Mumsy."

"I'm doing exactly what you say."

"My people're watching you. In the church, in between churches. We smell something wrong, I make a call and we do a fade. Get me? I'll fucking bury her. Then we do it all over again with someone else, and their people'll know we're not bluffing."

"I'll do whatever you say."

"You have five minutes to get to the church." He switched off.

Justin had passed this church just about every day since they'd moved to Pemberton Road. It was a 1950s building, big and ugly, put up at the height of the Catholic Church's dominance of Irish life. The car park off to the left of the church was empty when Justin drove in. Getting out, he looked around with as much nonchalance as he could manage, wondering if the gang had someone in a car across the street, or in a window overlooking the church, watching him. He leaned over and put his mobile under the left rear wheel.

There were two women halfway down the church, sitting together, speaking quietly. Up on the altar, a man in a cassock was polishing the tabernacle.

The women were late-middle age. Hardly material for employment by a kidnap gang. Justin looked around, found the first confession box on the left. The nameplate out front said

Fr. Thomas Daly. Justin looked back towards the altar. The man in the cassock had stopped polishing and was looking down the church, towards Justin. He turned back and resumed his polishing. Justin stood there, looking at him for half a minute, then he opened the door on the left of the confession box and went in. He found the mobile immediately, left the confession box and sat down in a pew. The phone was turned on, the signal bars strong.

The man on the altar finished his polishing, then moved away to one side, glancing down the church as he did.

The two women were still chattering. Justin sat with the phone in his hand, looking down at it, a small black Nokia. The screen said Vodafone, with the date and time underneath. His other hand rubbed his knee, over and over. He looked up and one of the women was staring at him, like she'd caught him doing something obscene. He stared back. She said something and her companion turned and looked across at Justin. The phone rang, a chirping bird noise.

"You got it."

"Where do I go now?"

"Leave the church exactly five minutes from now." Justin looked at his watch. "Turn right, drive for about ten minutes—you know St. Vincent's Hospital?"

The two old women weren't trying to hide their expressions of disapproval. Justin looked away from them. "Yes."

"Drive into the car park there."

"You'll be there?"

"Take your time. When you get to Vincent's, wait in the car until I ring you with instructions. There's a pub across the road from the hospital. There's another mobile to be picked up there. I'll give you the details when you get to the hospital."

The gang leader sounded slightly distracted. In the background, Justin heard a car door close.

"Can't we—"

The phone went dead.

Justin looked at the phone, then he put it to his ear again and it was still dead.

He looked at the screen. It said Call ended, then it said Vodafone, with the date and time underneath. He sat there looking at the screen for maybe ten seconds, then he shouted, "Jesus!"

He stood up and ran towards the porch, seeing from the corner of his eye the two biddies half risen, startled. When he got outside he saw a Pajero pulling out of the car park. He saw it and at the same time he saw the broken window of his LandRover, the open door. He screamed something incoherent and ran towards the Pajero, saw it accelerating, pulling out into the street, speeding away. He stopped, moved back towards his car, hesitated as he realised he hadn't got the number of the fleeing Pajero, started back towards the gate, then realised it was too late.

He ran to the LandRover. His mobile was gone from under the rear wheel. The two holdalls were gone from the back. He began to tap 999 on the Nokia from the church and saw that the numbers weren't registering on the screen, the keys weren't functioning. He made a sudden high-pitched noise.

"Is everything all right?"

The man in the cassock was standing a few feet away, concerned but keeping his distance.

"A phone," Justin said.

The man looked at the mobile in Justin's trembling hand.

"I can't," Justin said, "it won't—"

The man said, "This way," and led Justin back towards the church.

21

Y ou'd have to feel sorry for the poor bitch. Lock an animal up for a few days and it'll start whining. The hostage—what was it now, about five days?—was beginning to look like some kind of beaten thing.

Dolly Finn stood in the doorway of the hostage's room for a couple of minutes and she wouldn't turn round. Just lying there with her back to him. Silly wagon.

"Come on, missus," he said again, "don't be stupid."

The sandwich and the glass of milk he'd left by the bedside an hour ago hadn't been touched.

Dolly was alone in the house with the hostage. Frankie was in Dublin, hopefully getting his hands on the first chunk of money. This morning, the other two had driven into Wexford town for supplies.

Dolly went into the bedroom, around the other side of the bed, and looked down at her. She ignored him, continued to stare at the bedroom wall. He reached down to her and she erupted, jerking back towards the edge of the bed, staring up at him. She was staring like she might be able to burn away the woollen mask with her eyes.

"You have to eat," he said.

"You're the one," she said, in a flat tone. "You're the one who'll kill me. If your boss says so."

Dolly looked down at her. She said, "I can tell by the way you look at me. It'll be you."

He wanted to say, Not necessarily. They hadn't come to a

conclusion about who would do that, if it had to be done, which it probably wouldn't. But her accusation was so starkly made that he felt a surge of resentment. She had no good reason to say that. She was judging him. Like he was darker than the others, more sinful.

To hell with it. Poor cow. Only to be expected.

Dolly picked up the milk and the plate with the sandwich and left the room, locking it behind him.

He left the milk on the hall table and threw the sandwich in the bin outside the front door. He turned to go back inside, then stopped.

Looking out past the front gate, he could see a man—middle-aged, red striped sweatshirt, dark shorts and not a lot of hair—crossing the hump-backed bridge about fifty yards away. He was looking back towards Dolly as he walked.

Jesus fucking Christ.

Dolly leaned forward, pulled the balaclava off his head and when he looked again the man was out of sight.

Dolly ran back into the house, dropped the plate on the hall table, knocking over the glass of milk. He pulled on his bomber jacket, took his knife from an inside pocket, and then he hurried out of the house and ran towards the road.

When Dolly Finn got back to the house, Martin Paxton and Brendan Sweetman had returned from Wexford town and were unloading groceries in the kitchen.

"You left her alone?"

"Ten minutes, couldn't be helped."

Dolly told them about the walker, the balaclava, about running out after him. "I can't figure it. He was on the road, couldn't have walked far. By the time I got out there—no sign of him. I ran maybe a hundred yards up the road, no sign."

Brendan said, "Maybe he went into a house somewhere round here? Maybe he saw you coming, hid in the bushes."

Dolly shook his head. "I checked, both sides of the road." He took off his jacket, hung it on the back of a chair.

Martin said, "Anyway, Jesus, Dolly, what were you going to do with him if you found him?"

Dolly shrugged.

Martin said, "Where would you hide the body? What would've happened when he didn't come home, and his missus calls the cops and they start knocking on doors?"

Brendan said, "Maybe, looking at you from that distance, he didn't notice anything wrong, y'know, thought the balaclava was a hat?"

Dolly shook his head. "It's all over the radio, the papers. Then he sees someone in a balaclava."

Martin said, "Not everyone pays attention to the news."

Dolly was stroking his face, thumb and index finger running down the deep grooves alongside each side of his mouth. He shook his head.

Martin said, "We better decide what to do."

Frankie Crowe kept to a steady fifty, bypassing Ashford. He was in no hurry. He'd dumped the Pajero within minutes of taking the holdalls full of money and picked up a Volvo that Milky had arranged to have stashed within walking distance. Beyond Arklow, he bought a cheese sandwich and a Coke at a garage shop. He drove on until he found a picnic area with a view. He sat in the car, eating, listening to music on the radio. After a few minutes another car pulled into the halt. Frankie screwed the cap shut on his Coke and put the bottle down on the passenger seat. He let his hand rest near the pistol tucked down alongside his seat. A woman and two kids got out of the car and sat at one of the picnic tables. The kids were boys, quarrelling noisily. The woman said something sharp but they kept on snarling. It was more pushing and pulling than fighting, but it was loud and unending. Frankie started the car and drove away.

* * *

After they'd tried twice to ring Frankie on his mobile, and failed to connect, Brendan Sweetman said he thought they should get out of Rosslare.

"Safe side," he said.

Martin Paxton said, "We could be running for nothing. This character might have seen something from a distance. Or not. What's the chances he'll think twice about it, let alone go to the trouble of ringing the cops?"

Dolly Finn said, "It's taking a chance, staying here."

"Whatever we do, this whole thing, we're taking a chance. Where we going to go? Check into a hotel, bring the hostage in with the rest of the luggage?"

Brendan said, "Milky's place. He'd find somewhere, put us up until he does."

Martin shook his head. "Let's not panic."

After a moment, Dolly said, "Could have been the guy was daydreaming, never even saw me. Just, at the time—"

Martin said, "That far away, he sees a figure in the distance standing outside the front door, he's going to notice the mask? I can't see that."

The three of them said nothing for a while. The edge seemed to have gone off Dolly's anxiety.

Martin said, "Look, we've got the makings of a real belt-tightener. Are you on? Or do you want to dump it all in the bin, panic over nothing, and we spend the night in a ditch, eating Mars bars?"

Brendan said, "Fuck that."

Dolly shrugged. "Go ahead. I'll keep an eye out the front."

It had been a week since Martin had eaten a proper meal and he whistled as he worked on this one. He made stuffing for the chicken with breadcrumbs, herbs and butter, and he parboiled the potatoes and gave them a good shaking before put-

ting them in the hot fat and sliding them into the oven. He prepared the carrots and sprouts. No booze, stick to Frankie's
rule. Just Ballygowan. He spent a while sitting at the front window with Dolly, the most interesting thing on view being a couple of old guys with red faces and bare white chests heading
down towards the beach.

Martin had a shower and when he came out of the bathroom he went into the bedroom he shared with Brendan and
found him bent over the bedside locker, snorting the remnants
of a line of white powder.

"Ah, Jesus, Brendan, for fuck sake."

Brendan raised his head and said, "Don't tell Frankie,
OK?" He bent over and hoovered up the last few white specks.

Martin sat down on the end of the bed and watched the fat
man use the back of one hand to wipe his face. "You doing
much of that?"

"A bit. The last year or so."

"Not good. Last thing this situation needs is someone waving a shotgun and wired to the moon."

"I'm OK."

Martin remembered the feeling. I'm OK. Never better.
Strung out on whatever he could get his hands on, and feeling
fucking great.

"Just the coke?"

"Mostly."

For Martin it used to be coke, smack and weed when things
were flush. Otherwise, a handful of whatever assortment of
barbies he or his mates could stroke from a chemist shop.

Two years of it, before he knew what was happening.
Wising up didn't come suddenly, it came in flashes, like he was
glimpsing himself every now and then in a shop window. No
big eye-opener, just picking it up bit by bit, copping on he was
sometimes a little less together than he felt. Something he said
that didn't come out right, a good idea that suddenly seemed

more bother than it was worth, a day that started off going one way and he wasn't sure how it came to end up somewhere else. Knowing eventually that too much time, too much effort—too much of everything—was going into the job of stoking himself up. And knowing that a day without the stuff was too rough to think about.

Martin sat on the bed beside Brendan. "It's your business, but give it a miss until we're in the clear."

"My business. Keep your mouth shut to Frankie, OK?"

Martin shrugged. "Your business."

You come off it or you don't. The way things were in the Joy back then, the trouble with Bomber Harris and all, Martin was so ragged he needed all the comfort he could get.

Then, Frankie came along at just the right time to dismantle Bomber.

"Jesus Christ, Martin. Piece of shit like that." That was all Frankie said, the day before he paid a visit to Bomber Harris. Frankie and Martin had drifted apart since the Finglas days. Frankie got Joan pregnant, they paired off and he wasn't around the scene so much, playing happy families and building a reputation with Jo-Jo Mackendrick. That time he arrived in the Joy, Bomber Harris playing Mr. Big, Jesus Christ himself wouldn't have been more welcome on the landing.

"Piece of shit like that."

Next thing, Bomber Harris was being carted off to the Mater, Frankie's on report and he does a few weeks longer than scheduled.

Before he left the Joy, Martin got himself clean. It took a couple of months, and it wasn't as ferocious as he thought it would be. There was a social worker with a half-assed detox programme, but for Martin it was something you either wanted to do or you didn't. Live in shit long enough, maybe it gets so you don't notice the smell. That time in the Joy, what he saw was not just the world of shit he'd ended up living in but the fact that it was possible to go somewhere else. Frankie Crowe had plans, he had a road map, and if Martin Paxton wasn't at all certain where it was going, he knew what it was heading away from and that was what counted.

If Brendan was happy powdering his nose, fuck it, his business.

"Have you been in to check on herself?"

Brendan nodded. "Asked her if she was hungry. Sulky as ever. Wouldn't say a word."

"Wait'll she hears what's on the menu," Martin said. "Nothing like a good meal to cheer you up."

They went into the kitchen and Martin took the chicken out of the oven while Brendan filled the glasses with Ballygowan. Martin was checking the potatoes when Dolly came in from the front room and said, "Shit, lads, I'm sorry."

When Martin got to the front window and saw the two uniformed coppers getting out of the squad car he decided there was one last chance. Charm the fuckers. In their own minds, after all, the cops were most likely checking out the hallucinations of some local busybody. Give them a reason to believe.

Martin made a calming gesture to the other two and when the doorbell rang he took an oven glove in one hand and a dishcloth in the other and he went to open the door.

"Everything all right, guard?"

The younger cop stayed halfway down the front path, like he knew this was a nothing job. The other one had enough years behind him to know that most of what he'd do before retirement would involve going through the motions.

You could see it in their faces. Around here, the biggest deal is when someone throws a brick at a pub window and the local politicians kick up a row and Dublin OKs a shitload of overtime to deal with the crime wave. So, when there's stuff on the telly about a kidnap above in Dublin, naturally some old gobshite thought he taw a puttytat and the bluebottles have to put on their caps, straighten their ties and drag their arses down to check it out.

"Could you tell me how long you've been renting the house?"

"Just a couple of days. Myself and the lads, we're down from Dublin for a bit of a break. Is everything all right?"

"And how many of you would that be?"

"Four of us. We're bus drivers. Just down for a bit of drinking, few games of cards, check out the talent. Everything OK?"

First, the cops ask the questions they know the answers to. Once the busybody called in the report about a man in a mask, they must have done a check with the owner of the house.

Now, get to the point.

"Would it be OK if we had a look around?"

Martin waved a hand. "No bother, but is there something we should know?"

"Nothing to worry about."

Dolly Finn was sitting in the kitchen. He nodded when the garda came in. Brendan Sweetman stayed in the hallway, one eye on the younger garda, who didn't reckon it worth his while to come into the house.

The older cop poked his head through doorways, nodded, mooched on. When he spoke, there was no curiosity in his voice. "When'll you be leaving?" The body language said this was going to work out fine.

"Just a few days, soon as the booze money dries up. Listen, we haven't done anything wrong, have we?"

One last door. The cop tried the handle and found it locked.

Stay quiet, Angela. Not a peep.

"What's in there?"

Martin said, "That's the other fella, Liam, that's his room. Just a Dublin habit, I suppose, locking up when you go out. He went into Wexford earlier on, pick up a few things."

The sergeant nodded.

He knows.

Maybe something in Martin's tone or in his face. Maybe something about the way Brendan was hanging around the hall, looking like he was expecting a visit from the Holy Ghost. Whatever it was, the cop knew. No doubt about it. And he knew this was no time to be a hero. In his head he was measuring the distance to the front door. He said, "Well, that seems to be all right, lads. No problem, then."

He blushed.

He knows that we know that he knows.

The cop was moving towards the front door, his casual smile fixed now, his movements too deliberate. Then Dolly Finn was standing beside Brendan and raising his gun, pointing it at the sergeant. "We all know the score," he said quietly to the cop. "I'm sorry."

Martin said, "Don't—" and he saw Dolly's finger tighten on the trigger and he knew he was too far away to do anything. Brendan howled, "Fuck sake!" and pushed Dolly's arm away. The gun fired, the noise seemed to make the room shake. The smell of the gun's explosion swept through the air and Martin, having instinctively flinched from the shot, opened his eyes and turned towards the sergeant and there was no one there. Martin ran down the hall towards the open front door and he could see that the sergeant was halfway down the path, running in a crouch, as though he expected any second to take a bullet in the back of the head. The younger cop was almost at the road.

Brendan and Dolly came out of the house a step behind Martin. The sergeant was running past the squad car, screaming, "Leave it!"

The younger cop dropped the mike of the car radio and ran after the sergeant. They were forty feet away and only a few yards from the cover of the woods.

"Fuck it!"

Martin stopped. He turned to Brendan. "The cop car. Smash the radio, make sure the car can't move."

To Dolly: "Put the mask on her, get her into the boot, we're going."

"We should've done them. It was the only thing to do!"

"That's over with now, let's go."

"Why—" Dolly turned and called after Brendan. "Why the hell—"

Brendan jerked the cable of the radio mike out of the squad car's dashboard. "Killing two cops? You're not fucking serious, man. Jesus Christ." He brought his boot down on the mike and little bits of plastic scattered on the roadway.

"Move it!" Martin said. "It's done now, just grab what you can."

Brendan opened the bonnet of the garda car. The other two headed back towards the house.

"Prints?" Dolly said.

"No time," Martin said. "Torch the place."

The shooting in Rosslare was on the radio news bulletins within the hour. Brief and bare, just the news that two Wexford gardai had been fired on in an incident in a house at the holiday resort. "No further details are available." Frankie was approaching the Wexford roundabout on the N11 when he heard the news. He did a 180 around the roundabout and drove back towards Dublin.

Steering with one hand, he tapped Martin's number into his mobile. Nothing.

Could be they'd been caught. Could be Martin had left the mobile behind in whatever kind of scramble had gone on. An hour later, Frankie was stuck in the Gorey traffic jam when the next radio bulletin said that two Rosslare gardai were recovering from their ordeal at the hands of an armed gang. Garda sources believed the incident was connected to the kidnap of Dublin woman Angela Kennedy.

There was more of that kind of thing, none of which told Frankie anything he needed to hear.

Could be since then the cops caught up with Martin and the others. Could be the cops knew everything. Could be they knew nothing. Could be any fucking thing.

Frankie kept the radio on. When the next news bulletin came the opening words were exactly the same as they'd been an hour ago. "Two Wexford gardai are recovering—"

Frankie tried Martin's phone again. Nothing.

He needed to leave the money somewhere safe, somewhere he wouldn't have to babysit the two holdalls. Uncle Cormac's wasn't safe, cheesy bastard could come back early. Joan would never take it. He tried to think of who he could trust to hold on to two fat holdalls without getting nosy.

Frankie hadn't intended ever again coming near Harte's Cross after the fuck-up over the pub job two months ago. Now, he was driving a stolen Volvo down the main street of the small town with a million in two holdalls in the back of the car. He glanced at the pub as he passed.

Two miles beyond Harte's Cross, he turned off the main road and drove up a narrow track for a mile or more before he came to a farmhouse, with a shed to one side and a dilapidated tractor to the other. Leo Titley's home was a plain, grey, squat building, without adornment. Rectangular, with a shallow pitched roof, two bedrooms and a combined living room and kitchen. The house hadn't been painted in a couple of decades and the wooden window frames were cracked and the glass cloudy. When there was no answer to his knock, Frankie went round the back and broke in. He got the money from the car and five minutes later he was panting slightly, having hidden the heavy holdalls in the attic.

The kitchen smelled of cheap curry, and the unwashed plates on the counter had the hardened remnants of what might have been today's lunch or last night's dinner. The windows were too small, the rooms too dark. The furniture in the living room was sparse and ill-matched. Frankie was used to a small flat, but this kind of place would drive you mental after a fortnight.

When Leo got back from wherever he was, Frankie said, "You'd better fix your back door, OK?"

Leo was tall and stringy, wearing overalls and boots. His long hair was tied back in a ponytail. In his early thirties, he had the drained appearance of a man fighting a battle he no longer believed in.

"What's going on, Frankie?"

"You gave us bum information. But I treated you fair, even though the pub job was a fuck-up. Now, I'm in a bit of a fix and I need a place to leave some stuff. That OK with you?"

"What's going on, Frankie?"

Leo's life was being eaten away by the effort to make a living from a miserable few acres of land. When his father died, Leo had quit the haulage business and gone back to donate his stubborn loyalty to his father's hopeless legacy. It paid so little he spent most of his time labouring on other people's farms and doing odd jobs in Hartc's Cross. The sensible thing would be to sell the land, but economic logic is no match for pride.

As a truck driver, Leo had had a fringe role in several criminal projects, one of them involving Frankie Crowe, which led him to offer Frankie a tip about the vulnerable pub where takings from the bar and the concert gig accumulated.

"You owe me, is all," Frankie said, "and I need a place. No big deal. You come and go, I come and go. You say nothing to no one, we're square."

Leo stood there, silent, hands in his pockets.

Frankie said, "You know I pay my way, right?"

Leo thought for a few moments, then he said, "You want a drink or something?"

"I think you'd better fix that back door, and give me a spare key, so I don't have to break it again."

"You staying now?"

"I need to eat. Anywhere around here?"

Leo said he'd drive him to the Olive Grove, in Harte's Cross. "It's not the worst."

Getting into the pickup, Frankie said, "Not one word to no one, OK? You and me know I'm here. No one else. And stay out of the attic."

Leo looked at him for a moment, then he said, "Fair enough."

Three times on the way into town, and twice during his meal, Frankie tried Martin's mobile. Still nothing.

After the meal, in the pickup on the way back to Leo's place, Frankie switched on the radio.

"Two Wexford gardai—"

He was still listening to the bulletin when his mobile rang.

When he heard Martin's voice he said, "What the fuck is going on?"

Through the late afternoon and into the evening Martin Paxton, Dolly Finn and Brendan Sweetman stuck to narrow, twisting Wicklow roads, through mountains that resisted mobile-phone signals. Every bend in the road was a test of nerve. This wasn't car-chase country. If they stumbled across the cops around here, the jig was up. Twice they moved off the road, into woods, to take a break from the tension they all felt, and to let the hostage out of the boot for air.

Brendan drove, Martin stared at the screen of his mobile. Mostly it said No signal. Every now and then the signal bars would pop up, but would disappear before he could connect with Frankie. Finally, while they were taking a break, he got a strong enough signal. The conversation was short, and afterwards Martin could remember little of it. Mostly he remembered tough choices.

"Just bad luck," he told Frankie. "Tell you later."

Frankie said, "We might have to make some tough choices. You know what I'm talking about?"

Martin knew. He said, "Let's talk when we—"

"Where? No names."

"Can't stay in the open, can't just walk in somewhere."

"Where?"

"We're heading for—the guy who got us the butcher shop—his place, his home."

"When will you make it?"

"Another couple of hours. This is slow, the way we're doing it."

"See you there." And that was it.

Tough choices.

She knows my name. She may know Frankie's name.

The woman had not reacted when Martin let Frankie's name slip. Maybe she hadn't taken it in. Maybe, maybe not.

But she certainly knows my name.

Tough choices.

It was shortly after midnight.

One of Chief Superintendent Hogg's whizz-kids was addressing the emergency garda conference by speakerphone, explaining why the Wexford gardai sent two unarmed uniforms to check out a possible sighting of a kidnap gang. He was followed by another, reporting in more detail than was necessary on the failure to trace the identity of whoever rented the Rosslare bungalow for the gang.

"Technical through with the house?" Hogg said.

"Just about. The gang tried to torch the place, but it didn't take. Pucks of prints. Holiday home, there's bound to be. Most likely civilians, most of them. They're processing things as fast as they can."

The emergency conference at Carbury Street garda station was called as soon as Chief Superintendent Hogg found out about the gang managing to get hold of the first million of ransom money. Before the meeting could get under way, news came in of the Rosslare shambles and that put everything on hold. When the rescheduled conference began close to midnight, three of Hogg's men were in Wexford, a couple were following up the ransom screw-up. Four were accompanying ERU teams raiding the homes of the known gang members. The rest were in the incident room at Carbury Street, looking less gung-ho than the last time John Grace saw them.

Hogg maintained his air of calm, methodically taking his team through possible leads and areas of inquiry. Everyone in the room knew that the case could hinge on the next interview, the next phone call, the next bright idea. Everyone in the room knew that the case could as suddenly fall apart, a civilian might right now be finding a body in a ditch.

It was an image that John Grace found more plausible as this went on. Now that Frankie had a million, and he still didn't know he'd been fingered for the job, the option of taking his winnings and quietly killing the hostage must look more attractive.

Once the media blackout ended, I should have pushed Hogg on going public with the ID of Frankie and Sweetman.

A whizz-kid told Hogg why he'd concluded that the kidnappers' code word "sunflower" didn't have any significance. He kept running the fingers of one hand back through his hair as he explained how he wasted half an afternoon running the word through garda databases, looking for nicknames, companies or shops in Dublin that had any reference to flowers in their names, and running a check on the ownership of all florists within a mile of the Kennedy home.

When the reports were finished, Grace took Hogg aside. "Sir, I really think it's more important than ever to let Frankie know that we're—"

"I know, and it's happening. Frankie may already be getting word that the ERU are kicking in doors, but apart from that we'll be using the media."

Hogg shook his head, as though Grace had brought up ancient history. He continued. "Once Technical are through with the house in Rosslare they'll pass on anything that might be of use—a notebook, bits and pieces found on bedside lockers, stuff like that, even newspapers lying around. Same with anything we find in the raids on their homes. I want you in here first thing—it'll only take an hour or two—go over everything, every page, every scrap of paper—a name, an address, a phone number, anything that rings a bell."

At the top of the room, Assistant Commissioner O'Keefe drew everyone's attention by rapping his knuckles on the table. "Just to bring you all up to speed. As a result of recent events, Chief Superintendent Hogg and I have concluded there's a danger the gang might cut and run. Bury the victim somewhere, settle for the money they've got. It's important, therefore, that they realise we've identified some of them."

He nodded to Hogg, who told them he'd personally been on to TV and radio stations and the names would be going out at the top of every news bulletin that evening and into the night. "Snaps of Crowe and Sweetman are on their way to the newspapers, they'll be on every front page in the morning."

Grace found a chair and sat down, glancing at his watch. Bit late in the day, he thought. In more ways than one.

Keep your head, Frankie, stay cool. Let the woman be. Take the money and run.

Grace woke Nicky Bonner when he rang him at home.

"I'm heading off home now, but I've to be back at Carbury Street first thing in the morning. Hogg wants me to sniff through some stuff Frankie left behind. Can't promise anything, but—if you're still raring to go—maybe that hour of the morning you can poke your nose in."

"Terrific."

"All you have to do is be at my place first thing, give me a lift to Carbury Street."

"Lazy sod."

22

All Angela could see was a vertical line of light, no thicker than a hair. All else was darkness. She could hear in the distance, perhaps from a couple of rooms away, the muffled sound of a fierce argument. Twice since she was brought here she'd been out of this tiny closet under the stairs, to use the toilet. The night had passed and an hour or two of the morning. She had no idea where she was—what house, what neighbourhood, even what county.

The journey from Wexford had taken hours, travelling on twisting roads that had her sliding around inside the boot of the car. They'd stopped twice and she was allowed to stand in the woods, the mask over her eyes. The day had been hot, the car boot had left her sweaty, tired and sore. The air was cool in the woods, but it did little to penetrate the layers of grubbiness in which she felt encased. Standing in the woods, unable to see, brought back the terror of that first time, on the way down to Wexford, but it was a muted terror. It was as though the envelope of exhaustion that surrounded her was so thick that not even fear could get through. During one of the breaks, one of the gunmen opened a packet of salt and vinegar crisps and put it into her hand. While eating, she was allowed to push the mask up as far as her nose. She ate until there was nothing left, her index finger probing the bottom of the bag for crumbs. She licked the salt from her fingers.

Last night, when they'd arrived at this house, she'd been taken to the closet under the stairs and shut in. She'd heard a chair being pushed against the outside of the small door, jammed under the knob. Nothing but darkness and the vertical hairline of light. Jesus, what's her name, the Rockefeller girl, no—Hearst, Patty Hearst. One evening a couple of months back, Angela and Justin had watched a movie on television, the woman was kidnapped, kept in a little space like this. Movie wasn't up to much, so they'd switched off halfway through and gone to bed. Me and Patty. Living under the stairs. Then, remembering something from bedtime reading with Luke—Me and Patty and Harry fucking Potter. She made a small giggling noise.

Every now and then, someone walked past the closet, perhaps on their way to the kitchen. Whenever anyone went upstairs or came down, the sound of their footsteps hammered on the stairs just above her head. Such diversions were few, and as the hours passed Angela sank deeper into a dull timeless haze.

The closet was too small to stand up in. The cramped darkness made her all the more aware of her body. She could smell the dirt and sweat that encrusted her. She had taken the trainers off to find her bare feet chafed. This morning she got the first twinge that told her that her period was on the way.

Her night had been restless, consciousness coming and going, with her mind never entirely certain of the border between sleep and reality. The floor was tiled, hard and cold, she had only her bent arm for a pillow. Out of her tiredness, like a shape emerging through fog, a new fear began to make itself known. The panic in Wexford had disrupted the gang's plans. The pressure to cut and run must be greater than ever. No one said anything to her, but as she was taken in her mask to the toilet, she could tell by their voices that they were nervous and uncertain. When she was brought to and from the toilet, the hands that pulled her out from the closet and later pushed her back in were rough and impatient.

Now, elsewhere in the house, some kind of argument was

going on. The voices rose and fell and then there was an extended silence, as though a wave of anger had left everyone speechless. Angela sat with her back against the wall, her legs bent, her arms hugging her knees to her chest. She didn't have the tears to cry.

After a while, there was another session of raised voices, as though the gang had allowed the silent anger to accumulate to the point where it had to erupt. Angela had been staring at the line of light at the edge of the door. Idly, tentatively, she raised one hand until her fingertips were touching the door. The pressure she applied was so slight that she didn't feel the door move, but she saw the line of light thicken. One second a hairline, the next the hairline widening, the door moving away from her fingertips. Then the door was a full inch ajar, no chair to stop it opening.

In the living room, there were newspapers all over the place. The *Irish Independent* headline said, HAVE YOU SEEN THESE MEN? There were photographs of Frankie and Brendan. There was no photograph of Martin Paxton, but he was named. The *Irish Times* headline said, POLICE NAME KIDNAP SUSPECTS. The *Star* ran the pictures with the headline, THE BASTARDS WHO TOOK ANGELA.

Milky's panic when the gang turned up at his home the previous night had turned to rage and then a resolve to get Frankie and his wankers the fuck out of here.

"No," he told Frankie when he answered the bell and saw who was on his doorstep.

"The lads are on their way."

"No, absolutely not—fuck off, Frankie."

"Let's talk about this inside," Frankie said, and once he got in there was no getting him out.

"Where to?" he kept asking. "Where do you want us to go?" The rest of the gang arrived almost an hour later.

In this part of Killester, the houses were mostly bungalows, with high hedges in between. Milky's was a two-storey mock Tudor. Most of the streets were short and narrow, this one was wider and ran for a couple of hundred yards. There weren't more than half a dozen people on the whole street that Milky would recognise if he met them. It was one of those places where there was no higher praise than that you kept yourself to yourself. Milky's girlfriend, a twenty-five-year-old blonde model, threw a wobbler and Milky sent her to stay with his brother in Howth. There was hardly a waking moment since then that he didn't have a lighted cigarette in his hand. Frankie was amused to notice that Milky wore a check jacket even inside his house.

Milky's urgent task was to find a suitable rental somewhere to which he could shift Frankie and the rest of them. He'd begun making phone calls from first thing this morning, getting nowhere. It was the need for putting buffers between himself and the rental house that made everything more difficult. He needed someone to arrange for someone else to hire someone else to rent a suitable place from someone who didn't ask questions. A holiday resort would be difficult, now that the Rosslare balls-up was in the papers and everyone with a holiday home to rent was on alert. Best chance was another commercial site, something like the butcher's shop he'd used for the first couple of days.

Eventually, there was a possible, verging on a probable.

"Tallaght," the contact said.

"Fine."

"It's an old—"

"Whatever," Milky said. Some people couldn't help chattering on the phone.

"I'll know tonight," the contact said.

"This afternoon," Milky said. Get the place confirmed by this afternoon, shift them out by tonight.

"It'll be tonight. Late."

"Fuck it. Do your best."

Everyone was on edge. Several times that morning, casual comments were taken to be more than they were and arguments erupted. Milky said, "Line in the sand, Frankie. First thing in the morning—and I mean first thing—you're all out of here. If I have a rental, well and good. If not, fuck it, you're out. This is out of order, coming to my home."

"We'll need two cars."

Milky looked at the ceiling for a moment, then he said, "OK."

Frankie said, "It's over."

He was sitting at the head of the rectangular pine table in the kitchen. Around the table, Martin Paxton, Milky, Brendan Sweetman and Dolly Finn paid different degrees of attention. Milky looked like he was hanging on Frankie's every word. Dolly Finn's left elbow was on the table, his head bent, resting on his hand, his fingers stroking his forehead as though to soothe something wild inside. Martin Paxton was listening to Frankie, but watching Dolly.

Frankie said, "We've got the million—that's all we're going to get. Tough and fast, we said, and it's already been nearly a week. Take the money and run."

Not me.

Milky stared at Frankie.

Soon's they go, I wipe every inch of this place. I'm clear.

He'd had some money from Frankie up front, the rest he'd take when and if. The important thing was to get free and clear of this fuck-up.

Martin Paxton said, "What about her?"

"Take her with you," Milky said.

"Far as I know, she hasn't seen anything, right?" Brendan Sweetman said.

Frankie said, "What I think is, things stay as they are, it's best we just find somewhere that isn't used, an old shop, garage, something like that, leave her there. When we're well away, we let them know where to find her." He looked around the table, saw a couple of nods. No one said otherwise.

Frankie said, "I'll go get the money in the morning—where it is, it's a couple of hours down and back. When you know about Milky's new rental, you call me, I meet you there maybe at noon tomorrow, split the money, that's it. We leave the hostage somewhere, take the money and run."

Brendan Sweetman was staring at Frankie like he was trying to read his mind.

Take the money and run. The fuck that mean? Who takes the money? Who runs where? Couple of hours down and back, means outside Dublin—where?—and once Frankie's on the road . . .

"I think one of us should go with you. No offence, Frankie, we have to be sensible. I mean, none of us even knows where you're keeping the money."

Frankie didn't say anything for a few seconds, then he said, "No offence?" He looked at the other three. "Anyone else think I'm doing a runner?"

"That's not what I said, Frankie."

"Anyone else?"

Dolly said, "Fuck this." He got up and left the room. They heard him hurrying up the stairs and then a door slammed.

Brendan's face remained blank.

Shit.

If anyone was going to back him on this it was Dolly.

Martin and Frankie are joined at the hip. Milky doesn't care, long as we're out of here.

Brendan said, "Frankie, you know we all trust you. I was just saying. That's all."

"Saying?"

"I mean, if something happened to you—"

Martin Paxton was looking across the room, past Frankie. Through the open doorway he could see down the hall, past the closet where the hostage was kept. The door of the closet was half open, the hostage was casually, slowly, walking towards the front door. Frankie was telling Brendan that it was important that everyone keep their cool and this whole thing could still work out OK. Martin looked at Frankie. Then he looked at the hostage.

When the door of the closet opened an inch, Angela just sat there for several minutes. Her first instinct was to hook a finger around the edge of the door, pull it closed again. She found words for the weight of fear that paralysed her.

Leave well enough alone.

Leaving well enough alone at least wouldn't make things worse. It meant she would stay in this predictable hellhole until somebody did something and it all worked out one way or the other. Making a move might end this horror sooner but it also opened her up to the anger of the gunmen, and wherever that would lead.

The devil you know.

She had a choice, and she didn't want a choice.

Stay in here, her mind dulled by boredom and fear, her body soiled, her world reduced to a dark, stuffy closet, where she waited for an unknown outcome. Or make a break for it, end the tension, reclaim her life. That required going out there, where there were violent men, strength and hostility, anger beyond her experience and the petrifying risk of an immediate and brutal end.

A raised voice. "Fuck this," then she heard someone walk quickly past the closet, then the pounding sound of footsteps on the stairs above her head and the slamming of a door upstairs.

After a while, one hand steadying herself against the wall of the closet, Angela got to her feet, crouched, her head bent forward. She pushed at the door, it opened silently and she shuffled through the doorway until she could stand up.

She was in some kind of short passageway, all light blues and greens. To her left, the kitchen, the sound of the gang talking. She forced herself not to look that way. Instinct told her that if she didn't see them they wouldn't see her, and she knew that didn't make sense but she believed it completely.

To her right, the corridor led past an open door and then widened into a large hall, at the end of which was the solid dark wood of what had to be the front door of the house. She turned her back to the kitchen and overcame the immediate urge to run. She walked towards the hall, fighting to keep her step steady, to walk as casually as if she was going out to buy a newspaper. The plain blue carpet was cool on her bare feet. The material of her tracksuit pants was stuck to the insides of her thighs.

There was a large brass lock on the front door, some kind of latch. She had the door wide open, the sun blazing into her eyes, when she heard movement behind her and she didn't grasp the words that were spoken but she knew it was the voice of the gang boss.

What Frankie said was, "Close the door, now."

He tried to keep his voice calm. "Just close it and nothing will happen."

Angela took another pace, out on to the front step. Frankie raised his large black automatic and pointed it at her back.

Milky screamed, "Not here!" and Martin Paxton shouted, "No!"

Angela turned round. She raised one hand and touched the side of her face. The hand was trembling, there was sweat on her cheek. She put the hand out, palm towards Frankie, like a little shield.

Frankie said, "Come in, close the door."

Angela didn't say anything. She just shook her head. Frankie said, "That's how you want it." He looked along the top of the automatic, aiming at her forehead and Martin grabbed his arm and said, "No."

Frankie shook his arm free. "She's seen our faces, all of us."

Angela took a step backwards.

"So what? Our names are all over the papers. Rosslare, the cops saw our faces."

"Not mine, not Milky's. Besides, there's a difference."

The Rosslare cops, and maybe fingerprints, that was probably enough to put them away, but a victim standing up in a courtroom and pointing a finger and saying, "That's him," that closed down any loopholes.

"It's all over," Martin said. "None of this matters. We've got the money, we can divvy tomorrow, next week, whenever. Drop her somewhere, forget the rental, forget everything, let's just fucking go!"

Brendan said, "No, she's seen our faces. It matters."

Martin said, "Kidnapping's one thing. Be fucking sensible."

Frankie said, "Bollocks."

Dolly appeared halfway down the stairs. He seemed distanced from the scene before him, like he was watching a mildly interesting television programme.

Martin turned away and hurried back into the kitchen.

Maybe fifty feet away, there were two women in their twenties, stride-walking past on the other side of the road. They were in Nike tops and shorts, one was wearing a pink headband. Their arms stiff and swinging, they were walking fast, shedding calories with every stride. Had they glanced to the right they would have seen Angela at the front door, facing back into the house, one hand held out in front of her, and Frankie beyond her, pointing his gun at her face. Chatting, the two women walked on, out of sight behind the hedge.

Frankie made a gesture with the gun. "Come back in," he said.

Angela said, "Please."

Milky said, "Please, not here." He ran forward and awkwardly threw an arm around Angela and pulled her towards the hall. She grabbed the edge of the doorway, one knee braced against the architrave, and Milky punched her fingers and kicked at her legs. He clawed at her and she cried out. Brendan took a handful of her hair and pulled and she screamed and lost her balance and fell on her back on the thick blue carpet. Milky closed the front door.

Frankie stood over the hostage and pointed the gun at her face.

"I said no!" Martin was back from the kitchen, holding his gun down by his side. "Come on, let's take a minute, calm down."

Frankie looked at Martin and made a dismissive noise.

Martin shook his head. "I mean it. No killing."

"We're in a situation. You know that."

Angela's voice was high and wavering. "Please, Martin, don't let him kill me."

"Martin?"

Frankie's voice had an hysterical edge. "Martin?"

Martin said, "Look, let's just—"

"Fucking Martin, right? You told her your name? Holding hands, is that it? She's pulling your chain, mate." He was moving slowly around the hostage, the gun pointing down at her face. "Is that all she's been pulling?"

When Angela stood on the front step and turned round and the gang leader pointed his gun at her forehead, she looked into his face and saw her death. If she did as he wanted and came back inside he would take her somewhere in the house and kill her. If she stayed where she was, he would kill her.

From that moment, something inside her hunched over, braced for the killing blow. All thought was swept away by the rush of dread. She felt hardly any pain in the struggle to stop them pulling her back into the house. Each second was the last second before the end. She tried when she could to hold up one hand or the other, to position it between her face and where she thought the gang leader's gun was.

And when she was lying on the floor and the gun swung down and pointed at her head, a physical weakness swept through her and she felt her bladder empty.

"I said, no!"

She didn't take in what the two gunmen were saying as they argued about her life. She said something, a plea, and she wasn't sure if she said it aloud. Their voices became harsh.

Finally, Martin reached down and grabbed her by one arm and half dragged her back towards the closet, the gang leader still pointing his gun at her head.

Someone said, "Ah, Jesus, look at the fucking carpet!"

Martin pushed her roughly into the closet.

"Please—"

"Shut the fuck up."

"You have to get me out of here, he's—"

The gunman, his expression bitter and angry, slammed the door of the closet. She heard the sound of the chair being propped under the knob.

Afterwards, there was little talk about what happened. Martin and Frankie played it cool, let it all simmer down. That moment Martin walked back out into the hall, carrying the gun down by his side, careful not to point it at Frankie—that would always be between them. You could tell that from the politeness of the few words they exchanged afterwards. Anger would have been open to negotiation. Martin could have explained how just for that moment he wasn't sure where he stood with Frankie and he knew he needed to get his gun before he said anything else, and maybe that was the wrong thing to do but it was how it felt when the heat flared up.

"Killing her didn't make sense. You know that. It would have put us deeper into the shit."

Frankie said nothing, just shrugged. Martin nodded. The shrugs and nods and the short, polite sentences that followed emphasised the strain between them.

Later, one of Milky's people arrived with two sets of car keys. "They're parked down the seafront," Milky told Frankie. "Red Mégane, white Ford Transit."

Frankie gave the keys of the van to Martin, who was lying down upstairs. "For the morning. I'll take the Mégane, you'll need the van for the hostage."

For a moment, it seemed like Frankie was about to add something, then he nodded and went back downstairs. It was like they both realised there was nothing to be said about the craziness that wouldn't make things worse.

Around six o'clock, Martin came down wearing his jacket and said, "I told Debbie I'd be in touch today." Frankie nodded, Martin stopped like he had something important to say, then he said just, "OK," and he left.

It took twenty minutes of texting Deborah, watching her from a distance, directing her in and out of stores at the Omni Centre in Santry, before Martin Paxton was sure she wasn't being followed. He joined her in O'Brien's sandwich shop and there was an undertone of pleading in his voice. After he'd spoken for maybe five minutes she said, "No."

"Deb, think about it, please. It's the only way."

She said, "I have a family. I have a job. I can't just drop everything here and go off and maybe never see them again."

The tone of what he said changed, he spoke now of how he was entitled.

"It's my kid too."

"And he's going to be born in his own country."

"Deb—"

"There's no way I can learn another language."

"Sí, sí, señorita, mucho dinero."

She didn't return his smile.

"Come on," he said, "you'll pick up all you need in no time. This time tomorrow, I'll have my share, we build a whole new life."

She said nothing for a while. Then, staring at the table in front of her, she said, "You know it's what I want, the three of us together, but—it's no life, Martin. It's no life."

The honesty of her sadness was unmistakable and Martin realised he'd never loved her more.

After a while she said, "What are you going to do with that poor woman?"

"She'll be all right."

"What are you going to do with her?"

"What about the baby? I mean it. I have rights. I have to be able to at least see him."

She shook her head. "I don't know how we'll manage that, love. There's years ahead. Jesus, Martin, how do we arrange it? Where? How often? This is a lifetime thing."

"The cops, they get lazy—I know people who come into the country and go out again when they want. People come back. Slip in, find somewhere, settle right back in. Different names and stuff, you know. We can do it."

She closed her eyes for a few seconds and bowed her head and when she opened her eyes the pain he saw was answer enough.

He said nothing for a while. He took a sip from the still-full mug of coffee. It was lukewarm. Then he said, "Christ, what a fuck-up."

23

Milky was pacing his living room. "Bastard!" He said the word again and again. Brendan Sweetman was standing by the marble fireplace, his right hand making agitated patterns on his bristled hair.

"I told him," Milky said. "I fucking said it, again and again. Not here, I said, not here!"

Dolly Finn was upstairs in a small bedroom at the back of the house, sitting on the floor by the window, his back against the wall, his knees up and his hands cupped over his eyes.

From downstairs, from the kitchen, the noises had been coming for almost twenty minutes. They started maybe half an hour after Martin left. First, the sounds of struggle, then a scream, then a series of harsh, strained cries, then another scream. For some time, there were no abrupt sounds, no sounds of struggle, just a repetitive moan.

From the moment he learned that the police knew the names of some of those involved in the kidnap, Dolly Finn felt physically weak. It was only a matter of time before they fingered him. It was like some sinews in his arms and legs had slackened and couldn't properly function. Even the most routine thoughts had to push their way around the solid block of dread that settled inside his mind. Although capture or worse was possible in any such project, the sudden reality of being separated permanently from his home and his shop and the whole of the small, satisfying life he had constructed was paralysing. The police hadn't put his name on the radio or his picture in the papers, but there were too many who knew he was involved, and no one was going home from this.

England, he had a friend there, in Nottingham, friend enough to show him the basics. But even if that worked, he would never recover even a shadow of what he was losing. It wasn't the money that mattered, it was the shop and its merchandise and its customers and the role it gave Dolly in the culture that began with the instruments of faraway musicians, mostly dead now, and spread around the world through a network of people with the ears to appreciate the music. The shop and the flat and the routine they supported were Dolly Finn's life, and they were gone.

From downstairs, the endless Huh! Huh! Huh! Huh! of the hostage.

"No, wait," was all Dolly said to Frankie when it started. "Just wait."

Doing this didn't make sense. There was an argument for disposing of the hostage, if it meant saving all of them from disaster. You could weigh such drastic action against all the harm they might suffer if she was a witness, and that would be a reasonable decision. That was business. Not this.

This didn't make sense.

What this did was take them down beyond ruin, to night mare.

"Wait!" he said, his mind scrambling to find the words.

And Frankie said, "Fuck off," and Dolly stood there for a moment, then he left the kitchen and passed Brendan and Milky, standing in the hall, both of them looking sick. That was when Dolly came upstairs.

The Huh! Huh! Huh! Huh! of the hostage continued. Dolly Finn realised there were tears on his cheeks.

* * *

She knew, just from the way he stood when he pulled her out of the closet, what was about to happen. Standing there, the mask over his head, breathing hard, poised, almost inviting her to try to get away. Knowing it was hopeless, she tried to run and as she did she heard him grunt with satisfaction. He caught her in the kitchen, knocked her feet from under her, her thigh raked by the corner of a table, her back slamming against the tile floor.

Somewhere behind her, one of the others said something. The gang leader said, "Fuck off."

Slapping her face, pulling at her clothes, his knee pushing down the tracksuit bottom.

She cried out.

The punch in the face sent darkness rushing through her head, flecks of coloured light arcing and dying.

Then it was like she was waking suddenly, lying on the floor—seconds later, minutes, if she'd been unconscious at all—a rhythm coursing through her body, his weight on her, his panting, his rutting, her body rocking, the hard floor painful against her shoulder blades.

Jesus, Jesus, Jesus.

The kidnapper's eyes stared down from the holes in the mask. It didn't matter that she couldn't see the rest of the face—the eyes alone were enflamed with hatred. She felt liquid trickle along the side of her nose and down her cheek. He was making noises, in time with his thrusting, she cried out, he told her to shut the fuck up. He thrust violently, she screamed and that was when he punched her a second time and she felt something move inside her face. She didn't lose consciousness this time and after a while she became aware of her non-stop panting, Huh! Huh! Huh! Huh!

He had one hand pressed to the floor for balance. Her eyes glimpsed a familiar image. Inches from her face, the Rolex she'd bought for Justin's birthday said that it was just after seven.

She heard him whisper, Bitch!

Now he had one hand on her left breast, gripping hard, twisting. The other hand came up and his forearm pressed against her throat. The arm forced her chin up, her head back. The forearm pressed and relaxed in time with his thrusts. It was a crushing pressure. Her breath came in irregular gulps.

Knowing it would make no difference, she strained to plead with him not to kill her, but her mouth wouldn't make the sounds she needed. Blinking, sweat seeping into her eyes, she struggled to grasp the words, to put them in order. Half-constructed sentences broke inside her head and the words came out as a series of gasping noises.

From him, the panting had dissolved into just one word now, a pulsing hiss that kept time with his rutting.

Yes! Yes! Yes! Yes!

He hit her again, this time a clumsy glancing blow to the side of her head. He screamed, "Say it!"

Through the roaring of the blood coursing through her faltering brain she understood, and her mind scrambled to grasp the word and her throat forced it out through her quivering lips, more of a moan than a word.

"Yes—"

Within seconds, he bellowed and it all stopped and he was standing up, fixing his clothes. He bent over, grabbed her by the hair and by one arm, pulled her up and dragged her out of the kitchen. She wanted to plead but all that came out were wordless noises. He pushed her into the hall, pressed her head down and flung her backwards into the closet. Her back hit the wall, the top of her head collided with the underside of the stairs and she collapsed on to the floor. The door of the closet banged shut. In darkness, she heard the chair being slammed into place under the doorknob.

She realised she was making hissing sounds. She lay still, her wet cheek touching the cold floor.

* * *

Martin told the taxi driver to stop. It was a couple of roads past Milky's place and he walked back through the quiet neighbourhood. Way back when, this was the kind of area he and Frankie and their mates might canvass for opportunities. Maybe a fanciable car in a driveway, or a pitch-dark house that might be worth a visit through an upstairs window. Back then, you got to pick and choose. These days, they all had burglar alarms and reinforced windows.

Passing a gateway, he saw two people talking on a doorstep. At another house an open window let out a belch of canned TV laughter. Around the corner, a car passed and turned into a driveway. He looked at his watch—half nine.

A couple of years back, Martin and Deborah had been to view a house for sale on this road. Just for the crack. Even though the banks were shovelling money at borrowers, stoking house prices, there was no way a librarian and someone on the lower rungs of the thieving business could raise the kind of scratch it took to buy a place around here. Not that that mattered any more.

Before they left the Omni, when the conversation with Deborah had become no more than a muttered sentence every few minutes, Martin had given up trying to convince her. By now, his own belief in what he was saying had evaporated. When they parted, he held her close and they meant the things they said about the future, and they knew that nothing they said or meant mattered very much. Then they got into separate taxis and Deborah went home and Martin went back to Milky's house.

When he got there, he stood in the hall, his face pale, the fingers of one hand pinching his mouth, as Milky explained what had happened.

"Is she OK?"

"I had a look," Brendan Sweetman said. "She's a bit of a mess, but she's alive."

"Jesus, could none of you do nothing?"

"You know yourself," Brendan said, "I mean, when Frankie's like that. Christ, it's not like I know her or anything. I mean, interfering with something like that, when there's guns around—"

"Where's Frankie gone?"

"Just gone."

"And we're supposed to hang around here, cleaning up after him?"

"He's going to pick up the money, the place he hid it," Brendan said. "Soon as Milky knows the address of the new place, the rental, we ring Frankie, he meets us there lunchtime tomorrow, split the money, turn her loose."

Martin shook his head.

When Martin opened the door of the closet, the hostage leaned back from the light that spilled in. Martin hunkered down and said, "It's OK. Look, I heard what happened." He moved nearer and she made a shrill noise.

"I wasn't here. I didn't know. I knew nothing."

Silence.

"Look, let me help, please?"

Her voice was a whisper. "Go away." She moved her head into the light and Martin saw the bruised eyes, swollen cheeks, the eye on the right closed, a trickle of blood on her cheek. She was holding a piece of blood-smeared cloth to the left side of her face. It was hard to tell where the blood ended and the bruises began.

"Jesus, Angela, I'm sorry."

The whisper again. "Fuck off."

Frankie Crowe had a whole night to kill before heading off in the morning to pick up the money from Leo Titley's place.

He wanted to say goodbye to Joan and Sinead, but not tonight. Sinead would be in bed, Joan wouldn't want her disturbed. Anyway, there'd be cops watching the house from every angle, best to contact Joan away from there. Most of all, he didn't want to spend the night in Milky's house, with all the bullshit he could expect once Martin got back. After he'd told the others he was going to get the money, and he'd given them a mobile number to ring and told them how he'd meet them next day at the new rental, Frankie went down to the seafront and found the red Mégane.

He drove around for a long time, then he parked in a lane behind a string of shops in Santry, and settled down in the back seat. On one side of the lane were the backyards of the shops, on the other the backyards of houses. The walls were easels for the local graffiti artists, the ground looked like everyone in the neighbourhood who had a bottle to smash had brought it here. The only legitimate use the lane got was during the daytime, when deliveries were made to the shops. There were three security lights overlooking the lane and the one in the middle was broken, so Frankie parked directly beneath it. In the morning, he'd go see Joan and Sinead. Then, drive down to Leo's place outside Harte's Cross, collect the money from the attic.

He checked his watch and realised he must have dozed off for at least an hour. It was after eleven. He rolled down the window an inch or two and filled his lungs with fresh, cold air. He took out the imitation leather wallet Sinead had given him and found a scrap of paper. He tapped out a Belfast number on his mobile.

"It's me. That work out?"

"You're booked in, you'll pass as crew."

"You sure?"

"Ring me as soon as you get here. Wouldn't get a better service from a travel agent."

"Thanks. You're a lifesaver."

"Bring cash."

Frankie stretched across the back seat, used an arm to cradle his head, pulled his leather jacket around him and within minutes he drifted off again. He woke suddenly and thought at first he was in trouble. The car was rocking, there was a repetitive banging noise. Through the misted glass he could see a girl lying on her back on the bonnet, her long dark hair touching the windscreen. Frankie stared in disbelief. Above the girl, a teenager with a tight haircut, his chin up, his eyes shut tight, was pounding away between her thighs.

Frankie held his watch close to his face. It was after one in the morning.

Some fucking people.

He watched. It was like there was no end to it. The rhythm didn't speed up or slow down, it just kept going. Frankie slowly reached between the front seats, stretching until he could touch the key in the ignition.

Seconds later, the two were halfway down the lane, all jerky movements and little yelps, attempting to pull their clothing into some kind of order. It took a while before Frankie stopped laughing. Feeling the need, he got out of the car and pissed up against a wall.

Back in the car, he was wide awake. Not a good day, he told himself. Don't sweat it. Tomorrow, leave all this behind.

Well over an hour later Frankie was still awake. He turned on the radio, found a music station and curled up on the back seat. Things start out to go a certain way, people make moves, things go in another direction, and before you can straighten them out you're somewhere you never thought you'd be. Fuck them. All of them. Martin and the bitch. Dolly, Brendan and Milky, the whole fucking lot of them. Tomorrow, go see Joan, pick up the money from Leo's place, make tracks. Larne to Troon on the boat, take a couple of days moving down through

Britland to Dover, and then he had a whole continent to get lost in. Fuck them, each and every one.

Martin most of all. "Tell me the truth, Frankie, is this what you had in mind?"

Martin would never believe him. Things start out to go a certain way, then they go in another direction.

It's as simple as that, Frankie told himself.

Some moron DJ started cranking on about some stupid phone-in competition. Frankie climbed over into the front seat and switched off the radio. When he woke several hours later, he was still lying crumpled in the front seat, cold and aching.

24

As they got out of Nicky Bonner's car in the car park of Carbury Street garda station, John Grace said, "Anyone asks, you're here because you gave me a lift. After that you're on your own. Hogg himself comes along, he'll have you out on your ear."

Nicky said, "As my old dear used to say, it can't hurt to show willing."

Even in the lacklustre light of the early morning, the station had the air of excitement that went with a big case moving into a critical phase. Everyone involved in the inquiry knew that no matter which way it went this was one that would be talked about for years. There was a life involved. And in the wake of some thug's ambition, reputations could be made or broken. Grace was on no more than nodding terms with Hogg's regular team, he'd exchanged hardly a handful of sentences with any one of them. He could feel the competitive urge between them, and he shared it. He knew that, like the rest of them, he was stirred in equal measure by the hazard of failure and the excitement of opportunity.

Down the corridor from the incident room, in a small office assigned to them, Grace and Bonner were pulling on latex gloves when a uniform brought in a plastic bag and took from it a small pile of documents and several newspapers and magazines. "This is the Rosslare stuff," he said. "There's more on the way."

"Technical find anything?"

The uniform shook his head. It could have meant they didn't, or that he didn't know. He looked a little resentful at having to cater to a couple of outsiders. He proffered a chain-of-evidence form for Grace to sign, then he left.

The two detectives sat at opposite sides of a desk and Grace passed the newspapers and magazines to Nicky. "Phone numbers scribbled on the margins, names, directions, anything that might mean something."

On top of the pile of documents there were two passports. They belonged to the Kennedys. There was an ESB bill, again belonging to the Kennedys, AA renewal forms, bank offers of cheap loans, and similar domestic junk from the Kennedy house. The kind of stuff someone like Frankie Crowe, given time enough, could use to create fake papers. Grace did a quick shuffle through the rest of the documents, hoping there might be a ticket or a receipt that might point in a specific direction. Nothing of the sort. He went back to the passports and began to check everything, page by page.

Joan Crowe got out of her twelve-year-old Fiesta and watched Sinead scramble out after her, carrying her schoolbag. Joan locked the door and ignored the two plainclothes cops pulling up behind her in the unmarked Sierra. They just sat there, long faces and Action Man haircuts, staring at her, as they'd stared when she and Sinead left the house. Here, in front of St. Ciaran's, the street alive with parents herding their kids towards the school gates, they were as inconspicuous as a couple of clowns at a funeral.

As Joan passed through the school gates she felt her daughter's hand slip into her own. Since Frankie's photo appeared in the papers, Sinead had been distracted, surly and said no to anything Joan asked her to do. Joan had tried to talk about what was happening but Sinead made angry noises and turned away. She must have got some word from the other kids, but more likely she'd cut them off as well. Last night Sinead had come into Joan's bed in the small hours and while Joan lay awake beside her, she cried in her sleep. However this turned out, there was going to be a lot of that.

This morning, Sinead had very deliberately adopted a cheerful style and Joan played along with her chatter about a TV soap. They crossed the yard and rounded a corner into the school's prefab area. At the bottom of the steps up to the class-room, they kissed and Joan watched until Sinead was inside, then she turned back towards the school gate and she saw Frankie leaning against the wall of the administration building, smiling.

Peering around the corner of the administration building Frankie Crowe watched his daughter pass through the school gates and across the playground, holding hands with Joan. Five minutes to nine, bang on. Sinead liked to get into school a few minutes early, gave her a chance to chat with her friends before lessons began. He stifled the urge to step into the open and call to her. Much as he longed to see her face broaden into a smile, to watch her run to him, to feel her arms hugging his waist, there'd be no comforting her once she knew he was going away.

There'd be a time when she would run to him again. If he made it, he'd stay in Amsterdam for a year or two, put the money to use, then there were people in London, new papers, a new life. Eventually she'd be part of that, even if she just came on visits. It'd be awkward, and missing a chunk out of her life would be hard, like doing a couple of years in the Joy. But they'd adjusted to that before and they'd do it again, and he watched Sinead move away from Joan, up the steps to the prefab classroom, and he strained to see her face, fix it in his mind, and she was gone.

He watched Joan turn and he prepared to say the things

he'd thought through during his uncomfortable night in the car. About the way stuff happens that makes you do things that make sense at the time. And when it all dies down you come out the other end and it seems like there was a lot of strutting and prancing and the thing that mattered more than anything has turned into something else.

He put a smile on his face just a second before she looked up and saw him.

"They're outside the school," she said. "The house, too."

He nodded. "Fuckers're everywhere."

She moved to pass him. "Goodbye, Frankie."

"No, wait a minute, I've something to tell you."

Joan looked at her watch.

"I'm going," he said. "I've got a fella who can get me on to a ferry tonight."

"I don't want to know."

Frankie nodded, held his palms up. "All I'm saying is I'll be away a long time."

She said nothing, just looked at him.

"I'll send money."

"Keep it."

"Joan—"

The tone of his voice, the naked plea on his face, told her what he suddenly couldn't put into words.

"Don't be foolish," she said.

Frankie shook his head. He'd known the answer, but he couldn't go away until he'd heard her say it.

"If anything happens—" he said.

Joan said nothing, just stared at him like there wasn't anything he could say that she hadn't heard a dozen times.

"What I mean—"

Joan walked away.

Frankie moved to follow her, then realised that two more

steps and he'd be out into the yard, in view of the police watching for Joan to come back to her car.

For a second he almost stepped out.

"Joan," he said, but she was already halfway across the yard.

Cold-hearted bitch.

Frankie turned and headed towards the passageway that led to the back gate.

"Bugger all in that," Nicky Bonner said, pushing aside a small pile of magazines. A phone number scribbled on the back of a torn and empty envelope turned out to be the number for account enquiries at Dublin Gas. Two numbers on inside pages of magazines were traced to a Southside restaurant and a car valet service. An address written neatly in the centre of an A4 page belonged to a businessman whose dinner party the Kennedys had attended a couple of months earlier.

John Grace came across several sheets of A4 paper with scribbles on them. "Looks like Frankie was trying out different versions of a ransom note." He put them aside in a folder as potential evidence in any future trial.

After a while, the resentful uniform came back, this time with a cardboard folder of material just arrived from Technical.

"Finished?"

Grace nodded and the uniform took the original Rosslare documents and returned them to the plastic bag they'd come in. "That stuff's from Brendan Sweetman's house. As soon as you're done with that, there's a shoebox full of stuff from Frankie Crowe's apartment."

He was signing the chain-of-evidence form when Grace leaned across the desk and picked up the material he'd been examining. "What's this?"

The uniform looked at him like he always knew that plainclothes weren't the full shilling. "It's the stuff from Rosslare, the stuff you've just been through."

"The plastic bag. Did the documents and the newspapers come in that, or did you put them into it?"

"That's exactly how I got it from Technical, that's what I passed on."

Grace held up the plastic bag so Nicky Bonner could see. It had an illustration of a jolly butcher, announcing that there was no meat like Rafferty's meat.

"That's a Phibsboro address along the bottom," Grace said. "And it ended up in Rosslare." Nicky took a small Garda diary from an inner pocket, checked a number and thumbed his mobile.

Grace said, "Technical find anything on this?"

The uniform said, "Nothing useful on any of it."

Less than a minute later Nicky Bonner ended his call. "According to the local station, Rafferty's butcher shop's been out of business for a year or two."

Chief Superintendent Malachy Hogg was on the third floor of the Department of Justice when he got the call from Grace. He was providing a civil servant with a detailed update on the kidnap, for the information of the minister. The civil servant was slow at taking notes, and several times read the notes back to Hogg, for confirmation. Hogg felt like everything he said was being taken down to be used in evidence against him.

"Could be anything or nothing," he told Grace. "Give me the address of the butcher's shop. I'll get ERU to have a look and I'll join you there."

As he stood up and moved towards the door, the civil servant said, "I really believe you ought to finish your report before haring off."

Hogg said, "I'm sure you're right." He closed the door softly behind him.

* * *

By the time Grace and Bonner arrived at Rafferty's butcher shop, the ERU had been through the building.

"Looks like it's the place OK." Suited up and carrying an Uzi, the tactical commander introduced himself as Sergeant Derek Dowd. To Grace, he looked absurdly young to be in charge of anything involving firearms.

Dowd led Grace and Bonner upstairs to a room where a heavy panel of chipboard was screwed in place across the window. Nothing in the room except a single mattress with a Pokémon quilt.

"My lads have done a quick run-through, but there's nothing to find."

It took Grace and Bonner no time at all to conclude that Sergeant Dowd was right. If this was where Angela Kennedy was held, the gang had cleaned up before they left.

In the front of the shop, at the end of the counter, they found a roll of Rafferty's plastic bags, one of which had been used to wrap the documents taken to Rosslare. Grace bent and looked under the counter. Nothing except white wrapping paper. He pressed a key on an old-fashioned metal register and watched the cash drawer spring open. There was a decayed core of an apple inside. Grace shut the drawer.

In what seemed to have been some kind of staffroom, Bonner checked the fridge and found it empty. He looked in the cupboards and inside the microwave. When Grace joined him he was looking down into a waste bin. It was empty.

"Technical might get some prints," Nicky said.

Grace shrugged. "It's a dead end."

Sergeant Dowd came in to say that he and his ERU team were pulling out. Grace thanked him and said he and Bonner would secure the scene until the uniforms arrived.

Grace found a chair and sat down. Nicky, standing beside the television, poked a finger at a button on the front of the video. There was a whirring noise and a video cassette popped halfway out of the machine. Nicky exchanged a glance with Grace, then he took out the cassette.

"'A Few Good Men.'" He turned it over. "It's a rental job. Video Express."

Grace went into the front of the shop and came back with a phone book. He said, "Any numbers, codes, that kind of thing?"

"Yeah, here on the spine."

There were fifteen branches of Video Express in the Dublin phone book, nine of them on the Northside. The first call got them the information that the prefix on the cassette number belonged to the Clontarf branch. It took Nicky less than two minutes to ring that branch and get a name.

"It's overdue," he said, pocketing his mobile. He looked at his notebook. "Someone called Adrian Moffat."

Grace said, "No bells."

"Address in Killester."

"Who's this?" Neither of them had heard Chief Superintendent Hogg enter the room. He was standing just inside the open doorway, looking at Nicky but speaking to Grace.

"Detective Sergeant Bonner, sir. He was helping me go through the stuff from Rosslare." Hogg looked as though he was deciding if someone was trying something on.

"Sergeant Bonner's from Turner's Lane, sir. He's had as many run-ins with Frankie Crowe as I've had myself."

Nicky smiled. "I was hoping I might be of some help, sir, and—"

Hogg leaned forward, hands in the pockets of his overcoat. "Adrian Moffat. What's he got to do with this?"

"Sir?"

"The Milky Bar Kid. What's the story?"

* * *

Martin Paxton didn't sleep much and when he rose that morning his mind was made up. The others were talking shite.

Brendan Sweetman said, "Once we get to the rental, divvy up the money—those that want to go, go. I say we go for broke, hold on to her and have a shot at the second million. Situation we're in, it's not like we can afford to pass up that kind of chance."

Dolly Finn said, "Soon as I get my share, I'm off." He shook his head. "It's over."

Martin had already called Frankie's mobile half a dozen times that morning, and all he heard was the voice saying the number he dialled was not in service. No way on Christ's earth was Frankie going to show up to divide the money.

Milky's mind was focused on getting everyone—especially the hostage—the hell out of his house. The rental in Tallaght had been confirmed the previous night, first thing this morning Milky fetched the Ford Transit from the seafront and parked it in his driveway. By ten o'clock there was still no sign of the contact arriving with the keys of the rental.

"Come eleven, keys or no keys, I want you lot out of here," Milky said.

Brendan Sweetman's voice was as cold as his stare. "We'll go when we've somewhere to go to."

For Martin Paxton, going on the run was throwing dice. The chances of getting to a safe place were not great.

Whatever will be will be.

He knew that sooner or later the penny would drop for Sweetman and Finn. At that stage, they could go in any direction. Chances were, Dolly would run for the hills. Sweetman might run for it, too, or he might try to use the hostage to bargain.

Or, he might decide she'd seen too much.

We haven't killed anyone yet. Keep it that way.

A little more than half an hour later, the contact arrived with the keys to the rental.

"That's it," Milky said, waving towards the door, "shift yourselves. And take her with you."

25

When the lead car of the ERU pulled up outside Adrian Moffat's house, the driver realised immediately he'd made a mistake. The wide wooden gates were open and there was a white Ford Transit van in the driveway, facing out on to the road. The guy sitting in the van driver's seat—thin-faced, with a Fu Manchu moustache—saw the unmarked police car and you could almost hear his brain whirring.

"Shit," the police driver said. There were high hedges either side of the gate. Had he stopped anywhere else, they'd have arrived without warning.

A second ERU car pulled up behind the first. Inside that car, the unit's tactical commander, Sergeant Derek Dowd, was cradling an Uzi sub-machine gun below the line of the car window. A high hedge blocked his view of the suspect house. Situation like this, ideally you have even twenty minutes to suss it all out, figure how many, who and where. Today, he was dealing with a ticking clock. Could be a duff lead, could be the real thing—no time for niceties, go in.

Sergeant Dowd was halfway out of the car when he realised something was wrong. The lads in the car in front were sitting stock still.

* * *

The driver of the first ERU car made eye contact with the guy behind the wheel of the white van. The seconds were ticking. Could be Fu Manchu wasn't the brightest, maybe he figured this was a salesman come to make a special offer on replacing the gutters.

How are you going to play this?

A third ERU car bypassed the first two and came skidding to a stop.

"Ah no," the driver of the first car said, as the driver of the white van threw it into gear and the van jerked forward. The ERU driver watched the white van speeding towards him.

When the cops arrived, in their unmarked but unmistakable cars, Dolly was sitting in the driver's seat of the Ford Transit and the engine was ticking over. Behind the van, Brendan Sweetman was stepping down from the front doorstep, guiding the masked hostage towards the open rear doors of the van. Milky was standing at the front door of his home, with Martin Paxton in the hallway behind him.

The sound of two cars stopping made Sweetman pause. When the third skidded to a stop he pushed Angela's shoulder. "Hurry!" She was three feet from the back of the white van.

Dolly put his foot down and the van took off, leaving Brendan Sweetman standing, his mouth open. He was barely aware of the unseeing hostage walking on down the driveway away from him.

"Ah, shit!" Milky said.

The driver of the first garda car couldn't reverse, the second car was too close behind. With the third car in front, he had only a few feet to manoeuvre. He started forward. Dolly jerked the wheel to the right as the van cleared the gateway, but the gap was too narrow and the left front edge of the van clipped the rear of the police car.

There was a harsh metallic noise and the Ford Transit lurched down off the pavement and went into a spin across the road. The police car was knocked sideways, the two gardai shaken violently.

There were cops coming out of the other two cars, guns out, seeking targets.

At his front door, Milky was frozen. He stood straight, his hands down by his sides.

There was a loud smacking sound as the side of the van collided with a lamp-post on the far side of the road.

Brendan Sweetman put his pistol down by his side and moved, slowly at first and then in a stooped run, away from the front door and across Milky's front garden.

Martin Paxton called, "Angela!"

The hostage, now near the front gate, pulled the mask off her bruised faced. Blinking, she looked back towards Martin and then towards the gate. Off to the left, beyond the garden hedge, she could see the top of a lamp-post, bent at an angle.

She stared at it for a few moments, then she walked on towards the gate.

Which was when the shooting started.

When the van stopped moving, side-on to the bent lamp-post, Dolly got out, holding his automatic at arm's length, pointing it at the police. One shoulder had taken a wrench, but nothing serious. He walked backwards, fast, his back straight, his face blank, his arm moving this way and that, aiming in turn at each of the four plainclothes cops he could see crouched behind two of the cop cars. The two in the car he had rammed were slumped in the front seats. Seemed to be out of it. Dolly didn't pull the trigger, just let the cops know he was ready if they wanted to take this up a notch.

On a suburban street like this, they'd be reluctant to start the shooting.

One of the policemen shouted something.

Dolly glanced quickly left and right. More of them? Nothing. He moved sideways, stepping behind the brick gatepost of a house diagonally across the road from Milky's place. As he did so, one of the cops fired.

Dolly Finn looked around the gatepost and fired three times.

When he pulled his head back into cover, there was a fusillade, the bullets making chuk sounds as they hit the gatepost.

Angela was in the line of fire. She heard a shout, "Wait till you have a target," and something tugged at her left arm.

"Get down!"

There were men with guns, crouched, cars spread untidily along the street, their doors open.

"Missus. Get down!"

Angela looked to her left. She saw what she took to be someone kneeling in one of the gardens. Then she wasn't sure if there was anyone there.

"Mrs. Kennedy—get down, lie down on the road."

Angela looked one way, then the other. From behind her, she heard the sound of running. There were more shots.

Running forward, through the gateway of his house, past the hostage, holding his hands above his head and waving them, Milky reached the roadway and found himself staggering sideways, his balance gone. One second he was running, next second he hit the ground, back first.

Fuck that.

What happened?

He lay on his back and knew that there was wet somewhere down his left side.

Jesus, they shot me. Shit.

He felt pain where his back hit the ground, and nowhere else.

Winged and winded.

Where?

Somewhere down the left side.

Nowhere else?

He did a quick inventory. Both arms were working, one leg was caught under the other but he could move both of them, no pain. It wasn't his stomach, there was no blood on his chest. Most important, he hadn't taken a hit in the head. Definitely hit, no doubt about that. Somewhere down the left side, low down, but no sign of a dangerous injury.

Fuck you, Frankie. Fuck you and the horse you rode in on.

Dolly Finn moved quickly along the side of a house, kicked open a flimsy wooden door and ran across someone's back garden. At the bottom of the garden, he crossed into another back garden, then went through a side door into a front garden and stopped.

He brushed down his clothes, put the gun in his pocket and walked down the front driveway and out on to a street.

When the shooting started, Brendan Sweetman made it through a thin section of hedge, into the garden next door to Milky's house, crossed that garden and burrowed his way into a deep bush. His shotgun was in the van, gone with Dolly. First thing he did, he took his handgun out of his pocket and slid it into a tight-knit clump of roots. No way was he getting into a pissing match with a platoon of garda storm troopers. Best he could hope for was he might get to stroll out of here in the confusion.

There were bluebottles at both ends of the road, now. Squad cars parked here and there, and the toughies with shooters were coming down like dandruff.

Tripping over one another. Might be a chance.

Give it a couple of minutes, wriggle through the hedge into

the next garden, see where that leads. Try to make it out through a side entrance to a back garden, see if there's a way on to the next road. Maybe even stay here, keep the head down until it's all over, just walk down the next-door neighbour's garden path, on to the footpath, stroll across the road like a regular citizen. Play it right, it could be done.

"Hey, you."

Oh.

"You, in the bush."

Fuck.

From somewhere behind.

"Hey, fatso."

"Don't shoot. I'm not armed."

"Hands on your head."

"Yes, sir."

"Where's your gun?"

"I put it down, sir. Under a bush."

"Good boy. There's now a possibility that I won't blow your head off. OK, back out of there. Slowly."

Shit. Shit-shit-shit.

"That's it, keep your hands right up. On your head. Keep coming. That's it. Stop there."

"You want me to lie down?"

"That would be nice."

Dolly Finn was two streets away, standing in the middle of the road, his gun pointing at the windscreen of an approaching car, a boxy little blue Fiat. The car stopped. The driver was a young woman with short dark hair and a black business suit, and when Dolly got into the passenger seat she reached for the door handle beside her and Dolly said, "Drive!"

"Take the car, let me go."

"Drive."

"Please!"

Dolly looked back and saw a car come slowly round a corner maybe fifty yards back, passenger door open and a plainclothes copper trotting alongside, an automatic rifle held in the
crook of his arm. Dolly jammed his gun into the woman's side.
"No chat, drive now."

One of the bastards, the fat guy from the bushes, face
down on the ground, handcuffed and out of the picture. The
older guy in the green check jacket took a hit, from the look
of things he was out of it. The driver of the van—who the hell
knows?

How many does that leave?

Sergeant Dowd crouched behind his car, assessing the situation. The car was several yards down from the kidnap house.

"Hold your positions, everyone. Stay alert."

A voice in Sergeant Dowd's earpiece told him the driver of
the white van had been spotted hijacking a blue Fiat.

By now, armed back-up was on the scene, crouched uniforms were muttering into radios, sorting out roadblocks, the
area was being locked down. The victim was alive, standing in
the middle of the road, directly in front of the suspect house.
Sergeant Dowd's men were working their way in from all sides.
The two officers from the car that had been hit by the van were
still a bit groggy, but they were out of the car, taking cover.
None of the good guys seriously hurt so far. Time of the morning—kids at school, adults at work—no sign yet of curious
civilians spilling out to clog things up.

This could work out not too bad.

"Missus?"

No response.

Are they all gone? Or are they using her as bait, waiting for
a clear shot?

"Missus?"

Get her moving. Shooting starts again, we don't want her

standing there in the middle of it. Get her away from the front
of the suspect house. Move her down this way towards the car.

"Missus?"

Jesus, she's a mess.

The woman looked up, one eye puffed and closed, the
other looking directly through the sergeant.

Christ. The poor bitch. Can't let this drag on.

"Mrs. Kennedy?"

No response. Just standing there like she's waiting for her
turn at the supermarket checkout.

"Heads up, lads, I'm going to get her."

Sergeant Dowd stepped out from behind the car, into the
middle of the road.

Danger most likely to come from the left, the suspect house
and the gardens around it. But there was no telling. Too many
high hedges, both sides of the street.

He knew there were at least half a dozen police guns trained
on the house and the gardens around it. His own Uzi was firm
against the bend of his elbow, the muzzle pointing up at forty-
five degrees. Ready to turn in any direction.

Times like these, when there were guns about and he felt
the shadow of cross-hairs on his throat, the sergeant thought of
a superintendent named Oakley. Gruff but cuddly type of
man, everyone's favourite uncle. Face like a spaniel. A natural
sympathiser. He had a niche in personnel. Times like these, if
something went wrong, it'd be Oakley walking in the
sergeant's front gate, maybe an hour from now, Oakley walking up the sergeant's pathway. Oakley's compassionate face the
sergeant's wife would see when she opened the front door.

Twenty feet, fifteen, ten.

"Missus?"

The victim adjusted her gaze, she saw him. Good woman,
now don't panic.

"I'm a garda, missus. You're OK."

She said nothing.

He was with her now, and he gently manoeuvred himself between her and the suspect house. He never took his gaze from the house.

"You'll be fine, missus. Just take it easy. Move back down towards the car. Slowly. Step at a time. You're doing fine."

She said, "This way?"

He said, "Yes, that's it. Take your time. Towards the car."

She moved slowly, he matched her pace, still watching the suspect house. Two of his men hurried forward, one each side, closing ranks between the sergeant and the house. The sergeant turned and hustled the victim away, his men following, walking backwards, guns poised.

When he got her into cover he said, "How many of these men were in there?"

"My name is Angela," she said.

She looked with curiosity at the left arm of her tracksuit, torn and streaked with blood.

"What happened?" she said.

Silver lining. They shot an unarmed man. Play well in court. Shot an unarmed man. Upside to everything.

Milky reached into a pocket for his cigarettes and his lighter. He noticed that he'd lost a button from the front of his green check jacket. He looked up and saw a cop standing over him. Scruffy fucker, no uniform, jeans, woolly hat and a yellow garda waistcoat yoke. Some kind of fancy semi-automatic clutched in front of his chest. He was staring down at Milky, like he was point man on the first platoon into a vanquished city.

The house will go. The pub, the garage, too. These days, bastards've got laws lets them do that. Confiscate stuff.

Fuck you, Frankie.

They'll never find the bank accounts. Tear the kip apart, never find them. Bastards.

Shot an unarmed man. Worth a hefty slice off the sentence. Hell of a way to get sympathy, but fuck it.

Cape Town properties, can't touch those.

A casual associate of these men, Your Honour. My client has a clean record, apart from some youthful follies. Forced their way into his house. Threats. Fear. Then, fleeing to safety, shot by the police.

Play it cool, this'll work out.

He badly wanted a cigarette. Hadn't he taken the smokes out of his pocket a minute ago? They were—where?

The scruffy cop knelt beside him, made the sign of the cross, bent to his ear and began whispering.

"Say the Act of Contrition with me."

Milky stared at him.

Fuck off.

The cop was saying, "Oh my God, I'm heartily sorry for having offended Thee—"

Fuck that. Shove your Act of Contrition up the high hole of your arse.

"—I detest my sins above every other evil—"

Phone Dave, first thing.

No. Dave's fine for down the District. For this, need a lawyer gets off on suing the fuck out of people. Make back a chunk of whatever they take.

"—and I firmly resolve by Thy holy grace, never more to offend Thee—"

Jesus, get the right mouthpiece, might even come out of this with a profit.

He made a noise that might have been a chuckle.

He heard the cop's voice say, "He's gone."

Stupid fucker.

As consciousness melted into something else, Milky thought, Gone nowhere, I'm right here. Just resting.

* * *

She's so young, Dolly thought, in that business suit she looks like a little girl dressing up in her mother's clothes. He'd told her to take it easy, keep the speed down. So far, there was no panic. A little Fiat wasn't an ideal getaway car, but beggars and choosers. She'd followed his every instruction, taking a series of turns. There was no sign of the unmarked garda car. Dolly wasn't sure if the police had identified the woman's car as being connected with a fugitive.

The young woman looked straight ahead as she drove, as though loath to acknowledge his existence.

"What's your name?"

"Bonnie."

Dolly turned in his seat and looked back. Still no sign of the law.

Could be they're hanging back. After catching up with the Kennedy woman, last thing they need is they get a hostage back, get another one killed in a chase.

"You live around here?"

"Raheny."

Dolly's right hand was between his knees, loosely holding his gun. They were in a narrow, quiet street.

Maybe pull in, dump the Fiat here? Assume they twigged this one, take another car?

"What do you do?"

"I'm a supermarket assistant manager. Look, I—"

"You'll be OK. I promise."

"Please."

"Soon as we're away from here, I promise."

Ten feet ahead of the Fiat, a parked car suddenly lurched out from the left, into their path. At first Dolly thought it was some asshole bad driver, then he saw a couple of men with guns coming out of a garden on the right. The woman braked,

the Fiat stopped inches from the unmarked police car and
Dolly was thrown forward, his head smacking into the Fiat's
windscreen.

The woman screamed.

Dolly's gun was on the floor, where he'd dropped it. He
reached down with one hand, the other wiping blood away
from his forehead.

The window beside him smashed inwards and by the time
the door was pulled open he was sticking his gun into the
young woman's belly.

"Stay calm, do nothing stupid." The garda's voice was soft,
unexcited. He was wearing scruffy overalls and his hair was
long and unwashed. There were two others, one in front of the
car, one on the far side, both pointing pistols at Dolly.

The woman was making nervous noises. She was staring
down at the gun pushed into the folds of her pale blue blouse.

"Please," she said, high-pitched, teary.

Dolly said, "Back off, I'm telling you. I'll kill her. I'm not
kidding."

The long-haired cop said, "End of the road, one way or the
other. You choose." The muzzle of his gun was a foot away
from Dolly's temple and rock steady.

"Get back! Move away from the car!"

"Come on, what's the point? Stay calm."

"You'll be responsible." Dolly looked the long-haired cop
in the eye. Both of them were breathing heavily.

The cop said, "No one has to die here."

Dolly just sat there, thinking. He blocked out the woman's
mewling.

Choose.

They'd hardly shoot him. Too big a chance he'd jerk the
trigger, kill the girl.

Choose.

If he waited too long the cops might decide he was building up to something and end it all by shooting him and taking a chance that the woman would be all right.

Choose.

He nodded to the long-haired cop, then he slowly sat back and let the cop see that he was taking his finger off the trigger. He held the pistol loosely, making sure it wasn't pointing at anyone. On his right, the driver's door opened and the woman was pulled clear. Dolly could hear her crying as one of the cops hustled her away.

The long-haired garda had Dolly's gun now, stuffing it into a pocket of his overalls.

"Out. And put your hands on your head."

Dolly got out of the car slowly, and no one saw the knife until after it came up swinging and slashed the long-haired garda across the cheek. The cop screamed and dropped his gun and before it hit the ground Dolly was behind him, holding the knife to his throat.

Dolly was screaming now at the other two. "Guns down! Both of you! Now! Right now or I open him up!"

Nothing happened for a very long time, maybe ten seconds.

Dolly could feel the cop's blood wet and warm on his knife hand. He could see the other two figuring the angles. Was there enough of Dolly showing from behind their mate, would one shot disable him or would he be fast and strong enough with the knife?

"It goes one way, I walk away. For now," Dolly said. "It goes the other way, he dies forever."

His face was placid, as if the outcome was of little concern. "Decide."

One garda, then the other, pointed his gun away from Dolly, and put it on the roof of the woman's car. The woman was standing thirty feet away, one hand to her mouth, her legs visibly shaking.

Dolly kept the knife to the cop's throat until he reached into the cop's pocket and found his own gun. Then he said, "You can move away now." The long-haired cop was holding his face together, blood spilling between his fingers. He moved away, keeping his eyes on Dolly.

Dolly said to one of the other gardai, "Go look after her." The man looked back towards the young woman. He said, "OK," then backed away.

"You too," Dolly waved his gun at the other cop.

Dolly picked up the long-haired cop's gun from the roadway, unloaded the shells on to the ground and threw the gun into a nearby garden. He did the same with the two guns on the roof of the Fiat. As he wiped his bloody hands on the upholstery of the driver's seat he noticed an elderly man standing at the door of a house across the street, watching him, his mouth open.

Dolly turned to the cops and said, "Phones and radios." When he had smashed three mobiles and one handheld, he fired a shot into a front tyre of the woman's car. She screamed. One of the gardai held her tight, muttering calming words.

The engine of the unmarked police car was still running. Dolly got behind the wheel.

The long-haired garda sat on the kerb, holding his face together, watching him drive away.

The ERU took their time preparing the entry to the suspect house. By now, there were uniforms all over the place. They evacuated neighbours from several houses at either side and from across the road and from the houses on the street directly behind. They blocked off streets and the ERU marksmen targeted doors and windows. Sergeant Dowd used a loudspeaker, demanding that anyone inside the house or gardens show themselves. The house remained silent, nothing visible at any window or in the shadowed hallway beyond the open front door.

OK, do it the hard way.

Armoured-up, helmeted, they went in through the front door, slowly, covering one another, adrenalin raging. They used small mirrors on aluminium rods to peer around corners and into rooms. They found Martin Paxton sitting in the kitchen, elbows on the table, fingers linked, his chin resting on his hands. There was a gun ten feet away, on a countertop. He looked up as the first dark, militarised policeman came in. Then he looked away.

He got down on his belly when they told him to and when they had him cuffed and asked him his name he told them. They told him he didn't have to say anything and they asked if he wanted a solicitor. He didn't answer. They handed him over to the uniforms, who took him to Santry garda station, where he refused to make a statement or answer any questions.

Brendan Sweetman's solicitor, Connie Wintour, arrived at Clontarf garda station less than an hour after his client was put in a cell. Wintour, a small fussy man with blotchy skin and an air of weary superiority, talked to the arresting officer, then had a whispered conversation with his client. He then told the gardai that it might be in their interests if he was allowed a full private consultation with Mr. Sweetman before the interrogators went to work.

Mr. Wintour spent almost an hour with Sweetman and emerged with a handwritten statement, written by Wintour and signed by his client, to be greeted by two detectives from Chief Superintendent Hogg's team. Mr. Wintour told them he wished to read this statement to them in the presence of his client.

Ten minutes later Sweetman was brought in, looking pale and sweaty. His solicitor sat beside him. The two detectives sat across the table, pens poised over their notebooks. Mr. Wintour asked for a glass of water. While he waited, he quietly hummed Prokofiev's "Dance of the Knights." When the water arrived, and he had taken a sip, he began reading.

298 · GENE KERRIGAN

* * *

My name is Brendan Sweetman, of 15 Thornhill Crescent, Coolock, Dublin 5. DOB 16/6/1969. I am married, a father of three, and am in regular employment as a security officer in the city centre. Some weeks ago, I was offered a chance to take part in what I knew to be an illegal undertaking, the hold-up of a cash-and-carry premises in Crumlin. Although I had success-fully extricated myself from a lifestyle that involved criminal activity, for which I paid my debt to society, on this occasion I succumbed to temptation due to financial worries about the medical needs of my infant child. It was my belief that this undertaking would be carried out in a considered manner, with no personal injuries inflicted on members of the public. Only at the last minute did I discover the true nature of the project. I tried to withdraw but was subjected to threats from the ini-tiator of the project, Mr. Frank Crowe, and I reluctantly went along with it. The others involved with what turned out to be a kidnap, apart from Mr. Crowe, were Martin Paxton and a man known to me as "Dolly" Finn. Certain facilities were provided by the late Adrian Moffat—known, I believe, as Milky. At no stage did I hurt or threaten the victim of this crime, Mrs. Angela Kennedy. I took no part in making decisions and at all times acted on orders given under serious threat of physical harm. I was in the house when a violent assault was carried out on Mrs. Kennedy by Mr. Frank Crowe and I am willing to give evidence to that effect should it be necessary. I took no part in that assault and I wish to express my deepest remorse for my involvement in this unfortunate chain of events.

The solicitor took another sip of water. "My client has indi-cated to me his willingness to cooperate with the authorities in order to help bring this unhappy affair to a swift conclusion. To that end, he suggests that information in his possession may or may not be useful. However, it's my professional advice that he makes no other statement until such time as I feel it's in his best interests to do so."

One of the detectives leaned towards Sweetman. "Why did you go along with it? When you found out it was a kidnap, why did you—"

The solicitor shook his head. "I'm sorry, I must insist—"

Brendan leaned towards the detective. "Easy for you to say." He ignored his solicitor's upraised hand. "Not so easy when you're dealing with a nutter like Frankie Crowe. I mean, you don't know what he's like. He's fucking mad."

"That's enough," the solicitor said. "That's quite enough." He stood up. "Gentlemen, I must ask you to return my client to his cell." He put both his palms on the table and leaned forward. In a quiet voice he said, "If, perhaps, your superiors have anything to say about any mitigating statements they might wish to make to the court, during my client's eventual trial, I'd be available at the shortest notice. Delay on this matter, in my opinion, would not be in the interests of your ongoing enquiries. Nor, indeed, in the wider interests of justice."

The Minister for Justice was at the Westbury Hotel along with the Taoiseach and two junior ministers, attending a fundraising lunch for the party, when the call came through from Assistant Commissioner Colin O'Keefe. No, O'Keefe told the minister's aide, he would not like to leave a message. No, it wouldn't be all right if the minister rang him back when he had a break from his current duties.

O'Keefe said, "Just get him and no more bullshit."

The minister took the mobile and went into a corridor. O'Keefe told him, "She's out, Mrs. Kennedy is safe."

"Jesus. That's great."

"And she's OK. A bit bashed about, but alive."

"Thank God. What happened?"

"We got a lead, she was found at a house in Killester, there was a bit of a shoot-out."

"And?"

"One gang member dead, two in custody, at least one got away at the scene, and there was no sign of the leader, Frankie Crowe."

"The money?"

"No sign so far."

"My sincere congratulations, Assistant Commissioner. Listen, pass on my congratulations to Chief Superintendent Hogg. I'll formally thank him at a more opportune time."

The minister felt a tap on his shoulder and turned to see two of the guests at the fund-raiser preparing to leave. One was a public-relations consultant and the other a builder responsible for many of Dublin's new apartments. The builder pointed at his watch, arced a thumb down the corridor towards the hotel lobby, then turned the gesture into a thumbs up. The minister said "Sorry—" into the phone and he reached forward and shook hands first with the builder, then with his companion.

"God bless, take care—" He returned the thumbs up as he spoke again into the phone, "Sorry about that."

O'Keefe kept his tone even. "Apart from a serious facial wound and two members with minor injuries, there were no garda casualties."

"Fine, that's splendid. Should I—where is the, where's Mrs. Kennedy? Should I go see her?"

"The Blackrock Clinic. I don't think she's up to visitors. There's something else. She's having an HIV test."

"Fuck. What happened?"

"The gang leader, Crowe."

"Ah, Jesus."

The minister's voice took on the tone of a press release. "As far as I'm concerned, you're still free to authorise whatever is necessary in the way of overtime or additional resources. We've got the victim back, but there'll be no let-up until the leader of this gang of thugs is where he belongs."

26

S tephen Beckett, in black T-shirt and black underpants, grunted and sat upright on the edge of his bed. He straightened his back, ran a hand through his tangled grey hair, and took a long deep breath. Getting out of bed was one of the many routine activities he found troublesome these days. Performing each movement carefully, he let one knee down on to the worn green carpet, then the other knee, one hand on the bed, the other briefly touching a nearby wooden chair until he was sure his balance was right, then he was kneeling alongside the bed.

Jesus God, who'd've thought it.

It was the best part of seventy years since the days when kneeling by his bed, first thing in the morning and last thing at night, was a part of his life.

Gave up that oul shite before I got into long trousers, and now look at me.

It wasn't prayer that had him on his knees these days but the physiotherapist up in Dublin that his GP recommended. It was like something had worn away inside Stephen's back, and the pain that used to afflict him occasionally was now a nagging part of most days.

"First thing in the morning, it takes less than a minute," the physio said, "on your knees, loosen up the spine, you'll notice the difference."

From the kneeling position, Stephen went down on all fours, then slowly pushed his buttocks back towards his heels, feeling the stretch in his spine, stopping just the right side of pain. Five times back, then five times to each side, then another five times back, and he'd live to fight another day.

Using the bed and the chair to hold on to, he stood up, a tall man pushing eighty, big-boned, his hair as thick on his head as it was when he was young, but now even that dull grey crop looked tired. Big day ahead. Today he had to decide if he would kill a man.

On his bedside table, lying on top of a red and white hand towel, there was a dull grey pistol, a Colt .45.

Stephen had left Meath in 1942, when he was seventeen. He had the muscle and the ambition to thrive on the building sites in London. Bugger all for him at home. Strong and tall as he was, snagging turnips for pennies would have knackered his back long before now.

After a few months in London, he joined the army and in the weeks after D-Day he was among the thousands who broke out from the Normandy beaches, pushing the German army back, from hedgerow to village to hedgerow to town, and always another treacherous hedgerow.

"Oh," a man named Benny said, quietly. He was walking alongside Stephen Beckett, part of a patrol beyond Caen, on the way to Falaise, several weeks after D-Day. Following days of heavy fighting, things had been quiet all morning, apart from an intermittent mortar duel. Talking about it later, none of the soldiers remembered hearing the shot. One second Benny was there alongside Stephen, then he was on his knees, then toppling on to his side, rolling over on to his back, the dark stain on his chest growing bigger by the heartbeat, and within a second or two there was a machine gun's harsh burp and Benny's mates were scattering and he called weakly for help, his hands quivering down by his sides. He continued calling for help for the next twenty minutes, his life's blood pumping out of him, and every time someone moved to go towards him there was a blizzard of bullets from the German position. He didn't scream, just called out in a frayed voice for help, usually ending each appeal with a drawn-out "Please." The unit was isolated and pinned down. Attempts to break out to either flank cost two soldiers their lives and left another with a bullet-smashed elbow.

Benny's cries were relentless. Stephen saw one of the sergeants gesture to another, his suggestion obvious. A mercy shot? The other sergeant thought for a moment, then shook his head.

It wasn't long before Benny stopped begging and began cursing his comrades, screaming obscenities and damning them all to hell. Then he begged God for help and called for his mother, his cries growing weaker, intermittent and more bitter, the ground around him soaked with his blood. Eventually, the cries stopped and Benny died.

After a while, a Centaur tank came up the road and dealt with the Germans, about half a dozen of them grouped at the edge of an orchard on a commanding rise about three hundred metres away. Two of them were still alive when the tank had done its work. They surrendered, both of them wounded and bloody, and Stephen Beckett and his comrades talked about it for a while, a note of hysteria running through their chatter. Then Stephen and a blond bloke named Carter took the two Germans into a ditch and shot them. One of the Germans said nothing, the other—a private, hardly twenty—began praying aloud when he realised what was about to happen. Just before the bullet in the back of the head silenced him, he sobbed, his breaths coming in gulps. The other one, early thirties, a sergeant, a sullen, dark-eyed bastard with a hand wound, said nothing.

Before and after that incident, Stephen Beckett fought in several intense actions. He'd certainly shot at other soldiers and probably killed some of them, but none of that lodged in his mind like the image of that dark-eyed bastard. There was hardly a week since that Stephen didn't think of him, and the way he showed no fear as he waited. It was as if the man accepted that his life had come down to the remaining seconds in that godforsaken ditch, and he was determined he'd live it as whatever he chose to be, refusing to allow fear or hope or even anger to commandeer the small sliver of life left to him. When his comrade was shot he looked briefly at the crumpled body, then he examined his wounded hand, rearranging the grubby bandage. He waited with neither anxiety nor resignation, just watching what was happening, and then he died.

For a time, Stephen Beckett envied and admired the dark-eyed bastard's strength in the face of death. Later, when the sensations of his own war had been diluted by time, he understood how seeing and doing terrible things could leave a man like the dark-eyed bastard all hollowed out inside and all he felt for him was pity. In his long life, there were two major decisions Stephen Beckett made that he wished he could undo, and taking those two poor bastards into the ditch was one of them.

The second thing—well, that was more recent. And maybe he could make amends before the day was through.

Stephen considered a shower, then decided the hell with it. Time and energy he couldn't spare. For a man with so much time on his hands, it seemed to Stephen Beckett that he never had a minute more than he needed. Back when he was working, he could pack so much into the day and still have time left over for the family.

After the war, Stephen went back to the building work in London. He met and married a woman named Lily, a nurse who hailed from Kilkenny, and they had three boys, one of whom—the eldest—died at the age of six, a chest thing. In the booming 1960s, Stephen set up as a subcontractor, employing a handful of construction workers, never growing big enough to get rich but doing fine. Then Lily died. Stephen never knew what happened. The doctor said no more than "The gut, I'm afraid," and shook his head when Stephen asked what could be done. Six weeks later Stephen buried her.

His youngest sister Eilish came over to look after the kids. She'd been a baby when he left home and Stephen hardly knew her. Quiet and shy, she'd never been away from home for more than the odd weekend in Tramore. She stayed with Stephen long enough to see the kids through their teens, then she married an electrician from Kent and divorced him within a year. Last Stephen heard, she was running a B&B in Liverpool.

Stephen made a decent job of raising the boys. The older one became a policeman with the Met, the other went wild for a while but ended up in Cornwall, with his own small DIY store. One morning in the mid-1980s, shortly after his sixtieth birthday, Stephen lay on in bed, thinking for the first time since Lily died about what his life had become. Why did he bother working as hard as ever, pitching for jobs, arranging crews, pricing materials, filling his days with finding solutions for problems he didn't care about? The kids had their own lives, his needs were few, and he was tired. Not just physically, but drained by the pointlessness of it all. He was of an age when it was not unusual to think, in the final moments before sleep, of the possibility that he would not wake up, and he realised he was at ease with that.

It took him a while to make a decision, but eighteen months later he sold up the business and visited the two boys and their families. Despite their pleas that this was unnecessary, he insisted that they accept a cut of the money from the business. Then he sold his house and—at the age of sixty-two—went home to Meath to wait for death. His two eldest brothers were dead, the surviving brother was friendly enough but a stranger. Stephen rented a flat in Harte's Cross, the nearest town to the long-demolished family home, and it was there, one morning in July, sixteen years later, that he stood in Sweeney's Pub and said, "Leave her alone, you. Leave her alone."

When Frankie Crowe—Stephen didn't know the gunman's name then, but he knew it now—said, "Who the fuck're you, grandad? Sir Galahad?" and pointed the gun at his crotch, Stephen felt physical fear for the first time in decades.

Stephen Beckett's breakfast at the Olive Grove was the usual orange juice, coffee and two slices of wholemeal bread, followed by a bowl of porridge. Sean Willie Costello never got tired of wrinkling his nose in mock disdain at Stephen's breakfast. Every morning, Sean Willie cooked himself a fry-up in his single-storey house in Coulthard Lane. "Maybe if I ate rabbit food I'd live to get the president's cheque, what?" he'd cackle, "but it's no breakfast for a grown man."

Sean Willie had had his fry-up that morning before Sweeney's Pub was robbed. Then he'd arrived at the pub with his three Sunday-newspaper crosswords. Every week, no exceptions, Sean Willie did all the crosswords in the Sunday papers. He once won a Cross pen from one of them and newsagent Angus Tubridy cut out the crossword section of the newspaper the following week, with Sean Willie's name on the bottom where they printed the name of the winner, and stuck it in the shop window.

Every Monday, after breakfast, the two old men shared a pot of tea at Sweeney's, while Stephen helped Sean Willie with any clues he hadn't finished. The two had fallen into a host of such companionable habits.

Stephen Beckett and Sean Willie Costello had been classmates at the national school in Harte's Cross in the early 1930s. They played hurling together for a while, until Sean Willie lost the thrill of it when a length of ash laid against his forehead left him unconscious for two days.

A few years later, when Stephen left for England, Sean

Willie stayed on as a farm labourer. His parents had both died of TB before he got out of his childhood. Sean Willie had an uncle, a veteran of the war of independence who had worked for Michael Collins in Dublin. The uncle did his duty, and dirty work it was by all accounts, then he returned to Harte's Cross to manage a pub. When Sean Willie was orphaned, his uncle paid a neighbour to look after him. At the beginning of the 1940s, his uncle emigrated to Boston, and Sean Willie never heard from him again. Word came in 1963 that his uncle had died the previous year.

Back in the 1940s, Stephen had written home twice, encouraging Sean Willie to join him on the London building sites, but his friend wasn't interested. It wasn't just that he had enough work, he liked the work he did, labouring on local farms. Although he never grew much beyond five feet tall and he seemed slight and fragile, he had muscle enough to foot turf or scythe meadow, and he could spend the day bent over, remoulding drills and ridges after the weeding, and do it long after many a bigger man had given up. The way things were, he knew he'd never get a bit of a farm of his own, but he lacked the hunger for land that seemed to be rooted in so many around him. He liked the hard work, the rhythm of the year, the direct connection between the work and the consequent flowering of the fields. Even when he lay down exhausted, even in the truly bad years when the wages were hardly enough to keep him going, he could feel in his aching muscles the certainty of a deed done, a day spent. He was aware of his own poverty, and if he hadn't had the little house in Coulthard Lane that his uncle had left him he'd have been in trouble. Even those in the town who were well off didn't have a lot. A few families were prosperous, and labourers and servants were cheap, but back then there were no lords or ladies in Harte's Cross, and those who got above themselves could be put in their place with a mocking glance. Sean Willie felt at ease amid the streets of Harte's Cross and in the fields of the town's hinterland, and among the people he found there. The cruel certainties of a hard life at home were infinitely more attractive than a better life amid a jungle of strangers. Within a few years of his retirement, his weekly state pension was more than he'd ever received in wages. His needs were few and he had built up what he called a tidy sum in the Harte's Cross credit union.

After more than forty years away in London, Stephen Beckett had been back two weeks in Harte's Cross, and more than half convinced he'd made the wrong decision, when he met a small, stooped old man in an ancient felt hat coming out of Tubridy's newsagent's. The two old men looked at one another for a few moments, then Sean Willie grinned, took the roll-up from between his lips and said, "Sure, didn't I tell you you'd never settle down in that pagan nation? Welcome home."

They were very different men from the boys who'd been friends. Stephen had become a detached and sombre man, Sean Willie a thoughtful and mischievous one. They had little in common except memories of the old days, and later on when they talked about their youth each man sometimes remembered a Harte's Cross that was very different from the other's memory.

Sean Willie had never married. "I hadn't the time," he said. Stephen had an idea of what the marriage prospects might have been for a poor, slightly odd farm labourer in the Ireland of Sean Willie's youth.

"What did you do with your time?"

"I worked. I watched a lot of movies. And I read."

There was hardly a flat surface in Sean Willie Costello's small house that didn't have a book resting on it. He had shelves of paperbacks, blue Pelicans and orange Penguins, that he collected in the 1960s, and a selection of paperback classics. A catch-all collection, most of them second-hand, from

George Orwell to Mickey Spillane, from the *Wind in the Willows* to *War and Peace*, Jane Austen to Joseph Heller, Stephen Spender to Stephen King, James Thurber and *Myles na Gopaleen*. Books about history and books about movies, a book on how Houdini did his tricks leaned against a history of the 1926 General Strike in Britain, which was next to a volume of William Plomer's poetry. The pages were discoloured, some of the spines frayed. There were several favourite books he re-read every year and some of those had been replaced over the decades as they became tattered.

When Sean Willie was younger, he'd spent much of his spare time in the local cinema—which in the late 1970s closed down and was turned into the town's MegaMarket. He knew the dark streets of New York and the wide streets of Los Angeles as well as he knew the hot landscape of Monument Valley. He followed the careers of the John Waynes, the Robert Mitchums and the Humphrey Bogarts, but he also came to know the character actors, the Elisha Cooks, the Neville Brands and the Jack Elams, as well as he knew the bit players in the daily life of Harte's Cross.

Sean Willie was there in the scorching desert heat, watching Spencer Tracy stand up against prejudice, and down south in towns more inbred than his own, as Gregory Peck brandished his integrity. He skulked in urban alleys with Richard Widmark and Robert Ryan, went to prison with James Cagney and learned from Richard Conte that some smiles can't be trusted. In gangster movies and cowboy epics, he recognised diluted versions of the great classic stories and subjects dealt with in his paperbacks.

The decades of watching movies and reading made Sean Willie a good man to have on a pub quiz team. Always popular, in his old age Sean Willie became a town fixture, fondly respected. The movie man, the quiz man, the man who could tell you when any battle was fought and who won, or who got an Oscar for what role and which racehorse won the Grand National in any year going back to the 1930s.

Sean Willie's passion for Hollywood movies led someone to label him "Sean Wayne," and it never occurred to Sean Willie that the nickname, applied to a very small man, might contain an element of mockery. At least, it was not something he acknowledged. Whatever bit of ridicule might have been originally intended had long been erased by affection.

Over the past few years, he'd collected dozens of movies on video. Most of them he recorded from the TV, some he purchased from the bargain rack in the local MegaMarket. They were sorted into categories, mostly Westerns and gangster movies from the 1940s and 1950s. He had recently bought a DVD player.

Stephen Beckett had never had the cinema habit. It was all Hollywood mush, kiss-kiss, bang-bang. Under Sean Willie's guidance, he found himself drawn into a routine, watching one after another the movies of particular directors or stars, with Sean Willie explaining the background and the links between them. He described the differences between the kind of movies produced in the heyday of the big studios—the soft-focus romance of Paramount, the glamour of MGM, and his favourites, the dark, shadowy tales churned out by Warner Brothers. His heart, he said one evening, was with the Hollywood of the forties, fifties and sixties. "It's all over, now," he told Stephen. "There'll always be the odd good one, but mostly they want shite that'll amuse fat teenagers in Ohio while they're chomping on their hot dogs."

Stephen Beckett and Sean Willie Costello ate together, they drank together, they watched movies, they met most days and had rambling conversations and they went for long walks. For Stephen, it no longer seemed like he was killing time until death was ready to take him. He recognised in his old friend a funnier, sadder, more complex person than the quaint town character that his image suggested. For Sean Willie, it was a companionship he hadn't felt since childhood. The security of that companionship allowed him to acknowledge to himself the loneliness of the decades in Harte's Cross, though it was not something he could ever talk about, even with Stephen.

They sometimes talked about the lives they had lived. Stephen never liked talking about his time in the war, but Sean Willie was fascinated. Having Stephen to talk to about a great event he had read about in detail was like having a small bit of history in the kitchen of his own little house. One evening, over a bottle of Scotch, Stephen told him about Benny. He talked about how he often thought that it might have been him, not Benny, lying on a dirt road in France, his life seeping away. All it would have taken was for the German sniper to move his sights a fraction to the left. Benny would have had those years of work and family, all the good things and the bad things.

"Regrets?" Sean Willie asked.

For a moment, Stephen thought about the two German soldiers executed in a ditch, but he'd never talked about that to anyone and he wasn't sure he could explain what he felt, the small rightness and the huge wrongness of it, so he shook his head.

"Yourself?"

Sean Willie pointed to his temple. "It's all in here. A whole life, I lived it in here." He showed his remaining yellow teeth in a mirthless smile. "I suppose it was just the way it worked out. Maybe it was what I was comfortable with. I used to quote a thing to myself." Cigarette in hand, he gestured towards the bookshelves. "It's in there somewhere, a book of essays, blue Pelican. A fella writing about parades. The greatest pleasure, he said, belongs not to him that marches in the parade, but to the one that watches the parade from afar. I used to think that was true. Now that I'm in the home straight—a whole life watching the parade, that's what I think I regret sometimes." Then there was warmth in his smile. "But, only sometimes."

Sixteen years had passed since Stephen Beckett came home to Harte's Cross to die. They went quickly, and there was a lightness to his life that he had never known. It was an unexpected bonus at the end of a long innings. And then one morning, as he and Sean Willie Costello wrestled with the last few clues to the crosswords, a man with a gun came into Sweeney's Pub.

When the gunman pointed the weapon at Stephen Beckett's crotch the old man flinched. Knowing that death was in the room, he felt a dread of it that he hadn't felt for years. He was shocked to realise he wasn't ready.

Stephen knew from the war how random the choice was of who lived and who died, and his wife's sudden death told him that randomness was not confined to the battlefield. Death was perched above everyone's shoulder, preening and stretching. It would come for him when it felt the whim. Once the kids were reared he felt a relief. No emotional attachments, no one depending on him. Death could come now or come later, he was prepared.

In Sweeney's Pub that morning, he realised how much the sixteen years back in Harte's Cross had changed him.

His glance calculated the distance to the gunman. Without thinking, he was measuring the gunman's size, strength and weight against his own, working out the speed and angle he needed. Little fucker certainly wouldn't be expecting any trouble from an old man.

When the second gunman left the pub and the little fucker came closer, it was doable.

The others held at gunpoint were civilians. Stephen Beckett wore a uniform and carried a gun for just three years, almost sixty years ago, and he still felt some impulse towards a duty that civilians didn't have. He could see that Sean Willie was rigid with fear, and Mrs. Sweeney was close to shock. He forced himself to speak.

"Coming down here, waving a gun, why don't you work for your money, the same as the rest of us?"

When the gunman pointed the gun at him, Stephen Beckett's rage melted into fear. He knew what the gun could do and what it could take away, and he felt his every fibre flinch. When the gunman crossed to stand beside the booth, Stephen judged the distance to the man's gun hand, measured it against his body's frailties and the instant consequences if he failed, and he recoiled.

His surrender to his fears was the second great regret of Stephen Beckett's life. His failure to act, and his knowledge of what happened afterwards left him feeling like something had scooped away much of his insides.

The pub owner, Maura Sweeney, hadn't worked in the pub since the day of the robbery. She now dealt only with suppliers and sometimes helped out at lunchtime on the checkout at the family's MegaMarket. The barman who was there that day now worked part-time as a school caretaker.

Joe Hanlon, the young garda on duty that day in Harte's Cross, received the support of his colleagues and superiors in the wake of the hold-up. His uniform cap was found on a scarecrow, in a field near where the stolen Primera was burned out. "Nothing you could have done," his sergeant told him. "You'll be right as rain." A month later he was transferred to a station in west Galway. "Nothing to do with anything," the sergeant said. "They like to move people around." Two weeks after that Joe Hanlon quit the force and took a job selling advertising spots on a local radio station in his home county of Tipperary. He told his parents that he found the guards too regimented, too restrictive, and his parents said he was quite right to go for the kind of job where he was his own boss.

Of the two other customers in the pub, along with Stephen Beckett, the young woman with the baby seemed none the worse. The third customer, Sean Willie Costello, died three weeks later.

It was a merciful death. He went to sleep one night and didn't wake up in the morning. Every waking hour of the three weeks leading to his death was a fog of regret and shame.

The day after the hold-up, when Sean Willie went into Tubridy's to buy his *Irish Independent*, someone asked him what it was like in Sweeney's Pub during the hold-up and he shrugged and mumbled that it all happened so quick. Everyone in town was talking about what happened, and Sean Willie had been at the centre of it, and the man who always had a story had nothing to say. The following evening, in the back lounge at Hartnett's, Sean Willie ordered a pint and was watching it settle when one of half a dozen young men playing poker over by the fireplace looked up and said, "Hey, Sean Wayne, I hear you're auditioning for a part in Piss in Boots, what?"

Whether it was the pub owner or the young woman with the baby who told people about Sean Willie pissing himself, never mattered. Perhaps it was Garda Hanlon, or someone else who came to the pub after the shooting.

The other young men around the card table laughed and Sean Willie blushed. He walked out of the pub. The young lad who made the crack followed him out and apologised.

"It was just, Jesus, Sean Willie, it was just a stupid thing to say. I was being a smart-ass. Sure, you know I meant no harm?" Sean Willie nodded and said there were no hard feelings and he never went into Hartnett's or Sweeney's or any other pub again.

He hadn't recognised what had happened, not for a few seconds after the shooting, then he felt the wet on his trousers, the hot liquid running down his leg, and his whole mind screamed No! And when it was over and Garda Hanlon arrived and he was allowed go home, and no one seemed to notice anything, he didn't relax for a moment. Although Stephen had seen it happen, he never mentioned it. When a detective from Dublin came to Sean Willie's home the morning after the hold-up, to take a statement, he didn't mention it. The fear of it all coming back at him was like something heavy had been implanted in the back of Sean Willie's skull. When the kid from the pub made the Piss in Boots crack, the realisation slammed right through him that there wouldn't ever be a time when he'd be free of this. He told Stephen that evening about the kid in the pub.

Stephen visited Sean Willie every day after that and once managed to convince him to come for a walk down by the river, but that was all. Sean Willie stayed at home, had his few groceries delivered. He watched news bulletins and sport on the TV, but he didn't watch any of his movies. He never did another crossword.

Sean Willie never broke down in front of his friend, but one lunchtime he was cooking something at the stove and Stephen saw him grimace and close his eyes, as though the shame of it all had suddenly rushed through him. Sean Willie went into his front room for a minute and when he came out he continued cooking, without comment.

One evening, a week before he died, while they were playing a game of sevens, he put down his cards and he said to Stephen, "A whole life I spent spoofing. Then real life came along and I pissed in my pants and everyone knows what I am."

Stephen told him that was nonsense but he knew Sean Willie wasn't listening.

And one morning he didn't wake up. He was an old man, and there was no saying that what happened in Sweeney's Pub had hastened his death. But what Stephen Beckett knew was that those final three weeks demeaned a good life and tore the heart out of a kind man.

One lunchtime, three months after Sean Willie died, Stephen was crossing the main street on his way back home from the Spar shop. He paused to allow a Toyota pickup to accelerate past. His eye registered the driver—Leo Titley. Stephen knew his late father well, used to drink in Sweeney's. He stared after the pickup as it turned the corner and out on to the Kildorney road. He stood there for a couple of minutes, his breathing even, his senses suddenly icy clear, aware of everything around him with a sharpness he hadn't known since he was a young man walking down deadly country lanes in the French countryside.

The little fucker.

The last time he had seen the face of Leo's passenger was beneath the peak of a baseball hat with a cartoon character, and the little fucker was driving out of Sweeney's car park and smiling at him.

Feeling as though he'd been knocked off balance, he walked to the corner and looked down the Kildorney road, but the pickup was long gone. Off to Leo Titley's farm, a couple of miles down the road, Leo and his passenger, the little fucker.

He went home filled with the crystal awareness that seized him when he saw Leo's passenger and thought about nothing else all day. He ate only beans and toast and didn't sleep much that night. It never once occurred to him to call the police.

The following morning, sitting over his breakfast at the Olive Grove, Stephen read the headline of his *Irish Independent*. HAVE YOU SEEN THESE MEN? There was a sudden pressure, like something was rapidly expanding inside his chest, as he looked at the first of the two photographs below the headline.

Stephen crumpled the paper in his lap.

The little fucker.

Over the three months since Sean Willie died, Stephen had paid even less attention than usual to the national news. A few days back he'd heard something on the radio about a kidnap above in Dublin. Now, he read the details.

Poor woman.

Underneath the photo, it gave the little fucker's name. Frankie Crowe.

The other photo was of a chubby little thug by the name of Sweetman. That day back in July, there were two of them did the job in Sweeney's Pub and Stephen hadn't seen much of the one standing guard by the door. Maybe it was this chubby little hoodlum.

Stephen went to Hartnett's Pub that evening and sat alone. At nine o'clock the television news showed a house above in Dublin, armed gardai outside it. The Minister for Justice was telling a reporter how thankful he was that Mrs. Kennedy had been rescued safely. When the interview with the minister ended, there was a photo of the chubby little thug and the newsreader said that police were still searching for the leader of the gang, a Frank Crowe. They showed his picture and said that gardai were following a number of leads.

Stephen Beckett went home and got Sean Willie's gun down from the top of the wardrobe. A big grey Colt .45. He remembered the first time Sean Willie showed it to him, unwrapping it from the red and white hand towel. Standing in the front room of his little house, the big gun tucked into his belt, giggling like the kid he'd been when they'd played cowboys in the fields half a century earlier.

"OK, stranger, slap leather!"

Although Sean Willie's uncle was the only one of his family to get involved in the war of independence, his reputation as one of Michael Collins's gunmen gave the family a badge of honour among those who saw everything in the light cast by history. One evening in the mid-1970s, a local member of the

Provisional IRA came to the house and asked Sean Willie to look after the loaded Colt .45.

"I don't think there was anything going on at the time," Sean Willie told Stephen. "No reason why he couldn't have left the gun under his floorboards. It was like he thought I deserved the honour—being the nephew of the local patriot— the honour of doing my bit for the cause." He grinned. "Right spacer."

A few months later, this guy did a runner after a garda was wounded in a Provo bank robbery. There were rumours around town that he ended up working in a restaurant some-place outside Philadelphia. Never came back for the gun. Mustn't have told any of his friends that he'd left a gun with Sean Willie, and no one ever came looking for it.

After Sean Willie died, Stephen Beckett took three sou-venirs from the little house in Coulthard Lane. The gun, the Cross fountain pen that Sean Willie won in the crossword competition, and a tattered blue Pelican paperback, a book of essays he found on one of the shelves. He'd been reading it on and off since Sean Willie died.

Now, Stephen checked the weapon and the ammunition and found them in good order. He left the gun on top of the towel, on his bedside table, and stripped for bed. It was some time after three in the morning when he dozed off and when he woke the clock said it was just after seven.

When he finished his little bedside exercises, Stephen Beckett got dressed. He skipped breakfast at the Olive Grove that morning and just had a cup of tea at home, with Sean Willie's Colt .45 wrapped in the red and white hand towel on the table beside him. Then he put on his black overcoat, took up the gun and walked out of Harte's Cross and down the Kildorney road towards Leo Titley's farm.

After an hour sitting in a ditch above the Titley farmhouse, his thoughts darting around inside his head like small frantic animals, Stephen was still wrestling with his urge to kill the little fucker. He had it coming. He did what he did to the people in Sweeney's Pub that day, and he took that poor woman up in Dublin from her family, and God alone knew what else he did. Stephen thought, as he'd thought during the long, sleepless hours of last night, of the satisfaction of walking up to Crowe as soon as he came out of the farmhouse, and pointing the gun at his face and giving him a taste of the fear and humiliation that Sean Willie had suffered. Then he'd kill him.

The chances of getting away with it were not great. Someone—Leo probably—would see him. The police would ask locals if they had seen anyone in the area and the chances were that someone saw Stephen on the road. He could live with that.

Crowe needed killing.

Sometimes, there are people who need killing. Need it because of what they did and because of what they will do again and because the emotions and the pain of it all demand a bloody revenge. And Crowe, the little fucker, was one of them. Laying waste to people's lives.

Stephen sat in the ditch with the gun wrapped in the towel, resting it on his lap, telling himself that Crowe needed killing. And telling himself that if he didn't do it he'd be doing again what he did that day in Sweeney's—flinching, backing down from doing what ought to be done, out of fear.

The sun was shining but it was cold out here in the countryside. Stephen didn't notice the cold until a gust of wind blew across his face and he felt the chill of the tears on his cheeks. He was staring across the hedgerow, back down along the lane that led to Leo Titley's farmhouse. It took him a while to realise that inside his head he was staring across a different ditch, in the shadow of another hedgerow, on the road outside

Caen sixty years ago, the other time when the emotion and the pain of it all shaped the judgement that someone needed killing. The memories of Benny and of the two German soldiers in the ditch flooded through him and he felt sick at the thought of what he wanted to do. It was the right thing to do, and the worst thing anyone could do.

It was the loathing Stephen felt for his own murderous instinct that held him back. Sitting there, the towel in his lap, he recognised that it wasn't fear that was stopping him and it wasn't morality. It was because he knew that the weeks or the months he had left—and Stephen didn't think any more of his life as having any number of years to it—would be saturated with the anguish of killing. He knew that although rage made the killing right, the time that followed would make something else of it.

Useless old man. Do it, do something, one way or the other.

The door of the farmhouse opened and Leo Titley came out. He was chewing on something and he used the back of his hand to wipe his lips. He got into his pickup and after revving the reluctant engine, he drove away.

Stephen stood up, his spine bent. He made a puffing sound as he forced his back to straighten. In one hand he held the towel-wrapped gun, in the other a rock he'd picked up from the ditch. He approached the farmhouse from its blind side. He reached the back wall of the house and paused a moment, then he stooped down and inched along beneath a window, towards the back door. He found the jamb of the door broken, the door open a couple of inches. Stephen put the rock down gently. He unrolled the towel, cocked the pistol and went into the cottage. It took him less than a minute to check each room and see the place was empty.

Stephen Beckett couldn't know that Frankie Crowe had driven back to Dublin from Leo Titley's home two days previously, immediately after Stephen saw him in Leo's pickup on the main street of Harte's Cross. He couldn't know that Crowe spent that night in Dublin, in the home of a man named Adrian Moffat, and that last night he slept in a car in a lane and he wouldn't be back at Leo's farmhouse for another four hours.

Stephen went outside, and stood in the open for a while, the gun down by his side, his blank expression concealing his feelings of relief and frustration. He felt more than ever like a man alive beyond his time, beyond understanding the world around him, beyond any use.

He put the towel-wrapped gun under one arm and pulled his overcoat tight around him. His stiff knees, sore from the time spent sitting in the ditch, meant it would take him longer to walk back to Harte's Cross than it took to walk out here.

27

An hour after he'd read aloud Brendan Sweetman's statement, Connie Wintour turned up at Assistant Commissioner Colin O'Keefe's office and asked for a confidential meeting.

"My client, as you know, was placed in an invidious position, vis-à-vis the professional criminals who—"

O'Keefe said, "Let's take all that bullshit as read. What's he got to offer?"

Wintour looked slightly miffed at having to curtail his performance. "We're all aware that judges pay attention to what garda witnesses say about defendants. If there could be an understanding about the light in which your people cast Mr. Sweetman, my client might well—" and here Wintour paused to flick an invisible speck of dirt off the sleeve of his jacket "—have some additional information you might find interesting."

John Grace and Nicky Bonner spent the morning in the incident room at Carbury Street station. Hogg's team kept them in touch with events, and Grace was alerted that he might be needed at Santry garda station, where Martin Paxton was proving uncooperative. So far, Paxton was blanking everyone, but there was no harm seeing if he'd respond more helpfully to a familiar face. Awaiting confirmation that he was to go to Santry station, Grace was in the Turner's Cross canteen when his mobile rang.

"We have a lead."

Chief Superintendent Hogg was trying to maintain an even tone, but there was an edge to his voice. "Nothing more than informed speculation, but the best we have. Brendan Sweetman is dealing. He claims Frankie Crowe said the money was stashed somewhere, a couple of hours away, there and back. Frankie's strictly Dublin, but Sweetman says there's a farmhouse in Meath, near Harte's Cross, owned by a farmer by the name of Leo Titley. He says the farmer has previous with Frankie."

John Grace gestured urgently to Nicky Bonner, who was up at the counter getting them both a coffee refill.

Hogg wanted Grace down at Harte's Cross. "ERU are on their way. Could be nothing, could be Frankie's bolt-hole. If there's a stand-off, I want someone on the scene who knows him. If need be, soft-soap him. If he isn't buying, let the ERU lads take care of him."

Nicky was standing by the table, a tell-me expression on his face. John stood and began walking towards the exit, still talking to Hogg. He gestured to Nicky to follow. They took Nicky's car.

Grace and Bonner linked up with the ERU at the station in Harte's Cross and they'd been watching the house for all of ten minutes, as the ERU discussed how to approach the place, when a clapped-out Toyota pickup came round a bend in the track that led to the house. Almost on top of the police before he saw them, the driver stopped and started backing away, then thought better of it.

Grace and Bonner had been supplied with bright yellow garda identification jackets. They watched the armed squad pull the farmer from the pickup and push him to the ground, his hands cuffed behind him. Tall, stringy chap, ponytail. His name was Leo Titley, according to the local sergeant who led the way to the farm. The sergeant said Leo had returned to the area a few years back to farm the few acres his father left, and he wasn't making a very good fist of it.

"Quiet enough, mind you. Never known him to cause any trouble."

The farmer looked shocked now as the policemen threw questions at him. Watching from some distance away, Grace and Bonner couldn't hear what was being said. When the tactical commander brought Leo up the lane to the two detectives he said, "Mr. Titley here says he's got nothing to say."

John Grace looked the farmer in the eye. "You're being a fool. I don't know how you got involved with Frankie, but this thing is way over your head."

"I've no idea what you're talking about."

The farmer grunted as Nicky Bonner kicked him behind one knee and the leg went from under him and he stumbled and pitched forward. Bonner pushed him and he went over on to his back.

The ERU tactical commander shook his head and turned away. John Grace said, "Nicky—"

Bonner knelt down and slapped the farmer across the face. Bonner said, "Try again. Where's Frankie Crowe?"

"I don't know what you're talking about."

Bonner hit him again. "We're talking about people with guns. The gloves are off, boyo. We have to go into that house, and we're not going in blind."

Leo said, "I've nothing to do with any Frankie. I don't—"

Bonner got a handful of ponytail and jerked. Leo screamed. Bonner leaned close to the farmer's ear. "It's best if you know the score, so I'll set you straight. We've got to go in there." His voice was soft. "Anyone of us gets as much as a scratch—I swear on my mother's grave—you'll end up dead on your own doorstep and we'll put it down to Frankie."

Bonner tapped Leo on the nose, hard. "Do you understand what I'm saying?" The farmer stared at Bonner.

There was a small rock lying in the grass near the farmer's head. Bonner picked it up and smashed it into the farmer's mouth. The man screeched and blood welled up from his lips.

Grace turned away. There was a harsh sound behind him, as the farmer sucked in air and it came out in a sob. When Grace looked round he saw the farmer drawing another ragged breath. There was blood on his teeth and a stringy length of red drool on his chin.

"Do you understand me?" Bonner asked.

The farmer groaned, then he nodded.

"You have anything to tell me?" Bonner said.

The farmer shook his head. He grunted, his voice distorted. "I swear. Frankie hasn't been here in two days. There's no one in there."

There was no one in the farmhouse. The ERU smashed in the door and swept through the place. They opened closets, looked under beds and one of them stuck his head up into the attic and gave it a wipe of a flashlight. They went through the outbuildings.

"There's definitely nobody here," the tactical commander told John Grace. "Technical are on the way," he said. "Waste of time."

Grace said he'd have a look around the house until Technical arrived.

The ERU mounted up, with Leo Titley handcuffed in the back seat of one of their cars, and Grace watched until they were out of sight. Behind him, Bonner emerged from the house, taking off the garda ID jacket. "Could be this one's running away from us," he said.

"Could be," Grace said, still looking off into the distance. He felt like they'd come to the end of something. This was going to be one of those things that never got properly tied up.

Bonner said, "Most likely, Frankie's left the country by now."

"It's possible." The victim was safe, that's what mattered. Catching Frankie— they did or they didn't. Either way, there's always a Frankie to chase.

Bonner said, "Hope we didn't promise Sweetman too much for the tip-off."

They went back into the house. Bonner opened a window. The stale air held the scent of too many greasy meals half eaten and left lying overnight. Grace decided to have a look around in case there was something less obvious than a fugitive in a closet, or a foot sticking out from under a bed. Technical would do a proper search, taking photographs and finger-prints, the kind of stuff that might be needed if there was ever a trial. Meanwhile, it was possible that Crowe had left some small pointer to another hiding place. A note, a phone number, an address, a ticket, a receipt, a map. Within ten minutes, pok-ing through the contents of a drawer in one of the bedrooms, Grace decided this was pointless. This was the hovel of a bach-elor farmer. Frankie's stay was short, he left no trace. It's over, until Frankie turns up somewhere, sometime.

"Boss," Nicky's voice from the living room.

As quickly as the conviction had come that this was all over, it went. Nicky had found something.

The first thing Grace noticed when he went into the murky living room was the stillness of Bonner's posture in the decrepit armchair. The second thing was Frankie Crowe, standing just inside the doorway, casually holding a gun, point-ing it into the space between the two policemen.

There was a long silence.

Crowe's eyes were puffy. He looked like he'd slept in his clothes.

Trying for a conversational tone, Grace said, "This doesn't have to go the distance, Frankie. We can have a quiet finish, everything civilised."

"If I agree to sit in a cell for the next thirty years."

He gestured to Bonner. "You got a gun?" Nicky took off his jacket, turned round. Grace did the same. Neither man was armed.

Grace said, "Frankie, the way things are, we can—"

"You can shut the fuck up."

Crowe handcuffed the policemen together, back to back, then made them lie down. Grace, kneeling awkwardly, grunted as he felt a muscle twist in his leg. Rougher than he needed to be, and enjoying it, Frankie searched Bonner and took the policeman's car keys. He found Grace's mobile in a trouser pocket, threw it to the floor and stamped on it until it cracked open.

"Where's your mobile?" Frankie asked Bonner.

"Fuck off," Bonner said.

"Probably in his jacket," Grace said. "Take it easy, Frankie, no need for aggravation."

Crowe found Bonner's mobile and smashed it.

Grace was thinking about Technical—they'd be here in an hour, give or take.

How far will Frankie get in an hour? What direction?

"Traffic's pretty heavy this time of day, Frankie. You hit Dublin, you're crawling. Your picture's all over the place. The ports, the airports, ferries; not a hope."

Frankie ignored him. He used a length of wood with a hook at the top to pull down a spring-loaded rectangular panel in the centre of the ceiling. He unfolded the wooden Stira ladder attached to the panel and climbed up into the attic. A moment later he pushed a heavy holdall through the opening and let it fall to the floor. The second holdall hit the side of the table on the way down and knocked a half-empty teacup on to the floor. The cold tea soaked into the shabby carpet.

Frankie climbed down and left the ladder in place.

He got the two policemen to their feet, unlocked the handcuffs and cuffed them again, this time face to face, one of Grace's arms through the rungs of the wooden ladder.

Frankie grunted as he lifted the first of the holdalls.

Looking at the solid wood of the ladder, John Grace reckoned it would take a lot of shifting. Both of them working together, he and Nicky could maybe loosen a rung.

"Raping a woman like that, Frankie," Nicky said, "a woman with connections. Won't be a station in the country doesn't get a supplementary budget. All the overtime, won't be one of us doesn't have a summer home in Spain."

Crowe seemed distracted, and when he spoke it was as though he was talking to himself. "Send me a postcard."

Bonner said, "Up in Dublin, Frankie, your lads are queuing up to sing your praises. Martin Paxton, Brendan Sweetman—it was all Frankie's idea, Frankie got the money, Frankie raped the woman—how do you think we got on to this place?"

Crowe turned towards Nicky and he looked as though he was about to say something, but he remained silent.

Grace said, "Nicky—"

Bonner said, "They'll go down, but they'll go down easy, that's the idea. And when you're living in some squat in Amsterdam, waiting for the heavy gang to come through the door with their guns blazing, they'll get early parole."

Frankie Crowe stared at Bonner.

"What you reckon, Frankie, maybe the lads could take turns seeing if your missus needs a hand while you're away?"

"Nicky, cut it out," Grace said.

Crowe continued to stare at Bonner.

"Cat got your tongue?" Bonner said.

Crowe leaned over and spat in Bonner's face. As the spittle slid down his cheek, the policeman wore a broad smile of contempt, as though he'd won a small victory.

When the money was tucked away in the boot of Nicky

Bonner's car, Frankie Crowe made himself comfortable behind the wheel. He reached down and slid the seat forward a couple of inches and adjusted the rear-view mirror. He started the engine and thought about the safest back-road route to Belfast. Dun Laoghaire, Cork and Rosslare would be tighter than a duck's arse. Belfast gave him as good a chance as he could expect.

In the glove compartment he found an opened packet of Scots Clan. He took a toffee and listened to the engine ticking over. A solid car. Better than the piece of shit he'd had to use for the past couple of days. He sat there chewing until the sweet was all but gone. He took another Scots Clan, then he got out of the car.

Crowe was chewing when he came back into the house. He walked up to the two policemen and Grace didn't see the gun in his hand until he pointed it at Bonner and shot him in the face. A small dark hole appeared in Bonner's right cheek, an inch below the eye. It didn't bleed. He was breathing harshly. His eyes open, he stood there, stunned, staring at Crowe.

Crowe said, "Cat got your tongue, smart-ass?"

Grace, barely audible, said, "Jesus, Frankie—"

Crowe ignored him. He pursed his lips at Bonner and made a kissing sound. Still chewing, he took his time pocketing the gun, then he turned and walked out of the house.

Bonner's legs gave out from under him and he twisted as he fell. Grace's arms were jerked forward and the metal bit into his hands as Bonner's weight dragged at the handcuffs. Grace's face smashed against the side of the ladder. Bonner hung there, his arms above his head, his hands held aloft by the handcuffs, his face a few inches away from John Grace's wide eyes.

Bonner's eyes were still open, his face was calm and he wasn't breathing any more.

Grace was barely aware that he was making small, incoherent noises. He could hear a car moving off outside.

28

From the window of her room on the third floor of the Blackrock Clinic, Angela Kennedy looked down on a car park. She'd been staring at a fluorescent-green Volkswagen, trying to imagine who might have chosen such a silly colour. A giddy young nurse, maybe, full of the joys. Angela decided that if she sat by the window long enough she'd see the owner returning to the car.

She didn't turn round when the door of the room made its whooshing sound. A nurse came in, checked the charts and inserted an electronic thermometer in Angela's left ear. The instrument beeped, the nurse made a note of the reading, said something pointlessly encouraging and left the room.

In the hours she'd been here, she'd already become used to the whooshing of the door, the beep of the thermometer, the needle pricks, the tablets in the little plastic medication cup and the nurses' cheery routine. She felt herself to be the nodding, smiling cocoon of calm at the centre of a whirl of activity. If it wasn't temperature, medication or liquids, it was food, dressings or just How are we feeling? If it wasn't the nurses it was the doctors, or the police or the counsellor. Justin and the kids had been in and out, the bedside locker strewn with crumpled tissues.

The medical people were the easiest to deal with. They told her what to do and she did it. Just a while back, a doctor she didn't remember meeting before came to tell her, "I can assure you there'll be no lasting effects."

Angela stared at him. "In what—"

332 · GENE KERRIGAN

"The results were negative. All of them, and you already know you're not pregnant. All clear for chlamydia, HIV, hepatitis B, all the rest of it. You'll need a routine three-month follow-up, but I think we can set your mind at rest from that point of view."

She nodded.

The doctor looked slightly disappointed. Perhaps he expected the news to cause some visible lift in her mood. Apart from when she first saw the kids, her emotions didn't seem to be affected by the things she was told or the things she saw or thought. She wondered if among the cocktail of medication she was getting the doctors had slipped in something to soothe her mind. She hoped that was it.

She'd lost track of the doctors. Two consultants, for certain, maybe three, and another two or three brisk young men floating in and out. One of them told her about the hy-something that made her eyes red with blood. It would be gone within a week, he said. There was an area of numbness on her cheek. That'll pass in a few weeks, the doctor told her. "Or months," he added.

She had double vision. She found it hard to move her left eye, to look up. After an X-ray and a CT scan, another of the doctors told her there was something called a blowout, caused by the punches to her face. Fracture in the floor of the eye socket. That was what was causing the double vision, he said. On the back of a sheet of paper from her chart, he sketched something she couldn't figure out. Trapped tissue.

"It also accounts for the drooping eyelid," he said.

She hadn't known until then that her eyelid was drooping. She realised that no one had offered her a mirror, and she hadn't asked for one.

"The surgery is routine."

Angela nodded. Just do it.

There was a period of time to go through, pain and indignity, then she would see where she stood. Justin asked if she wanted to move house, but Angela said no. He told her he had a security consultant designing a new alarm system and it would be installed by the time she came home.

They spoke in only the broadest terms about what had happened. "You poor thing," he said. Again and again he said, "Those bastards." Something like this, she realised, they didn't share the vocabulary necessary to discuss the emotions she'd gone through. Maybe with her sister Elizabeth she'd be able to talk about the detail of what happened. When this was over, she'd go stay for a while with Elizabeth in Paris.

When there were people with her, Angela wanted to be alone. And when she had time to herself it went by in great silent, empty passages, her mind fastening on details that seemed worth her attention when she noticed them—like the silly colour of a car parked three floors below—and then left her wondering if there had ever been a time when she wasn't this woolly-minded.

"Have you decided yet?"

It was the most cheery of the nurses.

"Sorry?"

Nodding towards the menu left on the bedside locker. "For afternoon tea? Have you decided?"

"Well—"

"Ah sure, take your time. I'll be back in ten minutes. OK?"

As the nurse left the room, Angela turned back to the window. The luminous green car was still down there. She waited and watched.

Justin Kennedy met Kevin Little in the private waiting room down the corridor from Angela's room. Daragh O'Suilleabhain made the introductions. Half an hour earlier, Daragh had called with the news that Kevin was in the country for the afternoon for a meeting with the Minister for Finance. He'd heard the great news, was it possible he could drop in on Justin with his good wishes?

"Angela's not up to—"

"He wouldn't dream of intruding. He just wants to see you, wish you all the best, touch base. So many people are so pleased it's all—"

"That sounds fine."

"Kevin's an emotional man. It's like this happened to one of his own."

Kevin Little appeared at the hospital at the precise time he said he would. He spent two minutes expressing genuine warmth and concern to Justin, then he was gone. "We'll talk," he said as he was leaving. Justin nodded.

He rang Elizabeth, checked the kids were OK. When he got back to Angela's room a nurse told him his wife was having a nap—why not take a break, she suggested, maybe drop home and freshen up?

Justin shucked his cuff and glanced at his Patek Philippe. He shook his head. He'd stay. He wanted to be here when Angela woke.

29

A t the end of the narrow twisting road from Leo's Titley's farm, Frankie Crowe had a choice. Left through Harte's Cross and take the main road northwards, or right and take the safer but slower back roads. If the cops arrived sharpish at Leo Titley's farm and found John Grace handcuffed to the stiff, it didn't matter what route he took. Every boreen in Meath would have a roadblock within minutes. Speed was more important, so the better road was the one to take. Once he was clear of Meath, he could turn on to the back roads and take his time working his way towards Belfast. He turned left.

Have to find an out-of-the-way farmhouse, pick up a new car. Can't be sure when this one will turn red-hot.

The chances of getting out of the country were no more than fairly rotten. All it took was one roadblock, one copper who wasn't dozy, and it was all over. If he got across to Britain there were people ready to sell the help he needed to melt into a new name, new papers, in Europe. It would cost a bundle to get from England to Amsterdam, and more time to feel out the landscape. Kind of money he had now, there wasn't much he needed that he couldn't buy. But it would take time. Wander carelessly into a strange city with that kind of money and some early-morning stroller will find your bones picked clean.

He glanced at the Rolex. No matter how roundabout the route, he'd make Belfast before nightfall.

There wasn't much afternoon traffic in Harte's Cross.

Frankie drove carefully. Stay well within the speed limit, no sloppy moves.

Shit.

The petrol gauge showed the needle in the red. Would it last until he found somewhere to pick up another car?

He pulled into a garage halfway down the main street and filled up. He hadn't eaten all day. When he came out of the garage shop he was carrying two chicken sandwiches and two small bottles of Coke.

"Little fucker." The voice was loud but frayed.

He looked across the street and saw a tall old man, long black overcoat and wild grey hair, standing on the far pavement. There was surprise and anger and confusion on the old guy's face.

His voice rang out across the street. "You."

Culchie gobshite on day release from the local home for the bewildered. The country's full of them.

Frankie got into the car and put the food on the passenger seat, aware that the loony tunes was crossing the street towards him. He turned the ignition and reached for the door but the old man was holding on to it with one hand. When Frankie tried to pull the door shut the old man's grip made it feel like the door was set in concrete.

The old man said, "Get out."

Frankie let his hand fall naturally towards the handle of the gun tucked into his belt. He could feel the outline through his leather jacket.

No.

No fuss. Brush him off and it's just an old fool making a nuisance of himself. Pull a gun, everything goes ballistic.

He looked around to see if there was anyone who'd help him shift the fool. There was a car pulling in behind. He looked at the old man and saw that he was taking a parcel of some kind, a red and white towel, from under one arm.

"No time for chit-chat, pops."

The old man was unwrapping the towel.

Jesus.

"Get out."

The old man's gun was almost touching Frankie's temple.

"What the fuck's this about?"

"Get out."

Frankie slid out of the car. More freedom of movement, standing up. No way this could be settled now without a fuss.

Fuck it. Can't go any distance at all in this car now. Have to find new wheels just to get out of the county, dump that later, pick up another. Stupid old bastard.

The old man stepped back. Out of reach.

Frankie took a step forward. When the old man put the gun close to Frankie again, an arm swinging up fast would be enough to put the pistol out of the picture. After that, it was one-two-three. Punch in the throat, kick the legs from under him. Step on him. Whatever this was about, it had to be ended quickly.

Frankie glanced up and down the street. No sign of a uniform. The driver of the Toyota that pulled in behind, a plump young woman with short, dark curly hair and dark glasses, was unhooking the petrol pump.

Frankie said to the mad old man, "You're mixing me up with someone else."

"I know who you are."

Shit. The pictures in the newspapers.

"Nothing to do with you, old man. Mind your own business."

The old man jabbed the gun towards Frankie, like he wanted Frankie to stop talking. The old man's hand was trembling. Frankie's muscles tensed. Near enough now for a hand moving fast enough. Give it a second.

His arm down by his side, he made a fist.

One-two-three.

Something changed, a movement he didn't quite see, and Frankie was lying on the ground, on his side, facing the back of the car. The woman from the Toyota was standing twenty feet away with both hands clapped flat to the sides of her face. She was looking at Frankie, she was screaming, but Frankie couldn't hear anything except the hissing sound that seemed to come from inside his own head.

Burning smell.

There was something hot and wet on Frankie's face.

Jesus.

The old bastard was stepping over Frankie, the gun hanging down by his side. He looked right down at Frankie and he said something.

Frankie couldn't hear the words.

He tried to say something but he wasn't sure if any sound came from his lips and he wasn't sure what he wanted to say. The old man was bending down, leaning over Frankie.

Stupid old bastard, tears in his eyes.

Frankie saw the muzzle of the gun coming round.

Wait—

Twice Stephen Beckett declined the offer of a cup of tea. The third time, they brought it anyway. Now, it too had gone cold, and the ham sandwich they left with it remained untouched. For the first time since they brought him to the little room at the back of the garda station, Stephen stood up. The room was warm. It took him a couple of seconds to steady himself, then he took off his overcoat and the young uniformed garda standing just inside the door took it and brought it outside. When he returned he looked at the cold tea and the sandwich and he took those away, too.

Stephen sat down again in the chair behind the worn-out table. Over the couple of hours since he'd been brought here he'd been visited by a number of gardai, including a uniformed superintendent and a couple of detective inspectors. None of them had asked him anything about what happened. Mostly they asked if he was OK, if there was anything he needed. The superintendent asked if he had a solicitor. Stephen said he didn't want a solicitor. The superintendent said he'd better have one, anyway. By and by, a thin man in a grey suit came and introduced himself as a solicitor. He said something that Stephen didn't catch, then he said he'd be back in a little while and he went away.

The young uniformed garda brought in yet another cup of tea and left it on the table, then went back to standing beside the door.

"Won't be long now," he said. Stephen was about to ask him what it wouldn't be long until, then he didn't bother.

He was aware of a great calmness surrounding him, like the silence immediately after an explosion. He'd first noticed that sense of calm as he walked back from the garage, the sound of the second shot ebbing away, the crumbled figure on the ground behind him.

They'll ask me why, and anything I say will sound like an excuse.

He didn't want to make excuses, or pretend that what he had done was the right thing to do. He knew it was the wrong thing to do and he knew it was what he needed to do, he thought it was right that he should do it and he knew that in a couple of weeks he wouldn't believe that any more. He knew he could never explain this, he wasn't sure anyone could, and he knew it didn't matter to him now.

After a while, the solicitor was standing in front of Stephen, introducing a tall plainclothes policeman with the bearing of the officer class, but Stephen didn't catch the name. He saw that the uniformed garda by the door was standing with a very straight back.

The grand panjandrum.

Stephen noticed the detective's thin brown hair was dyed. The man nodded at Stephen, sat down, took out a notebook and said, "Let's get started, shall we?"

Acknowledgments

Thanks to Julie Lordan, who encouraged *Little Criminals* from the beginning; to agent Peter Straus, who took the book on; and to Jason Arthur, who published it. Their advice was invaluable. Along the way, Evelyn Bracken, Pat Brennan, Tom Daly and Rowan Rowth were generous with their support. Thank you all.

Gene Kerrigan is from Dublin. He is the author of several books, including the best-selling *Hard Cases*, and has twice been named Journalist of the Year.

Now Available from Europa Editions

Fiction

Carmine Abate, *Between Two Seas*
Stefano Benni, *Margherita Dolce Vita*
Steve Erickson, *Zeroville*
Elena Ferrante, *The Days of Abandonment*
Elena Ferrante, *Troubling Love*
Elena Ferrante, *The Lost Daughter*
Jane Gardam, *Old Filth*
Jane Gardam, *The Queen of the Tambourine*
Katharina Hacker, *The Have-Nots*
James Hamilton-Paterson, *Cooking with Fernet Branca*
James Hamilton-Paterson, *Amazing Disgrace*
Alfred Hayes, *The Girl on the Via Flaminia*
Jean-Claude Izzo, *The Lost Sailors*
Ioanna Karystiani, *The Jasmine Isle*
Peter Kocan, *Fresh Fields*
Sélim Nassib, *I Loved You for Your Voice*
Sélim Nassib, *The Palestinian Lover*
Edna Mazya, *Love Burns*
Alessandro Piperno, *The Worst Intentions*
Chad Taylor, *Departure Lounge*
Benjamin Tammuz, *Minotaur*
Edwin M. Yoder Jr., *Lions at Lamb House*
Michele Zackheim, *Broken Colors*
Christa Wolf, *One Day a Year*

Noir, Mystery, and Crime

Massimo Carlotto, *The Goodbye Kiss*
Massimo Carlotto, *Death's Dark Abyss*
Massimo Carlotto, *The Fugitive*
Alicia Giménez-Bartlett, *Dog Day* (Petra Delicado series)
Alicia Giménez-Bartlett, *Prime Time Suspect* (Petra Delicado series)
Patrick Hamilton, *Hangover Square*
Jean-Claude Izzo, *Total Chaos* (Marseilles trilogy)
Jean-Claude Izzo, *Chourmo* (Marseilles trilogy)
Jean-Claude Izzo, *Solea* (Marseilles trilogy)
Matthew F. Jones, *Boot Tracks*
Gene Kerrigan, *The Midnight Choir*
Carlo Lucarelli, *Carte Blanche* (De Luca trilogy)
Carlo Lucarelli, *The Damned Season* (De Luca trilogy)

Children's Illustrated Fiction

Altan, *Here Comes Timpa*
Altan, *Timpa Goes to the Sea*
Altan, *Fairy Tale Timpa*
Wolf Erlbruch, *The Big Question*
Wolf Erlbruch, *The Miracle of the Bears*
Wolf Erlbruch and Gioconda Belli, *The Butterfly Workshop*